ALL IN FOR
Christmas

One woman,
two lives—
but did she choose
the right one?

NEW YORK TIMES AND USA TODAY BESTSELLING AUTHOR

GINNY BAIRD

ALL IN FOR

Christmas

A MAGICAL ROMANTIC COMEDY

All In For Christmas
A Magical Romantic Comedy

ISBN 978-1-942058-48-9 *eBook*
ISBN 978-1-942058-49-6 *paperback*

Copy Edited by Sally Knapp
Cover and Formatting by Alt 19 Creative

Published by:
Winter Wedding Press

With the clock ticking
on Christmas magic,
can the past be undone?

CHAPTER
One

Cooper takes off down the high school corridor, his puppy dog tail wagging and his leash dragging behind him. His therapy dog vest is bedecked with shiny bells that *jingle-jangle-jingle* as he lopes along, and papier-mâché snowflakes dangle from the ceiling above him. "Cooper! Wait!" My pulse pounds fiercely. I was entrusted with his care for *five minutes.* Five seconds was all it took for him to break loose.

I scurry after him in my red tartan turtleneck and jeans. I've got a navy blue Paws and Read T-shirt tugged over my turtleneck. Its cute doggie pawprint logo is stamped inside a red circle on its front pocket below the white printed words "Paws and Read." Each paw pad resembles a book. Our librarian, Martha, thought that up. I was so pleased I hugged her, before remembering I don't do hugs. Outside my family, which is very small, just me and Mom. Otherwise, I'm super controlled, except for when I'm not. Like now. "Cooper! Here, boy!"

The rascally Jack Russell terrier glances over his shoulder with a sly look as I chase after him—faster and faster. But not too fast. *Whoa*—my sneakers skid on the damp floor, but I catch my balance with bent elbows just outside the darkened main office. It's after six and school has closed for the day, but our faculty holiday party rages on. Cooper's mostly white with a big brown patch around one eye, and exceptionally well trained. Only, by Beth—his handler—who's dashed back through the snow to her car to grab her ID badge.

I cannot blow introducing my program to the school. I've worked too hard for this by lobbying school administrators, then finally gaining school board approval. If there'd been this kind of program in place when I was a kid, maybe I and so many others wouldn't have fallen through the cracks. I was an embarrassingly slow reader, but—with the intervention of a kindly ninth grade English teacher—I landed on my feet. And now I teach English myself. Back then, I never could have imagined getting accepted to college, much less securing a teaching degree.

It started in kindergarten with the bluebirds. At first I was in the cardinal reading group, but then no. All the other kids could decipher the words on the page five times faster than I could. The pictures were great but the letters were one big stream of gibberish. I got to be a goldfinch next. The books had more pictures but fewer words. That didn't make them any less confusing, though. I gradually gleaned that some other kids had two parents, and many of them got read to at night. Mom was exhausted doing it all by herself. We watched TV. So. I landed with the bluebirds, a sad little group of fine-feathered friends. Our books had even more pictures and even fewer words.

Cooper hears the commotion in the cafeteria, trotting toward it and past the glass case of sports trophies and student awards. He clearly knows a good time when he hears one, the little scamp. Laughter booms through the cafeteria's double doors and light chatter sifts through the air like fluttery snowflakes.

"Cooper! Stop!" But Cooper has other plans. He's curious and interested, tilting his head from side to side at the noise while charging forward.

The doors part as a teacher pushes through them, leaving an opening for Cooper to dart through. "Oh! Sorry!" the surprised teacher says, her eyes tracking the dog. I dash after him and scan the crowd that's suddenly swallowed him up. Teachers dressed in holiday sweaters swarm toward buffet tables, filling sagging paper plates, and student artwork lines the walls, portraying views from our little mountain town of white-capped mountains and snowy valleys.

Walton High only opened this year, and everything's shiny and new, from the freshly painted concrete walls to the gleaming light fixtures. I shield my eyes with a hand and survey the area, peering around people and behind knees. Principal Peabody lords over the punch bowl dressed in a Santa hat and looking cheery. She sees me and I wave, nerves humming through me. *Dogs in the school won't be a problem*, I said. *They're very well behaved. And sociable.* Cooper's apparently the most sociable of them all.

"Cooper," I whisper hoarsely. "Cooper, where are you?"

Ahh, there he is! Jingle-jangle-jingle. I catch a glimpse of his puppy dog tail beyond a pair of chatting teachers and lunge forward—*oomph*—landing on my hands and knees. Cooper prances ahead of me as I frantically crawl after him. "Cooper! Cooper! Wait!" I hiss under my breath. Principal Peabody's laughing and smiling, glancing around the packed room. Her eyebrows knit together. *Noooo.* She's heard the jingle bells, too.

I crouch lower to the ground and crawl faster. Where's Cooper going? Aha. The treats table. Someone's dropped a pretzel on the floor, but I can't let him eat *that*. It's covered in chocolate and candy sprinkles and everyone knows chocolate's

3

bad for dogs. If he gets sick on my watch… My stomach churns. *No.* I crawl, crawl, crawl until I'm almost to him. He stops and sniffs the treat then tilts his head from side to side, bouncing on his front paws.

Jingle-jangle-jingle. Bark! Bark! Bark!

I pounce—then Cooper's airborne! …And being scooped off the floor and hoisted skyward. "Well, hey there, little buddy," a guy's voice says. "Where'd you come from?" Cooper's leash dangles beside me, its handle end coiling on the cafeteria floor. I swallow hard and goggle at the khaki pants legs in front of me, then sit back on my knees and look up.

A *very handsome guy* with short brown hair and a deep dimple in his cheek stares down at me and my breath catches. He cuts a familiar swath, like a movie star or a sports celeb. Someone I've seen billions of— My heart jolts like a sledgehammer's smashed against it. *Dean Burton.* Cradling Cooper in his arms and dressed in a dark red sweater. I had *no clue* he was back in town. Or at Walton. We met at a campus pizza place and dated my first two years of college. Last I'd heard, he'd moved to Boulder, Colorado.

A voice in my head shouts: *Surprise!* The word clanks around like a gonging cymbal, so loud my brain hurts. Of all the teachers at Walton, I'm the least likely to get surprised. Ask anyone who knows me. I organize; I orchestrate! I complete! Dot all the i's and cross all the t's. Plan out my workdays, my free time—my *dreams*, to be embarrassingly honest.

My pulse skitters. I did not plan for this.

Maybe he won't recognize me? Or remember?

Sweat beads my hairline.

A lopsided grin.

My heart hammers so hard it aches.

"Paige Pierce," he says. "This is a surprise."

I scramble to my feet and dust off my jeans. "Dean!" His

eyes fill with wonder, like he doesn't believe what he's seeing. I don't believe it, either. I'm melting in my snug turtleneck and T-shirt, and not in a good way. More like in the way my face is glistening. I tuck my stick-straight brown hair behind one ear, pondering Mom's advice. She's a hairdresser and forever urging me to spice up my looks. Add highlights to my hair, flirty layers! But that means being daring and taking chances. *Change.* And I don't change easily. My entire childhood was spent navigating rocky seas and I prefer calm waters. Although it kind of feels like my craft's been upended, and I'm drowning in Dean's deep brown eyes.

"Hey," he asks about the dog, shifting Cooper in his arms, "is he yours?"

"No, I'm minding him"—*and not very expertly*—"for Beth." I reach for Cooper and Dean passes him to me. Our hands brush and my stomach does a tiny twirl. *No, Paige. Just no.* I don't need Dean reawakening those old feelings. Where are they even coming from, anyway? I was so sure they'd been put to bed. I set Cooper down and pat his head when he sits properly by my feet. I hold on to his leash, very tightly, wrapping part of it around my wrist. "Beth is Cooper's handler for our program."

"Program?" he asks.

I pull myself together and proudly point to the logo on my pocket. "Paws and Read."

Dean chuckles and strokes his chin. "Nice play on words."

"Thanks! We tried out several options but this one was top-dog."

He smirks and my heart flutters. "Pretty doggone good." He notes the gray around Cooper's muzzle. "Guess you *can* teach an old dog new tricks?"

Cooper yaps excitedly, as though somehow aware we're talking about him.

"Dean!" I laugh and sigh, acting like I'm *dog-tired* of this conversation, which I'm *not*.

"So what do you do at Walton?" he asks lightly. "Other than, you know, run the doggie show?"

"I teach here. Ninth grade English."

"Really? That's great." His eyes shimmer so warmly I go all topsy-turvy inside. *Come on, Paige. Knock it off.* I'm about to ask him what he's doing here when a high-pitched squeal sounds, and someone taps a microphone.

"Can I have your attention, please!" It's Principal Peabody in her bright red Santa hat. Dean and I turn toward the short, stout blond. "I'm so glad we could all be here together at this inaugural holiday party. What a joyful occasion it is, having the entire faculty together under less stressful circumstances." She smiles. "No students!" Low chuckles ripple through the room.

Beth enters the cafeteria wearing her Paws and Read ID badge on its matching lanyard. Adrian's with her, and his dog Bailey's at his side. The mellow golden retriever spots me and Cooper, leading the others our way. As my volunteers join me, Principal Peabody remarks, "We have some special guests here tonight, volunteers with Paige Pierce's new literacy program, Paws and Read." I asked them to make a brief appearance. Employees and students will get a chance to officially meet them and the other Paws and Read participants at our launch party on the twenty-third.

People turn toward our group and smile. I hand Cooper's leash to Beth, and she and Adrian give hand signals prompting their dogs to obediently sit and stay. Dean nods in greeting at the newcomers and they do the same.

"But first," Principal Peabody continues, "I have a new faculty member to introduce: our new physics teacher, Dean Burton." I blink when Principal Peabody extends her microphone and

Dean starts striding toward her. "Dean, why don't you come on over and say a brief hello?" she says before ceding the floor. "Dean will begin at Walton after the break, but I've invited him here to join the party and meet you all beforehand. Please help him feel welcome."

"Thank you," he says. He's in the spotlight, amid a sea of waiting faces. He holds the mic, surveying the cheery decorations. "Happy holidays, everyone!" I'd forgotten how I love the sound of his voice, a smooth baritone. Plus, he's smart and great-looking. If he's not married by now, he's bound to have a girlfriend at least. Which is natural and to be expected. He no doubt assumes I'm involved with somebody, too. It *has* been six years. A thought bubble containing my nightly routine while working out on the treadmill blooms in my mind. Dating app letdowns. *Swipe left. Left. Hard left.*

A chorus rings back at Dean. "Happy holidays!" Teachers listen and watch politely. Everyone seems in great spirits. I'm sure winter break being right around the corner helps their mood. I know it bolsters mine. I've invested so much time in getting Paws and Read off the ground, it will be awesome to kick back and relax. Have chill time. Peace and quiet.

"Like Principal Peabody said, I'm Dean Burton, and it's so nice to be here." He beams brightly. "I look forward to meeting you all." He seems to notice nobody wears a nametag. "Just don't expect me to remember names right off the bat." Light laughter.

Dean finishes speaking and Principal Peabody beckons me forward. I approach her with my volunteers and their dogs accompany them in lockstep while others look on, impressed. "I'd like to thank you all for your support!" I state to pleasantly interested faces. "Our fall fundraiser was a hit and I'm happy to report—" I visually check in with Principal Peabody and she gives me a nod to go ahead. "—our superintendent's given us the greenlight to pilot the Paws and Read high school program at Walton."

Cheers and whistles erupt and I flush happily. I've wanted this forever. To make a real difference with struggling students. So many are in circumstances like I was in as a child, with working, single parents who are unable to help them with their schoolwork. Others come from homes where English is not the native spoken language. A few have skated along on such bare-minimum academic skills, if they're not helped soon, they'll be at risk for dropping out.

By the time I reached high school, I'd gotten *really good* at hiding my deficits. I was hardworking and articulate, so I could charm my way into passing grades. Then my caring English teacher realized I could only read CliffsNotes, and she taught me not to take shortcuts. To stay on the road. She set me up with a reading specialist and spent extra hours with me after school. I decided I wanted to be her one day, so I could help others. "The evidence is clear," I tell my colleagues. "Research supports the positive impact of having learning-challenged students read aloud to pup partners. What we haven't seen enough of is this sort of initiative taking root in the upper grades. I'm hoping we can change that here."

Several teachers have already signed up to have our dogs work with particular students or small groups in January and February, and my list for March is already filling up. "I'd like to introduce two of the volunteers in our program, Beth Chambers and Adrian Kearns, along with their dogs, Cooper and Bailey." People *ooh* and *ahh* at the sweetness of their canine faces, as Beth and Adrian smile and wave. Despite his sprightly gait, Cooper is a senior dog, nearly ten years old, while Bailey's an even-tempered youngster of four.

I continue my presentation. "Every volunteer with Paws

and Read is a trained therapy dog handler and each dog is fully accredited. The volunteers have also been vetted by our school system with complete background checks and will wear Paws and Read program IDs"—Beth lifts hers up and pivots it toward different areas in the room—"along with T-shirts like these."

I motion to my T-shirt and those of my volunteers, then say sunnily, "We'll have T-shirts for sale at our launch party next week. Paws and Read buttons, too. I hope you'll all join us in the gym after the assembly on Tuesday to get better acquainted with Cooper and Beth, and Bailey and Adrian, and our other dogs and volunteers."

After my talk, I thank Adrian and Beth for attending before squatting down to address their dogs. "And thanks to you too, Bailey." I scratch him behind his ears and he tilts his head sideways, laying his cheek in my palm.

Adrian grins. "Bailey likes you."

"And I like Bailey!" I say looking up. I turn my attention on Cooper. "That was very sneaky," I whisper, leaning forward and patting his head. "But don't worry, I won't tell." Cooper yaps merrily, bouncing on his front paws, and the bells on his vest jingle.

Beth's light eyes twinkle. "Cooper likes you too."

I stand upright, feeling happy and fulfilled. "Cooper's special," I say to Beth. I glance at Bailey, then Adrian. "So's Bailey." I deliver my heartfelt praise. "So are the two of you." Both are experienced with dogs-in-the-schools programs and served as my guiding lights by giving great advice. "Thanks for everything you've done, and thanks for coming tonight."

I bump into Dean by the punch bowl later. The light green punch has a frothy crown on top. "I think that's great about Paws and Read, Paige. Sounds like such a worthy cause."

I help myself to some punch and stand beside him, then we scoot out of the way as others crowd in, making our way to the treats table. "The idea of dogs working in schools has been around for a while," I say and take a small sip of fizzy liquid. It's tangy and tart, ginger ale with lime sherbet mixed in. "What's novel is expanding the concept beyond the elementary and middle grades. There've been some ninth grade programs, but those are fewer and farther between, because it's harder to get funding for the older age groups. But it's never too late to reach out to those in need. You know what I'm saying?"

He views me admiringly. "Yeah. I think I do." He selects a gingerbread person along with a red-and-green checkered napkin that says *Ho, ho, ho!*

I grab a napkin and an angel cookie, still in stunned disbelief that Dean Burton is here at my workplace and we're conversing after all this time. "So, " I ask casually, as we stand by a column wrapped with garlands, "how are your folks? Jenny?"

"All good." He takes a bite of gingerbread cookie. "Jenny graduates college this year."

"Does she? Wow. Exciting." I remember her as a teenager, but of course now she's grown up.

"How's Rosemary?" he asks about my mom.

"Great." I laugh and roll my eyes. "Same."

"Glad to hear it, I guess?" Dean knows Mom meddles in my life. He also understands how much I love her. The two of them really got along. She was very sad when we broke up.

The memory floods me like an old film reel in faded colors.

Dean and I stand on the stoop of my apartment building saying goodbye. Springtime breezes blow and flowers scent the air. A full moon hangs overhead. He's been granted an internship at the new STEM facility built on the site of the famous Arecibo telescope in Puerto Rico. He wants me to go with him, but I'm applying for summer jobs, so busy. Plus, I need to finish my degree, like he's finished his. He's two years older and graduated this year.

Dean lays his hand on my cheek. "Won't you please reconsider? You can take classes there and get them transferred—maybe complete courses online?"

"Dean, I can't just drop everything and go with you. What about Mom? If I leave, what will happen to her?"

He takes me in his arms and holds me. "Then I'll call and text every day."

Hurt wells in my throat when I share my hard truth. "You'll be gone a whole year, Dean. I don't think either of us should wait for the other."

"Wait." His eyes mist over. Are you saying we should end things?" His broken look ruins me. Shoots an arrow through my heart. But I've been thinking about this all week and I believe it's for the best. For him, for me. We're so young and our lives are just starting. We can't possibly last.

No man that Mom has loved has ever stayed, and the apple doesn't fall far from the tree. Dean might be the right guy, but this isn't the right time. I gently touch his arm. "I'm sorry."

He sets his chin and turns away. "Yeah, me too."

The light chatter of the party draws me back to the present, and a lead weight settles in my stomach. Might as well address the elephant in the room and clear the air between us. *Deep breaths.* "So," I ask, "Puerto Rico then? It all worked out?"

"It did," he says fondly. "That's where I met Wendy."

Oof. My chest hurts. Silly. Even though I broke it off, I'm not made of steel. It's hard to think he moved on so easily. Still. I force a pleasant face. Nod, like I'm interested. Like I *want* to know about Wendy. "Nice!"

"Wendy was my supervisor," he explains. "She was there on a fellowship from her private school in Boulder. She's the one who recruited me out west."

"Oh! So—?" I fan my face with my napkin.

"Our interactions were strictly business," he says with an amused air. "Wendy was *fifty.*"

And he was twenty-two. "A-*ha.* I see." I wind a lock of my hair around my finger, like I never assumed otherwise. Wrap it too tightly and my finger pinches. *Throbs.*

"I'm not exclusive with anyone, if that's what you're wondering." Humiliation swamps through me. *Gah, am I that transparent?*

"And you?" he asks. "Married? Kids?"

I shake free my finger from my hair. "Nope and nope!"

"All work and no play, Paige Pierce."

"Ha." *Nailed it.* Maybe I would be involved with someone, if the right person had come along. But no one's ever seemed just right and, after a few short months, each union's fizzled.

Chad Quesenberry walks over in a plaid button-down shirt and circular glasses. He's the lead guidance counselor at Walton. "Paige?" he interrupts politely. "I'd love to talk to you about your program." I spy others over his shoulder, approaching to speak with me next.

"See you around," Dean says quietly. His husky breath tickles my ear and electric tingles course through me. I really need to stop having these reactions to him. Especially since we're now both working at Walton. Thank goodness I'll have the weekend to get my head on straight. All I need is *a plan* for dealing with Dean, and I'm an excellent planner.

Maybe I can plug the problem into my dream journal? *Yes, there's a thought.* I've had success figuring out tough situations in my sleep before. It's like my subconscious is more adept than my conscious self at untangling those twisty knots. All I'll have to do is write down *professional relationship with Dean,* then my creative mind will fill in the blanks while I'm sleeping. *Aha! Problem solved!*

A high-pitched wail and a *tap-tap-tap* on the microphone startle us into attention a half hour later. "*Hel-lo!*" The room turns toward Principal Peabody. "This has been a very merry time having you all here, and getting to meet our newest addition, Dean." A round of applause. I search the room for Dean but don't see him. "Let's give a big thanks to the PTA for supplying these delectable goodies!" More clapping as parents standing by the door to the kitchen take a bow. "Now, the moment we've all been waiting for." She sweeps a hand toward a table holding prettily wrapped gifts. "Please pick out a package from our gift exchange as a fun memento from our party tonight. Happy holidays, one and all!"

Dean appears carrying a present. It's hard to look in his eyes and not think about what was, but I need to prepare myself for precisely that. "Paige, I want you to have this." It's a rectangular package wrapped in reindeer paper with a bright blue bow.

"Oh no, I couldn't. That's meant for someone else." When I opted into the gift exchange, I imagined selecting a random gift, not being given one specifically by Dean.

13

"I think it's just what you need," he says sassily. "A little dose of holiday cheer."

I cling to the package, trying not to tremble. *Darn it.* I'm not doing so great at separating the personal from the professional, but all I need is practice. There's nothing in the county handbook saying two teachers can't be friends. Which Dean and I should be, naturally. It's our history of having been *more than friends* that complicates things. *Dream journal. Right. On it.*

Dean nods at the package. "I found it downtown at the holiday market, and somehow it called to me. The older lady I bought it from was very mysterious about its properties, saying it can foretell the future, *change lives.*"

"Tall order," I say wryly. I don't mention that *change* is not on my top-ten list. I don't have to. I've been this way forever.

"The seller's assertion *was* a little out there, it's true. But hey! You never know, do you?"

"About?"

"Life?" He shrugs. "Fate?" He leans closer and his spicy scent washes over me. "Magical gifts from the holiday market?" There's an impish gleam in his eyes and I chuckle.

"Come on, you don't really mean it. Magic?"

"Why not magic?" he replies. "Stranger things have happened." Still the same old Dean. Powerfully optimistic. I was the realist between us.

"Have *not.*"

"Maybe not in your book, Paige, but there's still room for a bit of mystery in mine, and there's no greater mystery than Christmas magic."

I gasp playfully. "And this vendor convinced you of that?"

Dean holds open his hands. "She was dressed like Mrs. Claus, so fairly authoritative, I'd say." I chuckle at his serious look.

"What if I hadn't been here?" My eyebrows arch. "Who would have received your mysterious package then?"

Dean rubs his chin. "Someone in for a whole lot of Christmas magic, it seems."

"If you say so, Dean." I realize that sounds a bit flirty and my cheeks warm.

"I say so." The package shifts in my grasp and something moves around inside it. Maybe it's a set of tea towels? Or a tree skirt? Perfect. It can go with all the Christmas tree ornaments I own for the Christmas tree I never buy. But something that's actually magic? *Ha!*

I indicate the gift table. "Aren't you going to pick something out?"

Dean shakes his head. "I don't want anything this Christmas," he says, looking certain. "I'm already getting what I want. A once-in-a-lifetime chance." He glances toward the courtyard and up at the darkened night. "There's a big astronomical event happening tonight. The Christmas Comet. I suppose you've read about it in the news?" I shake my head no. "Some say it was the same light the Magi followed, mistaking it for a bright star." He gestures with his hand. "You should try to catch it. The clouds are supposed to lift later. It should put on quite a show."

"When?" I recall stargazing with him and being snuggled in his arms. But he's surely snuggling with somebody else now. Her name doesn't have to be Wendy and they don't have to be exclusive. My noses twitches anxiously and I rub it.

He squints, thinking. "Oh, around midnight?"

I sigh and answer, "I'll be fast asleep by then."

"Suit yourself. You're missing something special." The sparkle in his eyes makes me question whether I missed something special in him. "How about you?" he asks. "Want anything in particular from Santa?"

"I've already gotten my wish," I say happily. "Approval for my Paws and Read program. I'm so excited about starting it up at the beginning of next year."

"Good for you." He sinks his hands in his pockets. "You always had a fondness for animals." He must recall how I volunteered at the local animal shelter while in college. Growing up, I sadly never had a dog. We were on a tight budget and Mom said we couldn't afford pets. "Any dogs of your own?" he queries.

"Not yet." I shrug, adding hopefully, "But maybe someday?"

He smiles wistfully. "Yeah, same." The crowd in the cafeteria disperses, with PTA volunteers clearing the tables. It's obvious we need to leave, too. Though part of me hangs on, not wanting to go. Judging by the way Dean's gaze lingers on me, it's like he feels the same. Others pick out their gifts, walking toward the hall. No one seems to be opening their presents here.

"So I should just take this home and—" I lift a shoulder.

His eyes dance. "Enjoy it."

My face heats and I hug Dean's gift harder. "Okay then, thanks."

"Happy holidays, Paige. It's really great seeing you again."

His grin melts my heart in a way that is *not* good or helpful, when I'm trying so hard to stay over him, and the tiniest part of me can't help but wonder—how our lives might have been different if we'd never broken up?

CHAPTER
Two

Snow speckles the windshield of my burgundy-colored SUV, and the automatic wipers turn on. I peek at the darkened sky as snow strikes against the pavement ahead of me, my headlights painting the road. I hope Dean's right about it clearing up later, so he can see that comet he's so excited about. Of all the people in all the world, it's amazing he's at Walton. If I were the superstitious type—which I'm not—I might view our working there together as a sign. I recall the dreamy look in his eyes when we said goodbye, and sigh.

There was a time, with Dean, when I envisioned a different sort of life for myself. If things had gone differently, who knows? But they didn't, and I'm satisfied with how things turned out. Who needs kids and sleepless nights? A messy house…*laundry*? Not me, thankfully. I'm good where I am. My spirt flags, but I shake off the gloom. I couldn't let my path be swayed by romance. I had to chart my own course. Plus, I had someone else to think of.

The phone rings through my dashboard on my Bluetooth and the caller ID lights up.

Mom. What is she, psychic?

I press the answer button on the steering wheel with my thumb.

"Hi, Mom." The heater blasts, ushering in that clean, new-car smell. My one-year-old vehicle still gleams like new.

My SUV technically belongs to the bank, but in another four years, I'll hold the title free and clear. When the dealership offered me competitive financing, the splurge was hard to resist. My last car broke down every other *week*. I'm glad to have moved past my poverty phase and into a new one. Adulting.

"*Paige.*" She sounds as cheerful as ever. "How was the holiday party?"

"Good! And—" I pause a beat. "Surprising."

"Oh?"

I weigh how much to tell her, because I don't want her butting in. Then again, despite our differences, she's my best friend. I really miss my old college bunch: Kirstin, Mia, and Heather. We had such great times, but now they've fallen away with husbands and families of their own. We've tried *so many times* to get together, but between their obligations and my work commitments, we've never managed to coordinate our schedules. Sometimes I suspect they still get together without me. It shouldn't hurt my feelings and it doesn't. Except for the tiniest bit.

Naturally, they should meet up to discuss baby milestones and whatnot while drinking margaritas. I saw them at that Mexican restaurant once seated at an outdoor table, laughing and living it up. They all looked good and happy. Companionable. And I'm happy for them, I am. They have so much in common, and I'm—more or less, the odd one out.

So. I decide to let Mom know. Because, honestly? I'm dying to tell someone.

"Dean was there." I catch a glimpse of the gift on the passenger seat beside me with its big blue bow. An item portending change and Christmas magic. Ha. Ha. Ha. Or is that *ho, ho, ho*? Very funny. And impossible.

"Dean Burton?" She gasps audibly. "He's not in Colorado?"

"Apparently not anymore. He's taken a post at Walton teaching physics. He'll start there next semester."

"Well, well, well," she says cheerfully. "What a small world."

"Now, Mom." I know what she's thinking. "Don't get any ideas."

"Why not?"

"Because," I say like that's a full answer. I keep a firm grasp on the wheel as I drive. This windy mountain road's bolstered by guard rails. A craggy mountain ridge on my left sports frozen cascades and spiky icicle drips. Tall trees in the valley below are covered in white.

"Is he married?"

"No."

I can picture her clapping her hands together. "It's not over until it's over!"

"It's over, Mom." Even as I say it, my seatbelt feels too tight. Though I'd convinced myself that Dean was in my past, I sure didn't feel over him at the party. Those old feelings came crashing down on me like an avalanche, so hard my heart still feels the bruising. But there's no way to undo what happened back then.

Mom continues with her sunny tirade. "Well I, for one, take this as a very good sign. The two of you must have been put together at the same school for a reason."

"Yes," I say drolly. "That reason is called our former physics teacher, Edward Stone, who moved to Northern Virginia on account of his wife's business transfer."

"No," she insists stubbornly. "That reason is called fate."

Mom's a big believer in fate and romance. She thinks she wants happily ever after, but what she truthfully enjoys are possibilities. Reality is what she doesn't appreciate so much. Like when the bloom is off the rose, and they start leaving towels on the floor and dirty dishes in the sink. Not that I honestly blame her. Being single has its charms. Several of them, truthfully. Being single is good! More people should aspire to it! Like me! Oh, wait. I scowl as a salt truck passes by in the opposite lane. It's got its shovel raised, scattering chemicals in its wake.

"So, are we still on for lunch tomorrow?" I ask, changing the subject, although I suspect it won't be changed for long. Being two glass-half-full-type people, Mom and Dean shared a bond. Dean teaches science, but that doesn't keep him from seeing the outstanding possibilities in this world. I'm more about words and logical conclusions. Like when you dump someone six years ago, they're probably not eager for a fresh start. Just because they show up at the same school where you work. Coincidentally. And *not* on account of fate.

"Yes," she says about our weekly date. "I thought we'd try that new place, Beaumont's."

I've heard they have great burgers. "Sounds good."

Her voice takes on a happy lilt. "Can't wait to tell you about my new special someone." Mom's the perpetual romantic, forever searching for her prince. She's been searching for as long as I can remember. What I can't recall so well are the names of the many boyfriends she's had. I don't even know who my dad is, because she was never able to figure it out, and she doesn't seem to particularly care. I do, though. Or at least I once did. It's easier as an adult than it was when I was a kid. Still. There are moments.

"Oh yeah? Who is he?"

She chuckles warmly. "I'll tell you more at lunch. Want to say noon?"

"Okay. Noontime it is!"

Mom and I have gotten in the habit of exchanging early Christmas gifts. That way, we make the actual day more about togetherness and food. I try to get Mom what she wants, but she always says the same thing: earrings, because she thinks they're inexpensive. The one time I got her diamond stud earrings, she made me take them back. So I'm fine with our arrangement to only exchange trinkets. She generally gives me a Christmas tree ornament each year, even though I've never once put up a Christmas tree. It honestly *is* the thought that counts, and each one is special because I know she took care in selecting it.

Before we hang up, she stops me. "Oh, Paige?"

"Yeah?"

"I've got a little favor to ask about next week."

The first part of my week is busy with wrapping up the semester and my Paws and Read program launch, but I'll be there for her, naturally, if I'm able. She's quiet an instant too long, which is very unlike bubbly Mom. "What is it?"

"I have an appointment for a procedure, that's all. I'll be under anesthesia so won't be able to drive myself home after. I could ask my new fellow to take me, but honestly I'd feel better with you."

My heart's in a vise. The last procedure Mom had was to remove cancer from her spleen. They thought they'd gotten it all. She endured the rigors of chemotherapy and radiation nonetheless, and has just now grown back her curly red hair. "What kind of procedure?"

"I don't want you to worry," she says, meaning this must be worse than I thought. "It's just some additional testing." No, no, no, no. *No.* This can't be happening again. Not to

someone as goodhearted and kind as Mom. "An ultrasound
and MRI." They must have found something on the scans
she had done last week. She'd returned to her oncologist for a
routine checkup and was about to receive clearance for going
five years cancer free. Dean never knew about Mom. She got
sick my senior year of college

Wait. Queasiness roils through me. Mom would not need
anesthesia for those things. "Anything else?"

She blows out a soft breath. "Perhaps a small biopsy, non-
invasive, laparoscopic, but honey, the doctor says it's just a
precaution. He's very thorough."

Hot tears spring to my eyes and I have trouble seeing the
road. I wipe them back with a glove and pull myself together.
Me having an auto accident right now will in no way help Mom.
She needs me here. "When's your appointment?" I try to keep my
voice steady but fail. It shakes just a little and my chin trembles.

"Well, since you're so busy right before break, I asked them
to schedule me for Wednesday, on Christmas Eve morning. I
know school is closed then. I hope that's okay?"

The windshield wipers in front of me tick back and forth as
snow hits the glass. I dab my nose with a tissue and try to hide
my sniff so she can't hear it. "Of course, Mom. I'll take you."

"Great! And Paige?"

"Hmm?"

"Sweetheart. Everything's going to turn out great." She
pauses then adds emphatically, "Including with you and Dean!
Just you wait and see." I smile despite my tears. Still the same
old Mom. At least that part makes me feel good. And hey, I
should take a page out of her book and Dean's and start trust-
ing in happy outcomes. If I believe in my heart that Mom will
be okay, then she will be. I can't let her down. I need to stay
positive for her sake, hold on to that hope.

I pull into my condo building's parking lot, easing past the raised gate by the guardhouse. Lloyd is the off-duty cop who staffs it. He gives me a wave as I pass by.

I park under the high-rise building in my assigned spot and climb from my SUV, grabbing the package and my compact purse from the glove box. I brace myself against the cold as I hurry toward the glass enclosure housing the elevator. Its clear door holds a fake holly wreath, dripping with crimson holly berries and gold-spray-painted pine cones. A blast of heat envelops me when I step inside and press the elevator button.

A few minutes later, I'm upstairs on the sixth floor entering my condo. The large plate-glass window in front of me forms an entire wall beyond the adjoining living room and dining area. Snow slashes sideways against the glass and, below that, in the distance, the twinkling lights of Boone illuminate the foggy darkness. Boone's not a huge town, but it's at least four times the size of Piney Mount, where I am now. Boone is also where I went to college. My heart pings. *Where Dean and I fell in love.*

I flip on the recessed lighting in the hall and shut the door behind me. This place is tiny, but it's got everything I need. The galley kitchen to my left is divided from the dining area by a high countertop with two tall stools, and my round dining table's got two chairs. I ordered the set online from a Swedish discount shop, like most of my furniture here.

My sofa faces the gas fireplace with a TV screen mounted above it, and I've positioned two cozy swivel armchairs to appreciate the view. Elroy waits expectantly in one of them. I walk over to pet my shaggy white dog. He's the size of a large

23

baby doll and sits back on his haunches with his head raised in a frozen position of anticipation. "Hi, Elroy! How was your day?"

When my hand strokes his head he says, *"Arf, arf!"* and looks up at me with big glass eyes. He's a robotic dog, but his bark sounds convincingly real.

"Did you take good care of the place?" I pat his head again. "Arf! Arf!"

"Good boy! Extra treats for you tonight." I set the package from Dean on the coffee table, giving a voice command to my virtual assistant. Both lights on either side of the sofa switch on, as does the one by the armchair with its back to the window. My treadmill's beside the armchair and angled toward the television.

A single en suite bedroom is accessible from the hall, as is its connected bathroom through a separate door. The master has a similar plate-glass window framing the mountain views, which are gorgeous year-round, but spectacular in autumn. The peaks appear magical now, blanketed in snow.

I survey my tidy space, glad to be home. Winds bluster against the glass with a bone-chilling howl. I'm *also* glad I don't have to walk the dog—or pick up after one. Mom gave me Elroy, as somewhat of an apology.

"I'm really sorry I never gave you a real dog when you were a girl, but—considering your busy schedule—maybe this one will suffice for now."

"He's perfect!" I hug her and kiss her cheek. "The best pet I could wish for! No housebreaking. No vet bills," I say to make her feel better.

Tears glisten in her eyes but she still smiles. "Oh Paige." She laughs warmly. "You're impossible."

"Impossible not to love," I tease and hug her harder. "Thanks for the pet!"

That was the Christmas I gave her the diamond earrings. It was my first year of teaching and I felt flush with my newfound "wealth," meaning I was finally getting a regular monthly paycheck—even though a portion of it was assigned to paying down college loans. It helped that I shared the rent with Heather.

Mom had just begun managing her own salon and had a bit of extra earnings that year. Her new salon sadly didn't last. After her landlord raised the rent, she had to close her shop. Not all Mom's mistakes are of her doing. Some are plain bad luck. Like the torrent of medical bills that consumed the last of her savings.

That's why I'm planning to help care for her in her sunset years, and thanks to my school system 403(b) retirement account and other money I'm gradually setting aside, I'll manage. Mom's not much of a planner and has never had steady or high enough income to earn sustainable social security. But she'll never need to worry. *Although she doesn't. Mom's happy-go-lucky that way.* I'll have her back.

I approach the fireplace mantel and stare at my meager collection of Christmas tree ornaments. One looks like a snowman, another one is Santa with a sack of toys across his back. The third's a prancing reindeer with a bulbous red nose. I suspect that, this year, Mom will give me another. I hope she likes the pretty tin earrings I bought her at the holiday market. They're long and dangly in deep blues and greens and seem like her style.

I decide not to dwell on her procedure on Wednesday, thinking of the positives instead. She has a top-notch surgeon and is in very good hands. Plus, she's not alone on this journey. I'm right here with her, and this is where I'm going to stay. If she has another battle ahead of her, we'll fight it together. We won before and we will again.

My stomach rumbles and I realize how hungry I am. I'll microwave one of my frozen dinners to have with a glass of wine. The treadmill by the window summons me to be disciplined. But no. Not tonight. I'm worn *out*. I'll exercise doubly hard in the morning before meeting Mom for lunch.

A short time later, I'm settled on the sofa in my comfy pajama pants and sweatshirt. I hold my plate of hot lasagna and take a whopping bite. *Mmm.* Cheesy oregano flavors burst onto my tongue along with the taste of tangy tomato sauce and hearty pasta. I lift my wineglass off the side table and chase my food with a sip of cabernet sauvignon. Delicious.

The package on the coffee table captures my attention. It was sweet of Dean to insist I bring it home, and his hinting at its specialness does intrigue me. I set my plate and wineglass down and lean forward, picking up the present. Part of me feels like I should wait until Christmas, but no. I'm sure none of the other teachers are waiting, so why be the only one?

I turn over the gift in my lap and unseal the carefully taped flaps, before running my finger beneath the wrapping paper's seam. *There.* It pops loose and I remove the rest of the wrapping, flipping the box back over. I laugh at its oblong shape. It does look like a shirt box for real. A memory surfaces of me wearing Dean's large T-shirt, its fabric swamping me. I used to sleep in his T-shirts sometimes. They felt so cozy, like I was being wrapped in him.

Silly to remember that now. Stupid to keep looking back, when what I need to do is look forward to my newly approved Paws and Read program and the very many people it will help. My volunteers claim they benefit, too; training the dogs allows them to establish a sense of purpose in helping their communities, and most of the pups involved are working dogs, accustomed to needing a job to feel content.

I fit my fingers under the box lid and lift it off, setting it aside. Unfold the white tissue paper. *What?*

Oh my gosh, this is the cutest! A darling advent calendar nestles in the remaining tissue paper in the box. I carefully grasp its sides, holding it up. The roughly sixteen by twenty-two inch length of cloth unfurls before me. Its quilted, cream-colored material displays a fake wallpaper design and contains a green felt Christmas tree in its center. Below that, bright red pockets with gold braid trim line up in three rows of eight, numbered one through twenty-four in white stitching.

My heart does a happy dance at the fun surprise. I never had one of these as a kid, but I always wanted one badly. I have a vague memory of telling Dean something about that when we dated in college and discussed our childhood Christmases. Is it possible he remembered once he saw me at the school? If so, how thoughtful. But then, that's just like Dean.

Each numbered pocket contains a cloth Christmas tree ornament meant to be attached to the tree. The pocket labeled with the number twenty-four has two ornaments, though. One's of a chubby Santa Claus face with a snowy white beard, a cherry-like nose, and a cute Santa hat, and the other one's a star. I assume the star's supposed to go on last on Christmas Day, since there's no actual pocket labeled number twenty-five. The star's the finishing touch for the top of the tree after Santa comes on the twenty-fourth and the final sign that Christmas is here.

I remove the cute Santa face from the pocket and flip it over, seeing a strip of Velcro on the back. Aha! I press the Santa face to the tree, hold up the calendar—and Santa sticks! I chuckle. *Got it.* This is so darn cute. Though, honestly? Maybe better suited to a family with kids. I raise my chin, deciding I can be a kid at heart. Why not? I spend every hour of every day being so structured in so many ways. What's the harm in a little fun?

I tuck Santa back in the calendar pocket and happily shout at the ceiling, "Thanks, Dean!" Maybe things will go okay between us at Walton. And maybe the fact that he doesn't have a girlfriend is a good thing? He never said he wasn't seeing people casually. Merely that there wasn't someone serious. Still. Dean's handsome and well employed. Funny and smart. So there could be someone angling to become more involved with him romantically. Waiting patiently in the wings—to swoop in. I glower grumpily, although I don't mean to. *If that's the case, Paige, you only have yourself to blame.*

My heart thuds dully, but I bolster my spirits. Tonight, I don't want to think about self-blame and past mistakes. Tonight, I want to think about Christmas and possibilities! I freeze, worrying that Mom's rubbing off on me. *No.* I'm not throwing caution to the wind. It's just a holiday market advent calendar, after all. It doesn't *really* have the ability to predict the future— or change lives, least of all mine. I stand and grip the calendar in my hands, wondering where I should mount it. Maybe in the kitchen near the refrigerator?

I stride into the kitchen where the refrigerator holds only one thing: my daily schedule pinned down with magnets. The color-coded spreadsheet's neatly divided into blocks concerning professional and personal tasks. Today is Friday, so I've got "lesson planning for short week" written in the work block after "returning and discussing final exam" and "pick up dry cleaning" under errands. *Oops.* Forgot that. Then again, I wasn't exactly expecting the curveball of Dean showing up at Walton's faculty holiday party, either. No matter. I'll get the dry cleaning tomorrow, after my lunch date with Mom.

But now, to hang my fun surprise! I remove a framed piece of art from the wall and place it on the counter. A green ribbon at the top of the advent calendar attaches to a wooden rod from which the quilted fabric piece drapes. I loop the ribbon over the nail and straighten the calendar. It's so cheerful! It brightens up the space.

Okay. Today is December nineteenth, so I put up just as many ornaments. I select a toy drum from one pocket, a gingerbread man from another, a petite gift next. I've finally got them done when I think of Dean's Christmas Comet. My gaze snags on the star in the final pocket and I take it out, examining it in my hand. It's made of satiny gold fabric. How pretty! Why not put this one up tonight? I'll use it as a topper for the felt Christmas tree.

I press the star to the calendar with a flourish. "Here's your Christmas Comet!" I say out loud to Dean, as if he were standing right here. For an instant the item shimmers and glows, brilliantly bright. I blink and stare harder, trace a finger over the fabric star, but no. Now it looks normal. I must have imagined that somehow. This isn't *really* a magical calendar. That was all part of the vendor's spiel to give Dean's purchase greater allure.

My heart lifts; I know Dean would enjoy me getting a kick out of his gift. I stare out the window, seeing the snow has stopped and the dark clouds are parting. Looks like that Christmas Comet might make an appearance after all. A wave of exhaustion rolls over me and I yawn. I don't think I'll make it to midnight tonight. Not after the busy day I've had.

I prepare for bed and snuggle down under the covers with a pillow propped behind my back. I nab my spiral-bound dream journal off my nightstand and a pen. Last night, I wrote: *Dark Stretch.* That's what I write when I'm too tired to think about anything else. I just close my eyes and fall into blackness until my alarm goes off the next morning.

Tonight though, I've got a mission. I flip the notebook to a fresh page and position my pen against it, scrawling out December nineteenth. Then I write three words: *Relationship with Dean.* Sigh. And turn out the light.

•  •

A bright light beams against the window, waking me from my slumber and showering the room with a blistering brightness. I squint in confusion against the glare. *What?* Oh my gosh. I was so tired I forgot to draw the curtains.

I snatch the remote off my nightstand and press a button. Curtains glide toward each other, dragging on their tracks and darkening the room.

I check the glowing numbers on my bedside clock.

Midnight.

I pull the pillow over my head and groan.

Roll sideways.

And fall back asleep.

CHAPTER
Three

I hear faint music through the wall. Laughter. *Children?*

Did I leave the TV on? I'm aware of a snuggly warmth. So comfy cozy, huddled under the covers, drifting peacefully on a cushiony cloud, while a light scent fills the air. It reminds me of a Christmas candle, cinnamon and cloves, with nutmeg and a hint of vanilla. Ethereal. Floating. I never want to leave this euphoric place.

A strong arm wraps around me, cradling my back against a solid chest. My heart jolts. *Whose chest?* Long legs tuck up against mine, brushing the backs of my calves and thighs. I'm in some kind of heavy shirt, bare-legged, and *spooning? With whom?*

My bedmate stirs, holding me tighter. They're strong. Muscled. Heat coils in my belly. It's a guy, most definitely. Anatomy doesn't lie. My eyes fly wide, and I squint in the glare. This bedroom's foreign to me, sunlight filtering in through closed blinds. My heart pounds one, two, three times. Then it pounds harder. Manly fingers thread through mine, our hands interlaced on the bunched-up covers. *Freak-out moment!* We both wear wedding bands.

Deep breaths.

I did *not* pull a bender and wind up in Vegas. I've got no memory of traveling. Getting on a plane. I fight my brain fog, panic lodging in my throat. *Did I?* No.

Sweat beads my brow.

This isn't some fancy hotel room in a high-rise casino, either. It looks more like my late grandma's house, furnished with thrift store purchases. The cluttered dresser's missing a handle. The chest of drawers is scuffed. The threadbare chair in the corner's heaped with laundry. More clothing piles in a basket beside it. Child-size pieces and adult ones. Clean but not folded. Scattered dryer sheets poking out of the mix.

Wait. Is that a *dog bed* in the corner?

I frantically scan the room for any signs of a fur baby. The large, patterned rug could use vacuuming, and the hardwood floors hold dust bunnies. They appear to be real hardwood, not processed like you find in newer houses. The door to the bathroom reveals an older pedestal sink, a black-and-white tile floor. Toilet. The beginnings of a tub and shower combo, with an old-fashioned shower curtain bunched up at one end. Gone's my roomy walk-in shower with a rainfall showerhead. Gone's the stylish vanity. Gone's the primo lighting! I know what this is. A nightmare! *Yes.*

No. This feels extremely real. So does he. Pulling me closer, nuzzling his chin against my neck. Arousal hums through me, but I douse it—in very cold water. I don't even know who this person is, or where I am. Maybe…at an Airbnb? My anxiety spikes. Was I abducted? Doubtful. I peer at the door. I seem free to go. It's not even latched completely, standing open a lazy inch. Drugged? I gasp. Maybe someone spiked my drink?

Wrong. I've been *nowhere* in the past twenty-four hours, except to work and the Walton holiday party. He stirs behind me, cuddling me closer. Shifts and raises up on an elbow. Lightly kisses my shoulder. Heat floods my face. Then pools lower. Not good. I need to fight and flee! Assuming he's dangerous. Not melt into a slushy puddle of attraction. He does feel attractive, though. So solid, pressing against me. His forearm tightens around my chest.

"Morning, sunshine." His husky breath rakes over me, and my skin tingles all over.

Hang on. I know that voice. Incredibly well.

I peer back at him and his morning stubble. Slowly. Slowly. My heart races.

A solid jaw, that dimpled cheek. Dark eyes twinkling.

Handsome. Sexy. In-bed-with-me *Dean*.

Ahhh! I throw back the covers and sit up abruptly, pulling out of his hold.

"Paige?" His eyebrows knit together. "What's wrong?" He's in an undershirt and sweatpants. I'm wearing his large navy T-shirt and—I yank up the hem of the T-shirt to check—frilly satin panties that say "Friday" in bright red stitching. *Wait.* My butt feels bare. I'm in a thong? Seriously? I didn't know I had it in me. Mom would be so proud.

I drop the T-shirt in a rush, stretch it down toward my knees. Run my hands through my choppy hair. Wait! *What happened to my hair?* It sifts through my fingers in waves. My heart pounds and I spring off the bed, racing to the dresser mirror. Who is that person with pink highlighted hair framing her roundish face? My pale blue eyes are huge, my mouth puffy. I trace my bottom lip with my finger. I see Dean in the mirror behind me, looking perplexed. He sits there on the bed staring, like he's worried about me. Like he doesn't know who I am. That makes two of us.

33

"Did you have a bad dream?" His hair's askew, his mouth creased with concern. Bad dream doesn't begin to cover it. Bizarre hallucination might be closer. Is this on account of the advent calendar? Dean's mysteriously magical gift?

The door to the bedroom bursts open. "Mommy! Daddy! Yay!"

A child races in, and I wheel around. She's about five, I think, and has cute brown pigtails, hopping up onto the bed in baby blue pajamas. Dean pulls her into his arms, settling her in his lap, and she giggles. "Morning, pumpkin." He kisses her head as I gape at him. The two of them form such a pretty picture, like they're the perfect fit. She's clearly her daddy's daughter, with a dimple in her left cheek and big dark eyes.

"Mommy! Mommy!"

Two kids.

This one's a boy wearing dinosaur pj's. He's a few years younger than the girl, maybe two and a half or three. He flies through the open bedroom door and throws himself at my bare legs—*oof*—squeezing tightly, and my knees lock so I don't tumble over. He looks up. Big blue eyes and blond hair. Chubby cherub cheeks. Strikingly, he looks a lot like childhood pictures I've seen of Mom. "I'm hungry." He holds a stuffed Loch Ness Monster tucked under one arm. "Nessie's hungry, too."

Dean and I used to talk about traveling to the United Kingdom. Did we go, and I forget all the fun? How did we take that trip with kids? Did my mom watch them, or did his parents? Did we have a honeymoon? What about Puerto Rico? What about Mom's medical appointment Wednesday? My job at Walton? My super important program, Paws and Read? My brain scrambles to keep up as I stare at the room. I have a family? No. Not possible. Just a *very elaborate* dream.

My palms go damp. Which I didn't plan for. I distinctly

wrote in my dream journal: *Relationship with Dean.* My breath comes in fits and starts. *Oh nooo.* I left the "professional" part out. *Is this all my fault? How did this happen? Whyyyy?*

A shaggy white dog prances into the bedroom. He's midsize, maybe forty or fifty pounds, and looks like a big, lovable mop, fur falling over his eyes. He bounds over to me with a rolled-up newspaper in his mouth. It's in a clear plastic sleeve that's coated with snowflakes. He presses the icy mass against my leg and goosebumps raise on my arm. I reach down and take the paper roll numbly. It's damp, cold, chilling my hand—which is already slick with nerves.

I clutch the paper harder, so I don't drop it.

"Good job, Scout!" Dean praises the pup and gives me an odd look. The paper hangs limply from one hand and my other hand's on the little boy's shoulder. This stranger kid's shoulder. I yank it back. Hold it up in the air. Splay out my fingers then bring them back to together. A wedding band gleams up at me. The room glows blindingly bright, then dims.

Dean scoots to the edge of the bed and sets the girl down on the floor. "Eleanor, why don't you take Henry to finish watching your cartoons? Mommy and Daddy will be out in a bit."

She pouts but complies. "Okay, Daddy."

Eleanor? Henry? My head spins. *Daddy?*

Henry gives my legs a harder squeeze. "Can we have pancakes?" he asks plaintively. I can't say no. I mean, who am I? The Grinch? No. A different storybook character. One from classic literature. Ebenezer Scrooge. Although, honestly, I'm not *that* Scroogey. In fact, I'm not Scroogey at all. Frugal, of course, in a responsible manner. Organized, sure. But I don't pinch pennies at the expense of others. I'm reserved but giving and kind. So, what's this? A glimpse of my future? *Yeah, maybe.* So where's my spirit? My eyes dart around the room. I'm supposed to have three spirits showing me around. One each for Christmas Past, Present, and Yet to Come. I know that. I frown, feeling cheated. I've taught Dickens's *A Christmas Carol*, and read it, gobs of times.

"Uh." I blink blankly at the boy.

Dean meets Henry's eyes. "I think Mommy needs her coffee." He motions toward the door where Eleanor stands waiting. "Run along with your sister."

"O-tay!"

Dean winks at him. "That's o-*kay*, buddy."

Henry responds with a big bright grin. "O-tay, Daddy!"

They thankfully disappear and Scout follows, wagging his tail with a *woof, woof, woof.*

The room turns a quick revolution and I grab onto the dresser.

"Paige?" Dean's hand is on my shoulder. "Are you sick? Do you need to see a doctor? Go to urgent care?"

My voice squeaks. "No." He gently pries the newspaper from my clenched fingers and sets it on the nightstand by the bed.

I don't know what I am. Delusional? I can't tell anybody this. That I've invented an entire family! With a living-breathing-barking dog! *And laundry.* Nobody wishes for piles of unfolded clothes. Dean guides me back toward the bed and I sit in a daze. "Jeez Louise," he says. "How many margaritas did you have?"

My chin jerks up and I stare at him. "What?"

"Last night?" He speaks gently. "When you were out with the girls?"

"Er. Which girls are those?" I breathe heavily. "Exactly?"

He scrunches up his face. "Um. Your gal pals? Heather? Mia? Kirstin? The ones you have your girls' night out with on Fridays."

"We what?" I clasp my hands together. "We have a girls' night out?" Heat prickles the backs of my eyes. *Yes.* We worked it out! I knew there was a way if we put our heads together.

Dean seems oddly detached. Okay, okay, and slightly judgy. His jaw goes slack. "Did you drink *pitchers*?" His dark eyes are huge. "Do shots? What?"

"What? No!" I nervously lick my lips. Rub my twitchy nose. "I mean, maybe sometimes. But not—not last night." There were several times in college, truthfully. I'm less sure about now, with us having grown-up responsibilities. "Last night, I was at Walton's holiday party!" Surely he remembers. "With *you*."

"Paige." He sets his hands on his hips. "You know I wish it were otherwise, but it's not. I agree it's discriminatory to divide the faculty and staff and I—and some other teachers—have rallied against it, but—" I can't comprehend what he's saying. We weren't at the same party?

"But you were *there*."

"Sure," he says. "Attending the faculty party at six."

"And I was—?"

He crosses his arms. "Celebrating with the staff at three."

My mouth hangs open and I close it. "Staff?"

"Look." He shakes his head. "I realize working as Principal Peabody's assistant isn't the greatest job in the world—"

"I wh-what?" I blubber like a drowning fish. "I'm in admin and not a teacher?"

His worried expression rattles me and my nerves are already frayed enough. "Oh baby, I'm so sorry. Is this about your not finishing college?"

My head grows light and the room spins. "*I dropped out of college?*" I can't help the shrillness in my tone. No. I never would have done that. Something catastrophic must have happened.

Eleanor appears in the open doorway holding a toy Highland cow in one arm. It's got a curtain of bangs over its eyes and stuffed horns. Scout's with her, sitting faithfully at her side. "When can we have breakfast?" She rubs her tummy. Waits.

"Five minutes, sweetie!" Dean tells her.

Scout barks like he's hungry, too.

"Same for you, boy!" Dean promises and the pair skulks away.

I turn to Dean, my pulse pounding. "How old's Eleanor?"

"Almost six," he says like I should know this. I definitely should know this, assuming I am who he thinks I am. Which is what I'm still trying to wrap my head around.

"And, er." I anxiously rub my nose and ask, "When's her birthday?"

He drops the words like lead weights, "February. Ninth." I quickly calculate the dates. Can it be? Can she be? That had to have been right around the time Dean left for—

"Paige," he says sounding disappointed. "Are we back to Puerto Rico?"

I shrug helplessly.

"Sweetheart, we've settled that so many times. I'm not resentful I didn't go." *What?* "I'm really not. Things worked out. Our life took a different turn. A better one."

"But what about Wendy?" I blurt out, then cover my mouth with my hands.

He peers at me strangely. "Wendy?"

Where am I? How did this happen? This isn't a preview of a Christmas future. I'm *in the future* somehow. Our future, mine and Dean's. No, wait. Wrong. The present? An alternate reality, perhaps? This can't be the past. Neither of us is college age anymore. Dean looks exactly like he did yesterday. I cast a quick glance at the mirror. I've changed a bit, though. Maybe I did drink margaritas? No. It couldn't have been *that* wild a night. I was at home. My real home, not this one, and I only had one glass of wine with pasta. I press my palms to my temples when my head threatens to explode.

Dean's lips turn down. "Hon. Next time? Call an Uber. I mean it, seriously. I can't believe you drove in that condition."

A wave of heat crashes over me. Now he thinks I'm a lush! "No, it's not that," I babble. How can he not recall the holiday party? He was there, too! Right along with me. Of course, I was a teacher, not Missy Peabody's assistant. We didn't have kids *or a dog*, either. Fear grips me. Maybe I've died and landed somewhere that's *not* the Good Place. No. Dean wouldn't be here in that case, or those cute kids. And they are cute, even though they're total strangers. *How can I not know my children? I am such a bad mom!*

Dean studies me a long while. "Nothing some coffee can't fix," he says decisively. "And hey." A compassionate frown. "I'm sorry I judged you earlier. Who am I to talk? I've had those party moments myself." He plants a kiss on my lips, so swoony my pulse hums. "Just don't let it happen again without calling a car, all right?" he says warmly. "You've got a lot of people depending on you." Yeah, apparently. Three more than I knew. Four, if you count Scout. But he's not human.

I need to know about Mom. Is she okay?

"So, Mom?"

He pauses on the threshold. "She's expecting you at Beaumont's at noon," he says. "Which is why we need to fix you up."

"Dean." My breath catches.

"Yes, Paige?" But what can I say? None of this is happening. We broke up six years ago. Never married. Never had kids. Much less a dog. I'm a teacher at Walton, and not Missy Peabody's Girl Friday—and starting a brand new literacy program for students on top of that. He's right about coffee. Maybe that's all I need? A swift kick-in-the-butt java hit!

I need to process what's happening before I lay it all on him. "Coffee sounds good. Thanks." He smiles at me so fondly my heart bursts with joy. Then I remember none of this is real. It's just some far-out fantasy. Which I'm sure to pull out of soon enough.

He winks and says, "Stay right there."

As if I'm going anywhere. I don't even know where I am. Are we still in Piney Mount?

He shakes a finger at me but his eyes sparkle. "I'll be right back." Dean closes the bedroom door and I give an enormous sigh. This is probably a dream like I first thought, with extremely elaborate casting and detail. I'll think much more clearly after having my coffee and can decide how to proceed from there. Or possibly, I'll wake up first! I shut my eyes tightly and will it to happen. *Wake up, Paige! Wake up now!*

I open my eyes and grump. Sit back against the headboard and pull up the covers, settling in. Might as well check the newspaper to see where I am and what day it is. I grab the rolled up paper from the nightstand and slide it out of its plastic sleeve, dusting off the moisture from my hands. Then I hold it up, perusing the front page of the *Piney Mount Herald*. That seals it. Same town. Which I might have guessed from the fact that Mom is here *and* we're meeting at Beaumont's.

News snippets in the sidebar report hefty snowfall accumulations, boding well for the ski slopes in the surrounding areas. Above the fold, there's a large photo of a comet trailing majestically through the nighttime sky. My hands shake as I read the headline: "Rare Astronomical Event Graces North America."

Today's date glares back at me from the front page's masthead. December twentieth. Which is the day after the nineteenth, yesterday. Or the yesterday I think I had. Same year. My breath quickens. But now, everything's changed. My living quarters, my job, my relationship status—in a substantial way. Marriage? Kids? A family dog? At least he's well trained, and pretty adorable. But Missy Peabody's assistant? Really? And—*ooh, my heart aches*—what about Paws and Read? Is that even a thing here? Have I failed all those volunteers, dogs, and students?

The full laundry basket taunts me, giving me a glimpse of my low-end-fashion life. There are no nice teacher outfits for me here. Only outfits like we wear on casual Fridays. Blue jeans and long-sleeve T-shirts seem to rule the women's category. Apart from their rumpled state, Dean's clothes look more professional. Khaki slacks and oxford shirts. Those will take some ironing—not by me! I've never owned an iron in my life. Then there are all those little kiddie clothes. The majority appear to be unisex in nature. Small sweaters and jeans.

Smart move, so Eleanor's pieces can get passed down to Henry. Good gravy. I'm already thinking like a mom! Maybe it's not that hard? My mouth goes dry, and I stare at the door to the hall. What other surprises await me on the other side? Tension brews inside me. Surprises I didn't plan for. Can't control. My mouth gets dryer, like cotton's wedged inside it.

The kid part honestly terrifies me. I did some babysitting for the neighbor's kids as a teen, but that was ages ago, and those kids were older, eight and ten. Old enough to reason with and play board games. I have no idea what children Eleanor's and Henry's ages do, apart from what I've seen in the movies. They clearly watch cartoons and eat pancakes. So that's a start, though not a huge one.

Mom might not be much help. She was never much of a traditional mom to begin with. I hope she's okay, though, and not enduring any medical problems. I guess I'll learn more at lunch at Beaumont's. Does Mom recall my other life? Know about my seeing Dean at the holiday party? Can she possibly help me sort out this predicament? Will Dean, when I tell him what's going on? But how? I do a trial run in my brain.

Dean, I have something to tell you…

No. Sounds like I'm chronically ill. Or that I'm leaving him. Again.

There's something we need to discuss.

Nuh-uh. Too accusatory, and he's done nothing wrong. I think. Unless he's somehow caused this mess inadvertently? How? By giving me that advent calendar? I don't see it anywhere. I wonder if it's hanging in the kitchen, and what this kitchen looks like. Hopefully, it's not a wreck. And has a dishwasher. I'll die if it doesn't have a dishwasher. How barbaric. Is that even possible in modern times? At least Dean is equitably minded. I'm sure we share all the tasks around here. Unless stuff has changed about him, too?

No. He's still the same old Dean, as far as I can tell. Only much more of a family man And he's decently good at it! *I give him full credit!*

Okay. *Deep breaths.*

Something had to have caused this weird time split. It's like time moved backward and then forward again, but in a totally different direction. Could this really be because of the calendar? No, that's absurd. This has to be a dream. One I'll wake up from very soon!

I shut my eyes and wait. Count to ten—slowly. Open them.

Blow out a breath and try again.

Dean, I'm concerned we're… Wrong. That will concern him, too—about me.

The truth? Yes, always the best course. Why not?

I don't know what's happening, but—
My jaw clenches. *Ouch.* Maybe best to practice out loud.
"Dean," I say boldly. "I'm not who you think I am."
The door pops open.

CHAPTER
Four

I jump out of my skin. "Dean!"

He wears an amused smile. "Who are you, then?"

He enters the room leading with a full mug of coffee, balancing it carefully as he walks.

I blink as he comes closer. Music plays on the television in the next room. Little kid laughter tinkles like chimes in a music box. He approaches one of the two windows on the far wall. The dresser with a swivel mirror stands between them. I spot a large crimson-colored candle in a glass jar on the dresser top sandwiched between a hairbrush, perfume bottles, unruly stacks of books and magazines. The candle's label reads "Christmas Magic." So that's what's giving off the cheery cinnamon scent. We must have burned it last night.

"Mind if I raise these up?" he asks about the blinds, holding the mug in one hand. "It's snowing out there, really beautiful."

I nod numbly. "Sure."

He tugs at the cord and gorgeous white flakes twirl beyond the window, cascading against the glass and sailing through the air in dainty waves.

I remember the newspaper and the dog. "Still, Scout got the paper?"

"Of course," Dean reports. "It's his job." He raises the other set of blinds, and the room brightens exponentially. The wintry scene outdoors makes it feel twice as cozy in here with me snuggled under the covers. Though it's hard to understand about the dog getting outside to grab the paper on his own. I chuckle nervously, trying to picture it. "So. He just unlocks the front door with his teeth, and—"

Dean squints like that's absurd, and I suppose it is. "No. He uses the dog door in the kitchen."

"A-*ha*! Ha. Ha. Ha." I might have guessed that if I were used to owning a real dog and not a robotic one. Naturally, dogs are trainable. Just look at the stars of my Paws and Read program, Cooper and Bailey. Cooper is a little sneaky but smart as a whip and great at his job. So's Bailey. Evidently, Scout's equally skilled at his. Bringing in the paper. How precious.

Dean hands me the coffee mug and sits beside me on the bed. "Here. Maybe this will help. It's just how you like it."

I hold the mug and take a quick sip. Instantly spit it back out. So much sugar!

"What's wrong?" He peers closer. "Something with the coffee?"

I drag the back of my hand across my mouth. "No, no. It's good! *Sweet*."

"Two tablespoons is your normal amount," he says, sounding perplexed.

"Really?" I take another quick sip. This is not fat-free milk, either. It's cream. "Wow. Just throw in some flour and butter!" Who needs breakfast when you can drink a pastry?

"What?"

46

"Ne-never mind." I set the mug on the nightstand. "Thanks so much for fixing this for me." The breakfast of champions. I'm going to be so wired.

He shrugs. "Anytime." Dean studies my eyes. "How are you feeling?"

"Um."

He hands me the coffee again and I try not to wince. "Thanks!" I take a quick sip, strangely liking it better. I taste it again just to be sure. It's not *terrible*. I drink some more. Honestly, it's growing on me. Maybe this is how I get through my mornings with the kids? I stare at him over the rim of my mug. "Dean?"

"Hmm?"

Another sip of coffee, stoking my courage. Caffeine and sugar hit me with a *zippity-zap*. I blink like I've taken a belt of strong whiskey. "I need to tell you something," I say, "and I don't want you to freak."

His face seizes up and he grabs my free hand. "Oh no, Paige. You're not—" His fingers clench mine.

"Sick?" I fill in at the same time he guesses, "Pregnant?"

I choke on my coffee and set it on the nightstand.

"No!" I lick my lips. Glance down at my waist. "Neither." I hope. That would be a trick. And awful. I'm not adjusted to *two* kids, how on earth would I handle three? I never even thought I wanted any. Okay, okay. Perhaps one. Someday in the very distant future.

His tense expression eases. "Well, thank goodness you're not sick." He takes my hand. "Though, truthfully? Pregnant would be okay. Not catastrophic. We'd handle it."

I swallow hard. I'm not so sure about that. Prolonged bouts of morning sickness and bloating sound grueling to me. I don't know how my mom did it. How any moms do.

47

He leans toward me and says, "Just like we've handled all of life's other curveballs—together." The corners of his mouth turn up and my heart melts. He's so understanding and supportive. Such a gem. I'm so lucky to have him.

Only. I don't.

He lifts a hand to my face and sweeps back my hair. "Are you worried about last Saturday?" he asks quietly.

My stomach quivers. "What?"

"You know," he whispers. "When the kids were at your mom's?"

Sounds enticing. If only I could remember.

His hand glides behind my neck, fingers pushing up into my hair. "Things got kind of wild with me playing naughty Santa, and you sexy Mrs. Claus." His eyes gleam devilishly. "I'm sorry about the thong." My face heats. We what? Role-played?

"Oh!"

He kisses me deeply, and I hang on to his shoulders for dear life. Attraction ripples through me like a wildfire raging. His mouth fuses with mine in a dreamy meld, our tongues tangling. I don't know how he's gotten so much better at kissing when he was top-notch to begin with. Must be all the practice we've had.

"I'll buy you another," he says in gravelly tones. This seems to be happening so fast. So soon. *But only for me.* In his mind, we've been married for years. Together for longer.

"It's, um, okay!" My breath hitches. "Don't bother."

He gently peels back the covers. Casts a glance at my legs. Gently grasps my ankle. I warm all over, my pulse fluttering. "Maybe we should work on the other days of the week? Later, while the kids are napping?" I blush like a teenager, oddly embarrassed. Like we're oversharing. Physically. But we're not. OMG. We're married.

48

I tug his T-shirt lower on my thighs. "Sounds good!" I yank the covers back up and smooth them. I mean, he might recall last Saturday, but I don't, unfortunately. Thank goodness for Mom! Who knew she'd be such a great granny. "But, er. Maybe we should build up to it a bit?" I flush hotter and shyly raise a shoulder. "Quiet evening? Some wine?"

"You're right." He holds my hand and kisses the back of it. "Why rush romance?" I can't tell him it's already moving at breakneck speed for me. He'd never get it. Or maybe he will once I explain. I brace myself mentally for the enormous task ahead.

"You were going to say something?" he asks.

Okay. This is it.

Deep breaths.

"Dean," I say solemnly. "I come to you from the future."

He blinks. "Okay."

"Not our future, but my future. The one I have without you."

His breath catches. "Maybe I should call Rosemary."

This is so not working.

"Mom? No! Why?" I can't tell her this yet. I need to deal with my husband-not-a-husband first.

"Paige. Honey. Is this some kind of joke?" He rakes a hand through his hair, appearing pained. "Because I'm going to be honest with you. I'm not finding it funny."

"It's not a joke," I whimper helplessly.

He blows out a breath. "Oh boy."

"Dean! Please listen!"

He sits at attention. "Whoa, Paige, you're scaring me."

"I'm not trying to do that, honestly." I soften my approach. "I'm just trying to tell you the truth."

"You want a future without me?" he asks, sounding hurt.

"*Nooo.* That's not what—"

49

"Our family?" A sheen coats his eyes. "Are you saying you regret *us*?"

I can't stand his crushed look. The devastation in his tone. "Of course not," I whisper. "It's just"—I purse my lips—"sometimes life takes two paths. Diverges."

He stands from the bed and frowns. "I'm a divergence now? Wow." He shakes his head. Sets his hands on his hips. "Unbelievable. Next, you're going to tell me none of this matters. Eleanor, Henry." His raw tone pierces my heart. "Scout." He waves around the room. "Our great house. The one we scrimped and saved for. That we wanted for our family. The family I thought both of us loved." His jaw tenses. "I'm sorry you feel that way."

This is going so wrong.

I try appealing to his rational mind. "Dean, you're a scientist, right?"

He shrugs. "You could call me that, I guess."

"So you must have thought, at some point, about time splits and alternate realities?"

He rubs the side of his neck. "Like time travel, you mean?"

I nod and hold the covers against my chest. "This morning I had the oddest sensation when I woke up. Like I wasn't meant to be here, but somewhere else entirely."

"You were hungover, Paige."

"Dean, no." I clutch the covers harder. "This wasn't about that."

"Then what *was* it about?"

"It was like, um." I lick my lips. "I caught a glimpse of another world."

"A better one?" The way he searches my eyes breaks my heart.

"Er, not exactly," I hedge. "More like different."

"Did you like what you saw?" he presses.

"Some parts."

"But you were single, yeah?" When I don't answer, he hangs his head. "I see."

"Dean, please."

He gloomily looks up. "You're getting restless in our marriage, aren't you?"

He sounds so broken, I must protest. "What? *Nooo.*"

"Well, here's the thing, Paige." Hurt laces each word. "I'm not."

How can I do this to him? Someone so good and kind? The man who clearly adores me and our family? There's got to be another way. "I'm sorry, Dean. Everything I'm saying is coming out wrong. You're the very best husband and dad any woman could hope for."

Relief glimmers in his eyes. "Yeah?"

"Yeah."

I push back the covers and stand. "Dean, really. I'm sorry." I lay a hand on his arm. "Please forgive me." I broke his heart once and it nearly killed me. I can't do it a second time. My own heart won't let me. "That wasn't how it sounded."

"No?" He studies me, his expression worn. "Then how was it?"

I search my brain, desperate for answers. Any excuse. Some way to let myself off the hook that will go easier on him. "It was the, ah…" A shattered breath. "Margaritas."

His disappointment is so clear. "Is that what you ladies talk about? How you'd be better off without your husbands?" No. I don't imagine that of my girls' nights out with Kirstin, Mia, and Heather. They're all happy with their lives from outward appearances. I know appearances can be deceiving, but not in their cases. At least, I hope not.

"No, Dean. I swear." I stop and hang my head. "I just woke up confused, that's all. But the coffee's helping. It is! It's sinking in." So's this new reality. *Yikes*. There doesn't seem to be a great way out of it without hurting the people I'm supposed to love. But apart from Dean, I don't even know the people here. I've just met Eleanor and Henry. My lower lip trembles. "Can we just forget all about this for now?" Until I can figure out what to do next.

Sadly, I'm drawing a blank. Frustrating. But I don't want to frustrate Dean any longer or worry him. I can't stand hurting his feelings most of all. He pulls me into his arms and kisses the top of my head. "Sure." His embrace is so strong and steady I want to weep. "Just, next time?" He pulls away to stare down at me. "An Uber?"

He hugs me again, his heart pounding against mine, and I find myself melting against him. Oh gosh, how I've missed him. I didn't even know how much. I hold him tighter and close my eyes.

But no. I can't stay here indefinitely. I can't just jettison my real life for something so uncertain and new. I have a job. Responsibilities. Mom to take care of—now and in her elder years. Paws and Read to launch on Tuesday. Maybe this is just a weird time blip? A glimpse into an alternate world, like an extended dream of sorts, and when I wake up tomorrow I'll be right back in my old world, where I started.

Dean pulls out of our hug and says gently, "Why don't you shower and throw on some clothes? I'll start breakfast." A shower's not a bad idea. Maybe cleaning up will help clear my head.

"Thanks, Dean. That would be great." He really is the kindest guy. I'll miss this side of him, but it's not like I'll be staying long enough to get attached, anyway. Not to this *new Dean*. Not to the kids. The dog. The house.

"Pancakes all right?"

"Pancakes sound great."

He grins. "You've got it."

He leaves and I stride to the dresser, searching through the top drawer and my ample assortment of thongs. Good gravy! There are dozens. But only a certain number are holiday themed and labeled with the days of the week. I find Wednesday, Thursday, and Sunday. Monday and Tuesday peek out of the laundry basket. I select some regular old panties, which are still *a lot* lacier than my normal pairs, and find a matching bra.

What I don't pay for in outerwear, I seem to make up in undergarments. I've even got Spanx! Ew. A tight stretchy torso piece that covers the chest and mid-section, ending at the thigh. That looks uncomfortable, but maybe it works for dressy evenings? I stare around the messy bedroom, having trouble imagining us experiencing too many of those.

I pick out a pair of jeans and a black long-sleeve T-shirt, pulling them from the armchair and shaking out their wrinkles. Not bad. These will do. I check the closet next, considering what to wear to my girls' lunch with Mom. Maybe something a bit nicer, but not too fancy. *That's cute!* I find a flouncy dress with a fitted bodice and ruffled hem that reminds me of what a Dutch girl might wear, or Heidi. I giggle. Only older and all grown-up and sexy.

I hold the dress against my chest and peer down at the floor, spotting a fun pair of flat-heeled western boots. I sense a look coming together. Casual chic. I finish it off with tights and a nubby brown cardigan sweater, hanging that and the dress on the back of the closet door. The old me dresses much more conservatively, typically in neutral slacks and crewneck sweaters with stylish ankle boots. But I'm the new me now, and only temporarily. This fantasy state won't last forever. I'm not deluded enough to believe that.

Dean calls out to the kids in the next room and the shower sings my name. I stroll into the bathroom and remove Dean's large T-shirt, tossing it on the floor and glancing over my shoulder. Something colorful peeks up at me from my lower back. I gasp and turn around in front of the mirror above the sink, standing up on my tiptoes and trying to view it over my shoulder.

I have a tattoo?

I break a sweat.

When did this happen? Why? Was it on account of the margaritas? Did my girl group all get them together? I can't imagine getting tattooed with Mom.

But maybe?

The pretty butterfly spreads its blue and yellow wings right at the small of my back, above my panty line. *Oh my gosh. I'm a wild girl.* And a wife and mommy. Who has girls' nights with friends, *and* a really hot sex life with her husband, evidently.

I swallow hard and turn on the shower.

Okay. This is it, then. My brand new surprising life.

My heartbeats gallop away from me.

Until I can find my way out of it. Before Tuesday, so I can launch Paws and Read. The program's far bigger than me. It's about reaching a potential multitude of students. And, if the pilot program's successful, Paws and Read will benefit even more volunteers, pups. and pupils beyond Walton High—our entire community—when the program's taken countywide.

And I need to be back before Wednesday, so I can take Mom to her medical appointment. No way am I staying here and letting her go through that by herself.

I rub shampoo into my scalp, soaping up my hair. The hot water feels good, soothing my jangled nerves. Steam fills the room in billowy clouds around me and for an instant, I'm back at my condo, completely forgetting where I am.

The curtain scrapes open. *Wait.*

I scrub the suds from my eyes and *shriek*!

Eleanor! Grinning. "Breakfast time." She rocks on her heels, holding her stuffed cow. Scout's beside her. *Woof!* So's Henry—gawking. Nessie dangles at his side.

I twist my limbs over myself, my upper arms shielding my breasts, hands splayed low in front of me. Water streams down my face, glides off my nose, splatters my lips—and hips. Pools in my navel. My chin jerks up and I stare at the kids. "Mommy will be there in a minute." Wow, that sounded weird. I go lightheaded, but no. I can't fall. That will give them a full view of my butterfly—and butt.

Henry points to my splayed-out hands and asks with concern, "Where's your wee-wee?" His tiny eyebrows form a V. Of course he doesn't understand. He's a baby!

"Kids? What are you doing?" *Ahhh!* Dean's by the sink. Where did he come from? I lunge for the shower curtain and wrap it around me. It crinkles, all plasticky-like and sticky, the shower stream pummeling my back. "Sorry," he says and grimaces. "I just asked them to tell you breakfast was almost ready." He sternly glances at the children. "*Not* to invade the bathroom."

"Come on, guys, let's give Mommy her privacy."

Eleanor and Henry giggle at each other as Dean herds them away. He teasingly winks at the bunched-up shower curtain. "It's not like I haven't seen everything before."

Right. Maybe not.

But it's been a while since *I've seen him* see it.

"Ha!" I say sassily.

He chuckles and shuts the door. "See you in a bit."

CHAPTER
Five

I step into the living room and grasp the doorframe. It's like sensory overload in here. Christmas music plays through the speakers while the TV runs in the corner, the bright colors of an animated kiddie show bouncing across the screen. *Aww, sweet.* That looks like a real wood-burning fireplace with four stockings hanging from the mantel. No. Five. There's even one for Scout!

A glowing Christmas tree blocks a front window, but I'm sure it provides a cheery view from outdoors. It's loaded with shiny lights and homemade ornaments with wrapped presents stacked underneath. I walk over in a daze and lightly touch the Rudolph ornament Mom gave me. Locate the snowman on a lower branch, and Santa with the toys across his back near the star at the top. This is so surreal. How can *those ornaments* have landed in *this reality*? Then again, I've been catapulted here, too. Without much say in the matter.

I stare up at the ten-foot ceilings and plaster molding on the walls. An old-timey chair rail rings the room with its broad-planked heart pine floors. This house must be over one hundred years old. It's an antique! But with a bungalow feel and a charming ambience. The glass panes in the windows shimmer, and I get the impression they're original. A second window behind a rocker overlooks the postage-stamp-size front yard, and I note the house has got a covered front porch. Its railing and the entire lawn are coated in white, and more snow drifts from the sky.

I appreciate the tree-lined street and our neighbors' houses. They're older, single-story cottages like this one. Some have slanted tin roofs. None can be much more than fifteen hundred square feet in size. And yet, this house has three bedrooms. Our modest master and two kids' rooms across the hall, one barely big enough for a single bed, a dresser and some toys. From the dollhouse in the corner, the other room with matching twin beds appears to be Eleanor's. A tiny full bath stands on our side of the short hall that leads here, and—though it's equally small—we've got our own separate bathroom in the master.

The living room walls are painted off-white, like the walls in the rest of the house, and framed art prints showcase scenes in deep blues and yellows. Van Gogh's "Starry Night," "Wheatfield with Cypresses," and stunning "Vase with Twelve Sunflowers" complement the Ceylon blue upholstery and gold-and-navy carpet. I noted Monet's "Water Lilies" over our double bed in the master. Dean and I are clearly art fans.

Little kid laughter bubbles in from the kitchen through an open doorframe, as Dean chatters comfortably with Eleanor and Henry. I don't see any dining room in view, although I suppose you could squeeze a dining table at one end of this room if you became really determined about it. You'd have to work around the low-footprint sofa and love seat first. As well as the coffee table and end tables facing the fireplace.

The front door near the rocker leads to the covered front porch. There's a large welcome mat in front of it saying, "Love

Lives Here." And an entryway table holds a ginger jar lamp and two sets of car keys. A circular, gold-framed mirror with daisy-like petals hangs above the entryway table.

The scent of bacon frying floats toward me, and my stomach rumbles. I switch off the TV to the right of the fireplace and Christmas music swells, no longer competing with the clamor of the television. There are speakers on the jam-packed book-shelves framing the hearth, which are stocked with tomes of classic literature and contemporary bestsellers.

A few family photos are scattered around. Me with my arm around Mom. Dean's parents with our kids at a waterpark. Dean with his sister, Jenny, doing something daring like mountain climbing together. Dean and me with our kids, and Scout, on the deck of someplace sunny. The ocean tumbles in the back-ground and gulls dart through the sky. I sigh at the memories I don't have and investigate the cabinets below the bookshelves. There are board games and puzzles in one, and kids' building blocks and connecting toys in the other, stored in mesh bins.

The kitchen is surprisingly large, equal in size to the living room but on its far side, and opposite the bedrooms. Dean grins over his shoulder, cooking pancakes on a sizzling griddle. "There she is!" He's awfully handsome standing there in his sweatpants and undershirt, commanding the stove like a pro. The fact that he hasn't shaved gives him a sexy unkempt edge. I think of his role-playing comments and go hot all over. Santa and Mrs. Claus? Seriously? I wish I knew what that entailed. Beyond the broken thong. Obviously.

Scout bounds around Dean, staying close on his heels but without getting underfoot, miraculously. I like this domesticat-ed side of Dean, the daddy. If only I could keep him, but that would mean giving up too much. My education, my job, my literacy outreach program that's finally taking off, everything

I've worked for. My soul aches. My ability to help Mom through her current medical crisis and in her golden years. I have to be there for her, like she's been there for me.

Dean pries two flapjacks loose with his spatula and slides them onto a plate on the counter, which is already piled high. "Almost ready."

"Great." I take a sip from my near-empty mug, spotting the coffee pot and sugar bowl on the counter to the left of the kitchen sink and the right of the refrigerator. Naturally, my daily schedule's not posted there. A stick-figure drawing made in crayon hangs on the fridge instead.

The drawing shows a man and a woman, two kids, and a fluffy white dog. The awkward childhood lettering above them says "My Family." The F in "family" is written backward, resembling a flag. My heart catches in my throat. Eleanor must have drawn this. It's darling. A touching family portrait. A wave of melancholy washes over me, but I push it aside. Foolish to regret what I've never had. How much sense does *that* make?

Dean takes a pancake from lower in the stack and deposits it in the dog dish on the counter. "This one's for you, boy," he says, and Scout barks eagerly. Dean places the dog's dish by the side door, which contains a pet door in its lower panel, guarded by large rubber flaps. I peer out the window, seeing a short stoop with brick steps and an iron railing, all covered in snow. There are paw prints going up and down the stairs and trailing toward the drive.

The pup wastes no time in inhaling his pancake and happily licking his chops, then he paces over to the table where Eleanor and Henry sit near the back of the room. Dean's poured them both orange juice. Eleanor's in a regular chair while Henry's in a booster seat. Scout situates himself on the floor, stretching out between the kids with his head partway under the table.

Snow pours from the overcast sky in the window behind them, blanketing the picket-fenced backyard and burying a wooden kids' playset with swings. The wall to their left houses two Cézanne prints: "Still Life with Apples" and "Three Pears," which perfectly suit the kitchen.

Dean turns off the gas burner and moves the hot griddle aside. "Mind carrying this over to the table?" he asks, holding out the plate loaded with pancakes.

I set my coffee mug on the counter and take the plate from him, happy to be of help. "Sure." Their doughy scent fills the room. "They smell delicious." I spy the advent calendar suspended from its green ribbon on the wall and nearly drop the pancake plate. A wave of heat crashes over me, then an icy chill rushes through my veins. Relative to the refrigerator, it's hanging in roughly the same place as mine back home. *How is this happening? How, how, how, how?*

"It's great, isn't it?" Dean asks about the advent calendar. He places syrup and butter on the table as I stand there gawking. "I'm so glad we picked it up at the holiday market last week."

"Last week," I say, feeling dazed. "Right."

"That vendor was very mysterious," Dean goes on. "A calendar that can predict the future and change lives." He chuckles and admires his family. "What's to change here?"

I lift a shoulder and stammer, "Noth-nothing." Certain things are eerily the same. Like the star at the top of the felt Christmas tree on the advent calendar, *exactly* where I placed it last night. Other items have been added too, emptying all the pockets numbered one to nineteen. Today's the twentieth in both places, as far as I can tell. My heart races. If the other place still exists. No. I can't bear to imagine what that means. I couldn't have had my entire life wiped out in the blink of an eye. Or more like, in a solid night of heavy *Z*s.

I set the pancake plate on the table then go to refill my coffee. I need all the caffeine I can get this morning. Dean carries over the crispy-looking bacon on a plate lined with paper towels, joining the kids at the table. The minute he sits, he slaps his forehead. "Forgot the silverware. Hon?" He sees me standing by the refrigerator. "Will you grab some?"

"Er, sure!" The coffee maker's right in front of me to the left of the sink. I check the drawer immediately below me, but it's filled with coffee filters, a brush for dusting out the coffee grinder, a cheese grater. Hmm. I slide shut the drawer and try the next drawer over, as Dean engages the kids in conversation. "We'll have to add a new item to our calendar this morning," he tells them. "Whose turn is it?"

Shoot. This drawer is ice cream scoops and cake servers. A garlic press? What's with us? Must be on the other side of the sink.

"Mine!" Eleanor shouts while Henry cries, "Me, Daddy! Me!"

Dean rubs his chin and glances at me. "What do you think, Mommy?"

I yank open the refrigerator door and hide behind it, grabbing the skim milk. No. I hastily return it to the shelf, selecting the cream. When in Rome… I shrug uselessly at Dean, shutting the door. "Can't remember." *That's God's honest truth.* I dump in some sugar from the sugar bowl next, but I can't stir my mug without a spoon. Maybe silverware's in the drawer beyond the dishwasher to the right of the sink? I tiptoe over and slowly slide it open. *Ahh! Paydirt.* Knives, forks, and spoons nest in neat rows, divided in an organized holder.

"Found it!" I say, triumphantly holding up a teaspoon.

Dean wrinkles his forehead and stares at me. "Great going! Would you mind, uh…" He makes a circular motion over the table with his hand.

"Yes, yes! Right away." I grab three forks and three knives, dart a look at Eleanor. No. Maybe not a big knife for her. Oh, there. That one seems smaller and kiddie-size. I spot a fork with a handle shaped like a rocket ship. That must be Henry's. I grab the rocket fork and a smaller adult fork for Eleanor. It's a salad fork, I think, with a little diamond cutout below its prongs. *Wait.* Mom used to have this set.

Dean clears his throat and I slam shut the drawer. The cutlery inside jangles. "Coming!" I wear a bright smile and scurry back over to the table, doling out the silverware. I set each piece down and pause, waiting for someone to make a correction, or for Eleanor to call me out on it, precocious child that she is. Nobody says a thing except for Dean, who smiles and says, "Thanks, Mommy." So I sink down in my chair holding my coffee mug, my face flushed. Whew.

Dean crosses his arms and studies the advent calendar. It's so pretty and cheerful, identical to the one in my sleek condo on the sixth floor. Only it's not that one; it's this one here. Though I'm not sure why they'd be different, it's even tougher to understand how they could be one and the same. *So much to process.*

"I think it was your turn yesterday, Eleanor," Dean finally says. "Didn't you put up the gingerbread man?"

She slumps lower in her chair, looking guilty. "Maybe?" I can tell by the gleam in her eyes that she's hedging the truth. Though I can't blame her. Who wouldn't want to have all the fun and get tasked with decorating the advent calendar every day? I chuckle at her cuteness, unable to help myself. Even as an adult, I can relate to her feelings.

"Then it's Henry's turn today," Dean announces decisively.

Henry cheers with chubby little fists. "Yay!" He's a super cute munchkin with his shaggy blond hair and big blue eyes.

"We'll do that right after breakfast," Dean says. I timidly hold up my hand like a student in class. Dean eyes me curiously. "Yes, Paige?"

"Er. Who put up the star?" I probably shouldn't ask, but I'm honestly dying to know.

Dean chuckles in confusion and scratches the side of his head. "Why, you did, hon. Don't you remember? We were supposed to wait until Christmas Day with that one, but you said it was my Christmas Comet."

"Ah haaaa." Oh my goodness. This is so freaky. *What's happening? Did I somehow cause this time split by messing with the order of things?* I see the snowman's wedged in the pocket for day twenty. Same as it was at my place. Uh. My other place. Alternate place. Alternate reality condo. *Ooh, my head hurts.* No. This isn't real. Just an extended dream or hallucination of some sort. I swallow hard. I hope I'm not cracking up. Please, please, please, *please* don't let that be the case.

Dean serves the breakfast plates, starting with the kids', then mine. "Two or three?" he asks me about the pancakes. I release a shaky breath, pulling myself together. No one ever cooks for me at my condo. I don't even cook for myself.

"Two's great, thanks." I decide to go easy on the starchy stuff, planning to load up on bacon. It smells so fantastic, I can't wait. The salty, cured aspect might help balance out all the sugar in my coffee. I'm on my second mugful now, and it's growing on me. While also perhaps making me overly caffeinated, but maybe that's *okay.* I need to be wide awake to stay on top of all that's happening. Which is—a lot.

Dean slides Henry's plate in front of him, cutting the pancakes into child-size bites. "Go ahead." He looks at me and Eleanor. "You ladies dig in."

"Can I have some syrup, Mommy?" Eleanor asks. "Please?"

"Such manners!" I say with delight. I adorn her pancakes with an elaborate squirt, making a fun swirling motion as I trickle it on.

Henry sulks over his juice glass with big sad eyes. "Where's Mommy's wee-wee?" he asks Dean.

Heat seeps through me. Henry's evidently been stewing over this for the past several minutes, ever since seeing me naked in the shower. "I, er—"

Dean places Henry's plate in front of him and hands him the rocket fork. "We can talk about that later, buddy."

"No, no," I say, not wanting to make the wrong impression on the kids. They shouldn't be embarrassed about their bodies. *Says the woman who cowered in the shower.* But that was different. *I was surprised.* I glance at Dean. "It's fine. We can talk about it now."

Eleanor sits up straighter in her seat and informs her baby brother, "Mommies and daddies have different 'natomy."

Dean blinks. "That's very good, Eleanor, and correct."

The girl beams at me. "Mommy told me."

"I what?" I take a sip of orange juice. "Oh yes, of course."

She nods at her dad. "When we were changing Henry's diapers."

He's in diapers? Panic grips me. "But I thought." I peek at Henry's bottom half under the table. His pajama pants do look a bit baggy. I start eating faster without knowing why. I feel like a hungry beast that's about to get my food snatched away from me.

"Anatomy lessons, huh." Dean winks at me. "Silver lining to him still toilet training." *What? Oh, no.* I have the sinking feeling I'm going to get called into potty action. I mentally scroll through the ways to avoid it. None of them seem very mommy-like. I've never toilet trained anybody. They don't teach you that in teacher training programs! Maybe in preschool training programs. Or daycare. My forehead feels really, really hot.

I cover my remaining pancakes with more syrup. "How old is Henry?"

Dean wrinkles up his face. "Thirty-three months, but you know that."

"Haha! Right." *What? Nooo.* I've read up on this stuff. It could be a full half year before he's trained completely. Or more. I chew, chew, chew. Instinctively downing my food. Faster and faster in a form of self-preservation. I try not to focus on toilets and wiping bums, considering Dean's culinary skills instead. He's great at making breakfast.

"We'll get there soon enough," he says to Henry. "Won't we, buddy?"

Henry gurgles with laughter. "O-tay!"

This entire conversation seems to somehow plant a seed in Henry's brain. Because two seconds later, while I'm woofing down my remaining pancakes, he turns to me. "I go pee-pee."

My fork clanks against the plate and I steady it.

Dean winces, his shoulders lowered. "Power of suggestion?"

"Ha, yeah." I shove some crispy bacon in my mouth and then some more. Tasty. I hope I don't have to take Henry to the potty. Please let it be Dean. Please, please.

I want to shout, *I'm new here!* Of course I can't.

Dean pushes back his chair. Thank goodness.

But Henry hangs his head and pouts. "Mommy take me." Mommy. Great. I wait for Dean to relieve me. He doesn't. He goes right back to eating his pancakes in a leisurely fashion, like it's already been settled. He did cook, to be fair. However. Nobody warned me of the trade-off in advance.

"Ahh, okay." I wipe my mouth with my napkin and stand. Wrangle Henry out of his booster seat. My gosh, he's heavy.

What do we feed him? Loaded baked potatoes? Take him by his pudgy hand. Peek over my shoulder. "We'll be right back!" My jaw tenses. *Come on, Paige. You can do this.* He's just a little boy. *Your little boy.* I think I might faint.

"Don't forget the bull's-eye!" Dean reminds me. I have no idea what he means.

I'm crouched in the bathroom, madly hunting through the cabinet beneath the sink. There's not much under here but extra toothpaste and bathroom cups. Hand soap dispensers. A stash of training pants, which are something like heavy-duty diapers wanting to become undies with cartoon designs. Then I see Henry pointing to the shelving unit mounted above the commode. It looks like a tissue box but it's not. It's something called "Toilet Targets." Seriously?

I tug one out and it's very fine paper with colored rings and a bull's-eye in the center. I stare at Henry, and he points down at the toilet bowl. I flip up lid and seat and drop one in. It floats there waiting in the water, and Henry tugs down his pj pants and trainers.

I cover my eyes and peek through my fingers. "Need help there, Henry?"

"No." A steady whizz while I fixate on the ceiling.

Whew. I think he's got it.

I hear the toilet flush.

When I check, he's got his pj pants back up.

"Great job!"

He grins from ear to ear with pearly white baby teeth.

Toilet targets! Who knew?

Henry climbs up on the toddler stool to wash his chubby hands and I turn on the water. Squirt soap into his fat palm. Pass him a towel. Maybe this training phase won't be so bad?

Minutes later, we're back in the kitchen. "All good?" Dean asks.

"All good!" I shoot him a thumbs-up.

"Good job, buddy!" He holds out his hand and Henry slaps it, toddling by. Dean and Eleanor have finished eating. "Want more pancakes?" Dean asks Henry.

"No tanks."

Dean chuckles and shakes his head. "Paige, you need to finish your breakfast."

But I couldn't eat another bite. I stuffed myself with crunchy bacon. "I wish I could, but I think I'm done." Only the barest scraps remain on my plate. There's not much more to eat unless I lick it clean. I consider doing that for a fleeting instant. Bacon crumbles in syrup. *Mmm.* But no. Need to set the grown-up example.

Dean stands from the table and scoots back Eleanor's chair so she can hop down. "Okay then! It's time for our calendar." Both kids cheer.

A cell phone buzzes on the counter by a group of lined-up cookbooks. "You've been getting texts all morning," Dean says to me. "I think it's your girlfriends."

"Oh yeah?" I pick up the phone and a bunch of text message bubbles stare up at me.

> **KIRSTIN:** What a blast.

> **MIA:** Headache. Ugh.

> **HEATHER:** How many pitchers did y'all have?

> **MIA:** Says the one who's not drinking. You'd think she'd keep count.

Wait. Heather's not drinking? Are she and Peyton expecting their second kid? How exciting for them and their family.

> **KIRSTIN:** Not as many as when we got those tattoos.

> **MIA:** Truth.

Okay then. Confirmed. It *was* a wild night after all. At least for three of us. I hold the phone against my leg, not sure how to respond. We've been so out of touch, I feel intrusive suddenly chiming in. Even if they believe I was there, I don't recall a moment of it. So. I decide to like their individual messages with a thumbs-up.

> **KIRSTIN:** I think Paige is hungover.

> **MIA:** Lol. Same.

What? Way to talk about me like I don't exist! Although technically... No. I can't even.

> **HEATHER:** I told you girls to hydrate.

I grab my orange juice off the table and drain the glass.

"That them?" Dean asks, and I look up.

"Oh yeah. Ha. Ha. Just checking in!" I tuck my phone in my hip pocket and Dean hoists Henry in his hands, holding him around his barrel chest and underneath his arms.

"Okay, bud," he tells Henry, angling him forward toward the advent calendar. "Let's grab Mr. Snowman and put him on the tree!" He does, and Eleanor claps as Dean sets Henry down.

"Can we build a snowman?" She asks so preciously, it's hard to say no.

Dean and I glance out the kitchen window at the front yard and then at each other. "What do you think, Mommy?"

"Sounds like fun." I can't recall the last time I built a snowman. In college with Dean? I remember my lunch date with my mom. "Maybe when I get back?" There's no sense in *not* humoring the kids. I'm bound to wake up in my old life tomorrow. *So.* As long as I'm stuck here for the rest of today—and it seems like I am—I might as well make the most of it.

"We'll build one this afternoon, then," Dean tells the kids, and they bounce on their heels. "It will be fun." His dark eyes shimmer, and I feel a glow. He's always had that effect on me. In that way nothing's changed. Henry and Eleanor scoot out of the room in their pj's to watch the rest of their kids' show. I wonder about getting them dressed, but that shouldn't be too hard. I can sort through the laundry in the master and pick out pieces that fit. I'm not a total incompetent. I've got potty training experience now.

As I help Dean clean up the kitchen, I say quietly, "Dean, when we talked earlier." I lower my voice further, even though the kids are in the living room. "Why did you think I might be pregnant?" He rinses off the plates and hands them to me, and I load them in the dishwasher.

He leans closer and whispers, "IUDs fail, don't they?" I release a pent-up breath. An IUD—*of course I have one.* I'm responsible.

"They *can.* But that would be rare."

"Wouldn't be the end of the world, would it?" He bends

down to kiss me, and I can't keep from going breathy. In *this world*, where we're already a family. In the other one, that would come as a definite shock.

"No, I guess not."

Dean glances out the window over the sink at the street beyond our short drive. "The roads are still icy. You should probably take my jeep, since it's got four-wheel drive. I'll go and clean it off for you later. Warm it up. Get it ready to go." Just as I thought. No more pristine SUV. *Sigh.*

"That would be great. Thanks." His jeep doesn't appear to be new, but it looks younger than what's apparently my faded hatchback with a dented rear door. It's a miracle my car still runs. I wonder vaguely if Dean and I drive to work together. I want so badly to ask him how we got here. How we went from Point A to Point Z. What happened to his internship in Puerto Rico? How did he give up that dream?

But I can't hurt his feelings again, like I did earlier when I seemed to question our future. It will crush him even more to believe I don't remember our past. I know what I'll do. I'll ask Mom. Once I know more, I'll have a better sense about how to approach Dean about our being in an alternate reality. I have another thought, too. *Of course!* There are framed photos on the bookshelves in the living room. Maybe I'll find more pics on my phone?

CHAPTER
Six

I sit waiting for Mom at Beaumont's. It's a swanky place with chunky wooden tables and walls made from old wooden doors suspended from a heavy metal track. They're painted in rustic tones: reds, oranges, and browns. The flooring's washed stone. Brass lighting fixtures suspend from the ceiling like enormous hoods. I've ordered myself a glass of wine while I wait.

Mom texted she's running behind, which is honestly just like her. This gives me comfort, that she's still who I think she is in this decidedly different place. I scan through my photo app, flipping back through the years with my thumbs. Oh my gosh. There's Henry as a baby! What a precious nugget, tucked in his proud papa's arms. Looks like we're in the hospital from the bassinet behind them and the design of the swaddling blanket and the infant cap on his head.

I search for Eleanor's baby pictures next but find Scout's puppy shots first. I giggle out loud at his adorable baby snout poking out from his curtain of bangs. He snuggles on Eleanor's lap—tummy up—as she holds him, looking proud. She's got to be right around three. Her pigtails are shorter, not even hitting her shoulders. I scour back for her baby photos and find them, the shots of me as a first-time mommy filling my heart with more joy than I can fathom.

In between, there are vacation pictures. Our family at the beach. Scout frolicking in the waves with a tennis ball in his mouth. Me and the kids digging with shovels and buckets in the sand. All bright and sunny smiles, in bathing suits.

Happy holidays shared with Mom and Dean's family. Groups gathered around a larger table, maybe at Dean's parents' house. His sister, Jenny, holding hands with a college boyfriend. Dean beaming and slicing a turkey. The kids dressed for Halloween. Henry's a turtle and Eleanor's a ninja. I stumble upon my girl group next. All of us toasting with margaritas.

There's a shot of Scotland! Purple heather and rolling hills. Oh my gosh! We're on a boat touring Loch Ness! No, wait. That's not *us*. It's Dean's parents, standing side by side on a sun-splashed deck wearing warm coats, scarves, and sunglasses. The water gleams deep blue. Urquhart Castle's on the shore.

My heart aches dully. Of course Dean and I didn't make it to Scotland ourselves. We don't seem to be rolling in the dough here. His mom and dad must have gone and bought the Loch Ness toy for Henry and stuffed Highland cow for Eleanor. How could I have forgotten everything? So many beautiful memories? *It's because you haven't lived them, Paige.*

My eyes brim at the loss. I'm aware certain older people suffer when memories slip away. Though I understood that as sad, I never empathized fully as I do now. My grandma had dementia. I've always feared that Mom will get it, too. I couldn't bear to lose her that way. Or any other way. What about her health? Has she been sick here?

"Paige? Sorry, I was—"

I look up. "*Mom.*" I leap out of my chair and embrace her. Afraid if I let her go, she'll evaporate, like my old life has.

"My goodness." She laughs nervously. "Is everything okay?" She wears a paisley print skirt, a ruffled white blouse with puffy sleeves, and a wide brown belt with matching boots.

I place my hands on her shoulders and peer into her eyes. I have to know. I can't wait a second longer. "Are *you* okay? Your health? Your *everything*?" I can't bring myself to say "cancer."

"Sweetheart, yes." She leans closer and whispers, "I received my five-year cancer-free clearance on Wednesday. I told you all about it. The clinic threw me a party, with a cake and balloons. It was so sweet."

"Thank goodness!" The air whooshes back into my lungs and I *breathe, breathe.* Hug her tightly again then let her go.

Her big blue eyes go round. "Are *you* okay?" she asks me. "Because I have to say, Paige, you're acting a little strange."

"Yes, yes, of course! I've just missed you, that's all." I tuck my layered hair behind my ear, but it falls forward.

"Is that it?" she teases and takes a seat, setting her heavy purse on the floor. "Or do you miss my babysitting?" Relief crashes over me in big, sloshy waves. This is definitely the Mom I know and love. I'm so happy to see her and that's she's not sick. Nerves churn through me, though, because her state is still uncertain in the other place. Whatever happens here, I can't leave her to contend with that there all by herself. Is that other world still continuing? Are Mom and I having lunch at Beaumont's in an alternate realm? My head pounds as I try to sort through it, before realizing I can't. Not alone, anyway. Maybe Mom can help.

I sigh and sit down, too. "Thanks for last Saturday, by the way."

"My pleasure. You know I love spending time around the kids. You look cute." She surveys my outfit and hair. "I told you highlights would work."

I finger my feathery tresses, getting used to them. "Yeah, they're great."

"Glad to see you listen to me sometimes." Mom shares a teasing smirk, and I laugh, appreciating her in a new way. It's like we're bonded now that I'm a mom. *But not.* Twisted.

Our server stops by, and Mom motions toward my sauvignon blanc. "I'll take one of those too, please." She picks up her menu and scans it. "Everything looks yummy." She looks up and asks, "Have you had a chance to decide yet?"

On my food? Yeah. On other things? Not so much. Like how I'm going to tell Mom I'm in an alternate reality. "I was thinking I might have a burger." In my regular life, lunch is generally a boring sandwich, or a fruit and yogurt affair. So why not break out of the mold? I've already broken out big-time in every other way, it seems. *Butterfly tattoo? Really?*

She sets down her menu as her wine arrives. "I think I'll have a burger, too." We both order burgers with fries and all the fixings.

"Great choices," the server says, collecting our menus.

"So!" Mom says brightly. "How's your week been?"

"Er," I stall. "I've had a lot of stuff going on."

"Stuff?" She sets her wineglass on the table and taps it. "Mmm. This is good."

"Mom," I say and set down my wineglass. "My life has changed."

"I know, sweetheart."

I gulp. "You know?"

"You have a family now, a husband. A house." She sighs dreamily. "The wonderful life you've always wanted."

"What? No."

"No?" She wrinkles her nose. "Oh dear. Oh no. Paige," she rasps in hushed tones. "You and Dean...?" She gasps. "You're not having trouble? He hasn't strayed?"

I blink. "Dean? No, no. Nothing like that."

She leans closer. "You're right, that doesn't seem like Dean. Every time I see the two of you together, he appears just as much over the moon about you as he was in college, and vice versa." She sits back in her seat and studies me. "So what's going on?"

Hoo-boy. Here we go. "Mom, I don't know how you're going to take this, but, um. You believe in mystical stuff, right?"

"Mystical how?" She sounds a bit affronted.

"Sorry. I didn't mean that in a *bad* way. What I meant was..." I stare up at the ceiling and around the packed café. But answers don't rain down on me from above. I decide not to mention her medical procedure this coming week in the other place. Why get her all twisted up in knots with worry about the outcome, when I can carry that load myself?

"Paige?"

"Mom," I say urgently. "I'm in an alternate reality." I spit it out before I lose my nerve, focusing on the positive like Mom always encourages me to do. "Yesterday, I had another life and a great job teaching. I'm starting this new literacy program at Walton where students read to dogs. It's super wonderful and can help so many kids and volunteers. The animals get value out of it, too."

"Wait." She looks confused. "Does this involve Scout?"

Ugh, it's like she's not hearing me. "No, Mom. These are trained therapy dogs for my Paws and Read program."

"Pause and Read!" She smiles warmly. "I like that." *Finally,* she's coming on board.

"But I'm not implementing the program here. That was in my other world. My life was *different*. I was single and not married to Dean. I didn't have Eleanor or Henry, or Scout." She blinks but she's listening. "Then I saw Dean at this holiday party—"

"At Walton?" she asks.

"Yeah, there."

"But don't faculty and staff—?"

"Mom, *please*," I beg. "Let me finish."

Her pale blue eyes round. "All right."

I try to recall where I was. Oh yeah. Paws and Read. No. Party. "So when I saw Dean at the party, it was for the first time in six years. He and I broke up when he went to Puerto Rico—"

"Puerto Rico?" She gasps. "When did he go there?"

I hold out my hand like a stop signal, and she clamps her mouth shut. "Right after he graduated from college. That's what I'm saying. That's where he met Wendy."

"But I thought you said…" A worried frown. "Are you telling me he and this Wendy—?"

"No, no! She was his boss and much older."

"What?" I can see this is difficult for her. So many moving pieces. I try to wrap it up.

"My point is, Dean and I reconnected, and he gave me this special advent calendar. The woman he bought it from hinted at it being enchanted."

"Oh yes!" She brightens, happy to understand *one thing*. "I've seen it in your kitchen. It's very cute."

I sigh. "I think it might actually be magical."

"What?"

I drop my voice to a whisper, "I think it changed things. I think it *changed me* by transporting me here after I put up the Christmas star."

"What Christmas star?"

"The ornament that goes on the top of the green felt tree."

"Oh yes." She eyes me warily, like she's growing concerned.

I lean closer. "Mom, I went to bed last night *single* and alone in my condo. Then I woke up this morning next to Dean, *married* and with this family and a brand new life. Only, none of it is mine at all." Her mouth hangs slightly open. Her eyes look glazed. "Mom?" I wave a hand in front of her face. "*Mom?*" I swear I'm on the verge of tears.

She heaves a deep breath and say gently, "Okay, sweetheart. I'm sorry. You're clearly going through *something*. Have you tried talking to Dean about these…um…issues?"

"Yeah. Sadly, that didn't go well. I think I hurt his feelings by implying I want a different life."

"But you do want a different life, according to you."

"No. I just want things back how they were. I don't belong here."

As much as I love the thought of Mom being cancer free, I can't stop believing this is a temporary state, some kind of glimpse into an alternate world, like a thought bubble that's destined to pop. And when it does, I'll be back on the other side, left to contend with the fallout. I can't let my real life run off course when I have so many important responsibilities. At my school and most importantly to Mom.

"How can I have these kids when they don't even feel like mine?" I ask her. "When I have no memories of raising them? This must be some cosmic mistake, or a very unusual time blip. An alternate reality I've slipped into without warning." I set my chin, deciding. "I'm betting that calendar's got something to do with it, too. I just don't understand why it's happening or how to make it stop."

She takes a while to digest this. "I see what this is." Her eyes sparkle knowingly. "You're having regrets." What I'm starting to regret is having this conversation. I don't regret this life. How can I? It isn't even mine, except it is. Strangely. But if that's the case, what about my past, and why can't I remember anything at all about the last six years?

Our burgers arrive and we shake out our napkins, laying them in our laps. "I'm sorry, sweetheart," she says. "I'm trying hard to understand, honestly I am. Maybe this is a phase?" she suggests. "Postpartum depression?"

"For nearly three years?"

She holds open her hands. "It could happen, I suppose."

I lean toward her. "Can I ask you something?"

"You know you can ask me anything."

"It's about Dean and Puerto Rico." I ball up my napkin in my lap, wring it tightly in my hands. "He was offered a big opportunity in this world, too. Do you know why he didn't take it?"

"Sweetheart," she says softly. "It was because of you. You tried to break it off with him, but he couldn't end it. The next morning, instead of getting on that plane to San Juan, he came running back to you."

"*Nooo.*" I'm plagued with guilt. "I ruined his chances for the internship?"

She slowly shakes her head. "He made that choice, not you. And, if I'm being honest?" She peers deeply into my eyes. "I believe in your heart you were desperate for him not to go. He was the love of your life, you told me. The man you wanted in your future."

Pain courses through me, but not a recollection. "I said that?"

"I'm not exactly sure what happened during that make-up session of yours," Mom says coyly. "But roughly nine months later we all got a happy surprise: Eleanor. Dean wanted you to stay in college, but you didn't want to attend while pregnant. You chose a different sort of life. Came to work temporarily for me."

I gasp, unable to fathom this. "I styled hair?"

"No. You were my receptionist at the salon, and not so terrific at it, to tell you the truth." She fiddles with her beach-themed bracelet with seashells on it. "You said I got on your nerves."

I cover my mouth and giggle. "Oh gosh, I'm sorry."

She chuckles. "It's okay. I was a little pushy with my advice on childrearing."

"You've been the very best mom in your own way. Just because your way of thinking is different from mine doesn't mean it was wrong."

She reaches out and holds my hand. "Thank you for saying that, Paige."

We glance down at our juicy burgers, which smell delicious. "Do you think we should eat," she asks, "while it's still hot?"

"Yes, definitely."

Our burgers are loaded with lettuce, tomato, French-fried onion rings, sauteed mushrooms, and cheese. Gooey condiments squish out the sides when we take big bites. I could be one of those people whose appetite is adversely affected by stress, but I'm not. By the way Mom's tackling her food, it seems I come by it honestly. This heartens me somehow, making me feel less solitary on these shifting sands. I pop a French fry in my mouth and it's so tasty, likely cooked in peanut oil, with a nice crunchiness and the perfect amount of salt.

As we work on our lunches, Mom says seriously, "Paige, I think you should consider seeing a doctor. Maybe getting an MRI."

"What?"

She sets down her burger. "Honey, I'm worried about you. It's not normal for someone your age to start forgetting things."

But I know if I get an MRI, it won't show anything. I'm not sure how to convince Mom of that fact, though. She's speaking out of love and concern. "Tell you what," I say. "If this doesn't get better—"

"Quickly," she intercedes.

"Quickly," I agree. "Then I'll think about seeing a doctor, all right?"

"All right, sweetheart," she says pleadingly. "Please promise."

"I promise," I pledge, not sure how I'm going to keep it, or if I'll even be here tomorrow. But I want to make her feel better, not worse.

"How long did I work for you, anyway?" I ask, genuinely curious.

"Three months was all you said you could take," she quips. "Dean pulled some strings to get you an interview at Hillsdale, where he was at the time. Then when Walton opened, you both moved there."

"I see." So much is falling into place. I'm grasping the bigger picture of all Dean's done for me. The sacrifices he's made. I guess I made my sacrifices in this realm, too. Dropped out of college, put my focus on our family. But what about Mom? "How about you?" I ask her. A tender spot in my heart aches. "Are you okay?"

"Oh yes." She shimmies her shoulders and her big dangly earrings twirl. "I've got a new boyfriend now, Roger. He's a retired auto mechanic and very handsome. Paige," she says emphatically, "I think he might be the one." I can't help being pleased for her. She's radiant, with a sweep of color on her cheeks.

"Well, in that case, I'm really happy for you, Mom."

"I'm so glad you said that." She preens and pats down her auburn curls. "Because I don't want you to overreact when I tell you the news."

"News?" I ask with trepidation.

"Roger and I are moving in together," she says with a grin. "On his houseboat."

"Houseboat? *Mom*. Don't you know where we live?"

"Oh. His houseboat's not here in the mountains. It's down on the coast, in Wilmington."

My heart sinks like a stone. "You're leaving Piney Mount?" I can't believe it. This is her home. *Our home*, and has been forever.

"Darling," she says, sipping from her wine. "You have to go where love leads."

"Yes, but." I lick my lips, wanting to cry. "What about Eleanor and Henry?"

"I think they'll love learning to sail, don't you?" She misreads my panicked look. "Naturally they'll wear life vests. Safety first at all costs."

She's leaving me? No, this can't be. "Let's talk this over."

"It's not like we won't ever see each other, Paige. Heavens! I'll visit—with Roger, when he can join me. Otherwise, I'll come on my own, and you can visit Wilmington." My head spins and spins, like my whole world is spiraling away from me.

"What about your shop?"

"I'll open another. People need their hair done everywhere, my sweet girl, not just here."

Dread grips me by the throat. Is Mom planning something similar in my other reality? Is there a Roger there, as well as here? Is he who she was going to tell me about at lunch? And how does her medical testing play into all of this? Surely she won't flee with Roger to the coast if her cancer's back. Then again, maybe she will—deciding to savor what time she has left by doing exactly as she pleases. My heart hurts. I don't get it. I never would have left her. How can she abandon me? Us? My voice trembles when I ask, "When are you planning to go?"

"On Friday."

"This Friday?" It's like an entire house has fallen on me. "The day after Christmas?"

"Oh baby." Tears glisten in her eyes. "If you're sick, though, of course I'll stay. For as long as you need." But after that, she's going anyway? Who is this guy Roger? Worry claws at me. Maybe he's a scam artist, unsavory? Out to take advantage of Mom's sunny nature?

"I'd like to meet Roger," I tell her calmly, although my knees bob up and down. I sit up straighter and clasp my hands in my lap, so hard they ache. Press down on my knees so they stop jiggling. I'm not letting some random stranger whisk Mom away. Sure, I want her happiness, but not at the expense of her safety. Who knows who Roger is? Maybe a psycho, or an axe murderer?

"All right." She shrugs. At least that's something. "We'll check our calendar." *Wait.* They're a unit now? Already? Am I going to have to start calling them "Rogmary"? *Nooo.* How did this happen so fast? Where was I? Okay. Maybe in the other place. Not fair.

The server clears our empty plates. "Another glass of wine for you ladies?" she asks, noting our drained glasses.

"No, thanks." Mom smiles. "I'm driving. Maybe coffee?"

"Same. Make that two, please," I add.

While we're waiting on our coffees, Mom digs around in her purse and pulls out a small, giftwrapped present. "I brought you an early merry Christmas present."

I'm feeling far from merry right now. I'm frantic with nerves over the choices she's making. "I'm not sure if I..." I pull my purse into my lap and hunt through it. Yes. Her Christmas gift is there. I take it out and check the tag, which says, "For Mom." I hand it to her, wondering if it's those same tin earrings I bought at the holiday market in the other place.

84

"Should I go first?" she asks glibly like nothing's wrong, although my world's falling apart. I'm in a new reality that she doesn't understand. Probably because she's too besotted with Roger to contemplate much of anything else. I motion for her to go ahead, and she opens her gift.

"How lovely! Thank you!" She holds the pretty blue and green earrings up by her ears. "These will remind me of the mountains when I'm sailing the seven seas!" I hope she's joking, and they never moor their boat beyond North Carolina. I'm for sure meeting Roger as soon as humanly possible. She nods at the package she's placed on the table. "Now, your turn."

I carefully unwrap a Christmas tree ornament box, but when I turn it to face me, I want to weep. It's a miniature sailboat ornament with "Ahoy!" stamped on its hull. "Thanks, Mom." I work hard not to burst into tears. "I love it."

CHAPTER
Seven

ean's clearly astounded. "Your mom's doing *what*?" We're in the living room suiting up to go play in the snow. Dean and I wear ski pants and jackets. An assortment of hats, mittens, and gloves lie on the sofa beside me. I whispered the news to him while we gathered our winter weather gear from the coat closet near the front door.

Finally. Someone who sees the absurdity of the situation like I do. I guess my update on the houseboat finally sank in. "I know, right? What's Mom thinking?"

A houseboat in Wilmington? Besides the dicey nature of that living arrangement, given potential hurricanes, that's five and a half hours away. From Eleanor, Henry, and Scout. The dog lies snoozing by the fireplace, his head down on his front paws. From all of us, including me.

Dean's amazement is clear. "Wow. I think that's great!"

Wait. What?

"Great? *Dean*." I cut a glance at the kids, aware I shouldn't say too much about their grandma in front of them. "You can't mean it. Who relocates in December?" I choose "relocate" on purpose, guessing the kids won't know that that means.

"What's 'locate?" Eleanor asks. *Case in point.*

Ahh. I stare down at her, arriving at an answer. "It means moving someplace new."

Her bottom lip pokes out. "Grandma's 'locating?"

Not if I can help it. Someone's got to save her, even if that means saving her from herself. I know I shouldn't have a vote on anything, being as new here as I am, but she's my mom, after all, and I care, no matter what dimension we're in. I fret again about what's happening in the other universe. What if she takes off with Roger before I can return to stop her? What if I lose her indefinitely in both worlds?

Dean tugs on Henry's snowsuit, stuffing the boy's stubby legs into the pants portion like bulging sausages, while Henry sits on his lap. They're on the love seat while I help Eleanor from my perch on the sofa.

"Maybe this guy, Roger, is okay?" Dean suggests. "Hold up your hands, buddy," he instructs Henry before tugging on his mittens.

I'd like a chance to see that for myself. "I told Mom we want to meet him."

"Good. What did she say?" He adds a baby blue pom-pom hat with penguins on it that brings out Henry's eyes.

"She's checking their calendar." I huff and situate Eleanor's red reindeer hat on her head, straightening her darling pigtails beneath the fleece-lined earflaps.

Dean stands Henry on the floor in front of him, bringing the top portion of the boy's snowsuit up and over Henry's stout chest and securing the wide straps over his heavy sweater.

I work on Eleanor in the meantime, but she helps me, pulling up her bibs all by herself. I snap them over her shoulders.

Tighten the straps. Her green sweater's got candy canes on it. Henry's sweater is black with a snowman design. Both sets of kiddie snow bibs are navy blue. Dean and I wear red pants and puffy black jackets.

Before long we're all ready to go, but I'm still fretting. It must be obvious to Dean because he notes my frown. "Well, let's not worry about that right now," he says. "All right?" He corrals our group toward the front door. "Let's go build that snowman!"

He hands Eleanor a scarf and a floppy, black brimmed hat. Henry holds a carrot in his baby blue mittens. We'll scrounge pebbles from the drive for the snowman's eyes and "buttons" and use sticks for his arms.

The kids both cheer and I behold their cherubic faces. How can I be grumpy about Mom's move with this right in front of me? I can't. So I open the front door and an icy blast of wind bursts toward us, but we soldier on—out onto the porch.

Dean summarily studies the lawn, now piled deep with fluffy white stuff. "Troops!" he says, pointing toward the yard. "Onward!"

One hour later, Dean lifts Henry up to add the final touch to our snowman. He tilts Henry forward and the boy plunges the carrot in deep, right in the center of the snowman's face. Unfortunately, he sticks in the wrong end—the skinny one. So after a brief second, the carrot drops to the ground. Gravity. "No worries," Dean says, and he bends and picks it up. Hands it to Henry. Turns it around in the proper position in Henry's mitten. He leans toward the little boy and says kindly, "Let's try again."

Henry nods seriously and they do.

Success!

I clap my gloves together and cheer. So do the kids. Dean's incredibly handsome in the snow, his face tinged pink from the cold, his dark eyes shining beneath his black stocking cap. I've got on a white pom-pom hat and a matching scarf. They're both covered with snow and ice crystals. My nose stings from the chill and my fingers tingle beneath my gloves. "We should probably bring the kids indoors," I say to Dean, and he nods.

"Good idea."

He takes Henry by the hand, and I turn toward Eleanor, but she surprises me, holding a big snowball in her hands. "Eleanor! What?"

"Merry Christmas, Mommy!" she says and hurls it at me. She's short so it lands on my leg. I laugh.

"Oh, you little rascal." I tussle the top of her hat and she stoops down for more snow. "Now, wait one minute." I hold up a finger.

Dean enjoys the action from the sidelines. He makes a snowball for Henry. "Want to try it, buddy?"

"What?" I cry. "Not at me!" I feel totally ganged up on as Henry lumbers over, the snow halfway up to his knees. "Merry Kissmas, Mommy!" He hurls his snowball with both hands. It plops down in front of my boots.

I shake my finger at him and smirk. "Good try, though." Then narrow my eyes at Dean. "You're responsible for this malarky," I challenge, hands on my hips.

He thumbs his chest, all false innocence. "Who, me?"

I pick up Henry's dropped snowball and pound more snow into the orb. "Now you're going to get it," I tell Dean.

Eleanor chortles. "Go get him, Mommy!"

Dean playfully backs away then turns, darting behind the snowman with his arms outstretched.

"Dean Burton!" I shout. "Come back here!"

"Why?" he shouts, dancing away from me and springing from side to side so I can't aim properly at him. I try. *No—this way. That.* "So you can clobber me with a snowball?" He snickers. "Don't think so." I huff and decide I need a team.

"Here," I say, handing my big, heavy snowball to Eleanor. "This one's for you." Excitement lights up her face.

I make another snowball for Henry. "And this one's for you!"

Dean watches askance while I make my own snowball and motion the kids closer. They huddle in, lumbering through the snow. "Let's go get Daddy," I whisper slyly.

Eleanor's eyes sparkle but Henry just grins. I'm not sure he knows what's happening, but he understands this is family fun. "O-tay!"

Dean shouts with a glove held by his mouth, "What's going on over there?"

I continue whispering to the kids and they giggle. "On three." Solemn nods. "One," I say firmly. "Two."

Dean strides toward us, his boots crunching through the snow. "Is everything all rig—?"

"Three!" I shout and we wheel on Dean. I lob my snowball at him. It hits his chest! "Score!"

Eleanor shouts "Wheee!" and does the same. Her missile smacks her daddy in his middle and Dean gawks in surprise.

Henry gives it his best shot. His snowball arcs through the air—but only slightly—and lands on Dean's boot. The kids giggle in hysterics. I'm laughing too and holding my sides. The look on Dean's face is priceless.

He arches his eyebrows at me. "That was very sneaky, Mommy."

Uh-oh. He's making a new snowball of his own, and somehow I don't think he's targeting the kids.

"Dean!" I hold up my gloves and back away. "Enough's enough."

"Fine to say now." He strides toward me, and I start to run. He chases after me.

"Dean!" I scream but I'm chuckling. "Stop!"

He's closing in, but I run faster. Still. Not fast enough. It's hard to move in all this winter weather stuff, flailing about like a scarecrow. Dean lobs his snowball at my back and—*oof*—it lands dead center. The kids cackle when he grabs me by the waist. "Very funny." His husky breath is on my neck and my breath catches.

"It was funnier"—I huff and puff—"when *we* were throwing snowballs at *you*."

"Ha. *Ha*." He holds me snugly around the middle and kisses my cheek, and sizzling tingles shoot through me. "You're freezing!" he says in surprise. Except now, I'm all warmed up. My face burning. My heart hammering. *Oh nooo.*

I think I'm falling for Dean. I think I'm falling for all of them.

That's inconvenient.

Dean motions everyone toward the house, where our Christmas tree gleams prettily in the front window and icicle lights drip from the porch. "Great job with the snowman, everyone!"

Snow pounds us from above as he leads Henry by the hand. Eleanor reaches out, latching onto mine, and my heart thumps. I'm not supposed to develop an attachment to these children, because I'm bound to be leaving here soon. But it's hard not to be charmed by how Eleanor trusts me instinctively as her mom, and by Henry's darling garbled phrases. I hope I've been a good mom to them, and when they grow up one day, they'll look back with happy memories.

My brain freezes up like someone's jammed cogs on a wheel. I can't start thinking of Eleanor and Henry as mine. Only, in a very-hard-to-grasp way, they are. My heart twists painfully. Dean is also my husband, but that won't last, I remind myself. None of this is going to last, so there is no future in this realm.

Dean holds open the door, and we're enveloped by a cheery warmth when we step indoors. "How about we get the kids out of their snow stuff and light a fire? We can have an early supper and make some hot cocoa."

"Sounds perfect," I say and smile at him. Might as well enjoy the fantasy while I'm here, and that will be at least until bedtime, as far as I can see.

"Yeah." He smiles and I feel like we've spoken telepathically. That he's saying everything is perfect in our world. Which only makes my heart ache more, because I know what Dean doesn't. This isn't my actual existence, the reality that I came from and am more than likely destined to go back to, once this holiday magic ends.

Later that evening, Dean and I sit drinking our hot cocoa on the living room sofa. A real wood fire blazes before us, logs crackling merrily. Eleanor slumps against her daddy's shoulder, snoozing soundly and curled up in a sofa blanket. Henry's passed out with his head in my lap with another blanket draped over him. Dean's arm is around my shoulder and he holds me close, while Scout sleeps at our feet between us and the coffee table. "Hmm, this is nice," I say softly.

Dean sighs contentedly. "Yeah."

He added a jigger of bourbon to the adults' libations, and the effect's delightfully mellowing. Deliciously chocolatey with a nice warming kick. I survey my gorgeous husband and the family that resembles a holiday card. If only life were really this way for everybody—but it isn't for me. I'm experiencing what my life might have been like with Dean if we'd never broken up.

Still. None of this *feels* like an alternate universe. The heat of Dean's body next to me is so real. Could I honestly have had this life? I search the room for signs of my Christmas ghosts, but don't see them anywhere. If I did see a spirit, like one of the specters who visited Scrooge, I'd have someone to ask about what's going on. Failing that, I'll have to track down that holiday market vendor. Maybe she can explain how all of this happened, and how long I'm fated to stay. If I'm still here tomorrow, that's precisely what I plan to do.

"Dean," I ask as flames leap in the hearth, "can you tell me more about getting that advent calendar?" Maybe he can give me some hints as to where I might find its vendor.

He looks at me perplexed. "You were there with us when we bought it last week."

"Yes, but there's been so much going on this holiday season." I think up some excuses. "Between work." I sigh. "And Mom."

He chuckles warmly. "Do you really think she'll run away with Roger to go live on a houseboat?"

"Oh gosh, I hope not."

"I'm glad we're meeting him, though," he says. "Good call."

My heart twists because I'm so worried about her. "Yeah."

Dean watches the fire for a moment before turning toward me to answer my earlier question. "We got the advent calendar from the older woman at the booth near the end of the row under the big tent, don't you remember?"

I squint up at him and say vaguely, "Think so."

"You *have* been working too hard." He chuckles. "She was dressed like Mrs. Claus, so I would have thought she was pretty impossible to forget. Red Santa cap, nice round middle? White hair and wire-rimmed glasses?"

I start to picture her in my mind, and she does look jolly, with big round cheeks like her famous husband. "Oh-ho!"

"Oh *ho, ho, ho,*" he teases with a twinkle in his eye.

Though it seems superstitious to believe in a magical advent calendar, that's no more outlandish than my being here in this duplicate world, with its unique differences and nuances. And there's no denying it. Some of the differences here are pretty great. In only one day I've found myself falling for these children, *and Dean.* I steal a glance at his handsome face and my heart flutters. Our snowball fight was really fun and I felt so much a part of things. *A part of this family.*

Henry's tiny body's heavy with sleep, molding into me. I stroke back his golden hair, smooth down his pint-size brow. He's a beautiful child, and so is Eleanor, both even more special because of what they represent. The very best of the two of us. Of Dean. Of me. Of what we might have had together as a family. Hot tears brim in my eyes until they're full to bursting.

I stare down at the boy, remembering his actions earlier. "Funny that Henry put up the snowman on the advent calendar this morning and then we built one today, don't you think?" Maybe if Dean believes that calendar's magical, he'll trust me more about the dual realities.

"That wasn't really predicting the future. Come on." Dean shakes his head. "It's more like today's pocket item in the calendar gave us an idea about what we might do."

"I suppose you're right." I snuggle up against him, feeling happy through and through. "Still," I say. "What if that Mrs. Claus lady was on the level?"

He peers down at me. "What?"

I hold my breath, then plow ahead. "She didn't only say the calendar could predict the future, Dean. She also claimed it could change lives, right?"

"Paige," he asks warily, "are you back to that 'I came from the future' thing again?"

"No, no! It's not the future." I nervously rub my nose. "More like an alternate life."

"I thought it was the margaritas?" He goads me with a grin.

"Ha. *Ha*."

"If other things start happening, though," Dean teases about the calendar, "I might be tempted to believe you." He shrugs. "I think a poinsettia's in the pocket for tomorrow, the twenty-first, and we sure haven't got one here."

I glance around the room and at the brightly lit Christmas tree. No poinsettias in sight. It's hard to see how one of those might materialize from out of the blue. "Well, we certainly can't grow a plant in these conditions," I joke. Snow still falls heavily outside the windows, coating the night sky.

"Nope." He kisses the top of my head. "That's true."

My cell phone dings on the end table beside Dean. He reaches over, passing it to me. "Looks like your mom," he says, seeing her text pop up the screen.

"Looks like we're having company!" I tell him.

CHAPTER *Eight*

*ean blinks at* my phone. "What? Now?" He checks the clock on the bookshelf. "It's nearly nine o'clock."

"Not tonight," I answer, scanning Mom's text. I look up at Dean. "She's asking about them stopping by in the morning for coffee around ten o'clock?"

"I don't see why not," he says.

"I agree. I'd like to meet this Roger guy. The sooner the better." *Assuming I'm still here.* If I land back in my condo world, I'll just have to find Mom there and learn what she's up to. I can't believe I'm getting used to the idea of me having existed in two different realms.

My heart sinks again at the idea of leaving this place and this family, which is ridiculous, I know. I've been here less than twenty-four hours, but I can't help the unexpected tug on my heartstrings. I'd have to be made of stone not to feel my heart gently prying open and overwhelming emotions flooding in. I glance at Eleanor and Henry sleeping angelically and sigh

97

deeply. No matter where I wake up tomorrow, all will look clearer after a good night's sleep. *I hope.*

"Getting tired?" Dean asks.

Once he's put the idea in my head, I yawn. "A little."

He studies me carefully. "I know we didn't sleep much last night, waiting up for that comet." His disappointed look surprises me. "Too bad we missed it."

"What?"

He shakes his head. "I'm just sad that it kept on snowing. The weather report promised the storm would lift before midnight."

Wait. We *didn't* see the comet? Yet another difference between my former reality and this one. I distinctly recall being awakened by a very bright glow in my condo.

"But the Christmas Comet was still up there," Dean continues wistfully. "Today I read it was visible in many locations. Somewhere high above the earth, it was lighting the way for all those serious astronomers out there."

"You're a serious astronomer."

"Yeah, not really." He winces. "Sure, I thought about it once, but, as you know, my life took a different course." He shrugs. "I'm happy with how things worked out."

I know what that means. Without Puerto Rico and Wendy, a job out west, his life experiences have been different. He did circle back around to Walton in both realities, to be fair. And he appears content in both places. When I saw him at the holiday party, he seemed good and happy. I wonder if he surmised the same thing about me.

Dean blows out a breath, his mind still on his missed opportunity with the comet. "I know we could have seen it with the naked eye, but it was really great of Chad to loan me his extra telescope. Seeing it through a lens would have been fantastic."

I'm surprised Dean doesn't own a telescope of his own. Maybe in this world he sees that as a splurge and thinks we can't afford it. "I've already packed it up," he says, "and will take it back to him on Monday."

"Chad—Quesenberry?"

"Yep, he's the one."

"But isn't he a counselor?"

Dean nods. "Yeah, sorry. I thought I'd told you about him being a big stargazer buff. He's got all sorts of equipment. Some that I envy, honestly. He doesn't even teach science, but he probably could if he wanted to. The man knows a ton about galaxies and black holes. He's fun to talk to." I'm glad Dean has friends at school and wonder if I do.

It's heartening to know I've reconnected with my old friend group from college. Or rather, that we never disconnected here. When I return to the other world, I think I'll reach out to them. It may be hard at first, but worth it. I've missed those girls so much. It shouldn't matter that our lives have evolved, and that we've chosen different paths. What matters is the love we share in our hearts and our longtime history as friends.

The logs in the hearth crackle softly and the fire burns down low. Christmas stockings hang on either end of the mantel, out of harm's way from the heat and flames. Dean's stocking and mine are on the left, with the two for Eleanor and Henry on the right. Scout's stocking is next to Henry's. All the names are done in swirly lettering and in sparkly silver glitter. The DIY project looks kind of rough, like we might have made them as a family ourselves, but the results are still charming.

Dean smiles over at me. "What do you say we tuck these munchkins into bed and get ready for bed ourselves? Maybe watch some TV in our bedroom, or read?"

I find myself yawning again and cover my mouth. "Sounds good."

I wouldn't mind more chill time to process the day. Mentally plan out my goals for tomorrow: a Plan A for this world, and a Plan B for the other. Though I feel certain if I typed up any kind of schedule, Dean would find that weird. A light bulb goes on in my brain. A computer! Brilliant! I can go through its history and bookmarks to piece together more of my past.

"Dean?" I ask. He's peeled back the sofa blanket from Eleanor and holds the sleeping girl in his arms. "I seem to have misplaced my laptop. Any idea where I might find it?"

He chuckles softly so as not to disturb Eleanor. "Are you hinting to Santa again?"

"Santa? What?"

"I know you've wanted your own laptop forever, and I'm sorry we're still sharing the one Walton issued me."

"Sharing?" My head spins.

His shoulders slouch. "Yeah, it stinks we couldn't count on that old one you had from college to last forever. But soon!" he says. "Keep the faith! If I get my teacher bonus this year, we might find a way."

I'm speechless. I don't have a laptop? That's not something frivolous. It's a necessity. How strapped for cash are we? "But don't I get a laptop with my job?"

He cocks his head. "Hon, you've got a desktop at school."

"Er. Right!" I force a laugh. "I knew that."

"Paige," he asks worriedly, "are you feeling all right? Because lately." He purses his lips in a pause. "You seem to be forgetting things."

I heave a breath. "That's because—"

"You want a different life?" he asks, sounding beleaguered. "Is that why you're mentally scrubbing this one?"

The way he puts it sounds *horrible*.

"*Nooo*. No, no, no. I would never do that on purpose."

"Your mom texted me earlier. She sounded worried about you." He wrinkles his brow, hugging Eleanor against his chest. "Are you sure you're not sick? Experiencing other symptoms?"

"No, no."

"Or." He glances at my stomach.

"Definitely not." I swallow hard.

"All right." He smiles warmly. "It's good we've got winter break coming up. Sounds like you're due for a little downtime." He arches an eyebrow. "Or at least a slightly less hectic time than we typically have around here."

Things haven't been that bad. A bit busy with the kids, but they seem to go to bed early. They get up early, too. I yawn again and cover my mouth, drained by the events of the day. Waking up next to Dean, toilet training Henry, lunch with Mom at Beaumont's, then playing in the snow with the kids. No wonder I'm exhausted. And it's the weekend.

So, no computer. *Sigh.* Well, at least I've got a cell phone. Some kind of lifeline to technology, meaning the modern world. I pick it up and examine it, realizing it's a model from several years ago. *Doesn't matter! Still works!* The screen goes black and I panic.

"You probably just need to charge it," Dean says before he leaves the room.

"Of course!"

He carries Eleanor to bed, and I carefully scoot out from under Henry's heavy head. No way. I birthed that? His head's the size of a bowling ball! No. It was smaller then. My palms go damp. Surely.

I remove his blanket and gather him up in my arms. He sags against me when I stand upright, so cushiony soft and babylike. And yet, he's growing up. Potty training. Tears burn in my eyes, and I blink them back. I can't take credit for his progress. I only helped him to the toilet once. Clearly there were other times that everyone else recalls. Everyone but me.

I don't know which is worse. Being unexpectedly thrust into this alternate reality or being painfully unaware of the memories I've made here. I sniff back my emotion and straighten my spine, carting Henry to his bedroom. I lay him in bed, tuck him under the covers. Yawn again, because goodness gracious, I'm zombie-like with exhaustion myself.

I switch off lights in the living room. Note that the fire in the fireplace has mostly burned down to purplish embers. Take my cell phone into the kitchen, find my charger, and plug in my phone. No signal. No battery icon. Maybe it's so far gone, I need to charge it overnight for it to restore itself?

As I leave the kitchen, my gaze snags on the advent calendar. I've got a sneaking suspicion that my landing in this alternate world has an awful lot to do with the shimmering star I pressed to the top of that green felt Christmas tree. I'm just not sure how.

"What do you know about all of this?" I ask the calendar.

But of course it doesn't answer.

I find Dean in the bedroom, in his sweatpants and T-shirt. "Do I need to lock up?" he asks me.

I shake my head. "I did it." I hunt around for Scout because he wasn't in the kitchen or the living room. He's tucked himself into his doggie bed. "Does Scout need to go out?"

"He takes care of himself," Dean explains. "That's how we trained him."

He's trained exceptionally well to go in and out the door to the side yard, where there's no fencing. "He's very good to never run away."

Dean chuckles as if that's impossible to imagine. "Old Scout's not going anywhere," he assures me. "He knows how good he's got it." I find myself relating to Scout. But no. He's a dog, and I am human. Not trained to this reality in the least. Although, it does seem I'm catching on a lot more quickly than I might have guessed.

I get ready for bed in the bathroom, where I find the large T-shirt of Dean's I slept in last night hanging from a hook on the back of the door. Brush my teeth. I can't find my electric toothbrush, so I use a regular kind, the sort the dentist gives you at check-ups. The green one is obviously mine since the blue one looks wet, like it was recently used by Dean. Floss my teeth, wash my face, change into the T-shirt.

When I reenter the bedroom, Dean's sorting through streaming choices on the TV that sits on the chest of drawers. "What do you think, hon?" he asks me as I approach the bed. "A movie or one of our shows?"

The instant I'm under the covers, my eyelids grow heavy, and I have trouble keeping them open. I can't imagine making it through an entire film. "Maybe a show?" I suggest. "Your pick." But even that demand is too great. I yawn again without meaning to, and then another time. Soon darkness closes in, and Dean turns off the TV. Grogginess settles over me like a warm blanket. I hear a snort and I startle. Is that me? Gosh. No. I don't snore now, do I?

Hmm, maybe.

Or maybe it's sheer exhaustion kicking in.

My body grows heavy and heavier. Limp. Then there's nothing but the sound of the snow pattering against the windows. A *click* and Dean switches off his light. The mattress sags and he burrows under the covers, gently tugs me into his embrace. I melt into our spooning position with him behind me, like we've done this our whole lives. And maybe we have. Sleepiness creeps over me and Dean holds me tighter. Despite the winds that rage outdoors, I'm safe and warm. In a good place.

My eyes pop open and shadows cloak the room.

I forgot all about my dream journal!

Do I even keep one here?

Doubtful.

Dean's already breathing more deeply, falling asleep behind me. Him giving way to slumber makes me drowsy, too. I let me eyelids fall closed, hug his arm draping over me. Wrap the blankets over my shoulders and drift like the snow.

I do not wake up in my shiny condo with views of the snowy valley and neighboring Boone. I'm snuggled next to Dean, which is nice and cozy. Until the kids burst into the room.

Jump up on the bed.

Eleanor. Henry. Scout. *Woof, woof, woof!*

"Mommy! Mommy! Wake up!" Eleanor. Her bony knees digging into my back. *Ouch.* She's bouncing and bouncing on the bed while vigorously shaking my shoulder. So hard, she's going to dislocate it, if she doesn't watch it.

Henry peels back the comforter from my face and collapses on top of me. *Oof.* Just like a bag of sand. "It's Kissmas!" he says very close to my ear, his stubby arms circling my neck.

Dean sits up partway on his elbows from lying on his back. "Not yet, buddy." He's so handsome with his hair mussed up and in his dark morning stubble.

Scout crouches between Dean's legs on top of the blankets, lowers his head between his stretched out front paws, and says, "*Woof, woof!*," his tailing wagging high behind him.

The bed isn't even that big! It's just a double. How's it holding all of us?

Dean and I stare at each other and he grins.

"Guess everyone's hungry," he says.

Okay, I'm still here.

My mind buzzes as I mentally prepare for another day.

CHAPTER
Nine

I learn Sunday breakfast is my time to shine. I view the carton of eggs on the counter by the stovetop, not sure where to start. I've never made French toast before, though I've partaken of it often, slurping up its buttery, high-fat goodness. So, butter, yes. I set a stick of that on the counter by the stove. I know it's got bread. Obviously. Do I toast it first? No. That would be silly, but maybe prevent it from getting too soggy? I don't know. I'm no cooking expert.

Truth is, I rarely cook at all. There's only me typically. So.

Dean walks over and hands me a mug of coffee. "Feeling any better this morning?" He kisses my cheek, and I can't help liking this domestic bliss. Until it's my turn to do the cooking. I take a sip of coffee and am jolted awake by the sugar and cream.

"Ah yeah! Yeah, thanks."

Dean's got the little ones settled watching whatever it is they watch on TV. I suspect it's educational, given that both of us work for a school. I'm a bit nervous about going into my job tomorrow, to be honest. Will I flub it up? Make a mess of things?

Doubtful.

It's more likely I'll be supremely organized! Yes, that. Assuming I'm here tomorrow again like I am today. At this point, it's hard to know what to expect.

Dean extracts syrup from a cupboard and sets it down beside me.

"Er. Maybe we should have cereal this morning?" I say.

"Cereal?" He puzzles out the word. "That's usually for weekdays, but okay. If you're not feeling up to it—" He tries to remove the frying pan from the stove, but I clamp down on his wrist with my hand. "No, no! I can do this."

Dean rubs his chin. "It's not rocket science, you know. It's just French toast."

The skillet gleams up at me, questioning my abilities.

"Stop it," I hiss.

"What's that?" Dean turns toward me.

"Oh, no." I tuck my hair behind my ear. Some of it falls forward. *Right, layers.* "I mean, all's good! I wasn't talking to you. I was addressing the—skillet."

"The skillet?" He screws up his face and picks out a spatula from a utensil jar nearby. He holds in under his chin like a microphone. "Mr. Skillet," he addresses the frying pan. "The public would like to have your thoughts on breakfast."

"Oh stop!" I swat his arm but I'm laughing.

He hands me the spatula and shrugs. "I can take over if you'd like. I really don't mind."

He's being so sweet, but I'm sure I can do this one thing. I mean, come on.

It's only French toast.

I turn the burner on high. The French toast I've had always has a nice crisp patina. Whisk up some eggs. Dump out several slices of precut bread and lay them on the counter in an orderly fashion. Unwrap a whole stick of butter. I mean, we *are* four people. Toss it in. Heavens! It sizzles! Splatters! Flames!

"Fire!"

The smoke detector wails and wails and wails and I yank the skillet off the burner, the melty pool of burnt sludge hissing at me.

Dean rushes into the kitchen through the cloud of black smoke. "What happened?"

Eleanor and Henry stand in the doorway. Scout's with them. The three of them have wrinkled up their noses. Even the dog, I swear. Fact is it does not smell delicious in here. It smells burnt. Dean throws open a window. Hits the smoke detector with a broom handle. Shoos the kids away and turns to me.

I stand there by the stove and see it's glowing, purple flames circling the gas burner. I lunge forward and turn it off. Wince at Dean.

"Ahh, want me to take over?" he offers.

"No." I lick my lips and act like I planned this. "Just warming up."

"Uh-huh."

I put my hands on his back and gently push him out of the kitchen.

I will not be bested by some stupid skillet and a stove! No! I run over to my phone to look up cooking instructions for French toast. Crap. It's still dead. Then I spy something unusual. A row of hardcover cookbooks, the sort my mom never used to have. Although I've seen them on television, and naturally for sale in stores. I may not be super-duper experienced in the kitchen, but I'm, at long last, a decent reader. I delve into my kitchen library and start again.

"*Paige*," *Dean says* appreciatively, "I think this is the best French toast you've ever made." We're seated around the kitchen table and breakfast is almost over. After my initial false start, I did better the second go-round.

I beam proudly. "Thanks!" The kids are scraping their plates. Reading directions wasn't that hard. I'd have thought of that earlier if I'd been more organized. *Eeep. What's happening to me?*

Dean stares at my white-knuckled hold on my fork. "Everything all right?"

"Oh! Yes. Absolutely." I square my shoulders. "Glad you like the French toast." I enjoyed it quite a bit myself, having had four pieces. I relax my grip, set down my fork. It's not like I need it any longer anyway. My plate is empty. Oh, wait. Except for that last, syrup-drenched nibble. I stab it with my fork and gobble it up. This recipe really is to die for. It's got a touch of vanilla in the egg batter and the finished product is dusted with powdered sugar and cinnamon.

The doorbell rings and I jump. Stare down at my bare legs and fluffy fur-lined slippers under the table. With my prolonged cooking efforts, I've neglected to change out of the big T-shirt I slept in. Dean checks his watch. "That must be your mom and Roger."

He's not dressed either, though slightly more presentable than I am. Eleanor scoots out of her chair and races to the advent calendar, nabbing the fabric poinsettia out of its pocket for Day Twenty-One. "Can I put this up?" She clearly fears she'll miss her opportunity otherwise.

Dean nods hurriedly and scoops Henry out of his booster seat. "I'll get the door," he tells me. "You go and change, then we'll switch."

"What about all this?" I survey the messy kitchen. Dirty dishes, bowls, and utensils are everywhere.

"We'll pick up later," he says, holding Henry in one arm.

Eleanor huffs loudly because we've forgotten about her standing there.

Dean and I both stare at the child and say, "Yes!"

She presses the poinsettia to the felt Christmas tree near the bottom of the advent calendar, which is about as high as she can reach, and I scoot past her out of the kitchen, scurrying back toward the bedroom, when I see Mom peering through the glass panel in the front door. I change quickly into a sweater and jeans, forgoing my shower until later, run a brush through my hair, and emerge in the living room to spell Dean.

He's visiting in the entryway with Mom and Roger as they peel off their coats. Through the window by the rocker, I see they've left open umbrellas on the porch. Eleanor and Henry watch Scout busily sniff Roger, who keeps trying to push his doggie nose away from several strategic areas.

"Mom, hi!" I rush toward her and give her a hug while Roger holds their coats.

"Darling," she says, "so good of you to have us over."

Dean takes their coats from Roger to hang in the coat closet, and I smile at the older man with a reddish beard and hair. He looks younger than Mom but not by much. One of his cheeks is scarred and he's got another narrow scar by one of his bushy eyebrows. "Roger, I'm Paige. So nice to meet you."

He smiles with uneven teeth. "Same."

A man of few words. Okay.

I shoot Mom the side-eye, but she doesn't respond.

Roger lifts something off the entry table he'd apparently set down earlier. He hands a big leafy plant with bright red petals to me. Green foil covers its flowerpot. I glance at Dean.

He raises his eyebrows, but it's probably just to humor me.

"What a beautiful poinsettia!" I turn to Roger and Mom. "Thank you."

Dean points to the back hall. "I'll just go and, um, change."

Mom seems to notice for the first time that the kids are still in pajamas. "Did we come too early?" She checks the clock on the bookshelf. It's a quarter past ten.

"Not at all," I tell her. "Please come on in and have a seat."

As she walks past me she leans closer and whispers, "Looks like everything's all better?"

"What?"

"You know." She keeps her voice down and darts a glance at the hall. "Between you and Dean?"

"Oh, uh. Yeah." I can't help being deflated by her question. When I confessed my time-travel troubles to her over lunch, she clearly didn't believe me, chalking up my distress to more mundane marital woes. I point toward the kitchen. "I'll just—go start a fresh pot of coffee."

Dean pokes his head back into the living room from the hall. "Might want to grab some of those Christmas cookies from the freezer, too." His sunny smile sparkles and Mom gives me a satisfied look.

"Mm-hmm," she says, taking a seat beside Roger on the love seat.

"Christmas cookies," I repeat. "Right!"

Dean beams at my mom and Roger. "Paige and the kids made some really yummy ones."

"Ooh," Mom says. "Sounds great!"

Roger rubs his thick hands together and nods.

When I open the tin from the freezer, I can hardly believe my eyes. There are snickerdoodles smelling deliciously of nutmeg, slightly lopsided gingerbread people releasing heady bursts of ginger and spice into the air, and chocolate-dipped pretzel sticks with green and red sprinkles on them. Some sort of white chocolate covered sandwich cookie, too. Each one of those has two chocolate coated candies on top, one red and one green.

I take sneaky bite of a sandwich cookie to taste it. *Ooh.* The crunchy round and salty crackers hold a big dose of peanut butter inside. *Yum.* I made these? I'm immensely impressed. I'm also going to gain ten pounds during this fantasy visit if I'm not careful. But if it's a fantasy, and not real, what's the worry? I seem to carry a few extra pounds no matter how much I exercise, so why not own it? I down the remainder of the sandwich cookie, then scarf down another. So tasty. I've got no treadmill here, but maybe I don't need one, since we're always chasing after the kids.

I set an assortment of treats on a plate, ignoring the messy kitchen, which is a bit hard. It looks like the aftermath of a cooking show disaster in here. My fingers twitch, itching to clean up the mess, or—at the very least—load our plates in the dishwasher. Thank goodness, yes. We do have one of those. But no. Not now. I force myself to turn away from the disarray on the countertops and kitchen table and carry the treats into the living room.

Roger's engaged in conversation with Henry. "What's your name, young fellow?"

Scout noses his way in and Roger pats him on the head. Scout sits, keeping an eye on the situation and Roger. Good boy.

"'Enry," the little boy tells Roger.

"That's *Henry*," my mom informs him, enunciating clearly.

Roger speaks to the boy. "And how old are you, Henry?"

Henry holds up two fingers then asks, "Do you have a wee-wee?"

Scout cocks his doggie head, waiting on the answer.

Roger's neck colors and then his face. "I—I'm quite sure I do."

"Oh!" Mom covers her mouth and giggles.

"Henry," I cry, mortified. I pass Mom the cookie plate and Scout eyes it. "No, boy," I say sternly before rushing over to pick Henry up. I deposit him by the cabinet where the connecting toys are. Squat down and pull out a mesh basketful. I blink at the child and speak in sweet mommy-like tones. "We're not supposed to ask that of *everyone*, Henry." I snap a yellow piece and a blue piece together and hand them to Henry.

He catches on right away and starts hooking pieces together himself. Scout follows Henry, plopping down beside him and the basket of connecting toys.

"Sorry," I tell the grown-ups with a grimace. "He's still learning."

"'Bout 'natomy!" Eleanor crows proudly, standing right in front of Mom, her back to the coffee table. She crosses her arms to inform Roger, "Mommies and daddies are different."

He strokes his beard. "You don't say."

Mom holds Eleanor by her shoulders. "What a bright girl." She pulls her into a hug. "Eleanor's six in February," she tells Roger, "and growing up so fast." Her eyes go misty.

"In kindergarten?" Roger asks.

Mom replies, "Next year."

"Eleanor," I call. "Want to help your brother build something fun for Grandma and Roger?"

She shrugs. "Okay." She sits cross-legged by her brother and starts snatching away his toys. Henry blubbers out some tears. "Eleanor," I say in horror. "Share."

She hoards more of Henry's connecting blocks, piling them in her lap. "I'm sharing."

Okay. Maybe this was a bad idea. I run my hands through my hair. "Sweetie." I hold out my hand and Eleanor reluctantly gives me one of her pieces. Then two. In ridiculously slow motion. I roll my eyes at her and she giggles.

"Okay," she finally says. She hands Henry a fistful then gets a fresh batch for herself from the basket. Henry's over his momentary sadness and gleefully hooking things together again. *Whew.* I feel like I need a break!

I dart a glance at the clock. It's only been five minutes.

The coffee beeps that it's ready as Dean enters the room. "I'll get that," he says.

"No, no," I answer hastily. "I'll go!" I glance at the kids and Mom and Roger. "Why don't you stay here?"

"No need," he responds breezily. "I'm already on the way."

Right. I stand upright and smooth back my hair. Sit on the sofa closer to Mom. "So, Roger," I say. "Mom tells me you were a mechanic?"

He nods.

I wait for him to offer something more. He doesn't. "Did you work locally?"

He nods again.

Mom adoringly pats his arm. "Roger had his own business! For over thirty years!"

He nods a third time. I'm starting to feel like I'm talking to a bobblehead.

"How great!" I respond. I look at a Roger, hoping to draw him out. "What was the name of your business?"

"Roger's Automotive," Mom says sunnily.

"Ahh. Nice!" I try to give Mom a look encouraging her to can it, so Roger will open up. She doesn't take the hint.

"It's over on Twelfth and Vine," she supplies next. "At least it was. Roger sold the business, and a new tenant has it. They're putting in something else." She turns to Roger. "A coffee shop, is it?"

He nods.

Arghhhh.

"Do you have kids, Roger?" I ask him directly.

Nod.

"How many?"

Nod. Nod. Nod.

"Three?" I guess—accurately, I suppose, because he nods another time.

"Roger's a very succinct speaker," Mom says besottedly. "He's got ten grandchildren."

"Ten! Wow! What fun!"

He nods.

Oh. My. Goodness.

I'm not going to ask him their ages, because I don't want to count the nods. Or have Mom answer for him. Which she seems perpetually inclined to do.

Dean returns bearing coffee. He hands a mug to Mom and another to Roger. "I forgot to ask you how you take yours, Roger?" He glances at Mom. "I know Rosemary drinks hers black."

"Roger does too!" Mom informs us.

Roger freaking nods.

I jump to my feet. "Why don't you sit here with Mom and Roger?" I tell Dean. "I'll go get ours."

"But I don't mind it."

I practically shove Dean down on the sofa. "No, sit!"

"What?" He screws up his face.

"I mean." *Deep breaths.* I apologize to Mom and Roger. "Sorry. I just take my coffee in an, um—very particular manner. So I'll fix it!"

CHAPTER
Ten

I scurry toward the kitchen and Dean peers at me as I scuttle away. I run the kitchen tap water cold and splash some on my face. *Nod, nod, nod. Nod!* What does Mom see in him? Maybe that he's agreeable?

Oh my goodness. I dry my face with a hand towel. Dab at my neck and brow. Maybe I should have worn a long-sleeve T-shirt and not a sweater. Who knew meeting Roger would be so taxing? It's not that he's not a nice man. It's more like it's hard to tell what sort of person he is. Getting to know him is like pulling teeth. Another idea occurs. It's possible he simply doesn't like talking about himself. There *are* people like that.

I prepare my coffee and fix some for Dean. He takes his with cream but no sugar. I noticed that yesterday morning. My view roves to the advent calendar and the poinsettia piece Eleanor added today. *No. That can't mean anything.* Silly. Still. It *is* odd, when you think about it. If I can prove the calendar's making magic about the future, Dean will have to believe me about how I got here.

When I return to the living room, Dean and Roger are *laughing*.

"This guy's a stitch!" Dean says, motioning toward Roger.

"Is he?" I hand Dean his coffee.

"Roger was just telling me about his houseboat."

Wait. The man spoke in full sentences, and I missed it? "Oh! I'd love to hear about that too!" I enthusiastically tell Roger. "Would you mind repeating?"

Mom leaps in. "Roger said he's ready to chart his own destiny now. Take charge as the captain. Set out on the sea of life!"

My jaw drops. "Roger said all that?" I ask Dean.

"Well, no." Dean rubs the side of his neck. "Not directly." He casts a look at my mom. "Now that you mention it, Rosemary told me. But!" Dean smiles. "She was merely repeating what Roger told her earlier. Isn't that right, Roger?"

Roger—nods.

My teeth clench, *hard. Ow.*

"Well, Roger," I say. "That's quite an ambition. To retire to a houseboat." I try to keep my tone airy, light. "Have you had this dream for a while?"

He nods and I stare at him stone-faced, trying hard not to scream.

"For the past five years," Mom tells me and Dean. "And now?" She latches onto his arm, leaning toward him. "He's wanting to share that dream with me, aren't you, honey bunch?"

Dean and I silently mouth to each other, *Honey bunch?*

"I like honey!" Eleanor pipes up from by the cabinet. She's done fine work building a house. Henry's not making anything in particular. He's just snapping and unsnapping pieces and having a great time with it, apparently.

"Oh yes." Mom drags a hand down Roger's arm and says in sultry tones, "Me too."

I try not to look grossed out. I reach for the treat plate and shove it under her face. "Cookie?"

"All right." She picks up a snickerdoodle and I extend the plate to Roger. He takes a sandwich cookie, *and nods.*

My smile's so tight it pinches. "You're welcome." I set the plate on the coffee table and return to my seat on the sofa.

"So Roger," Dean says. "How long have you had this houseboat?"

Roger holds up a hand, pumping his fingers.

"Five years?" Dean guesses.

Roger pins his thumb to his palm.

"Four?" Dean tries again.

Roger nods and Dean stares at me helplessly. Now he's getting it. I widen my eyes at him and Dean stifles a chuckle. That makes me giggly, too. I purse my lips and finally ask Mom, "You didn't mean it, did you? About moving to Wilmington?"

"Oh yes!" She preens prettily and fusses with her curls. "I can't wait. Roger, too. Isn't that right, honey bunch?"

He nods.

Oh wow.

"And when is this happening?" Dean asks her and Roger.

"The day after Christmas, on Friday," Mom answers for them. At least that gives me some time to try to talk her out of it. Not a ton of time, but I'll take what I can get, in either reality. Ooh, I hope, hope, hope this isn't happening in the other world. Am I even there, or did my disappearance leave a great big hole? My heart seizes up. Poor Mom! She must be frantic in that case, worrying that I've gone missing.

Did I skip our lunch at Beaumont's? Will she be okay on Christmas Day? I roll my eyes toward Roger, wondering if he's the kind of man who can be two places at once. I didn't know I had that capability until recently. And maybe I don't.

Maybe there's *only one me* and I've left the other realm for this one, and Mom is texting and texting my phone. Calling and fretting when I don't answer. My heart aches. I can't do that to Mom *there*. But I'm also worried about her *here*.

Oh my goodness, this is unnerving.

Roger finishes his sandwich cookie and sets his mug on the coffee table. "So, Paige." Two whole words! "And Dean." *Four.* "Rosemary says you're teachers?"

Hallelujah! The skies part and angels sing.

The man speaks. I was seriously starting to doubt.

Dean nods. *Oh nooo, it's catching.* "Physics."

I try not to move my head. Or chin. Stare straight at Roger. "I'm a staff." *Wait.* That came out wrong.

"Which kind?" Roger asks. The man is *conversing.* Okay. Maybe I judged him too quickly. And maybe it's that he doesn't like talking about himself. He seems to do better when the attention centers on others.

"I work for the principal, Missy Peabody."

"Drives an old Cadillac?"

Dean *nods*, then winces at me like he didn't mean it. "That's right." He sips from his mug. "Did you work on her car?"

Roger nods.

I try to be grateful for the minor progress we've made.

"Will you look at the time!" Mom says brightly. We all turn toward the clock. It's nearly eleven, but they haven't been here that long. "Roger and I have got to get going if we're going to make it to church." Mom has never set foot in a church for as long as I've known her, meaning my entire life. When she and Roger stand, she grabs his arm and says, "I just love the Christmas hymns this time of year."

"Those *are* nice," Dean concurs. I know his family are all regular churchgoers, but I'm not sure where we stand on things.

"Paige and I generally take the kids to the Christmas Eve service with the pageant." That answers it. "Eleanor's an angel this year and Henry's a shepherd." I'm stunned Henry has any kind of role at all, at his tender age. I hope he doesn't go asking others at the manger about their wee-wees.

"Oh yes!" Mom says like she's aware of this event. "We'll be there. We wouldn't miss it. Would we, Roger?" Her eyes twinkle at Roger and he—

I shut my eyes briefly then open them, help Dean escort Mom and Roger to the door. "Thanks for coming by, and thanks so much for the pretty poinsettia," I tell Roger.

I hold my breath and brace myself for another nod.

Dean looks like he's doing the same.

At long last, Roger bows his head.

Then, mercifully, they go. Before the door shuts, Mom leans back in and stares at me. "You and I will have to catch up!" I guess she wants to talk about Roger and ask how I resolved things with Dean. "Maybe coffee before Christmas?"

"Coffee before Christmas sounds good!"

"We can meet at that cute place, Cuppa Joe, the morning of the twenty-fourth. Eleven o'clock? You'll be off from work then."

"Sure, it's a date!"

I fall back against the closed door and blow out a breath.

"Oh. My. Goodness."

Dean nods, nods, nods. "I know."

"Do you think the nodding was a nervous tic?" I whisper so the kids don't hear.

Dean shrugs. "Guess your mom finds him easy to get along with."

I shove his shoulder and laugh. "Oh boy. What are we going to do, Dean?"

"Us?" he answers solidly. "Nothing."

"But Dean, we can't let Mom—"

"Paige." He gently holds my face in his hands. "She looks happy to me."

I sigh because the truth hurts my heart. "Yeah," I admit hoarsely. "To me too." I glance out the window as their car drives away. "But how can she stand it?"

He kisses me on the lips and his affection calms me. "Different strokes?" He chuckles. "Seems like they get along." I know what he says is true. Still. I don't get it.

I stare up into his very dark eyes, shining like I mean the world to him. It's amazing to believe he feels that way, and wrenching to know deep in my heart I don't really belong here. I need to find that vendor at the holiday market, the woman dressed like Mrs. Claus and learn—once and for all—what's going on.

I trudge through the snowdrifts, winding my neck scarf around me. The colorful lights of the holiday market glimmer in the distance, distinguishing the tented town square area through the gloom. I parked on a side street because the two busy parking lots in the quaint downtown area were jammed full. Two smaller tents and one large one form a U shape framing our town Christmas tree, which stands facing the courthouse, its widespread limbs adorned with shiny white lights. An outdoor skating rink is stationed in front of it, and skaters link hands, gliding across the ice.

My boots leave tracks on the sidewalk as I hurry along, crossing the street at the corner. No crosswalk or light. This is Piney Mount, North Carolina, population five thousand. We've got one stoplight at the edge of town where Main Street joins the bypass. It's midafternoon with dusk closing in, the twinkling lights of the market glowing brighter as darkness falls.

People crowd among the vendors offering holiday finery. Fun trinkets like nutcrackers and carved wooden reindeer. Stacking Russian dolls and rustic handmade crèches. Tables loaded with ceramics, platters, vases, and mugs, many of them Christmas themed. I draw nearer and scoot under a tent, shielding myself from the snow. A vendor nearby sells hand-stitched Christmas stockings; another displays festive holiday wreaths adorned with fresh pine cones.

An old-fashioned popcorn machine that looks like a red pushcart stands upright ahead; its glass case displays the popping corn hopping its way out of a suspended tin contraption inside. Two workers stuff paper bags with fresh-popped popcorn and deliciousness fills the air, along with the smell of hot apple cider. Shoppers stroll by holding paper cups with lids. Some drink cider, others coffee. I know one seller in particular who specializes in French hot chocolate, which is—*ooh la la*—to die for.

Is that same vendor here?

I survey the meandering crowded, scanning the various booths. Dean's home watching the kids, and I told him I had to run some errands. I didn't say what, but he probably—rightly—believed those had something to do with Christmas.

Or "Kissmas," as Henry calls it so winningly. I sigh when I picture his precious face, and Eleanor's adorable mug when she's hogging toys. I can't help rooting for Eleanor. I admire her gumption. She goes for what she wants, and that's a good thing. Dean and I just need to encourage her to do that kindly, without steamrolling others in the process.

I pause at a table selling handmade puppets that are worn like oven mitts. I tug on a happy elf and cheery Santa, thinking Eleanor and Henry might like these and find them fun. There are others, like an angel and a snowman. Three wise men! How cute! A reindeer, too. I'd love to buy these for the kids and decide to pick two up on my way home. These would look precious poking out of the tops of their Christmas stockings.

Ooh! I find someone selling gourmet candies, including Christmas goodies I recall from my childhood, like large stick-type candy canes and licorice whips. Those would be fun to get for the kids, as well. Maybe Dean would like some treats? *Hang on*—I spot a special mug on the next table over in a booth selling ceramics. It's dark blue and shows the darkened mountains, the night sky speckled with dozens of yellow stars. How perfect. I bet he'd love this. I'll come back for that too, but I can't forget my mission. Finding Mrs. Claus.

I traipse down the aisle, squeezing past others admiring trinkets and flowing scarves. Earrings, like the ones I bought for Mom. I stop walking and back up, return to a particular booth. "Happy holidays," says the artist who makes the earrings. I pick up a pair that resemble the ones I got for Mom and admire them.

"Oh yes!" She smiles cheerfully. "You were here last week."

"Was I?"

She adjusts her holly wreath vest. She wears a bulky turtleneck underneath and has short, choppy brown hair. "You bought something for your mom?"

"Yes, yes. That's right." I *did* buy those earrings for Mom, both here and in my other reality. Certain things seem consistent leading up to the time split, others not. *If only I could understand why it happened, and how to get back to my old life.*

"Looking for something special?" the woman asks me.

"Yes, actually." I glance around. Under the big tent, Dean said, near one end. I peer in both directions. "I'm looking for the lady who sells advent calendars. Do you know her?"

"Why sure!" Her smile sparkles. "That's Mary Christmas."

"I'm sorry?" I ask, thinking I've misheard her.

She chuckles, clearly having been through similar conversations before. "First name's Mary, M-A-R-Y. Last name's Christmas. Or so she says. She sure dresses the part."

She laughs and I chuckle right along with her. "*O-kay.*"

"You should check out her advent calendars," she says. "I hear they're very special. Everyone raves about them."

"Thanks!" I say cheerfully. "I will." I turn and I'm greeted by a sign for the booth across the way. "French-Style Hot Chocolate." My mouth waters and I know I'll have to buy a cup. I wait patiently in line, and as I stand there, I spot a storefront across the way, on the other side of the sidewalk fronting the square.

It's a consignment shop called Second Chances, and something special catches my eye in its front window. A handsome telescope stands on a tripod base, and I instantly think of Dean. What an awesome gift. It would be so much fun to surprise him. But first things first. Anyway, the consignment shop is closed, like most of the places surrounding this town square on a Sunday.

"Can I help you, Miss?" I look at the hot chocolate vendor, seeing the line has inched up and it's my turn. "Yes," I say happily, "I'd *love* one of your cups of hot chocolate."

He fixes it for me. "Whipped cream on top?"

I shrug, smiling. "Why not?" I dig in my purse for my wallet, flip it open, and hunt for my debit card. What? Gone. Credit card, too. Hmm. "Just one minute," I tell the man who holds up my cup of hot chocolate with a frothy white peak. It smells fantastic. I count out my paper bills and ask, "How much?"

He answers, and I've barely got enough cash. Embarrassing. I hand him the largest bill I have, which isn't that large, honestly, and he makes change. "Thanks!" I say, dropping the loose coins into the zipper pocket in my wallet. How broke am I?

I tuck away the receipt the man gives me in a separate section of my wallet. Ah, there! I spot the plastic card sporting my bank's logo. So I do have a debit card after all. I wonder if it still works and whether I can check my balance at the bank. A branch for the one I use is located beside the consignment shop.

I accept the steaming cup of hot chocolate and take a sip. It's hearty and delicious. Also, piping hot, and it warms me up in the chilly afternoon air. Snow continues falling around me in the square, twirling toward the ground in big heavy flakes and crowning the tops of the downtown buildings. None of them are very tall, only two or three stories. These old masonry buildings are historic, having been constructed in the eighteen hundreds. "Thank you!" I tell the man. "Merry Christmas."

"Merry Christmas," he says before addressing the next person in line.

I glance at the bank beside Second Chances, thinking I should check my balance before making my holiday purchases. But first! I need to track down Mrs. Claus. I keep getting distracted. I meander down the row, sidestepping past happy shoppers. Everyone seems to be in a great mood as they appreciate the handcrafted wares being sold by the individual vendors.

Finally! I spy the top of a red Santa hat, then its white pompom tip hitting a woman's shoulder.

CHAPTER
Eleven

"*Hello, dear,*" the older woman says as I approach. "Merry Christmas!" She has kind blue eyes behind round wire-rimmed glasses. Her thick white hair is pulled back in a bun below her Santa hat. She's dressed in a red tunic with fluffy white fur on the cuffs of her sleeves and at her neckline. It resembles what Santa might wear, but as I draw closer I note the tunic's actually a dress, not a top worn with slacks. It falls to her knees, and she's paired it with black tights and ankle boots.

I nod, unsure whether she's issuing a greeting or introducing herself. "Merry Christmas," I say, admiring her work. The table in front of her is loaded with advent calendars like the one we've got at home. There's an entire stack of them at one end. She has a display of several hanging up on a pegboard behind her. "Your advent calendars are so pretty."

"Are you enjoying the one you have?"

I startle, not having been prepared for her remembering me. "Why yes!"

"You were here last week with your husband." Her eyes twinkle. "And two young children."

"Oh?" I hadn't realized the kids were with us. But of course, why wouldn't they have been?

"You'd just come back from church and rehearsing for the pageant." She nods at the gray stone church behind her with broad wooden front doors and a high steeple.

"Ahh, yes," I say, although I have no memory of this at all. "That's right."

She's arranging the advent calendars on the table as we speak. She takes the items out of the pockets in one and places them back in the pockets in a different order. "Sometimes children get busy with their little fingers and mix these up," she explains merrily. "Not that I mind their curiosity."

"Are you saying the order matters?"

"Oh yes. Absolutely." She slides her glasses back further on her nose to stare at me. "Everything in its place and all things in good time." I think of how I put the Christmas star up early on my calendar back at my condo. I apparently did the same thing with the calendar here.

"Mrs. Christmas," I say, amid the hubbub of chatter around us. Though the market is busy, I'm the only one at this booth for the moment. "I need to ask you about something you said about my calendar." I swallow hard. "I mean, ours. The one Dean and I bought for our family. You said something about it predicting the future?"

The dimple in her chin deepens. "Has it?"

The snowman can be explained. I'm not as certain about the poinsettia. "I'm not sure," I tell her honestly. "I've only been here two days."

She takes this in stride. "I see."

I lean toward her and whisper, "Do you believe in time travel? Or in alternate realities?"

"Well, I certainly believe in traveling at the speed of light."

She chuckles warmly. "My Kris does that every year." She's talking about Santa Claus. Great. Now I'm not sure who's more loony tunes, Mrs. Christmas or me. I'm glad no one's recording this conversation. "Have you traveled somewhere?" she asks.

"I'm—not sure." I grimace. "It could be that I'm dreaming."

"You look wide awake to me," she says, observing my cup of hot chocolate.

"Ha, yeah." I lower my voice. "Waking up's how it started. Yesterday morning with Dean. And then, there were the kids. *And* the dog." I heave a breath. "And, oh my goodness, Mom!"

"What's Rosemary up to these days?"

"Wait." I blink. "You know her?"

"Of course, dear. Kris keeps careful track of everyone on his list, even the older ones who've lost their faith." She wags her finger. "But not your mom. She never did! She's always believed in the power of magic," she says wistfully. "And love."

Sounds like my mom all right.

Hang on. "Mom didn't have something to do with this?"

"With what?" She finishes stuffing the calendar pockets. "With your being here?"

I nod.

"Well of course she did! She gave birth to you!"

She reads my troubled frown. "Oh! You mean about your being *here* here, in this different reality. No, no," she quickly says. "You're your own agent."

"So *my* actions caused this change?"

"Indeed." She tugs on her Santa hat. "How are you enjoying your early dose of Christmas cheer?" *An early dose of Christmas. Of course.* I recall how the Christmas star ornament seemed to shimmer and glow when I pressed it to the advent calendar in my condo. Did I upset the cosmic timeline somehow by jumping the gun and putting that particular ornament up early?

"So my being here—in this alternate reality—was caused by the advent calendar?"

"In part." She straightens her glasses. "The other part has to do with the wish you made in your heart."

I gasp, feeling like she's peeked into my head. "What wish?"

"You were wondering about Dean. Considering how your life might have been different with him if the two of you had stayed together. Isn't that right?"

I shrug sheepishly, because I can't very well deny it. Not when this woman already seems to know so much about me and my motivations, without me totally understanding how. Can she actually be *the* Mrs. Claus? Married to the jolly old elf himself? *Nooo.*

"Mrs. Christmas?"

"Yes, Paige?"

I ask because I must know. "Are there two of me now? One here and one there? Back in my old world?"

"Heavens, no," she says with conviction. "Every soul is unique."

My heart thumps painfully. "You mean, now that I'm here, I've disappeared from the other world?"

"I'm afraid it's much worse than that," she says, jangling my nerves. "Now that you're here, there is no other world."

A huge knot forms in my throat. "My job? My condo? My SUV?"

"*Poof! Poof! Poof!*" She makes flicking motions with her fingers. "All of that gone!"

My mouth hangs open. "My Paws and Read program?"

She shrugs. "Not happening."

"Mom?"

"Disappeared!"

I gasp. "Dean?"

"Finito!"

Impossible. I've destroyed them all? "But Dean's got a great life! He went to Puerto Rico. Lived his dream!"

"How do you know his dream couldn't have been different?"

"So wait." I swallow hard. "Are you saying that things are said and done? That my other life has disappeared forever?"

"No." She shakes her head and the pom-pom on her hat sways. "I never said that. I merely said you can't be in two places at once. Gracious!" She claps her hands together. "Even my Kris can't accomplish that." She winks slyly. "Which is why he has to move so fast."

"So if I go back to my other reality—"

"It will pick up just where you left off." Meaning Mom will need my support, and I'll be there to launch Paws and Read.

The terrifying truth dawns. "What about Eleanor? Henry? Scout?"

"*Poof! Poof! Poof!*" she says, again motioning with her fingers.

My heart breaks into tiny pieces. "What a horrible choice."

"It's not so horrible, really," Mary Christmas says. "Your heart will lead the way."

I try to put things together, but can't quite get there. "If nobody can be in two places at once, then how come Dean and the kids, Mom—my family and friends—all seem to remember the past here? Everyone sees it but me."

Mrs. Christmas nods, getting what I'm asking. "That's because when you transferred into this reality, it became a complete world breathed into life by the love you and Dean once shared. This life is the *only life* the rest of them have ever known, because this is your life as things might have been.

"In your case," she continues, "things are different because you're living on the cusp of two realities between *here* and *there*. You're trying to discern whether you've made the very best choices, and the universe is giving you a little kick in the caboose to urge you along."

"So then, you think I chose wrong the first time?"

"Nope." She shakes her head. "Didn't say that." She stares directly at me. "What I'm saying is that whichever existence you choose, you can't leave room for doubt. You have to be all in, totally convinced, with one hundred percent of your heart that the path you've selected is the right one."

"So if I go back to my original world and this realm disappears, will Dean—?"

She shakes her head. "He won't remember this place."

I frown at the difficulty of this outcome. "That seems so unfair."

"Unless!" She holds up a finger. "The two of you share something unique here, an unbreakable bond. But that bond would have to be *very special* to cross the boundary between two realities. Almost unheard of, really." She sets her jaw, thinking. "But possible."

"How about Mom? If I go back to the other place, will she be okay?"

She frowns solemnly. "I'm afraid I can't answer that, Paige." I feel like an anvil's settled on my chest.

"And Paws and Read?" I ask. "Can that still happen here?"

"That's not up to me to answer." Her countenance brightens. "I can tell you one thing, though, and listen up because it's *very important*." She holds open her hands. "The advent calendar's magic only lasts through Christmas Day."

"And then?"

She addresses me like a schoolteacher questioning her class. "What comes after?"

"Er," I hedge, then answer. "December twenty-sixth?"

"Bravo!" She dons a grin. "Then the rest of your life."

"So wherever I am on December twenty-sixth, that's where I'll stay?"

"There'll be no more need for the advent calendar then, will there?" She sighs, gazing dreamily at the gloomy sky. "Although Christmas will be over, its magic will live on."

"Yes, but." I tuck my layered hair behind my ear. "Will I be here or there?"

She folds her arms, looking at me. "Only you can decide that."

But I feel so helpless about impacting anything.

"Oh, you're not helpless," she says. "Far from it."

My forehead warms beneath my hat. "I didn't say anything."

"No, but you thought it, and thinking is just as good as saying." She whispers sneakily, "Only quieter."

Incredible! Now I've got to watch what I'm thinking? "So there's nothing I can do to influence my future?"

"Of course there is!" Mary Christmas says brightly. "Take each lovely moment as it comes. Enjoy!" She goes back to arranging her advent calendars on the table, and smoothing out their creases. Checking pocket items and tucking them back in.

My mind whirls at her advice. How can I enjoy when I don't know what tomorrow will bring? When I can't plan for it and organize? When my future is so uncertain? When I don't know whether I'll be *here*, or *there*? "Mrs. Christmas, one more question, if you don't mind. It's about Dean. Will I ever be able to share with him about what I've been through—I mean, in a way that he'll finally believe me and understand?"

She winks and says sweetly, "Everything in its place and all things in good time."

My head reels as I stand at the street corner letting a few cars pass by. I dump my empty hot chocolate cup in a public waste can then cross the street with a group of pedestrians. Some hold umbrellas, others hunch their shoulders against the pounding snow. Almost everyone wears hats and gloves or mittens. Many have winter scarves like mine.

The telescope in the window of Second Chances gleams in the reflection of the glass. It's a sturdy specimen, with a long, eggshell-colored tube and a lens cap on the section tilted toward the ceiling. A smaller lens cap covers the eyepiece. I know almost nothing about telescopes, but from outward appearances, this seems like a good one, with no noticeable nicks or dings. I crane my neck to peer at the price tag dangling from the tripod. That's not a huge amount, but it's not cheap, either. Surely I've saved up *something* from my work as Missy's assistant and my earnings haven't all gone to family expenses.

I expectantly stand at an ATM machine, waiting for my balance to print out after inserting my card. The slender white piece of paper churns out and I rip it from its dispenser slot, staring at the numbers. My mouth hangs open. No. I had five times this amount in the bank last week. Not only that, I had a savings account! I reinsert my card and try again. Ah, yes! There's a joint checking account shared by me and Dean.

I select "Print Balance" then blink at the results. This is evidently the account into which our paychecks go, and the one we use to pay our mortgage and other monthly expenses, like utilities, groceries, and childcare. The resulting balance provides evidence we're living on the edge. Disappointment seeps through me. Unless Dean's got a bundle in his personal account, and somehow I doubt that; we're far more cash-strapped than I thought! I check our joint savings next and find barely the minimum balance there.

134

I stare longingly at the telescope, wishing there were a way. But no. I can't zero out my personal account. That would be irresponsible. And I certainly won't take from one of our depleted joint accounts to buy Dean an extravagant surprise. I examine the balance in my personal account again. There's not a ton of money there, but it seems plenty to pay for a modest selection of gifts from the market. I'll buy a few things for the kids and Dean. I saw a vendor selling organic dog treats, so I can pick up a bag of those for Scout's stocking, too. Since I very well may be here through Christmas, it's best to be prepared.

I withdraw some cash and slip it into my wallet. Turn and view the bustling market across the street. I can see Mary Christmas's booth from here. *Enjoy*, she said, encouraging me to make the most of things. She clearly wasn't aware of how little I have. I picture Dean and the kids in my mind. All of us gathered in the front yard building a snowman, with Scout happily bounding around us. *Or maybe, Mrs. Christmas understands more than I guessed.*

When I return home, Dean's in our bedroom digging through the laundry basket and yanking stuff out. Two oxford shirts and pair of khakis. Socks. Underwear. "Hey hon. How were your errands?"

"Good." I take the opportunity to stash my shopping bags from the market on the high shelf in my closet when he's not looking. I wish I could talk to him about seeing Mary Christmas and what she said, but now's not the time. The kids are around.

Henry stands by the bed, running a toy race car across Dean's nightstand and making vrooming noises. Scout's with Eleanor in her room across the hall, lying beside her while she plays with her dollhouse. I'll need to find the right private moment to speak with Dean about alternate realities and real Christmas magic. But I'll have to figure out a way to do that gently, so he'll believe me. *Everything in its place and all things in good time.* But when will the right time be?

I shut my closet door and turn, nearly stumbling into a metal structure with a flat top. "Ack!" I point like an alien's landed. "What's that?"

Dean's forehead wrinkles up. "An ironing board?" He steps toward me and sniffs my breath.

I stare at him, aghast. "What are you doing?"

"You weren't out meeting the girls?" he asks concernedly. "For midday margaritas?"

"What? *Nooo.*" I can't believe he'd think that of me. I straighten my sweater, slightly offended. Of course I know what an ironing board is. It's not like I haven't seen one. I've just never seen one in my house.

Dean sets his two oxford shirts and khaki slacks on the ironing board and pats it. "Here ya go."

"Here. I. Go?" I cluck out the words like a stunned chicken.

Dean holds his chin in his hand and tilts his head. "Um. Paige?"

"Yes?"

"You act like you've forgotten how to iron." He gurgles out a laugh and strides into the bathroom.

"Iron?" I call after him. "Who? Me?"

He returns with—yep—a stinking iron.

Who is he, Houdini? Where did the contraption materialize from? Certainly not the shower, or under the sink.

"Where did you get that?" I ask suspiciously.

"From the bathroom closet, where it always is."

I wonder if he's trying to trick me by testing my knowledge

of our domestic supplies. I *do* know there's a vacuum in the coat closet. I've seen it. "And *why* isn't it in the laundry room?"

Dean scratches his head. "The laundry room we don't have?"

I set my hand on my hip. "So where's the washer and dryer?" It's evident we've got them, based on the heaps of clean laundry and dryer sheets in the basket and on the chair.

Dean gives me an odd look and retreats into the bathroom, swinging forward the door. He motions behind it with the iron in his hand. I creep forward to peek behind the door. He peels back a hanging curtain hiding an alcove in the wall. What're a stackable washer and dryer doing in there? I must have missed them somehow.

"*Vroom, vroom, screech!*" Henry runs his race car across our pillow shams then down the quilt covering our bed, mussing things up a bit, but that's okay. He's keeping himself entertained and not upending the bed completely. Dean and I made it this morning together, after Mom and Roger left. So, see! We're not totally piggy. Merely untidy in a selective fashion because, honestly, who has the time to fold clothes and—I gulp at the iron in Dean's hand—iron.

"Is it my turn or something?" I ask meekly. Dean's so equity-minded, that must be it.

"Sweetheart, it's always your turn."

"*What?*" I don't mean to shriek, but this seems extremely prejudicial. "Because I'm a woman?" I ask.

"*Nooo,*" he says kindly, "because I'm abysmal at it. Remember how I scorched that brand new button-down shirt you bought me? The one I was supposed to wear to Jenny's high school graduation?"

No.

"And my nice pair of dress slacks?"

No again.

He could be making this up, and I'd never know the difference.

My heart softens to the truth.

That's not Dean.

"So I—offered to do this?"

He wears a jokey smirk. "Hey, are you trying to hint I don't do enough around here? You know I do other things in return," he continues in cajoling tones. "Keep up the cars. Change the oil, top off fluids. Clean and wash them."

Gosh. I just take my SUV to the oil-change shop and the car wash. Maybe those things represent unnecessary expenses here. Like, apparently, dry cleaning.

Dean shakes his head. "Look, it's no big deal. If you're not feeling up to ironing for whatever reason, I'm happy to take a stab at it again." He sounds nervous about it, though. He gives the iron a wary look, like it might bite him. "We've only got two days of school left, so it's a fairly small job."

Guilt harangues me.

I'm such a bad domestic partner.

But ironing?

Wahhhh.

Why can't I go back to making French toast?

"No, no." I step forward and take the iron from him. "No worries. I'll do it!"

The appliance sags in my hand. Jeez. What does this weigh? As much as Henry's bowling-ball-size head? I check the settings dial and note it's got an off and on switch, and a very long cord.

Henry toddles up to me and tugs on my arm. "I gotta poo," he says and frowns, hugging his saggy bottom.

I grimace at Dean and hold up the iron.

"Right." He shoves his hands in his pockets and nods. "I'll take him since you're busy here."

"Great! Thanks!" I turn the iron around to study its flat underside. Hmm. Well. It can't be that hard, can it? I blow out a breath and plug the darn thing in.

CHAPTER
Twelve

I had no idea how relaxing weekends were until I hit Monday morning, *and yep. I'm still here.* "Enjoy," Mary Christmas said. "You're your own agent." Sure. Maybe in getting here, but not in understanding what to do next. I'm sad about losing Paws and Read and the familiar world I left behind, and yet this new place is growing on me daily. Mary Christmas acted like I have a choice about whether I go or stay, but she never told me how to make it. Instead, she said to take each lovely moment as it comes. And in *this moment*, we're running late.

I scramble to shove snacks into the kids' backpacks in the kitchen. Dean rushes in and sets down his coffee, picks it back up for another quick sip. Dumps the remnants from his mug in the kitchen sink and slides the mug into the dishwasher and mashes a button, starting the machine. He checks his watch against the kitchen clock. "Five minutes," he says. *Right.*

When he turns I spy the back of his blue oxford shirt, which is *not* expertly ironed. A set of double creases goes all the way down his back, protruding out like fins, and his slacks poke out sideways, giving the appearance of jodhpurs around the hips and thighs. Yikes. How did that happen? At least nothing's scorched. "Er. You might want to wear a sweater!" I urge. "Chilly out."

He grins over his shoulder. "Good point. I'll go and grab one." Great. At least that will conceal half the problem. He pretends not to notice his khakis. Or maybe he really doesn't. Things are rather hectic around here. *Grumble. Grumble. Ironing.* Who knew that would be on my schedule? Obviously, I was not prepared.

I zip the tiny backpacks and hurry into the living room. Eleanor and Henry sit on the sofa stuffed into their coats and snow boots. I tug on their small hats. Dean grabs the borrowed telescope in its case and carries it toward the front door. It's stopped snowing at last, but frigid blasts of air blow through the front door before he shuts it.

"I know you usually drop the kids off at daycare," he says, holding the door ajar and battling back the wind. *Except I have no clue where that is.* "But today, maybe we should ride together in the jeep? Give the roads another day to clear before you take the hatchback?" *Whew.*

"Great idea!" I pull each child off the sofa into a standing position. It's harder with Henry, and he topples forward slightly. I steady him by his shoulders until he stops rocking back and forth. "Okay, Henry?"

He grins sweetly. "O-tay!"

Aww. I tug him into a hug and embrace Eleanor too. I can't leave her out. She's already mildly jealous of her little brother, but that's normal. She'll grow out of it. I'm so proud of her for knowing about 'natomy and everything. She's sure to go far. I'm thinking brain surgeon or cardiologist. It's too soon to tell with Henry, but I have an inkling he'll stay a sweetheart his whole life through. I'm not supposed to get attached to these children, and I'm not. *I wince internally at the lie.* Merely appreciating their obvious attributes.

Dean hurries back inside to grab his work bag and computer. I've got my stuff piled on the love seat. Scout tries to trail after Dean with a tennis ball in his mouth, but Dean waves the pup aside. "Later, boy," he says before addressing me. "I'll switch the car seats to the jeep." He glances over his shoulder. "You do the house check!"

"Hmm?"

He holds up his fingers and enumerates. "Coffee pot off. Toaster. Stove. Your cell phone. I've got mine," he says, patting his pocket.

"Right!" I spring into action, racing into the kitchen.

"Side door locked!" Dean calls after me while Scout tags along at my heels. I take my cell phone off the counter. *Groan.* Still not charging. And last night I used Dean's charger, in case that was the problem. Awesome time to have it die. I'll have to text Mom and my girlfriends from Dean's phone, saying my phone's on the fritz. I return my phone to the counter and Scout sits alertly, barking at the advent calendar.

He's right. We forgot to put something up! Maybe it's not so important, but after my meeting at the market with Mary Christmas I'm no longer sure. She urged me to make the most of this reality, not screw it up. If we miss a day with the advent calendar will something bad happen? Will we all go *poof*? I don't even want to entertain the possibility.

I throw the bolt on the side door, which Dean left open when he hauled out the trash. I'm somehow in a nice top and black stretch pants with flat boots. My hair looks decent too, which is amazing. I merely dried it with a blow dryer. Took five minutes. I've got my makeup routine down pat. Eyeliner, brow brush, blush and lip gloss. I must have mastered speed primping when the kids were even younger. My usual routine takes me twenty minutes, start to finish. No time for that here.

Scout barks again and I see his water bowl's empty. Maybe he wasn't calling my attention to the advent calendar after all. Now that I've noticed, though, I can't unnotice. I quickly fill Scout's bowl from the kitchen sink. Check the coffee pot, which is on. Turn it off. Unplug the toaster. Stove knobs are all in the correct position. Meaning, not leaking gas into the house. That would be disastrous.

I dash into the living room, where Dean stands by the door. The kids are with him. He glances at my purse and work bag on the love seat. "Ready?"

"Er—no!" I glance at the kitchen. "The advent calendar! We forgot to add something for the twenty-second."

Dean stares at his jeep in the driveway. He's left it running, warming up. "Can't we do that when we get home?"

I grimace. "Better not wait."

"Fine." He picks up Henry and hurries him into the kitchen. It's Henry's turn. But he can't get the object out of the pocket wearing his mittens, so Dean has to yank one off. Great! He plucks out the pillow-like item picturing a pair of ice skates and plants it on the advent calendar extra hard. The whole thing tilts and I reach over and straighten it.

"Can we go ice skating?" Eleanor asks hopefully.

Dean winces and replies, "Sometime, sweetie. Sure! But probably not today."

She pouts and skulks out of the kitchen. "That's what you always say." She makes a grumpy face and says to Henry, "Tamica's family always goes."

Henry grins at his big sister. "Merry Kissmas!"

"It's not Christmas, Henry." She grumps some more. "Santa probably doesn't even know where we live." Uh-oh. *Someone* woke up on the wrong side of the bed this morning.

"Of course he does!" I chime in and grab my things off the

love seat. "And he'll be here Christmas Eve."

"That's right. So." Dean winks at the kids and lilts into song. "You better watch out—"

"You better not cry!" I sing in return.

"You better not pout," Dean croons is a deep baritone. Wow. He's got a voice! "I'm telling you why."

The two of us join in on the refrain: "Santa Claus is coming to town!"

Eleanor and Henry stare at us, stunned. Both their mouths hang open.

I chuckle at Dean. "Not bad, Daddy. Not bad at all."

He laughs and opens the door. "I'd say the same for you."

We load the kids into their car seats and snap them in from either side of the jeep. I've got Henry. Dean's got Eleanor. "When did we learn to sing?" I ask, amazed.

Dean chuckles and shakes his head. "Must have been all those karaoke nights in college."

"Yeah, must have been." I do remember those, and they bring a huge smile, along with happy memories. We often went with our friends. Sometimes it was just the two of us.

As I buckle myself into the passenger seat, I catch a glimpse of the kids in the rearview mirror. Eleanor's over her funk about not getting to ice skate and tracing designs on her frosty car window with her mitten. Aww. Now she's made a smiley face. Henry hums an unknown tune, lost in his own world, his blue eyes shining. It must be fun to be Henry. Although, frankly, I'd rather not toilet train again. *Personally.* I see Dean's cell phone sitting on the console charger. "I think my phone died."

"Bummer." He centers his hands on the wheel, checking the backup camera as we exit our drive and onto the icy street. It's been plowed, but there are slick patches. "Maybe we should take it to the phone store for testing? Since tomorrow's a half day, we can stop by after work then?" He frowns uncertainly. "If you can make it that long without it?"

I've amazingly lasted so far. The old me had everything organized on my cell phone calendar and printed out in a neat display on my fridge, but I evidently don't plan as meticulously here, so somehow the phone doesn't seem as great a loss. Or maybe I've simply had so much else to keep me busy, the lack of technology has been harder to notice. He turns the jeep, heading north, and we putter down our sleepy snow-covered street. Once we hit the main roads, we'll have nothing but clear asphalt ahead of us. I fold my hands in my lap and say surely, "I can make it."

We pull into the school parking lot a short time later, after settling the kids at Wee Winks Daycare. Huge piles of snow are pushed into mounds, making way for employee parking spots. "Okay," Dean says and hands me the keys. "These are for you to pick up the kids later. Then you can come back and get me at four."

"Wait, what?" I ask as we climb out of the jeep, and I lock the doors.

"Paige," he explains gently, "today I host the Science Club after school."

"The Science Club, yes!" I say like I'm remembering.

He leans toward me. "You're not still having regrets?"

"What?"

"Trying to mentally scrub our life?"

I hate it when he puts it like that. I force a cheery grin. "Of course not!" *What I'm trying to do is figure out how to tell you what I'm going through, and have you believe me.* If there's a magical way to explain my dual realities to Dean without hurting his feelings or making him think I'm trying to "scrub" our relationship, I haven't found it yet.

"So you're happy with where you are?" Dean asks, putting me on the spot. Chilly winds blow around us, stinging my cheeks and eyes.

I squirm as we walk toward the building, but not in a way he'd notice. "Um, sure!" Missy's assistant. *Gah.* But the rest of it's okay. I peer over at Dean and my heart twirls. Better than okay. Fantastic.

"Not wishing you had a different life?" he presses. "One without me and the kids?"

My forehead grows really, really hot. "No, Dean. No." I mean, what else can I say? Every time I've brought it up he seems to get more worried. He has a right to worry, honestly, because if I leave here somehow—even without meaning to—then this whole world goes *poof.* This is so messed up.

"So what do you have going on today?" I ask, trying to be chatty. Acting like I'm not torn to shreds over what might happen to this life if I'm suddenly wrenched away.

Dean's eyes gleam as we stride toward the building. His arms are loaded down with his teacher bag, his computer satchel, and the telescope. "Today, we've got our Christmas party in Science Club," he says, sounding upbeat. "The kids are bringing snacks."

I'm glad he's over his temporary annoyance with me. Dean was never the sort to hold grudges. "That sounds like fun."

"Should be!" He goes a bit melancholy. "Although I know everyone will be just as disappointed as we were about our missed opportunity with that comet on Friday night."

"Yeah. I'm sure." Before we reach the front entrance, he pauses by the flagpole.

"Paige?" he asks seriously. "Are you sure you're okay?" He looks a little wounded. Okay, so maybe he didn't come back from thinking I wanted to scrub our life as easily as I thought. "Are you sure *we're* okay?"

My nose twitches anxiously and I rub it. "Yes, Dean. Sure."

He smiles softly and gives me a kiss. "That's good." He kisses me one more time for good measure. "Have a great day."

It's impossible not to be buoyed by his support. "Thanks, you too!"

He's such a terrific husband, and I'm very lucky to have him—for as long as I have him. That's what I need to focus on, the here and now. Not all those nail-biting what-ifs about switching back to my other reality. *Enjoy*, Mary Christmas said. *Take each lovely moment as it comes.* And it's all been amazing. Okay, except for maybe the ironing.

My euphoria lasts, *ohhh*, about five minutes, until I reach the principal's office.

I find my desk sitting in an anteroom in front of it, and it's piled with so much paperwork, I can't count the stacks. Mounds and mounds of manila folders teeter in high towers. I thought everything was automated these days. Done on computers!

What happened?

I can tell this desk is mine by the name plaque positioned near the front of it beside one precarious stack of files. It says, "Paige Burton." My heart jolts. Burton? Oh gosh, of course. I must have changed my last name to Dean's. I guess I haven't thought all the details out.

Missy emerges from her office with a coffee mug in her hand. Its logo says "Boss Lady." "Morning, Paige."

"Er. Good morning." Do I call her Missy here, or Principal Peabody? I opt for neither just in case.

"Looks like you've got your work cut out for you again."

"Uh-huh."

"You were very smart to think of verifying our student records after Thanksgiving."

"Verifying? What?"

"You were spot on in thinking we should double-check each student's paper file to make sure nothing got lost in the transfer from their old schools to Walton's electronic system." She nods and continues, "And we're grateful for the oversights you've found so far, like some of the students' updated medical information not being included in their electronic files. I don't think I have to tell you how catastrophic things would have been had we not known about Billy Conway's peanut allergies, or the Epi Pen Myra Welch needs access to in the event of a bee sting." She folds her arms across her chest. "It's one thing for the nurse to have the information, but it's critical for the entire school to be aware of students' special needs. Emergencies happen."

"Yes, yes, they do."

"You're an excellent administrative assistant. Walton's lucky to have you." She smiles broadly. "So am I." She holds a clutch of colorful sticky notes with handwritten scrawl on them. I take the handwriting to be hers. "These are my appointments for today. I know you set my calendar, but I had to make a few changes. I'm sure you won't mind."

My head throbs.

"I can't see the Wilcots at two. I'll be in a specialist meeting then with our ESL teacher and one of her families. So we'll have to reschedule the Wilcots for afterward or earlier today, or tomorrow morning, but not tomorrow afternoon, since tomorrow's a half day. Please, no appointments after lunch. Things will be hairy enough with that being our last day of school before winter break."

My eyes glaze over as she hands me a yellow sticky note. "I need you to call this list of parents first. The top pair wants to preview the school as they're looking at homes in the area, but if you could put them off until after the break that would be ideal. If not, then have them come tomorrow morning first thing." She goes on to explain the rest of her itinerary.

"So, ah. This isn't entered on an electronic calendar?"

She furrows her brow and says suddenly, "You've never complained about my sticky notes before."

I keep my eyes open extra wide so I don't blink. "Sticky notes, right! How clever!"

"Yes, that." I peer into her office and see sticky notes over-populating nearly every piece of furniture, including the metal filing cabinets. She nods. "Makes it so much easier when things need to be moved around. So! Here you go! These are the rest of your tasks in priority order." She lays one sticky note in my hand, then squints and picks it up.

"No. Wait. That one goes second." She fishes for another sticky note. This one is pink. "Pink goes first," she informs me. "Which means last! Least important. That's why I've labeled it with a number four."

My temples pound.

"Then blue. Which is number three. Third in importance. Green. Two." She lays those sticky notes down on top of the others in my hand. "And finally!" She looks up, wielding a yellow sticky note in the air. "There's this one! Yellow, like the first one I gave you! So obviously"—she rolls her eyes—"these are my number one priorities for today!"

"Great." I grin tightly. "Thanks."

CHAPTER
Thirteen

Dean drops by to see me on his lunch break. "Hey, tiger. How's it going?"

I sigh and look up from my peanut butter sandwich. "Like it's good I packed my lunch."

His peruses my desk. "Looks like you're making progress, at least." He thumps the doorframe with one hand. "The piles look shorter this week."

"Really?" I ask hopefully.

He makes an inch-wide motion with his thumb and index finger. "A little?"

I blow out a breath. "I had no clue how tough this job would be," I muse to myself.

Dean's forehead wrinkles. "What's that?"

But I don't want him to feel bad about this. He's making the best of our circumstances. So should I. "Nothing. I was just saying I'm happy to see you." I playfully bat my eyelashes at him. "Handsome husband that you are."

He laughs. "Yeah, well. I'm happy to see *you, beautiful wife.*" He walks over with something concealed behind his back. "I brought you a surprise."

"What? Oh!" I'm so touched he'd think of me. It's the middle of his workday, too.

He lays a candy bar on my desk. I'm guessing he bought it from the vending machine. It's my favorite kind. "How sweet!"

He winks. "I figured you'd need the energy," he whispers softly. "Working for Missy."

"Oh, Paige!" She appears in her doorway. Sticky notes are in both hands and some snake up her arm. "I have a couple of changes for tomorrow."

I hold my breath then say, "Of course."

"I'll see you later this afternoon." Dean waves from the doorway out of Missy's view and mouths, "Hang in there."

Missy watches Dean leave, then she sees the candy bar on my desk. "Did he bring that by?" When I nod, she sighs. "What a sweet husband." She strolls over and shuts the door to the hall. "Now, I need to ask for your advice." *Wait.* She scoots a chair beside my desk and says in hushed tones, "Remember what I told you on Friday?"

"Friday?"

"Oh please don't make me repeat it." She blushes and takes a seat. "It's too embarrassing."

"No. I—wouldn't dare."

"Thank you." She clasps her hands in her lap and asks, "So have you thought about it?"

"Um."

She leans toward me and continues, "About what I should tell Phil?"

Hmm. Intriguing. "And Phil is—"

"The ninth grade English teacher at Hillsdale?"

What? That's my old job.

"But of course you know that," she continues quietly. Missy

goes all breathy. "I told you about what we've done and made you pinky swear."

Pinky swear?

What are we, four?

She holds up her hand and leans forward. "Paige," she says desperately. "Please."

"Er. Pinky swear, sure." I hold up my hand and she hooks her pinky around mine. *Ouch.* Awkward.

"You're not to tell a soul about the hotel."

This is sounding juicy. Missy Peabody? Who knew?

"No, I—wouldn't dare."

Her face turns red. "Or about Phil's—*proclivities.*"

Now she's piqued my interest, darn it. "Proclivities?"

"Paige!" She titters and waves her hand. "I'm not going into details—*again*. You bad girl! But no." She straightens her skirt. "That's not the point. The point is, he wants me to run away with him. Can you believe it? Although, honestly?" she says wistfully. "When we're together, he makes me want to surrender *everything*."

"Oh! So he's—?"

"No. That's *meeee.*" Her eyes gleam darkly. "Madam X. That's why he gave me my coffee mug. 'Boss Lady.' I require him to surrender first."

"Wow." I'll never look at that mug the same way again.

"Paige," she begs me. "I know we're not friends, but I feel like we've formed a bond."

I can't help wondering if she chose the word *bond* on purpose.

"I've told you so many personal things and you've listened."

"Uh-huh."

"Plus, you're so experienced. Two kids and everything. You also have pink hair!" she whispers hoarsely. "The color's very cool, truthfully. I'd try it myself if I weren't so chicken. But!" She squares her shoulders. "Phil *is* emboldening me."

I really don't want the details. No. I thought I was curious, but not *that* much.

"The next thing you know, I'll be getting a tattoo on my back like you've got."

What? I told Missy about that?

How chummy are we?

I blink at her, having lost track. "So, what was your question?"

She clears her throat and says, "Should I run away with Phil, or not?"

"And, uh. Leave both schools in the lurch?"

"You're right," she agrees thoughtfully. "Now's not the best time. We should wait until after the holidays."

I can't wait for two thirty to get here. I think this day will never end. The mound of paperwork is endless, and comparing paper files to electronic records is painstakingly grueling. My unexpected conversation with Missy also wore me thin. I had no idea she leaned on me this much for relationship advice. It's daunting. I hope I didn't steer her in the wrong direction.

The school dismissal bell rings loudly, and students filter into the hall in boisterous groups, holding or wearing their backpacks and preparing to exit the school. Missy's office door opens, and a pair of parents walk out. It's the couple who wanted to tour the school and we managed to fit them in near the end of the day.

"Thanks for visiting Walton!" she says as the couple leaves. "I hope to see you and Jocelyn here next semester!" I know that's an empty promise, since she's angling to elope with Phil then.

They leave and I start packing up for the day. I thought my homelife was demanding, until I got a load of my life at this office. After working for Missy, taking care of sweet Eleanor and Henry will feel like a break. I stare at the candy bar Dean brought me but that I didn't have a second to eat. Being around him will feel like heaven. It's so easy being by his side. In an awesome way, he's my best friend. I slide the candy bar in my purse and lift my work bag off the floor, as Missy plunks a long, giftwrapped package down on my desk. There isn't a ton of room, but I've freed up some space beside a family photo of me with Dean and the kids.

"Oh my!" I tell her. "That's so sweet."

I'm swamped with guilt that I don't have anything for her. "Don't feel like you have to return the favor," she says as if reading my mind. "You're not supposed to give to your 'Boss Lady,'" she jokes, and I laugh. Missy is so quirky, but she's also all right. I find myself warming to her, and starting to regret that she's leaving, assuming she really does run away with Phil.

"Well then, thanks, Missy." I hold up the gift. "Thanks so much."

"Go ahead and open it. It's something you should use right away." She nods at the package. "Some people like to give gifts. I like to give experiences."

"Oh yeah?" I try not to think about the experiences she's had with Phil and hope this present has nothing to do with their private life. My nose twitches nervously and I rub it. No. Missy's not going to give me something untoward or steamy to use with my husband. She's my principal, for heaven's sake.

I unwrap the paper and open the flat narrow box. It holds four printed out tickets inside. They're for ice skating. My eyes heat at the thoughtful gesture.

"The downtown rink is only open through early January," she explains. "So I thought you and your family might enjoy using these beforehand. I know your boy, Henry, is a bit young—"

I leap to my feet and hug her around the neck. Even if it's not professional. Even if I'm not supposed to. We're probably not supposed share pinky swear secrets either, but we have. "Missy, thank you. Eleanor will be thrilled! She's been begging—"

I catch my breath and remember this morning. The *ice skates* on the advent calendar. So wait. Yes. Maybe the calendar *is* predicting the future. I can't wait to tell Dean. Maybe we can go tonight?

We have a lot of trouble getting Henry to stand up on his ice skates. Although there are kids who look as young as he is on the ice, those types were obviously born to it. Dean crouches low and holds Henry's hands, trying to stabilize him. Henry's skates start to splay out sideways, and Dean grabs him under his arms in his puffy coat. Turns to me and chuckles. "I think you were right."

Henry grins from ear to ear, staring at his dad. "Merry Kissmas!"

Dean and I laugh. I'm holding hands with Eleanor. She seems to be doing a lot better than Henry. Maybe he'll have to wait until he's her age. I clomp forward in my skates and pull her along. She latches onto my coat sleeve with her mittens and swings away from me in a wide arc. "Wheee!" she says, skating back toward me as we glide forward.

Dean nods ahead of us and scoops Henry into his arms, taking care with his skate blades. "You two take a turn around the rink. Henry and I will go over there and buy some supper." He glances at the food truck parked by the curb in front of the courthouse. "Hot dogs or tacos?"

"Chili dog for me!" I answer and Eleanor bounces up and down.

"Chili dog, yay!"

"Okay," Dean replies. "We'll get four of those," he says speaking for himself and Henry. They clomp off the ice, and I hang on to Eleanor as we make a careful circle around the rink. She's doing quite well, and—though I haven't skated in a while—it's coming back to me.

"This is fun, Mommy!"

Chilly air nips my nose and ears. "Yeah, it is!"

When we come back around toward the entrance, I spy a familiar couple skating onto the ice. Mom and Roger. He leads first and nods—naturally—holding out his glove. She takes his hand, and he pulls her toward him. She's laughing, her face flushed. "Oh Roger," I hear her say. My heart pitter-patters. She does look happy, and in love.

"Mom, hi!"

She looks over and sees me and Eleanor skating toward her. "Oh my goodness!" She and Roger turn in our direction.

"Well, hello!" he says. His mouth turns up and his breath clouds the frigid air.

"Hi, Roger. Fun to see you and Mom here."

They scoot aside near the railing, and Eleanor and I join them. I'm able to stop myself and catch Eleanor by her shoulders when she keeps going. "Grandma!" she says, hugging Mom's legs. Mom pats the top of her pom-pom hat. "Hi, sweetheart. Where're your brother and dad?"

"Getting chili dogs!"

Mom chuckles at Roger. "Sounds like the right idea after a bit."

He nods.

This time, instead of getting annoyed, though, I begin to see his charm. Mostly that involves how he seems to make Mom *feel*. Uplifted and cared for.

Mom turns to me. "Didn't expect to see you out on a school night."

I shrug. "It wasn't planned." The words freeze on my lips and in my brain. But no. *It's okay not to plan everything.* "Principal Peabody gifted us with the tickets."

"How nice." Her blue eyes sparkle. "A tad of spontaneity's good in my book." She glances at Roger. "Isn't it, honey bunch?"

I wait for him to nod.

Instead, he takes her hand and presses the back of her glove to his mouth in a kiss. "Sure is." He's clearly as smitten with her as she is with him. All right. I'm done judging and making assumptions about Mom and Roger. I do want her happiness, I do. And I haven't seen her glowing like this around a guy in years. She shines so brightly, she puts the town square Christmas tree to shame. Understanding settles in my heart. I can't hold Mom back from her dreams. She's never stopped me from pursuing mine.

"Your cell phone still out of commission?" Mom asks me.

"Yeah, sadly. I'm hoping to get it fixed tomorrow."

Dean plods back over through the snow in his ice skates, holding Henry and a large paper bag. "Rosemary!" he says seeing Mom. "And Roger." He grins at the older man. "How great to see you both."

"Looks like you've got your hands full," Mom says. She waves at Henry. "Hi, Henry!"

"Merry Kissmas," he says, and she chuckles.

"Oh my." Mom addresses me and Dean. "A little young for the ice?"

I lift a shoulder. "Yeah. A little."

She and Roger exchange a look and he nods. "Why don't you let us sit with Henry for a bit on a bench, so the rest of you can have a go?"

Dean answers almost at once. "Thanks, Rosemary. That would be nice."

Eleanor tugs at my hand as the scent of chili dogs wafts toward us. "I'm hungry."

I laugh warmly and glance at Mom. "All right if Eleanor sits with you, too?"

"Of course," Mom says.

Dean peeks at the food truck. "I need to go back for the drinks I ordered." He surveys Mom and Roger. "Could I sell you two on a couple cups of coffee?"

"And two chili dogs?" I pipe in, getting his drift.

"I wouldn't mind a bite," Mom says.

Roger agrees breezily. "Same."

"Great," Dean replies. "You can eat with the kids while Paige and I skate. Then we'll switch off."

"You don't have to ask me twice about spending time with my grandchildren," Mom says merrily. My chest aches, but no. I can't hold it against her if she wants to move to Wilmington. She'll come and visit, like she said. And maybe the kids will get even more quality time with their grandma, if she's staying with us at our place.

Dean goes back to the food truck for the beverages, and I help Mom and Roger get settled with the kids on a park bench overlooking the ice skating rink. Another family has just cleared out from sitting there, so it's already been dusted clean of snow. No more white stuff falls from the sky, but the entire town square is coated in white, the lights on the holiday market tents making everything appear more magical. It's after five, so the sky is dark, but the skating rink is rimmed with lights, and the tall town Christmas tree stands nearby.

I think of Mary Christmas and what she said: *Enjoy.*

But then my soul twists like a sheet in the wind.

It's hard to enjoy what might get snatched away from me at any second. Frightening not to have control over my destiny. When I first landed in this existence, I was so thrown by the sudden changes all I could think about was returning to my former life. But now, this new reality is growing on me. Despite my crap job, old clunker car, messy house, there's—my heart sighs—my amazing husband and family.

Dean takes my hand and stares at the ice skating rink, where groups and happy couples skate by. "What do you say, Mommy?" he asks sweetly. "Want to give it a whirl?"

Just looking at him calms my inner turmoil. It's hard to stay stressed when I'm around Dean. He has a way of making everything seem easy, like it will be all right. A smile tugs at my lips. "Absolutely, Daddy." It should feel awkward calling him that, but it's not. The word trips off my tongue like I've been referring to him as Eleanor and Henry's dad for years, and of course—in this world—I have.

Maybe if I'd known how good things could be going forward, I'd have made different choices— but no. Knowing me, maybe I wouldn't have. I'd still have wanted to finish my degree and do the responsible thing. Although there can't be any huger responsibility than helping run a family.

I consider my teaching job and Paws and Read, pondering the differences between the two realities. In this world I have an incredible homelife and family, but no memories of how we got here, which is super sad. But Mom is healthy and happy, which is a blessing that's too great to ignore. In the other world, I have all the accomplishments I've worked for and a safe, stable life, and am planning financially to look after Mom. Plus, I'm establishing a worthy literacy organization, with memories galore.

It feels like the only way I could set up Paws and Read in this realm would be by going back to school and becoming a teacher. But, with our family's financial demands, money's incredibly tight. It's hard to see how I could justify outlaying additional funds for educational expenses with our bank account balances being so paltry. Maybe if I got a scholarship? No. It's still hard to see how that would work. I'd need to keep my job working for Missy to help keep us afloat.

My mind turns to the world where I'm already a teacher. Now that Dean and I are working at the same school in my other reality, if I were somehow transported back there, could we have a second chance? The more pressing question is, could things be as awesome between us there as they are here? And what about our kids, and Scout? If Dean and I started dating and eventually married, would Eleanor and Henry come along someday? Our sweet shaggy pup, too? My gaze tracks to Mom and Roger sitting on the park bench with our children. And what about them? Would Mom's medical tests come out okay, and could those two have a future?

CHAPTER
Fourteen

*D*ean holds my glove in his, and we glide around the ice, going faster and faster, weaving in and out of other skaters, and with each turn around the rink, my spirits grow lighter. No sense in fretting over things that may come, when I can't control them. The key lies in listening to Mary Christmas and truly learning to *enjoy*. And I am enjoying this outing, so much. It's fun to cut loose and have this wintertime adventure with my family. I laugh, feeling carefree. "This is great!" I call as winds muffle our voices. "So much fun!" We went on lots of ice skating dates in college, so this is a natural for us.

"Yeah!" Dean concurs. "Thanks to Missy for the tickets!"

"Thank you, Missy!" I call out into the night. Dean holds my hand tighter, then suddenly he slows, dragging me over to the side of the rink, by the railing.

"Dean? What is it?" I see Mom and Roger on the far side of the rink with the kids on their park bench, chatting happily and chomping down on their chili dogs. Henry sits on Mom's lap and Eleanor sits in the middle, between Mom and Roger. They form a picturesque group in their winter hats and coats.

He pulls me toward him in a hug, my bulky coat pressed against his. "I wanted to ask you a question."

"Oh yeah, what?" Skaters bustle past us, obscuring Mom and Roger and the kids from view. Dean's head dips toward me, his mouth hovering over mine. My heart skips a beat at the dreamy look in his eyes. The nearness of his kiss. And suddenly, I so badly want him to kiss me.

"Paige Burton," he says. "Will you go out with me?"

My cheeks warm. "Aren't we already going out?"

He glances around the crowded ice skating rink. "You mean here?" He shakes his head. "I mean on a *real date*, just the two of us." His gaze washes over me, filling me with so much contentment and joy. What if there were no other reality and this was my new world forever? Could I adjust to the transition? Three days ago, I thought not, but now my life is changing. *I'm changing.*

A lump forms in my throat and I glance at Mom sitting on the park bench with the kids and Roger. Mary Christmas said she couldn't promise what would happen to Mom if I go back to the other realm, or my program if I stay here. And yet, I'm frustratingly not being offered a real choice here, am I? And since I'm not, I'll just have to make the most of each moment I'm here until I learn where I'm bound to stay.

I stare up at my handsome husband and his dark eyes dance. "There's nothing I'd love more than going out with you," I say, meaning it absolutely. How could I not want to spend time alone with this totally amazing man? I tilt my chin and quip, "On a real date."

Dean brings his lips to mine in the sweetest, most tender kiss. "Good."

"When?" His arms are still around me. Others skating by are starting to stare, or sneak glances our way. Do they imagine us as new lovers? It kind of feels like we are. Brand new yet familiar. Wonderful and warm.

"How about tomorrow?"

I gasp because that's so unplanned. Practically spontaneous, and how much spontaneity can an always-planning woman take in one week? Still. I suppose *I am* being given twenty-four hours' notice, and—assuming I'm still here tomorrow—my schedule's clear. My stomach quivers with excitement over going out with Dean. Just the two of us, like a serious romantic couple. "What about Henry and Eleanor?"

"I already spoke with my folks," he says. "They're coming over to babysit."

"Then it sounds like we're set."

He holds me close and kisses me again. "I was hoping you'd say that, because I've got a special surprise."

"Oh?" My heart beats erratically. Is he giving me an early Christmas gift? I've got almost nothing for him. Just a simple coffee mug. I stare across the town square and past the holiday market. Though I can't see Second Chances from here, I know that it's there, holding that telescope in its front window. How I wish I could find a way to buy it for Dean. "What is it?"

"Now, I can't tell you that, can I?" He kisses the top of my head. "Then it wouldn't be a surprise."

We have a great rest of the evening, and it's not long before the kids are worn out and ready for bed. Dean tucks Henry under the covers and settles the blankets around his shoulders, laying the storybook he's been reading on the nightstand. Henry's just moved up to his "big boy bed," apparently. After his crib, we kept his mattress on the floor for a while before adding the low bed frame that resembles a yellow and red race car. Toy cars line the shelving along one wall. These were Dean's when he was a kid, and his parents saved them. He recently passed them on to Henry, once Henry was old enough to understand he wasn't meant to eat them.

"Didn't make it to the end of the book?" I ask Dean from the doorway.

He tiptoes out of the room, turning off the light. "We can finish tomorrow."

Eleanor holds my hand in the hall. "Can I have a story, too?" She's dressed in a cute pink flannel nightie with a dainty silk white bow at the neckline and buttons on the bodice. The nightie is long, falling past her ankles and nearly to her fluffy puppy-dog-face slippers. She still wears her pigtails, but they're pulling apart in places after her busy day.

"You bet you can," I tell her, "but first let's brush your hair."

We already brushed her teeth in the bathroom after finishing up her bubble bath. Dean gave Henry a quick bath first, taking pains not to linger since the boy's eyelids were drooping already. Dean creeps toward the hallway, leaving Henry's door partially ajar. "Should I build us a fire?" He views me longingly. "I can open some wine?"

"That sounds really good." I consider my sterile condo with its gas fireplace and where I have only Elroy for company. I shake my head at the thought. A robotic dog. Then I see our real dog, Scout, curled up in the center of Eleanor's bed. I place a hand on my hip and scold him. "Scout! What are you doing?"

He lazily lifts his head and blinks, having been roused out of his slumber.

"He's sleeping, Mommy," Eleanor informs me.

"I see that," I tell the girl. "Only, Scout's not supposed to sleep here. He's got his own bed in Mommy and Daddy's room."

Eleanor covers her mouth and giggles. Scout hops off her bed and trots over before sitting down at her feet. He cocks his head and says, "*Woof!*"

Eleanor and I both shush him on account of Henry.

Eleanor holds a finger against her lips. "Don't tell, Scout," she whispers. "It's a secret."

I sagely scan the girl. "What kind of secret, Eleanor?"

She shrugs and says sweetly, "Sometimes, when you and Daddy are sleeping, Scout comes in here and sleeps with me."

"On your bed?"

"Uh-huh."

"And you like that?"

"Oh yeah," she says seriously. "Scout's my best friend."

I laugh and hug her, not sure of what else to do. If this is already a habit between them, it's going to be hard to break. We keep Scout clean and bathed. He stays on flea prevention medication, too. I wrinkle up my nose and tell her, "I'll have to talk to Daddy and be sure he thinks it's all right. We'll both have to agree."

She nods like she expected this response and respects it. Evidently Dean and I present a united front before the kids. "Okay, Mommy."

I lift her hair brush off her dresser. "Now, come here," I say gently. "Let's undo those pigtails and run a brush through your hair." She stands facing the mirror as I brush out her long brown hair, her pretty, dark eyes gleaming back at me. She reminds me so much of Dean in miniature, it's uncanny. My heart swells with pride that we made her, and that I had something to do with the outcome. She's bright and as cute as a button. *My little girl.*

A lead weight settles in my stomach.

The child I'd lose by leaving here.

I'd also lose Henry. Baby heartthrob that he is. So precious.

What about Mom and Roger? They seem so good together here, but their fate's uncertain in the other world. So is mine—and Dean's. Tears prickle the backs of my eyes. Even though Dean and I are single in the other reality, I don't know how I could ever explain to Dean what I've learned by being here.

Scout's interest in the hair-brushing session wanes, and he goes off to find Dean in the living room. Meanwhile, I pull back Eleanor's covers and help her scoot into bed in a sitting-up position. I note the selection of books on the short bookshelf beneath her window. "Which one shall it be tonight?" I ask her.

She points to the top shelf. "The one about the princess!" she says eagerly.

I trace my finger along the book spines. *Princess. Princess.*

"That one!" she says, and I stop. Pull out the book and remove it from the shelf.

It's got a lovely, illustrated cover with a princess commanding a schooner, standing at the ship's wheel like a formidable captain. She wears a tiara but is dressed like a pirate otherwise. "This one looks adventuresome," I tell her.

Eleanor bubbles excitedly as I walk over, "She lives on a boat like Grandma's going to do."

I sigh, resigned to this outcome. "Your grandma's adventuresome, too."

Eleanor stares up at me with love in her eyes. "So are you, Mommy."

She doesn't know how wrong she is. I'm the person who always plays it safe and never takes chances. Until now.

"What makes you say that, Eleanor?"

Her grin lights up every dark corner of the room. "You said marrying Daddy was your greatest a'venture of all!"

"Did I?" A tear leaks from my eye, and I wipe it back. "Oh."

Eleanor frowns when I sit down beside her on the bed, my former world drifting away like tiny snowflakes flitting off in the wind.

"Are you sad, Mommy?"

"No, no. I'm happy." I hug her tightly and my heart weeps with joy. "So happy, Eleanor." This is so much more than I could have imagined. It's a brand new feeling, being adored by these kids, who are melting my heart so completely I can't help adoring them, too.

She hugs me and her muffled voice says, "I love you, Mommy."

I hold in my building tears. "I love you, too."

When I arrive in the living room my eyes still sting, but I've pulled myself together. Dried my leaky tears. Dean looks over in concern from where he's crouched by the fireplace. The lights are low, with only one lamp burning on the entryway table and another on an end table by the sofa. The rest of the room's illuminated by the multicolored lights on the radiant Christmas tree. "Everything all right?" Scout sits beside him, patiently watching his every move.

I nod because everything's so perfect. More perfect than I ever thought it could be. "Yeah." I sniff and center myself. "Eleanor was just being really sweet."

"She has her moments," he jokes. He stares fondly down the hall toward Henry's room. "They both do."

"They're great kids," I tell him.

He stuffs bunched-up newspapers below the grate, where he's laid a fire with logs and kindling. "I agree." He winks and my heart flutters. "We're lucky to have them."

My breath hitches on the truth. "They're lucky to have *you*."

Dean strikes a match and holds it to the newspaper in the hearth. It ignites with a flare, flames raking over crackling twigs, catching their spindly limbs on fire.

"Hey, Paige? I really do want to know." He stands and walks toward me. "Is something going on?" He gazes at me sweetly. "Because you can tell me, you know."

"Dean." I stare into his swoony dark eyes. "There's so much I want to tell you."

"Oh yeah?" He brings his arms around me and holds me close. "Then spill."

My heart pounds in my throat when I say, "I do think that calendar's magical. Just look at the snowman, the poinsettia, those skates."

"Hmm. Could be. Those occurrences were rather mysterious." He pulls me nearer and gazes into my eyes. "You want to know where the real magic is?" He gently strokes my cheek with his thumb. "Right here, between us," he murmurs and kisses me so tenderly I go all melty inside. *Yes, I believe that with my whole heart.*

The fire behind him builds, purplish flames lapping against the logs. He's laid the fire expertly and it fills the air with the light scent of cedar, issuing in a cozy warmth.

Dean takes my hand and leads me to the sofa. "It's been a very full couple of days," he says, "and you're still adjusting to the news about your mom and Roger. Why don't we sit and have a glass of wine?"

I see a bottle of cabernet sauvignon on the coffee table next to a corkscrew. He's brought out two wineglasses, too. I sink down on a sofa cushion, not believing I've earned any of this. He opens the bottle and fills my glass.

When he hands me my glass, I ask, "Whatever did I do to deserve you?"

"Paige." He raises his wineglass to mine. "I'm the lucky one." His face is so handsome in the shadows. I trace the line of his dimple with my fingers. Excitement ripples through me at the feel of his skin and his late evening beard stubble.

We clink glasses and I say, "Maybe we're both lucky?"

His lopsided grin bathes my soul in happiness. "Here's to us, then."

"Here's to us!"

We clink glasses again, and he leans forward and kisses me. So silky soft, my heart pounds and my head grows light. I open my eyes and catch Scout slipping down the hall. Dean peers at the dog. "Looks like Scout's calling it a day."

"He might be sneaking into Eleanor's room."

"What?"

I nod. "I have it on good authority, he's been sleeping on her bed."

Dean chuckles and shakes his head. "What do you think?"

"He's a tame, mature dog. Plus he loves those kids." I lift a shoulder. "I don't see any harm in it. You?"

He smiles affectionately. "Same."

The fire burns brighter, its heat spreading toward us.

Dean takes our wineglasses and sets them on the coffee table. He holds both my hands in his. "Have I told you lately..." His voice goes raspy. "How much I love you." His eyes shimmer in the firelight and my heart soars. While I can't recall these past six years in this dimension, I'm certain of one thing. I do know Dean. I know *this* Dean like the back of my hand, or the other half of myself. And no, he's not the type of guy to hide his feelings. He's the sort who would have told me many times.

"I'm sure you have."

"That's good," he says softly, "because that's something I always want you to remember. One thing that will never change."

"I don't like change," I tell him honestly, and the truth slays me. Because it's *change* that's brought me here.

"Then let's not change anything, hmm?" He wraps his arm around me and says huskily, "Unless it's for the better."

Now I can't fathom wanting to change anything at all. I have a husband who adores me and two wonderful kids. A sweet dog, and a passel of girlfriends I'm close to. I've also got Mom, who is cancer free, and for the first time in forever she's truly happy in a relationship. Everyone here seems happy! Even my boss, Missy Peabody. And happiness is all I could ever want for anyone. Emotion blooms in my heart until it's so overwhelming I find the words spilling out of my mouth. "Dean," I murmur as the fire crackles low, and the Christmas tree shines brightly, "I love you, too."

"That's good to hear." His lips brush over mine and I sigh in his embrace. Let his kisses sweep me away as he holds me closer. So close it's just the two of us and our rapidly beating hearts, growing nearer and nearer, warmer, my skin igniting at his touch. He reaches over and switches off the light, gently easing me down on the sofa. And suddenly, that other reality feels very far away.

CHAPTER
Fifteen

I wake up hugely happy and—I peer under the covers.—naked. I'm not wearing a thing, not even my Monday thong. *Oh!* There it is on the floor beside the bed. The bedroom door pops open. Eleanor! I snatch the undergarment off the floor and tuck it down under the covers beside me, wriggling it on. Backward. Ugh. That's no good. I scoot if off my ankles, and *kick, kick, kick* with my feet, turning it around. Dean's awake now, too.

I peek beneath the sheets. Also naked. *Oh wow*, no wonder I'm happy. Okay, *focus* on the kids. I blink as Henry barrels into the room. "Merry Kissmas!" he cries, pouncing onto the bed. *Oof.* Dean pulls on his sweatpants under the covers. He sneakily hands me his T-shirt and I peer at him in our dark tent. Henry bounces above us. Elbows and knees. Sharp edges. "I'm hungry!"

A heavier bounce. "Mommy! Daddy! It's snowing!" That's Eleanor.

Dean tugs up the covers above us and I slip his T-shirt over my head. Manage to get it on. *Wait.* My arm is stuck. "What are you doing?" Eleanor asks, trying to pull back the sheets.

"Waking up!" Dean hollers back to her. He tries to help by grappling for my elbow, but he shoves it in the wrong direction.

"*Ouch*," I whisper. "*Dean*."

"*Woof! Woof!*" That's Scout—trampling my legs. Dean helps me tug down the T-shirt. My face flames as we finally peel back the covers and I stare at the kids. Sit upright in bed. Straighten the covers. Dean does the same. "Morning, everyone!"

"Mommy! Yay!" Henry throws his arms around my neck, knocking me backward toward the headboard. A stash of pillows catches us.

Eleanor sits back on her knees, her pink nightie bunched up. "Do we have school today?"

"School?" Dean's eyes grow wide as he stares at the clock. "Yikes! We're late!"

"Merry Kissmas!" Henry yells into my ear. He kisses my cheek. A sloppy wet kiss. So sweet. Though my head smarts from his yelling. Or maybe it was the wine. We opened a second bottle. Scout prances up to Dean and the mattress sags beneath him. He drops the wet rolled-up newspaper sleeve in Dean's lap.

"Good boy!" Dean pats his head and glances at me. "We've got to get going."

"Right!" We scoot the kids and dog off the bed, and I yank up the covers, dumping the clothes basket on the bed. Why haven't we folded anything? Is this how we live? Dean races for the coffee pot to switch it on. God love him. Scout doesn't know who to follow, Dean or me. He darts back and forth, barking.

"Can I wear red?" Eleanor asks, pointing to some stretch pants and a Christmas top.

"Of course you can!"

I hunt for something for Henry.

"I have to pee!" He's got his hands on his pajama pants over his crotch.

"Hold it!" I hurry him along into the bathroom. "Eleanor, can you grab your and Henry's backpacks and take them into the kitchen?"

"On it!" she says like the very grown-up person she's not. She races out of the room in her pink nightie and Scout runs after her. "*Woof! Woof!*"

I herd Henry into the hall bathroom, find the toilet targets, drop one in the bowl. *Whew!* We make it just in time. Then I catch a glimpse of myself in the mirror over the sink. Who is that ridiculously happy women with the pink-tinted layered hair? Oh yeah. Me. I feel like I've been hit by a wild tornado. The storm of a different reality.

But I'm kind of digging it, truthfully.

Now I know why Dean calls me "tiger."

I was like a wild animal last night. *Grrr.*

Okay, we both were.

And I'm still throbbing everywhere.

Pleasantly.

I try hard not to squeal at my reflection.

Life is good.

* ❄ *

We're dressed and in our coats, halfway out the door. "Let's ride together again," Dean says. "Since it's a half day and we're both getting off early. That will make it easy to stop by the phone store."

I huff and puff, hauling the kids and their stuff along. "Sounds good." I check my coat pocket to be sure my cell phone is where I put it earlier.

"Wait!" Eleanor wails and we all freeze. "We forgot the calendar."

"She's right," Dean says. "We should do it. But quickly!"

We hurry back into the kitchen en masse. "Whose turn is it?" Dean asks.

I wheeze, breathing heavily, hands on my knees. "I've lost track. Eleanor?" I stare at the girl. She shrugs in her pom-pom hat.

"Henry?" He holds up his baby blue mittens.

"You do it," Dean says in brisk tones.

I locate the item for Day Twenty-Three in the pocket. It's a pretty Christmas candle with a holly design on the candlestick base. "What can this have to do with the future?" I ask Dean.

"No idea." He nods at the calendar, and I press the decoration onto it.

"Okay." Dean smiles at our group. "Let's rock and roll!"

"Are you and Mommy going to sing again?" Eleanor asks as we hurry toward the door.

"I think we should *all* sing," Dean tells her. He starts a chorus of, "Jingle bells, jingle bells—"

Eleanor and I join in. "Jingle all the way!"

Scout barks happily by the tree and tries to come with us.

"Sorry, boy," Dean tells him, pulling the door closed. "We'll be home soon."

"Jingle bell!" Henry says thirty seconds too late on the front porch.

"That's right, Henry," I say and hug him hard. "Very good!"

Dean and I stare at the wall of shiny new cell phones, getting discouraged. The price tags have soared since the last time I bought one, but that doesn't deter the crowd of others clamoring toward displays to get closer looks. Dean holds Henry in his arms and Eleanor stands between us. We're waiting on the sales associate to return from the back room where he's testing my phone. He finally arrives and hands me my cell phone. The guy's tall and thin and wears a black collared shirt. "I'm sorry to say it's a goner."

"Already?" I gasp. "It's not that old."

The sales associate winces. "Sorry. That model hasn't been made in five."

"Months?" I ask.

"Years," the salesperson replies with a grimace.

Dean heaves a deep breath. "We should get you another." He's trying to look solid, but he's gone a bit pale. I know what he's thinking. It's the holidays and we already have extra expenses. I haven't seen any Santa gifts around the house but suspect we must have some hidden somewhere. We're the kind of parents who'd dote on their kids, even if it meant running up the credit cards during the season. But buying a new cell phone is something else. "I suppose we could finance through the store?"

"I don't know, Dean."

"It's not exactly like you can be without a phone," he argues reasonably. "The daycare might need to reach you about the kids, when they can't reach me. We both need to be available."

"They could always call the school."

"Yeah, but. We're not always at school." He sighs and says sweetly, "Paige. We need this."

The sales associate senses our financial predicament. "You could try buying a refurbished phone online?" he suggests kindly. "You can get some really great deals, I hear."

Dean and I exchange a look. "That could work," he says. "What do you think?"

"Let's check online when we get home."

Dean and I sit at the kitchen table later with our coffee, looking up secondhand cell phones. The light snow that was falling this morning and earlier today has stopped, and a fresh pretty blanket of white covers the fenced backyard visible through the window. Scout snoozes by our feet and both kids are napping. "What about this one?" he asks, pointing to a sleek model. "It's only a year old."

I frown. "Are you sure we can afford it?"

He gently lays his hand on my arm. "We can't not afford it, Paige. Your having a phone is a safety concern, not just for the kids but also for you."

I nod and check the cell phone's price. It's less than half the cost of a similar phone we saw at the store.

"It can be here by Friday," he says. "The day after Christmas."

"Dean?" I ask. "About the kids and Christmas. Their Santa gifts—"

"No sense worrying about what we spent when they're all taken care of and paid off."

"What?"

"Like you insisted." He squints at me. "I guess knowing what we know now, it's a good thing we bought early this year and charged it with the plan to chip away at the balance and get it cleared before Christmas, huh."

I square my shoulders. "How responsible of us."

He smiles warmly. "I can't imagine how bad off we'd be if you weren't managing our family finances." Oh my gosh, our paltry bank balance is my fault?

I press my lips together. "I checked our account balances on Sunday. It honestly doesn't seem like we're doing that great."

He takes my hand. "Are you kidding me? A family of four with a house of our own and two paid-off cars. Honey." He squeezes my hand. "We're doing fantastic." His eyes sparkle. "Just think of all we have."

My heart brims so full with all the blessings, and I concede we have a lot. "So the kids' Santa gifts? Are you sure they're enough?"

He nods. "Eleanor's getting what she wanted. The new bike with training wheels. And Henry's getting his Hot Shot."

Hot Shot? "Er, nice! I bet he'll love that!"

"Yeah." Dean chuckles. "Let's just hope he doesn't tear up the house. We'll need to be sure he rides it outside."

Ahhh. It's some kind of vehicle? "I'm so excited for Henry and Eleanor both! We ordered so long ago, I've nearly forgotten the details."

"Oh, here!" Dean checks his computer bookmarks and pulls up some links. One showcases a small red bike with a sparkly seat and training wheels. Colorful streamers hang from the handlebars, and there's a darling basket in front with plastic daisies on it. I can see we purchased a kiddy bike helmet with it.

"Aw, she'll love that."

Dean whispers, although the kids are out of earshot and most likely soundly sleeping. "And here's the one we landed on for Henry." He opens the link, and a toy car appears that looks like a blue hot rod with flames painted along the sides. It's got a roof and a micro steering wheel and doors that open and close on either side. It's made to seat one person of about Henry's size and is propelled forward by the child's feet.

I chuckle imagining Henry inside of it. "Watch out for our mini speed demon."

Dean laughs. "I know! Christmas morning's going to be fun."

"Where will they ride?"

"I'll be sure to clear the snow in the driveway. At least enough of a path for them to go back and forth." He's such a good dad.

"I found a few stocking stuffers at the market," I volunteer. "Some cute puppets and candies."

"Perfect," he says and holds my hand. "It's not like they won't have enough. Our Christmas tree is loaded with packages from my parents and your mom. And I've got something special for you."

If only I had more to give him. "You didn't have to." I blush. "I mean, maybe we should just let the cell phone be my gift?"

"Too late," he says and shakes his head. "Already bought it."

"Can't wait to see."

"You'll just have to sit tight for one more night."

"Oh!" *Wait.* "On Christmas Eve?"

He grins happily. "I liked our idea to exchange our gifts the night before, and make Christmas morning more about Santa and the gifts from our parents." He shifts in his chair. "You haven't changed your mind?"

"No, no." I firmly grip his hand. "I can't wait for our private gift time."

He peers out the window to the backyard and glances at the street beyond the kitchen sink. "Maybe I should get a head start on that snow shoveling? Don't want to leave it all till tomorrow, and my parents aren't coming over until six."

"Do you need any help?" I ask, because I've got some experience in the shoveling department. I used to shovel our neighbors' drives as a teen to pick up extra cash.

"The best way you can help is by staying right here and keeping toasty and warm, while also keeping an ear out for the kids. We should probably go ahead and have them bathed and in their pj's when my folks get here. Do you mind handling that?" Three days ago I might have been daunted by that prospect, but now I feel like a domestic goddess champ. "No problem," I say with gusto.

By now, it's clear I've missed my Paws and Read launch party in the other realm, and I'm very bummed to have let all those pups and people down. But there's an upside to my new situation. Mom's healthy here and has no need for further doctors. Maybe I'll come up with a different way to give back if I stay in this world indefinitely. For the moment, though, I'm just grateful to be here for one more day.

Dean suits up to go outside and I check on the kids, who are still napping. They dozed right off when we came home from the phone store but never seem to sleep for more than an hour in the early afternoon. I can't help feeling excited about my special night out with Dean. It will be the first date we've had in forever. Longer ago in my mind than in his, obviously. I head to my closet to check out my wardrobe choices.

There's a slinky black dress that is strapless. A cropped black jacket accented with swirly gold stitching hangs beside it. Now this looks vintage. My pulse quickens. How lovely! I must have bought it as a splurge one time. I pull its hanger from the closet and take out the dress, holding both pieces in front of me in the dresser mirror. The dress's fabric is super clingy. I could wear tights with it and slingback heels. I press the fabric to my tummy, which is not exactly flat. There are bound to be bulges.

A light bulb goes on in my brain.

Spanx.

I lay the dress and jacket on the bed and pull open my top dresser drawer.

The Spanx lie there beside some lacy underwear that I'll *of course* have to wear! I choose a sexy red thong and a matching push-up bra, my face heating. The old me never would have— no. Stop. I'm *this me* now. The girl with the lower back tattoo and pink highlights.

I pick up the Spanx, which are disappointingly heavy. I bet the garment pinches in places, but maybe some pinching will be worth it to see the look on Dean's face. I tug at its taut cylindrical shape, wondering how I'm going to insert my midsection into this contraption. I'm not exactly a small person. On the short side, maybe, but plenty curvy. It's got stout legs cut to the midthigh and a bodice that covers the stomach, back, and breasts. I wouldn't own the darn thing if I weren't capable of squeezing into it somehow. So! I'll give it the old college try. Ha.

I start to close the drawer—but wait. A tin box with a floral design on top sits below where the pair of Spanx was. I pick it up and something heavy rattles inside. Sounds like marbles? Stones? What? I sit down on the bed and pry open the lid. A wad of cash springs out of the box. Bunches and bunches of lower denomination bills. There are coins scattered in the bottom of the tin.

I've been squirreling money away! I pick up some currency. Fan it out in my fingers like a deck of cards, and—something drops out from the middle, fluttering to the floor. I pick it up. It's a picture of a telescope! No, wait. An advertisement from a local store. Second Chances. I gasp and my heartbeats race away from me. A secret surprise! I've been planning to buy this for Dean!

I count the money, wondering if I've got enough. It's very close. If I made a modest withdrawal from my personal account, I'd have this. I glance at the clock and it's nearly three. The kids will be up at any minute, and I'll need to get them—and myself—ready for tonight. Tomorrow, though, I'll finagle an excuse to run an errand. Assuming I'm still here, and all indications are that I will be.

A grin tugs at my lips, so huge it hurts.

I can't wait.

I think of my old life, but it's getting farther and farther away. Growing fuzzy like a fading dream I'm having trouble recalling. I didn't plan this. Didn't intend to be sitting here two days before Christmas in some alternate reality while holding a lap full of cash money and Spanx.

Fear suddenly grips me like an icy glove, latching onto my heart and squeezing harder.

Just as breezily as I was dumped here, I could be yanked the other way.

But I'm not ready to leave.

I press my palms together and beg of the ceiling.

Please, not yet.

I want to be here to see the kids' happy faces on Christmas morning, and to tell Henry that yes, "Kissmas" is finally here. I want to buy Dean that telescope and see his dreamy smile light up the room. I want Mom and Roger to be happy, and for all of us to have a merry Christmas. And that kind of Christmas can only happen here.

CHAPTER
Sixteen

Eleanor shouts and raises her fists in glee. "Gammy and Poppi are here!" She bounces on her heels by the front door, having peered out the window by the rocker.

Henry toddles up to the door. "Gammy! Poppi!"

We all heard their SUV's door shut in the drive.

Dean opens the door, and the middle-aged couple appears, dressed in winter coats and hats. Only Poppi's hat looks like Santa's and Gammy wears a green elf hat.

"Hel-lo!" Gammy grins around the room. "Good to see everyone."

Dean hugs his mom and one-arm hugs his dad. "Thanks for watching the kids."

Gammy rolls her eyes. "As if you have to ask!" Dean takes her coat and she's fashionably dressed in nice camel-colored slacks and a cream-colored sweater. She's got short dark hair and Dean's dark brown eyes. "Paige!" She hugs me tightly. "It's been a while."

I pull back to smile at her. She looks good and hasn't aged a bit in the past six years. "Yeah, it has."

"When was it?" she asks. "The week before last at the pageant rehearsal?"

"Ah, yep! Must have been then."

Dean's dad, Jack, hugs me, his coat draped over one arm. "Paige, always good to see you." He's gone salt and pepper around the temples and has Dean's same deep dimple on his left cheek. His eyes are lighter brown than those of Dean's mom, Miriam. Jack's kept himself fit and is shorter than Dean, with him and Miriam being nearly the same height, around five foot ten.

Scout excitedly bounds between us and Miriam bends down to scratch him behind his collar. "Hey there, boy! Have you been behaving yourself for Santa?"

Scout sits back on his haunches to reply. "*Woof! Woof!*"

"He has!" Dean says as Jack fondly pats Scout's side.

"Scout's always been a good boy," Jack says. "Ever since he was just a pup."

Dean hangs up their coats and the kids throw themselves at their grandparents.

"Who do we have here?" Jack asks, scooping Eleanor up in his arms. "Is this a Christmas elf?" He thumbs her nose, leaning his face closer to hers. "Or are you the Grinch?" he asks in fake grumpy tones.

She giggles and whispers, all raspy voiced, "I'm the Grinch!"

"Are you really?"

He playfully tickles her side. "Poppi!" She cackles. "*Stop.*"

Miriam holds Henry, jostling him in her arms. "How about you, young man? Are you ready for Santa?"

He presses his sweet baby forehead to hers and whispers, "Merry Kissmas."

"Oh my goodness!" She throws back her head and roars. "You," she tells Henry, "are adorbs."

The group makes its way into the main living area near the sofa and love seat. Dean's built a fire, and it burns brightly. "I've put in the order for the pizza," he tells his dad. He reaches for his wallet in his hip pocket, but his dad stops him.

"Don't even think about it." Jack holds up his hand. "Tonight's on us."

"Well, thanks, Dad." Dean pats his shoulder. Nods toward the hearth. "Extra logs over there in the holder if you'd like to keep it going."

Miriam snuggles Henry closer. "Everything's so nice and cozy." She admires the Christmas tree. "Beautiful tree this year."

"Thanks!" Dean and I say together, because the house does look very nice and festive now that the living area's all picked up.

Miriam glances at our clothing. "You two run along and get ready. We'll hold down the fort with the kids."

"Thanks, Mom," Dean says.

"This is such a great pleasure for us," Miriam's declares. "Really!"

Eleanor stares up at her grandpa. "Want to see our 'day calendar?"

His forehead furrows seriously. "My, that sounds intriguing."

I laugh. "That's our advent calendar."

"Aha!" Meriam speaks cheerfully to the boy. "Shall we take a look, Henry?"

He claps his hands together. "O-tay!"

Dean takes my hand and tugs me toward the bedroom. "Reservation's at six-thirty."

"You never told me where we're going?"

"Riazzi's."

"Ooh, fancy." It's the nicest Italian place in town, farm to table with house-made pasta.

His grin melts my heart.

"Nothing's too good for my girl."

Ten minutes later, I've gotten on my Spanx. Oh my goodness, that was work, but worth it. I admire my reflection in the bathroom mirror. Stand up on my tiptoes to check my image front and back. All super smooth, no bulges. Only sexy-looking curves.

I open the door to the bedroom, where Dean stands putting on his necktie. "Wow," he says when I walk in. "You look— amazing." Tingles shimmy down my spine to my toes and I enjoy the glow. I love being appreciated by Dean. He makes me feel special, no matter what I wear. But the way he's looking at me now makes me feel extra glamorous.

I sashay out of the bathroom, staring at my great-looking husband in charcoal gray dress slacks and a white button-down shirt. "You clean up pretty well yourself."

He kisses me firmly on the lips. "Thank you." Dean finishes knotting his crimson necktie and flattens it down against his starched shirt. This one clearly didn't come from the laundry basket. He'd concealed it and his nice suit in a laundry bag in his closet. So we evidently visit the dry cleaners sometimes. I glance at our piles of laundry. Although it's clearly not a general habit.

Deans lifts his suit jacket off the bed. "Ready?"

I grab my purse off the dresser, my heart feeling happy and light. "I am."

Dean's reserved us the best table in the house. It's a special two-top nestled in a bay window overlooking the street. We can see the town square from here and the glowing lights of the holiday market. The town square Christmas tree and the ice skating rink are in the distance, and passels of skaters crowd the ice. Occasional people pass by on the shoveled sidewalk in front of us, families and couples huddled together against the cold. But it's cozy indoors in our very romantic spot.

A bottle of Chianti sits on the table and we both hold full wineglasses. I lift my glass and hold it up toward Dean. "This is so nice, thank you." As awesome as our family is, it's a treat to be out alone with my handsome husband.

He lifts his wineglass as well. "Here's to us."

"To us!"

We clink glasses and sip from our wine. We've both ordered yummy-sounding dishes. I got pasta Alfredo and Dean, the chicken piccata.

I note the candle on the table between us. "Dean," I say, and he sees what I'm staring at. The tall red taper sits in a white candle holder that includes a holly design with green ceramic leaves and red berries on its base. It looks exactly like the holiday candle on our advent calendar. The one we put up this morning for Day Twenty-Three.

"That's—got to be coincidental." Dean looks up and meets my eyes.

"Like the snowman, you mean?"

He rubs his neck. "Not as sure about those ice skates, though." He darts a glance out the window at the ice skating rink, and I do the same.

"Or, the poinsettia," I remind him, thinking of Mom and Roger's surprise delivery.

He chuckles warmly. "Okay, you've got me there." He takes another sip of wine and sets down his glass. "Maybe that lady dressed like Mrs. Claus was the real deal?" But he sounds like he's joking.

"I spoke with her, you know. Mary Christmas."

"Wait, seriously? Merry Christmas? That was her name?"

I wryly twist my lips. "M-A-R-Y Christmas, yes."

"Aha." He shakes his head. "When was this?"

"On Sunday, while I was out running errands. I asked her about our advent calendar and its supposed properties."

Dean takes a piece of bread from the basket on the table and butters it. "And?"

"She was *very mysterious*, hinting that the magic of our calendar might end on Christmas Day, but that the magic of Christmas will live on."

"Hmm. Intriguing."

"Maybe there is something to that special advent calendar. I wouldn't put it past that Christmas decoration changing a life or two around here." I wait to see how he reacts.

Dean chuckles and takes a bite of his bread. "Sure."

Darn. Well, I'm not going to hint I want to scrub our life again. That's for certain. I select some bread for myself. It looks and smells freshly baked and is still warm. I slather my piece with butter too and taste it. "Mmm, this is delicious."

He munches on his bread as well. "The best.

"So wait," he asks suddenly. "What were you doing at the holiday market?" Dean snaps his fingers. "Oh right. Buying presents for the kids."

"And Scout. I got something for him, too."

"That's very thoughtful."

I think of the consignment shop, Second Chances, on the far side of the square. Though we can't see it from here, I know precisely where it is. I wish with all my might that the telescope is still in its front window, or at least available and for sale. I'll try the store first thing in the morning when it opens. There's nothing I'd love more than buying that telescope for Dean.

"Paige, speaking of change… I wanted to talk to you about something." He shifts in his seat, appearing anxious. "And I hope you won't think I'm overstepping."

That doesn't sound good. "Is something wrong? Did I—?"

"Sweetheart, no." He reaches out and takes my hand. "You've done everything right. That's just the thing." He seems to gather his nerve. "You remember the other day when we were talking about changes? You said you didn't like them, and I know that about you. But then I said—"

"It's different when the change is for the good?"

"Yeah, that." I fall into his gaze, considering the tremendous leap I've made in entering this reality. After the initial bout of disorientation, I've found my way in the woods. And it's not dark and scary here. It's a happy and protected place. An existence where I feel heard and sheltered. It's getting harder and harder to imagine ever wanting to leave.

He swallows hard. "So. Here's what I've been thinking."

A server arrives holding two hot plates of food with oven mitts. "The chicken piccata?" she asks. I motion to Dean and she sets the plate in front of him. "And pasta Alfredo for you, ma'am." Incredible garlicky and creamy, melty cheesey aromas rise from the steaming dish.

"Oh my gosh," I tell the server. "This looks wonderful."

"Mine too," Dean says.

Another person arrives with a pepper grinder to sprinkle our dishes with fresh cracked black pepper. Yet a third tops off our ice waters.

"Great service here," I mention once we're on our own.

"Agreed." Dean considers me fondly and picks up his wine.

"So, you were saying?" I dig into my dish with my fork.

He takes a sip of his Chianti and returns his wineglass to the table. "I was talking about change, and how not all of it is bad. Sometimes it's good and can present new opportunities."

I take a nibble of heavenly pasta Alfredo, savoring its richness. *Oh yum, so tasty.* "I one hundred percent agree."

"Do you?" He blinks in surprise. "Well, great. I mean, that's good. Because, Paige," he says, "I have a proposition to make and I want you to think about it seriously."

I'm confused about where he's going with this. I lay my fork on the side of my dish. "I'm not sure what you're saying, Dean?"

"I'm talking about your future. Your dreams." He slices a piece of chicken and spears it, twirling pasta on his fork. "Look, I know you always wanted to teach."

"I *did*, but then life," I shrug, "had other plans, right?"

He enjoys his food before saying, "Right, but that doesn't mean you don't still have options."

"For?"

"Paige." He takes my hand again. "I hope you won't be mad at me, but I took the liberty of poking around. Did some investigating in the county, and"—he heaves a deep breath—"I think you should go back to school."

My wineglass shakes in my grasp, and I set it down. "But Dean, we can't afford—"

"Oh yes we can," he insists. "Since you're already employed by the school system, they'll reimburse the cost of your taking teacher education courses. All you'd have to do is maintain certain grades, and I've no doubt you would. You always did so well in college. You'd breeze right through."

"But we've got the kids and such a full schedule."

"I'll help in every way I can," he says. "Find a way to make it work. The great thing is that a lot of these courses are offered online, so you could do them at home, in the evenings or on the weekends. I'll spell you with the kids. Give you all the time you need." He's being so kind. So generous. But neither of us is made of money.

"*Reimburse*, you said. Where would we get the money to begin with?"

"Maybe student loans?" The thought of taking on more debt scares me. Maybe our vehicles are paid off, but we still have a mortgage and daycare expenses. Although, it's true—next year, Eleanor starts public school, so her schooling expenses will go down.

My head reels with the possibilities, but I know our financial situation. This seems like too big a reach. "But won't there be other expenses? Maybe supplies? I'd surely need a computer of my own. Even if we found one secondhand, it could be costly."

He nods like he's thought about this. "I've got good news in that department," he says and grins. "I learned this morning my teacher bonus was approved. So sometime before the end of the year, I'll be receiving a nice extra paycheck."

"But that's your money, Dean. You earned it."

He leans toward me and says, "Wrong. It's ours. And I'd choose to use it for the betterment of our family. Paige," he says firmly, "I want this for you. I want you to be happy."

"But I *am* happy." When I say it the truth dawns in my heart. "I've never been happier than I am right now, here with you."

"You could be happier still," he replies stubbornly. "I've been thinking a lot these past few days and about those comments you made concerning another life, a different reality."

My heart clenches. Oh no.

"Paige, honey," he says gently, "I get it. I do. I understand what you've been going through. Some kind of crisis about where we are. The things you've missed. But sweetheart, I want to help you fix this." He holds my hand tighter. "Look, I know Principal Peabody isn't scatterbrained on purpose, and at heart she's a nice person, but she makes your support job twice as difficult as it needs to be. Plus, you've taken on extra responsibilities. Gone above and beyond your stated role. It would be one thing if you really loved your job, and that's what you wanted to do, but it's not, is it?"

I hang my head, unable to look at him. He runs his thumb along the top of our linked hands. "Paige?" he asks, and I look up and meet his eyes.

"There are trade-offs."

"There don't have to be," he says. "That's what I'm telling you. Paige." He stares at me pleadingly. "You're the woman I love. I want you to have everything *you* love. And there's one thing I know about you—in here." He pats his chest. "You'd make an incredible teacher; I believe that profoundly. The kind students remember. The sort who helps shape lives."

My eyes prickle with tears. "Like you are," I murmur.

"I hope I make that kind of difference." He sighs, his fingers lacing around mine. "I guess only time will tell." He gives me that lopsided smile that I adore. "So what do you say, Paige Burton? Will you think about it?"

My breath catches. "I don't think I could be any more in love with you than I am right now." Talk about a dreamboat. If I'm dreaming, I hope I never wake up.

His whole face is a sunrise. "Then your answer is yes?"

Could I really have it all? A husband and kids I love, and the job I've aspired to forever. It seems too big of an ask of the universe. How could I get that lucky?

I see the answer sitting right across from me.

I got lucky when I met Dean.

"Thank you for supporting me." My lips tremble. "For loving me." Tears form hot pools in my eyes. "For being who you are." I can't believe that I've finally found my right life. It rips me to shreds that I might lose it. That I might lose Eleanor and Henry. Lose Dean.

"Of course I love you," he says with so much conviction, my heart aches.

Tears leak from my eyes then gush harder, pouring out like rivers. Rushing down my face, dribbling down my chin. I wipe them back with my cloth napkin, my mascara smearing the white linen fabric, and I sniff. Dab at my nose. Try so hard to still my rapidly beating heart.

"Paige?" Dean's face creases worriedly. "Are you all right?"

"Yes, fine." I collect myself and say, "Thank you for being so sweet."

His voice grows husky and I know he means it. "Thank you for being my wife."

I stare out the window at the lights of the holiday market. Though it's closed for the evening, its lights still glow. I need to go there first thing tomorrow morning and find Mary Christmas. If I beg, she'll have to tell me how I can stay. This can't be only temporary. I don't want it to be.

I want my unbelievably amazing husband. I want precious Eleanor, and sweet Henry, and loyal Scout. I want Mom to have found Roger. I want Dean's folks to be charming Gammy and Poppi. I want us all to have a very merry Kissmas. My breath shudders. I don't want to scrub this existence. I have to fight for my new life.

CHAPTER
Seventeen

*D*ean and *I* sit on the sofa holding hands by the light of the Christmas tree. Orange and purple coils of flame circle the logs in the fireplace and soft holiday music plays. A stubby pine-scented Christmas candle burns on the mantel, its short flame flitting back and forth and casting shadows along the walls. Between the scent of the candle and our natural Christmas tree, this part of the house smells like a lush pine forest. So holiday cheery.

After we got home, I changed out of my sexy dress and the Spanx—*thank goodness*—so I could breathe, and into some comfy sweatpants and a sweatshirt. Dean did the same, shedding his nice clothes for sweatpants and a T-shirt. I've still got my flirty underwear on, and it makes me feel daring, like I'm guarding a secret from Dean.

I hope we'll wind up in bed together again like we did last night, because Dean was amazing, and sweet, and sexy. My pulse hums. It was like no time had gone by between the two of us. Like we're meant to be together, and that's how it's always been.

"I'm really sorry I got emotional at dinner." I can't have him thinking I'm a basket case, falling apart at every kind gesture. Although, in fact, I am. He makes me feel so cherished, like I'm his fated one. It's a feeling that I'll never take for granted anymore.

"Don't even think about it." His eyes shimmer in the firelight. "I get emotional myself."

"Do *not*."

Caring? Thoughtful? Yes.

Direct with your emotions? Absolutely.

Overly gushy? No.

His mouth pulls into a lopsided grin. "Okay, fine. But that doesn't mean I don't feel things, too."

Maybe when we were younger, I didn't understand what we had. Maybe neither of us did completely. Now that our relationship has matured, it's only gotten better, it seems. He undoes me with his kindness, and the way he kisses me sends me to the moon.

"I know you do." My fingers tighten around his. There's so much I want to know. So many gaps I want filled in. He's poured us each a scotch and our glasses sit on the coffee table, ice cubes melting in the heat from the fire and turning the straw-colored liquid a paler gold.

He's such a wonderful dad to Eleanor and Henry, and I believe him when he says he wouldn't take any of this back. If I could remember this version of my past, I'm sure I wouldn't have regrets, either. Still. I want him to have more. Everything he needs.

"Dean?" I lean my shoulder against his arm and lay my head on his shoulder.

"Hmm?"

"I know you say Puerto Rico doesn't matter, but I'm still sorry you missed the opportunity. It doesn't seem right that I can go back to school and recoup my teaching dream when you've lost yours."

He dips his head to peer in my eyes. "I haven't lost mine."

I've been thinking about this ever since we left the restaurant. I want to be able to support Dean the way he supports me. Assuming I'm allowed to stay here, and I intend to leave no stone unturned in making that happen.

"Maybe there's still a way for you, too?" I say. "A fellowship or something, like Wendy—?"

"Who's Wendy?" He wrinkles up his face. "Wait. Didn't you mention her before?"

I purse my lips. "Er. Did I? Hmm. Funny. I'm not sure? I thought you'd said she was a colleague of some sort. Someone who'd gotten a physics grant?"

He considers this and shakes his head. "No. Don't think so." He reaches for our drinks, handing me my short tumbler and picking his up. "Maybe I'm remembering wrong," he says, leaning back on the sofa.

But I'm the one with the memory issues, not him. I want him to know everything. How my life has changed, and how much being here matters. How I've fallen head over heels for him, and our kids, and our dog, but that sounds so wrong. He'll be crushed that I can't recall their births and the intricate details of every birthday, the holidays and anniversaries we've shared, and the memories of the family we've created together. What I can do is encourage him to make the most of this life, like he's been encouraging me.

Part of me is dying to tell him about my other world, the place that I've come from, but my heart aches because I know he won't understand. He's already reasoned it out to believe my crisis was about giving up teaching, and now he's trying to help me reach that dream. I can't bring the alternate reality up again at this point, because that will only make him believe I'm unhappy in our marriage again, when nothing could be farther from the truth.

I'm happier now than I've ever been. Giving Dean any indication to the contrary would be a lie. I also can't hurt him. I won't. And if that makes our being together in some ways tougher on me, so be it. I want to make things easier for him.

I rest my glass of scotch on my sweatpants leg, and the tumbler's weighty, a bit chilly. "What I'm trying to say is, maybe you should look into it? There could be research or work opportunities for high school science teachers. Summer programs? Fellowships?"

The dimple in his cheek deepens. "What about you and the kids?"

"We'd come with you! Make it an adventure! Eleanor hasn't started kindergarten yet and will be out during the summer anyway."

"And Scout?" He stares at our sleeping pup by the fire.

I sigh. "Maybe your folks wouldn't mind watching him for a short while?"

"You're right. They really love that dog; they'd probably take him in."

"So?" I ask. "You'll think about it?"

He winks and happiness grows inside me. "Sure."

I can't wait to get to the consignment stop tomorrow and purchase that telescope. I'm even more determined about speaking with Mary Christmas, too. If anyone can help me, it's got to be her. Could the Christmas candle on the table at the restaurant really have been a coincidence? I know it's a nice Italian place and candles on the table are typical there, but not *that kind of candle* in such a specific-looking holder. *Enjoy*, Mary Christmas said. I am enjoying being here—so much. But I'm wrecked that I can't know the building blocks of this life. I wish I could remember the many moments that brought us here from that night on my apartment stoop when I was twenty years old and saying goodbye.

Curiosity niggles at me about our past. "What made you come back?" I ask Dean, hoping he won't mind sharing. "That morning when you were going to the airport?"

He takes a sip of scotch and sighs. This seems like a story he's shared with me before, but it's a bittersweet memory. I can tell he doesn't mind repeating it, as part of our history that helped shape where we are.

"I was already at my gate after having gotten through security," he says. "Then they started boarding the plane. People needing assistance and those with young children first."

He turns to look at me, and the fond recollection plays out on his face. "There was this cute young family. A mom and dad with a toddler girl in a stroller. They seemed to be juggling all sorts of baby paraphernalia, including a large diaper bag. They appeared somewhat disheveled, and very harried. And yet. Their love was so clear. For each other. For their family."

He sets down his glass and takes mine, placing it beside his on the coffee table. He turns toward me on the sofa, speaking gently. "That's when I knew," he whispers, "I wanted that kind of life with you."

A lump forms in my throat.

"I couldn't lose you, Paige." His hand cups my cheek, his face so near. "You were the love of my life." A tender smile. "Still are."

"Oh, Dean."

He sweeps back my hair with his fingers, centers his palm at the base of my neck. "I knew I couldn't go," he mutters hoarsely. Electric tingles course through me, making me feel so alive, so cared for. Adored.

I lick my lips. "So you came back."

"You were so surprised when I knocked on the door and you saw me standing there with my duffel bag. But you didn't hesitate, not even for a second. You leapt right into my arms and started crying, saying how badly you hadn't wanted me to go. Holding on so tightly my heart exploded with happiness, because I knew I'd made the right choice.

"That's when I said I'd never leave you." He leans closer, his breath raking over my lips. "And I meant that." He gently brings his lips to mine in a kiss so silky smooth, my insides melt like butter. I don't know *what* I was thinking. How could I ever have believed that our breaking up was the best thing for the two of us? What's best for me and Dean is the two of us together.

He wraps his arms around me, and I hold on to him, never wanting to let him go. I let him go that one time, but I shouldn't have. If he hadn't come back for me, maybe I should have gone after him. But no, I couldn't do that, because I didn't want to destroy his dream. Rob him of his future. The future I believed he'd wanted until now. He kisses me again, and I sigh into his kisses as they become stronger, deeper. A different sort of future becoming clear. I'm overcome with emotion, love, and longing.

"I love you, Dean," I murmur between kisses.

"I love you, too." He holds me closer. "So, so much." He tugs my sweatshirt over my head and my bra straps slip on my shoulders. "Nice," he growls softly. "Sexy." His finger trails down my cleavage and the bra's fabric dips.

"Just wait till you see the thong."

His laugh is gravelly, low. "Can't wait." I lean back on the sofa, and he helps tug off my sweatpants. Flames leap through me like brittle twigs catching fire, spreading heat across my breasts and down my torso and thighs.

In an instant he's out of his T-shirt and sweatpants too and wearing only his briefs. I cast a glance at the hall. "Should we go back to the—"

His mouth meets my stomach, moves lower in traveling kisses. Tantalizing nibbles. Heat pools in my belly and seeps lower.

My pulse flutters. *"Dean."*

"Love the thong." He looks up and slides his hands under my bare butt.

We hear a scuttling sound in the hall.

Henry.

Ahhh! I clamp my knees shut, trapping Dean's head between them, and Dean wrenches free from their stronghold—*yank!*— sending his hair spiking skyward, his eyes wild and wide. He grabs my sweatshirt off the floor, hurling it on top of me, and I quickly cover my chest, search for my bra. *On the coffee table. There!* I snatch it up and shove it into the sweatshirt's front pouch, scoot into a sitting position.

"Buddy, hey," Dean says coolly. "What are you doing up?" The child stands between the hall and the fireplace, rubbing his eyes with a fist and holding Nessie by the neck in the other.

"I'm t'irsty," Henry says like a sleepy little nugget. Dean scrambles to the floor and into his sweatpants, tugging them up over his briefs. "I'll take him," he says. "You wait here."

I giggle at the situation, positioning the sweatshirt around me, stretching it out here and there to cover strategic places. "Maybe I should wait in the bedroom?"

"Ah yeah. Good point!" He winks and scuttles toward Henry. "All right, buddy. Let's get you a drink from your bathroom cup." My insides stir at the sight of Dean striding bare-chested across the room. He's incredibly well built, trim but muscled.

I bury my face in my hands, thinking that was a close call. Things clearly aren't like they were in the old days—pre-kids. We'll need to be more careful. I tug on my sweatshirt and pick up our drinks, carrying them down the hall. I pass Henry and Dean in the bathroom on the way.

"I gotta pee!"

Dean pulls a toilet target from the box as I sneak past them, angling my bare backside away from the open door. I pause and peek into Eleanor's room, where Scout's crept up on the bed. He's curled himself into a big furry ball and sleeps peacefully at her feet. I quietly crack open our bedroom door, carrying both glasses of scotch to my bedside table. The lights are off except the one in our bathroom, which sheds a tempered glow across the carpet and bed. I creep over to the cinnamon candle on my dresser and strike a match, holding it to the wick.

When Dean returns, I've removed my sweatshirt and wait under the covers. "Sorry about that." He strips off his clothes in the faint, wavering light, and I get a glimpse of his incredibly fine form. Hunger stirs inside me, a deep, primitive need. We might be Mommy and Daddy to Henry and Eleanor. But between the two of us, we're still lovers. We've never lost our touch. Thank goodness. I chuckle at the memory of Dean saying he'd broken the other thong.

"Now. Where were we?" He cradles me in his strong arms, and I scooch into position underneath him, his chest hair teasing my bare skin. The weight of him so solid against me. My excitement builds. I hike up my hips. "Right—here?"

His eyes sparkle sweetly, and he kisses my lips, easing himself lower. Lower. My pulse pounds and my head whirls.

I am so ready.

He reaches down to peel off my thong, and I help him. Working harder. Faster. Pushing, shoving. Tugging. My fingers claw over his, grab the writhing fabric. He grabs too but pulls in the opposite direction.

Wait.

I shake my leg when the thong tightens around my ankle. "Ow."

It twists harder. "*Ouch!*" I hiss quietly. "*Dean.*"

"*Ooh! Sorry!*" he rasps, but still, he yanks.

He tugs harder and my leg shoots skyward, my knee locking and tenting the covers. "Dean!" I dart a glance at the closed bedroom door. "I'm losing circulation." The darn thing's like a tourniquet.

"That's why I ripped the last one," he grumbles. "Hang on." He throws back the bedclothes and I huddle my arms across my chilly chest. But the more he seems to pull, the tighter the tourniquet winds. Tighter. Tighter. "Ouch! Ow. *Ow-wee.*"

"Dean." I clench my teeth. "Stop."

"Your foot's turning blue," he comments.

I sit up and stare at the frilly thong, knotted impossibly around my ankle. No wonder. You can't even tell it's an undergarment anymore. It looks like one of Missy Peabody's torture toys. Okay, I flush that thought from my mind. I do *not* need to be thinking about my eccentric "Boss Lady" and her sexual exploits right now. I need to focus on mine. I open my nightstand drawer and hand Dean the scissors.

"Aha!" he says like he's done this before.

I cower back on my elbows when he grabs my foot. "Careful."

Then—with a *snip-snap*—he frees my leg. Tosses the dastardly thong on the floor. "There goes Tuesday," he says as we both watch it fall.

I chuckle and collapse against the pillows. "*How* did we ever make Henry and Eleanor?"

"Want a refresher course?" he asks, clambering on top of me.

I nod eagerly.

"All right."

I melt into his kisses, my heart so full.

He pulls the covers over us and takes my breath away.

CHAPTER
Eighteen

I ***creep out of*** bed while Dean's still sleeping. My handsome, bare-chested husband snuggled under the covers. Just thinking of him as my husband fills me with a happy honeymooner vibe. I traipse quietly to the bathroom and shower and wash my hair. I'm so excited for this day and what it will bring. *Christmas Eve.*

The kids slumber peacefully when I pass their rooms. Scout hears me in the hall and perks up his head, slowly climbs down off Eleanor's bed and lopes across her room. "Morning, boy," I whisper and gently pat his head.

He follows me toward the kitchen, and I note the Christmas tree lights still shine. We forgot to unplug them last night, but the fire in the fireplace has burned down to ash. A piney scent fills the air. *Eeep!* I tiptoe over and blow out the candle on the mantel then unplug the Christmas tree. I smile to myself, knowing Dean and I were in such a hurry to get to bed after Henry's minor interruption, we forgot nearly everything else.

Sigh. Kids.

Double sigh. My super sexy husband.

Scout and I trot into the kitchen, and I feed him his kibbles from the giant can with a snap-on lid near the door. Give him fresh water. I'm waiting on the coffee to brew and mentally planning my morning when something cold presses against my blue jeans above my knee. I laugh and look down. Scout's brought in the paper.

"Good boy!" I take the paper from him and set it on the counter, sliding it out of its plastic sleeve and opening it to the front page. The date and year seem accurate, but everything else about this existence is new and almost too *awesome* to be true.

I've got to find a way to stay here. I don't want to go back to my ultra-planned life. Even if I have to postpone starting my charity, I've decided that's okay. *Everything in its place and all things in good time.* There's no reason I can't undertake the same steps at Walton to establish the Paws and Read program here like I did there. It will just take longer. I'll need to earn my degree first and become an established and respected teacher before I can propose starting something as ambitious as a countywide literacy initiative.

Going back to college will be extra work, but not as much as it seems, because I've basically done those same teacher courses before. Same with setting up Paws and Read. The first time was a learning curve. The second should run like clockwork. And since Mom's healthy here, I can take pains to ensure she gets regular checkups so she stays that way. I want this life—complete with its chaos and extra family demands, its unfolded laundry. Our cute little house and our very sweet dog. I'm going to speak with Mary Christmas to see if she can share some clues about how I might change things. Not just for the better, but *for good*.

The coffee maker beeps that it's ready and I fix myself a cup, adding sugar and creamer. The new concoction has grown on me, truthfully, and the one-two punch of sweetness and caffeine does a stellar job of waking me up. The advent calendar catches my eye and I see it's nearly complete. Just one more item needs to be added to the felt Christmas tree: the jolly Santa Claus face.

I take a sip of coffee, bracing myself for the day ahead. It's going to be busy, between my errands this morning and meeting Mom for coffee. We've got the kids' Christmas pageant at church this evening, then it's hopefully an early bedtime for them so Dean and I can get Santa gifts ready. I hadn't realized we'd need to assemble Eleanor's bike and Henry's riding car. Those things could take work, and time. But I don't mind volunteering for either thing. As long as I'm with Dean, I'm happy. It will be a project night for the two of us together.

I fix my husband his coffee and carry it stealthily down the hall and into the bedroom. He groggily opens his eyes and sits up partway when he sees me walk through the door. "Well, hey! You're up early." He blinks and stares at my wet hair. "Have you showered already?" He props himself up against the headboard using some pillows and I take him his coffee.

"I have." I hand him his mug. "I've got some errands to run this morning," I say, strolling over to partially raise the blinds. It's snowing again, but not heavily.

"More errands?" he teases. "Mysterious."

"Ha. Yeah." I sit down beside him holding my coffee mug. "Plus, I'm meeting Mom for coffee." Before, I'd planned to use the occasion to talk Mom out of running away with Roger. Now that I've seen how happy the two of them are together, I simply can't do that. Not when I understand what it feels like to be head over heels in love myself.

"That's right. You're finalizing your Christmas menu." He sips from his mug. "What kind of salad is she bringing this year?"

"Umm, not sure, actually."

Dean's eyes shine when he says, "Everyone's looking forward to your world-famous lasagna."

"What? We're not having turkey?" I saw the photo evidence on my phone of Dean carving a great big bird.

He laughs and shakes his head. "Good one."

I wasn't joking. "Sorry?"

"Paige, are you getting your holidays mixed up? You know we always have turkey at Thanksgiving. We're doing what we do every year," he answers. "Having my folks, my sister, Jenny, and your mom over for Christmas dinner."

"For lasagna?" I say, still wrapping my head around it.

He wrinkles his brow. "Are you worried about the groceries? Oh gosh." Dean frowns. "You haven't had time to shop yet, have you?"

I raise a shoulder. Not unless I did that before December twentieth. "Ahh."

"Tell you what," Dean says kindly. "Why don't you let me do the grocery shopping while you run your errands. I can take the kids with me. It's no big deal. I'll get everything you need."

"You don't, um, need me to make a list?"

Please say no. Please, please, please. Please. I have no clue about what goes into my "world-famous lasagna" besides, well, obviously lasagna noodles and sauce. I hope it's not too much of a bear to make. Maybe I use a premade sauce?

"Nope," Dean says. "I've got it." His eyes twinkle warmly. "Including all the ingredients for your delicious homemade sauce."

My nose twitches anxiously and I rub it. "Yay!"

"Don't worry about the rest of the meal," Dean says. "My folks are bringing dessert and extra wine, and I assume your mom's supplying her usual bread and a salad. Though this year…" A dimpled grin. "I suspect she'll bring Roger as well."

"Sounds spectacular."

"Always is." He leans forward to kiss me. "And don't worry about any mess you might make. As per our deal, I'll do the cleaning up."

"Mommy! Daddy!" Eleanor rushes through the doorway holding her Highland cow and pouncing on the bed. Dean and I steady our mugs when our coffees slosh. Scout follows her with leaps and bounds and a "*Woof! Woof! Woof!*" as he lumbers onto the bed and scrambles over Dean's legs tucked under the covers.

"Morning, pumpkin," Dean says and tussles the top of Eleanor's head. Her hair is long and loose this morning. Before I go out, I'll braid it and get her dressed. I'll also help get Henry ready for his day, too. Since Dean will be watching them later, it's the least I can do. Dean strokes Scout's back. "Did you get the paper for Mom?"

He barks and sits down, and I confirm with a nod. "He did."

Henry stands on the threshold with his Nessie, grinning from ear to ear. He throws up his hands, squeezing Nessie around the neck on one side. "Merry Kissmas!" he shouts, his toddler cry bouncing off the ceiling.

I set down my coffee mug and hold out my arms, and Henry rushes toward me, scrambling up on the bed. I tug him into my lap and hug him as he giggles. "Almost." I kiss the top of his head.

Dean winks and my heart warms. "Tomorrow, it will be a Merry Kissmas for real."

"I know," I say happily. "Can't wait."

A short time later, we stand in the kitchen by the advent calendar. Upon reflection, Dean and I calculate that yesterday should have been Eleanor's turn when I put up the Christmas candle instead of her, so she should go today. But Eleanor generously steps aside. "Henry can do it," she says in such a sweet way my insides go all mushy. *Our little girl is growing up.*

Dean smiles at me and then her. "Very nice of you Eleanor," he says, picking up Henry. "Okay, buddy! Go for the Santa!" Henry digs his chubby fist into the pocket for Day Twenty-Four and plunks Santa near the top of the tree when Dean hoists him higher.

Eleanor cheers, "Yay!"

I grin at the kids and say, "Santa comes tonight."

Dean takes the jeep to get groceries with the kids, so I drive my old hatchback. It's not a far distance to downtown from our house and mostly flat driving, so the old clunker does fine. I park at a curb near the town square and more snow starts up the minute I get out of the car. My purse hangs from the crook of my arm and it's heavy, weighted down with currency. I intend to stop by the bank before visiting the consignment shop. It won't do for me to make the purchase in numerous coins and low-denomination bills. But first, I need to find Mary Christmas.

The festive lights of the holiday market are ahead of me, and I keep my eye on the large tent as I approach. I pass the person popping popcorn and the vendor selling French hot chocolate, peering through the crowd. Mary Christmas's table should be straight ahead of me, right at the point where this larger tent joins one of the smaller ones in the U-shape. But funny. I don't see her, or her trademark advent calendars, anywhere. My boots scurry beneath me as I start walking faster. I felt so sure I knew where her booth was, but I must be remembering wrong. I stare around the vibrant space but still don't spot her. Where is she?

I stop by the table of the artist who sold me the tin earrings I purchased for Mom. "Excuse me?" I ask her. "Have you seen the lady who sells the advent calendars?"

"I'm sorry, who?" Her face is blank, and my panic spikes.

I know I saw Mary Christmas here only a few days ago. I didn't dream her, even if I'm dreaming this! *She was in this dream.* "Mary Christmas?"

The artist smiles warmly. "Merry Christmas to you. Hey, didn't I sell you a pair of earrings last week?"

"Yes, yes. And they're so pretty. Thanks so much. My mom loved them. But I was here on Sunday, too."

"This past Sunday?" She narrows her eyes, searching her memory. "Hmm."

That was only three days ago, but I suppose her booth stays busy with lots of customers. I attempt to jog her memory. "I asked you about the advent calendar lady. You said her name was Mary Christmas, spelled M-A-R-Y."

She adjusts her colorful scarf with gold threads woven through it. "I'm not really sure—"

I'm starting to feel desperate. "She was dressed like Mrs. Claus?"

"Oh!" She glances at the other side of the tent. "You mean the woman who helps Santa?"

"Er, yes. Maybe?" I nervously shift my weight from one foot to the other. "That could be her."

The artist points to a person dressed as Santa Claus sitting in an area set up to look like the North Pole. Kids gather with adults to get their photos taken with the jolly old elf. "You might want to check down that way?" she says.

"Okay. Thank you." I sidestep through the crowd, my heart pounding. Where is Mary Christmas and that booth of hers? The one with all the advent calendars? I reach a younger woman in an elf hat. She looks like a teenager taking a winter-break job. She's busy organizing photos and sliding them into envelopes. They're of Santa with various children. "I'm sorry to bother you," I say.

She looks up. "I'm afraid the line to take photos with Santa is over there." She gestures to an area by a velvet rope where guardians and kids wait patiently for their turn with Santa. Another worker, also in an elf hat, helps guide them along. A third wields a digital camera, maximizing photo ops with each new child.

"Uh, no. You don't understand." I loosen my wool scarf. "I'm looking for Mrs. Claus."

The teenager laughs. "You'll have to ask Santa about her."

"Haha, yes." Normally I wouldn't mind this light banter, but at the moment it's making me antsy, like I'm wasting my time, when what I need to be doing is finding Mary Christmas. I glance over at Santa. "Do you think it would be okay if I ask him a question?"

The teen checks her watch. "If you don't take long. We don't want to hold up the line."

"Great, thanks!"

I bustle to the head of the line, inviting scowls from a few kids and more than one mom. "Oh no! I'm not butting in," I tell them. "I just have a quick question for—" I turn, and Santa's stood from his chair, hands on his hips.

"I'm sorry, ma'am," he says. "You'll need to wait in line like the others." He doesn't seem very Santa-like. He doesn't even give me a *ho, ho, ho*. I can tell the beard is fake. So is his snowy white hair. My spirit sinks. He's an actor.

"I just wanted to ask you a quick question, *Santa*." My heart deflates like a balloon with all the air going out of it, because I know I'm grasping at straws. What would a paid actor know about real holiday magic, or time splits? Likely nothing at all.

"You're taking time away from the kids," he whispers behind his glove. "Will you please move aside?"

"But!" Two elves walk toward me like sports bar bouncers. "I just want to know about Mary Christmas!" I realize how loony that sounds. "The lady who sells the advent calendars?"

Santa gives me a steely look like I've landed on his naughty list. Gee. I hold up my hands and back away. "I'm sorry. I've made a mistake."

Santa holds his round middle and smiles at the child behind me. "Ho, ho, ho! Who's next?" he asks as I retreat.

Tears brim in my eyes. I'm at such a loss. This can't be the end of things. It can't.

Someone taps my shoulder. "You're looking for Mary Christmas?"

I turn and it's *her.*

"Yes! Thank goodness!" I say with a grateful sigh of relief.

Her eyes twinkle merrily behind her wire-rimmed glasses. "What can I do for you, Paige?"

"I—don't want to go back! Please, not yet," I say, the truth pouring out of me. "Tomorrow's Christmas Day, and I want to stay here."

"*Here* here?" she asks.

"With all my heart. Mrs. Christmas," I gush out, "I thought I had a good life, a life I worked for. I had important responsibilities too, but there are things *here* I can't let go. I've fallen in love with all of them. With Dean. With Eleanor. With Henry. And Scout. With this wonderfully happy version of Mom, and Gammy and Poppi. For goodness' sake, even this new version of myself!" I'm babbling so hurriedly, I'm tripping over my words. "I don't know exactly how your special advent calendar changed my life. But whatever kind of miracle it was that brought me here, I don't want it to end."

"So you believe you've earned your chance for this Christmas?"

"Yes."

"All right!" she says and my spirit soars. I can't believe it was that easy.

I throw my arms around her in a hug and stumble forward through thin air.

What? I blink and stare around the tent. "I'm sorry," the teenage elf says, "you're blocking traffic. You'll need to clear out of the way."

"But—but, Mary Christmas," I inform her. "She was right—"

The girl scrunches up her face and eyes me dubiously. "No. It was just you."

"What?" Impossible. I gawk at Santa in his chair and the line of parents and kids. No one pays me any mind, almost like I'm not here myself. I pat down my arms and the front of my coat to make sure I am. I feel real enough to me. But where is Mary Christmas?

"Ma'am?" the teen elf says.

I step aside numbly, not knowing what's happened.

Did it work?

Have I claimed my new life?

CHAPTER
Nineteen

put my purchase for Dean in the back of my hatchback and shut the door, so grateful to have still found the telescope in the window of Second Chances and available for sale. Cuppa Joe's not far from here, only a few blocks away and down a side street. Snow lightly drifts through the air and passersby wear happy faces. If only I weren't racked with nerves about getting to stay in this reality. I hope I'm right in thinking that Mary Christmas has granted my wish. I decide to try talking to Mom about my situation one more time in hopes that she can reassure me.

She's already sitting at a table with her coffee when I arrive. I wave and order a cup of coffee for myself before joining her. She watches me dump packets of sugar in my cup. "When did you start taking your coffee like that?"

"On Saturday." It's so hard to believe that was less than a week ago, since my whole life has changed. I can't imagine how different I'll feel after an entire month's gone by, *a year.*

"Well, watch the sugar," she says. "It will make you edgy."

I might need to be souped up for this conversation, but I

decide to ease into it and not drop the whole wad on her at once. "The kids' pageant is tonight."

"Yes, I know." She sits back in her chair. "I'm really looking forward to it."

"Yeah, us too." I smile at how time has flown. "Santa comes tonight."

"And tomorrow's Christmas," she says with a happy sigh.

I snap the lid on my coffee cup after stirring in the cream and sugar. "So you're bringing the salad tomorrow?"

"Yes. I was planning to go simple. Will a Greek salad be all right?"

"That sounds yummy."

"We'll also bring a couple of baguettes." She drinks from her coffee. "Roger can't wait to try your lasagna. I've raved and raved about it."

Ah, so here's my opening. I take a sip of coffee and set down my cup.

"Mom," I say honestly. "I really like Roger."

Her face lights up. "You do?"

"So does Dean."

She grins happily. "You don't know how glad I am to hear it, Paige. He makes me feel like a teenager falling in love for the first time all over again."

I reach out and touch her arm. "It shows."

She lifts a shoulder. "So you're okay with things then? About my move?"

"I want you to do what makes you happy."

"Oh, Paige."

"But, Mom," I say earnestly. "Please wear a life vest."

She laughs warmly. "Of course!"

I spin my coffee cup around in my hands, gathering my nerve. "Mom?" I ask seriously. "Have you ever had a situation where you were so happy, you were afraid of it being taken away from you?"

I expect her to say no, because Mom is never afraid. She's happy-go-lucky. A glass-half-full kind of girl. She stares out the café's front window at the falling snow. After a beat she says solemnly, "Yes. I've always worried about losing you."

My heart hammers. "Me? Mom." I'm almost too stunned to speak. "That will never happen."

Her eyes glimmer sadly. "There was a time when you were a teenager when I felt like you were drifting away. You didn't understand me and maybe judged me for being different."

"Well, I'm sorry about that now." I take her hand on the table. "I really am."

"You're a very good daughter, " she says. "You know that?"

"Thanks. You're a great mom."

"Paige?" She looks down at the table and then up at me. "Is everything okay between you and Dean? Because when we went to lunch last Saturday, you said some things that concerned me. Then I saw the two of you together on Sunday, and your relationship appeared better. You two were even more together-seeming at the ice skating rink."

"Oh Mom," I blurt out. "I love him so much, I do."

"Well then." She holds open her hands on the table. "What's the problem?"

I blink back the heat in my eyes. "The problem is I fear it won't last."

"Honey." She meets my eyes. "Dean adores you and your family."

"I'm not talking about him." I purse my lips. "I'm talking about me."

"Oh." She looks startled. "I see." She lowers her voice and asks quietly, "Have you found someone else, Paige?"

Yes, me.

The me I love better.

But I can't tell her that.

"No. It's just, Mom. I know you didn't believe me about being here from another reality when we had lunch the other day—"

"Oh dear, sweetheart. Are you on that again?"

Tears brim in my eyes. "But what if it's true? What if I wake up tomorrow, or the next day, and everything I love is gone?"

She sets her chin and says gamely, "Well then, you'll just have to get it back, won't you?" Understanding settles over me.

She's right. I can't give up. I gave up on Dean once before and that was wrong.

I'm not going to do it again.

"You hold on to what is good, Paige Burton." She winks warmly. "Never forget that."

I cross my fingers and lay them against my heart, not wanting to forget. Not wanting to let these things go. Knowing that Mom is right. I've got to hold on to the great things in my life, no matter what it takes. "Thanks, Mom."

Dean and I hurry the kids out the door and into the drifting snow, Eleanor's puffy coat pulled around her shoulders and over her pretty powder blue gown and shimmery angel's wings. Henry's got his shepherd's garb on, and Dean carries him along with his short shepherd's crook through the darkened evening. Their Gammy sewed their costumes and did a great job. Dean opens the back door to his jeep so we can situate the kids in their car seats. "I can't believe it's Christmas Eve."

"I know. It came up so fast!" Everything has been a whirlwind since I landed here. Has it only been five short days? I woke up in this life in total shock, but already I can't imagine myself anywhere else. I don't want to be anywhere else. I hope that Mary Christmas was right and that I'll get to stay. It would be devastating to leave all this behind.

Dean and I buckle ourselves in and he navigates the jeep out of the drive. As many times as he's shoveled the driveway, the snow keeps on coming. Although the layer on the driveway now is extremely thin. We should be able to clear it enough tomorrow for the kids to try out their new toys, even if only briefly. I can't believe I'm making a lasagna. I've never made the dish from scratch. Hopefully it won't be too taxing. And it's nice that Dean's folks and Mom are bringing the rest of the meal.

"What time is dinner tomorrow?" I ask Dean. That will be a lot of people to pack into our cozy cottage, but I suppose we'll manage, likely by eating buffet style. The kitchen table's not large. We can't all squeeze in around that.

He stops at the end of the drive before backing onto the street, checking both ways—and in his rearview camera—for traffic. The windshield wipers sweep back and forth across the glass and the heater blasts full force. "Don't we usually say four?" he answers. "That's for folks to arrive, then we sit down at five."

"Yeah. Sounds good." Also sounds like plenty of time for me to get the lasagna together, after sharing a nice, relaxing Christmas morning with Dean and the kids. I glance at our homey house before we drive away. We've left the Christmas tree lights on and they cast a cheery glow against the front window. We've also got the holiday icicle lights draped from the roof of the front porch and a cheery Christmas wreath on the door. Scout puts his paws up on the windowsill by the rocker and peers out at us. "Bye, Scout!" I say.

Eleanor waves with her mittens, and Henry waves, too.

I love our little house.

I love our *life*.

I don't want to lose it.

Dean and I sit by the aisle in one of the front rows at the church. Mom and Roger are beside us, and Miriam and Jack are on the other side of them. This old stone church is historic and smallish, so we take up nearly an entire pew, which seats eight in a crunch. Christmas greenery lines the center aisle and LED candles glow on the windowsills below tall stained glass windows. A manger scene's been established in front of the altar and an older boy, probably upper elementary age, reads Scripture from Luke 2:8–14. New King James Version.

"Now there were in the same country shepherds living out in the fields, keeping watch over their flock by night."

A group of children parade down the center aisle dressed as shepherds. An older girl helps Henry along, guiding him by the hand. My heart swells with pride and I nudge Dean. We grin at Henry, who grins, too. Mom and Gammy and Poppi wave. Roger—nods.

"And behold!" the reader says. "An angel of the Lord stood before them." Eleanor arrives down the center aisle, positioning herself near the empty wooden cradle and facing the shepherds. "And the glory of the Lord shone around them, and they were greatly afraid. Then the angel said to them…" Eleanor opens her arms, holding them high, and her wire wings flutter. "'Do not be afraid, for behold, I bring you good tidings of great joy.'"

I peek at the grandparents and Roger, who watch raptly.

The reader continues, "'There is born this day in the city of David a Savior, who is Christ the Lord.'" Two kids dressed as Mary and Joseph carry a baby doll down the center aisle and place him in the wooden cradle, kneeling silently behind it with their heads bowed forward.

A tear escapes Roger's eye, and he wipes it back.

"'And this will be a sign to you: You will find a Babe wrapped in swaddling cloths, lying in a manger,'" the reader says.

Eleanor gestures grandly to the cradle, and her wings spring back and forth at her shoulders. "She's a natural," I whisper to Dean.

He takes my hand and holds it. So happy. The proud dad.

The reader completes the passage. "And suddenly there was with the angel a multitude of the heavenly host praising God and saying: 'Glory to God in the highest, and on earth peace, goodwill toward men!'"

The reader closes his Bible, and the minister rises to the pulpit. Turns up his palms when the organ plays. We stand to sing "Angels We Have Heard on High" while children holding wicker baskets distribute narrow white candles with protective paper discs at their bases to the crowd. After another hymn, a family lights the final candle in the advent wreath on the altar, and the minister encourages the congregation to share their light—and the good news—with the world.

The lights dim as adult congregation members walk down the center aisle holding flickering tapers and lighting the candles of those standing closest to the center aisle in the pews. Each person in turn lights the candle of the person standing next to them.

Dean lights mine and I light Mom's. Mom lights Roger's…

Soon, we're singing "Silent Night" and holding our candles high.

The children's minister bends low and instructs the kids in the pageant. They disperse to join their families in the pews. "Great job," Dean tells Eleanor as she scoots in between us. Dean moves over a bit and Henry squishes in on his other side. "Nice going, buddy," Dean whispers, patting his back. Candlelight wavers among us and sweet, sonorous tones fill the air.

I stare down at the kids and then over at Mom, Roger, Miriam, and Jack. Everyone's faces hold happy glows, and I'm filled with a sense of peace. Like I'm in the right place and at the right time. I close my eyes and say a silent prayer, wishing to stay here—always.

CHAPTER
Twenty

ho knew assembling a bike could be so hard? Dean and I fixate on the directions spread out in front of us on the floor. I squat, anchoring the seat on Eleanor's bike with my hands. Dean attempts to secure it.

He grabs a wrench and a bolt. "I think this one goes—no, wait." He squints and picks up another bolt, holding it up to examine it in the light. We're in front of the fireplace, and Dean's built a fire. The coffee table's been moved to the far side of the room, and we have boxes open. Since I hadn't spied any large packages around the house, I should have guessed Dean had stowed these larger gifts in the garden shed.

"Try that one over there." I hitch my chin to a spot by his knee.

"Aha!" He holds it up and tries it. His grin melts my heart. "It fits."

Thank goodness.

He gets the seat fastened tightly and tests it. "Okay." He dusts off his palms. "Almost done. What's next?"

I take the directions and flip them over. "Streamers for the handlebars, then the basket." I lift a shiny object off the floor. "And this bright bell." It *dings* when I move it, and Dean and I freeze. Set our jaws. Listen for footsteps. Stealthily peek at the hall. He sends me a look and I'm ready. If it's one of the kids, he'll somehow cover up things in here as I dash them back to bed.

Scout lazily lopes into the room, blinks, and surveys his surroundings. Dean and I don't move a muscle. The dog slouches low and turns, heading back down the hall.

Dean blows out a breath. "Whew."

I sigh. "When are we going to have that eggnog?" I ask, because he mentioned it earlier, saying he'd bought some at the store.

"As soon as we finish the bike."

Henry's Hot Ride stands by the tree with a gigantic blue bow on its roof. That one was a *lot* easier to put together than the bike. All we had to do was snap on the wheel brackets and doors. I fish the streamers out of an oblong box and pass one set to Dean. They have cone inserts on one end that fits right into the handlebars. Dean and I each take a side. Then I work on attaching the basket. I let him tackle the bell. I don't dare take a chance on touching it again.

We stand back to admire our handiwork. Eleanor's cute red bike shines in the firelight, steadied on two training wheels.

Dean beams happily. "I think she'll love it."

I cross my arms and ask, "Stockings next?"

"Yeah, why not?" he says. "Let's get everything wrapped up and then relax with our drinks."

We pick up the mess in the living room and return the coffee table to its spot. Dean said he and I were going to exchange our gifts tonight, and I'm ready. I giftwrapped his telescope while he was out shoveling snow this afternoon and hid it in my closet. I'll stuff his Christmas stocking with the candies I bought him and the starry night mug. Also, an orange, because that's apparently what we do around here.

We quietly carry some packages in from the bedroom, and I show Dean the hand puppets I bought the kids at the holiday market. A Santa puppet for Eleanor and an elf one for Henry.

"Those are cute." He puts the Santa one on his hand and says, "Ho, ho, ho, Merry Christmas!"

I stand up on my toes to kiss him. "Oh, you." My heart is so full I don't know how it can get any fuller. Playing Santa with Dean is so much fun.

He grins. "I can't wait to see Henry's face when we tell him it really is 'Kissmas.'"

I chuckle. "I know what you mean. He's at such a precious stage." My heart warms thinking of him and his sister. "Eleanor is too."

"All their stages are precious," Dean says.

"Maybe up until now," I warn him. "We don't know how they'll behave as teenagers."

"True." He shoves candies and toys into the kids' stockings while I fill Scout's with doggie treats and a superbly durable new ball.

I top Eleanor's and Henry's stockings with their puppets and Dean hangs them back on the mantel. There are two empty stockings left, his and mine. "So," he says casually. "Should I go make our eggnogs?"

"Eggnog sounds good."

"Bourbon or rum?" he asks lightly.

Yum, both sound scrumptious. It's hard to decide.

"Ooh, bourbon, please."

Dean plucks one of the empty stockings off the mantel and tucks it in his rear jeans pocket.

"Wait," I say. "Where are you going with that one?"

He thoughtfully rubs his chin. "Oh, somewhere."

"Mm-hmm." I cross my arms and ask him, "We still exchanging our grown-up gifts tonight?"

"Unless you want to change things?"

"No, no." The fact is I can barely wait another second to give him my big surprise. "Tonight will be great."

He nods and his eyes sparkle cheerily. "That works."

While Dean's making our drinks, I hurry into the bedroom with his empty stocking and fill it on the bed with the items I'd hidden in my closet. I grab his big present from the floor of the closet next and cart both things into the living room, setting them on the love seat. He's still not back from the kitchen. "Need help in there?" I call softly.

"Nope. I've got it!" He walks through the door holding two full glasses of eggnog and hands me one. He's dusted the top of the frothy liquid with nutmeg. I take a small sip. "Yum. Delicious. Thanks." He nods and sets his drink on the coffee table, spying the box on the love seat. "Whoa. What's this?"

I proudly hold my eggnog. "Just a little something."

He raises his hand. "I've got a little something for you."

He goes back to the kitchen and returns with my full Christmas stocking. He places it beside the other one and his package on the love seat. "Shall we sit and have a toast?"

I nod and he makes himself comfortable beside me. "Here's to a very merry Christmas," he says, lifting his glass.

I clink my glass to his. "Merry Christmas."

He takes a drink then says, "This is what? Our eighth Christmas together now?"

"Counting the time we dated in college, I suppose so." I sip from my drink too, enjoying it. Enjoying Dean's company. Enjoying this life, like Mary Christmas suggested I do. If only

I could have my memories from the rest of it, things would be ideal. But I'll take what I can get, near perfect.

He leans back and wraps his arm around me, snuggling me close on the sofa. "There's nobody I'd rather spend Christmas with than you."

My heart dances. "Thanks, Dean. I feel the same."

"So that lasagna takes you what? Five? Six hours to put together? Between making the sauce and cheese mixture and creating all the layers."

My panic spikes. "Hours? What?" The assembly line imagery starts coming together in my mind and I grimace.

"I included baking time," he says. "Often with those super deep pans you say cooking takes a while."

"Ha! Good thing I follow a recipe!"

"What recipe?" He angles forward to scan my eyes. "I thought this was your original? You said you never write anything down."

Wonderful. Maybe I should have—last time.

I start running numbers backward. If we're sitting down at five, the lasagna will need to set out and cool for a while first, so it needs to be done by at least four-thirty. I twirl a lock of my hair around one finger. "How long does it cook?"

Dean rubs my shoulder. "With that big a batch, one and a half, at max two hours?"

"Aha." So in the oven by three. Which means getting all that sauce and the noodles together first. "Guess I'd better get cooking by one?"

He nods. "That's the usual, but Paige. Hon. Seriously. If this year it's too much—"

"No, no!" I press my lips together. "Erm. Sorry. What were you going to say?"

That heart-melting grin. "I was going to offer to help you. You've never taken me up on it before, but—"

"This time I say yes!" I blurt out. My face burns hot. "And thank you."

He chuckles and holds me tighter. "No problem. More hands make lighter work." He reaches over and passes me my stocking. "Want to see what Santa brought you?"

I study his handsome face, feeling like I've already received the greatest Christmas gift of all being here with Dean and our family. Still. It's exciting to think he's picked out something special just for me. "Sure." I peek down at the stocking in my lap, prying the top of it open. A prettily wrapped box sits inside. The bottom of the stocking is filled with an orange and candy. Sticking an orange in each Christmas stocking is apparently a holiday tradition from Dean's side of the family and we've carried it through over the years.

I take the gift box out and hold it in my hands. "This is so nice. Thank you." I admire his expert giftwrapping job before poking my finger under the ribbon and sliding it off. I remove the wrapping paper and find a small jewelry box inside. My pulse pounds because, whatever it is, we probably can't afford it. I look up and into his eyes. "Dean."

He shrugs happily. "Open it."

I remove the jewelry box lid and the most gorgeous ruby heart necklace rests inside on a satin pillow. I lift it by its delicate gold chain to appreciate it in the firelight. The colorful sheen from the Christmas tree causes it to almost glow. I gasp, enchanted. "It's beautiful."

He gently strokes my cheek and gives me a kiss. "I wanted you to know you'll always have my heart."

"Is this a ruby?"

He nods and tears form in my eyes. It's my birthstone. "I love it so much." My breath catches. "But how could we—?"

"Afford it?" he guesses accurately. He stares at me with love in his eyes. "I saved up."

"Hmm. Good plan." I pass him the necklace and lift my hair at my nape, turning my back to him so he can help put it on. He closes the clasp and the pretty chain drapes from my neck, hitting the front of my gray sweater.

I lay my hand on top of the pretty heart pendant. "I'll treasure this forever and ever."

"So?" he asks sassily. "What'd you get me?" He casts a glance at the package on the love seat and his loaded stocking, and I laugh.

"Stocking first," I say, standing and handing it to him.

He scoots forward on the sofa cushion and centers it on his lap while I sit back down beside him, resting the larger box on the floor. He digs into his stocking and extracts an orange. "What a surprise!"

"Keep going," I urge, and he finds a fistful of candy next.

"Nice. Chocolates." He reaches in further and pulls out the mug. It's wrapped in tissue paper. He peels back the tissue, revealing the starry night sky painted above the darkened mountains. "*Stellar*," he quips, and I wryly twist my lips. "Seriously?" His eyes meet mine. "I love it. Thank you." He kisses me full on the lips.

"Here's something else." I pass him the large package and, when he takes it, his hands sink.

"Wow. Heavy!"

"Uh-huh."

He smirks. "You look like the cat who swallowed the canary."

"That's a horrible expression!" I giggle.

"Maybe so," he comments, "but, at the moment, accurate."

He pulls back the giftwrap and stares at the box. Second Chances had the original packaging, and I was grateful for that. Dean slowly looks up in wonder. "Paige?"

I can't contain my excitement. "It's a telescope," I squeal with glee. "Secondhand, I'm afraid, but it looks in good condition."

His eyes grow misty. "But how?"

I shrug. "I saved up."

He sets the box on the floor and takes me in his arms. "This is the best Christmas gift ever. Thank you so much, Paige. You don't know how long I've wanted one of these."

"So," I prompt gently. "Take it out of the box."

He does and sets it up on its tripod, standing it beside the coffee table. He uncaps the lens and takes a peek through the eyepiece. "This is amazing," he says, smiling broadly. "What an awesome surprise."

My heart brims with joy. "I'm so glad you like it."

"I love it." He holds out his arms and I stand, embracing him. "And I love you."

I stare up into his incredible dark eyes. "I love you, too."

He nods to my Christmas stocking on the coffee table. "You didn't finish opening your stocking."

"What?" I gasp. "There's more?"

"There might be an item or two beneath the candy."

"Oh!" We both sit on the sofa and pick up our eggnogs. Take and drink, clink our glasses and say cheers. I'm probably happier than I've been in my life. Everything seems merry and bright and I'm so lighthearted. Like all is right with my world. I need to trust what Mom said about holding on to the good things. Mary Christmas basically assured me that my wish would be granted, so I don't need to fret over bad things that *may* come. I need to be more like Mom and Dean and focus on the positive. The joy I have here, and now.

"I think it's probably good we're opening these by ourselves and not around the kids," he says teasingly. There's a hint of *naughty* in his tone.

"Oh really?" I reach into my stocking, clearing out more candy and setting it on the coffee table. When I stick my hand back into the stocking my fingers find something silky. Material. "Dean?" I gaze at him curiously and he chuckles.

I pull the slinky item out. It's a thong!

"You were missing Saturday," he remarks matter-of-factly.

I roar with delight.

He points to the stocking. "I replaced Tuesday, too."

I dig Tuesday out next and see more wadded-up bundles in the toe of the stocking.

"What the heck," he says when I look up. "I went for the whole week."

Oh. My. Gosh. I adore him.

I laugh and find Wednesday, twirling it around on my finger. "Shall we see how it fits?"

"I'll try not to break it," he growls huskily. "No promises."

CHAPTER
Twenty-One

"*Yay! Santa came!*" Eleanor's happy shout rockets me awake.

My eyes fly open and Dean rolls toward me. "Merry Christmas," he says, kissing my cheek. His light beard stubble leaves a delightful tingle. *Christmas, yes! I made it!* I peek under the covers. Also, Dean and I had the presence of mind to get dressed before falling asleep last night. I pull up the hem of my T-shirt to double check. For the record, he did *not* break my new thong. Heat stirs in my veins. Close call, though.

"Merry Kissmas!" Henry stands in the doorway, holding out his arms. Nessie hangs from one hand by its tail. I beckon him toward the bed, patting the mattress, and he scuttles over before leaping up and tackling me. This is the moment I've waited for.

"Merry Kissmas!" I say holding his pudgy self against me. His back is to my chest, my arms around his middle. He squirms and I hold him tighter, kissing the top of his head. The side of his neck. His cute little shoulder. "Merry Kissmas! Merry Kissmas! Merry Kissmas!" I cry over and over, and he giggles. Giggles. Giggles.

Dean lies on his side, propping himself on his elbow. He grins at Henry. "Merry Kissmas, buddy." We hear a *ding, ding, ding* in the living room. The bell on Eleanor's bike.

Eleanor comes racing in and Scout too, with a "*Woof! Woof!*" But it sounds more like a "*Moof! Moof!*" because he's got his new ball clenched in his teeth. Eleanor jumps on top of our bed and leaps at her daddy. He sits up and catches her midair. "Daddy! Daddy! Santa brought me a new bike! With training wheels!"

Dean holds her up with his hands below her armpits, lifting her higher. "Did he really?" he asks, before settling her down in his lap.

She nods eagerly. "Uh-huh, uh-huh!" Eleanor beams at me and Henry. "It's red."

"What about you, buddy?" Dean asks Henry. "Did Santa bring you something too?"

Henry laughs, throwing his head back against my shoulder. "A Hot Tide!"

"Nice," Dean says and winks at me. "We can't wait to see, can we, Mommy?"

"Scout got a ball!" Eleanor chirps.

"I see that!" I respond cheerfully then yawn. Scout drops his new ball on the floor and prances out of the bedroom, his wagging tail held high.

Dean turns to me and asks, "Coffee?"

I nod gratefully. "Coffee."

Scout returns in a flash with the rolled-up newspaper in his mouth.

I smile at Dean. "Looks like he hasn't forgotten his job in all the excitement." Scout pounces up on the bed, struggling to find an empty spot. He wedges himself in between the kids and us and drops the paper on Dean's legs, since Eleanor's in his lap. Dean laughs and pats Scout's head. "Good boy! Merry Christmas."

We get the kids suited up and herd them out in the snow. They're dying to give their new toys a try, and we don't blame them. Scout can't decide who he wants to trail more, Eleanor or Henry, as they ride up and down our short driveaway. Dean chases alongside Eleanor, holding out his arms. Despite her training wheels, he's concerned she'll skid on the ice, even after shoveling again and scattering sand along the driveway's surface. We agreed on only ten minutes to give the kids a taste of fun, but it's been almost twenty. They're having such a great time with their Santa gifts, we hate cutting it short.

Henry doesn't mind slip-sliding sideways in his Hot Ride *at all*. I hang on to the roof with my gloves, trying to keep him from careening off course—and into the bushes hedging our house—and he giggles. The vehicle's made entirely of heavy-duty plastic with rubber for the wheels. There are no real windows to speak of, just openings where the windshield and the windows would normally be.

"Keep your hands on the wheel, Henry!" I advise, because he's honestly not steering, just looking around at the neighbors' kids in their front yards, trying out their new stuff. One kid's got a skateboard, another a pogo stick. *Really?* I thought those were old-school. The kids on the other side got a toboggan, and their dad tugs them across their front lawn, giving them a ride.

Everyone's happy and cheerful, *and cold*. I've never seen this many parents with their pajama pants tucked into boots outside at this time of the morning, and there are others across the street. *But hey, it's Christmas*, and Christmas isn't only about one day. It's about all the days before and those that come after. The Charles Dickens line occurs to me: "I will honor Christmas in my heart, and try to keep it all the year," says Ebenezer Scrooge in *A Christmas Carol*.

Scrooge might have arrived at this understanding overnight, but he didn't achieve it on his own. He had the help of three mildly frightening spirits. Though I've had no ghost guide here, I'm *so glad* I was able to say "Merry Kissmas" to Henry. That made my year. Watching Eleanor get her balance on her new bike with Dean hovering protectively nearby lifts my heart, too. But it's chilly outdoors, below freezing with a cloudy gray sky and a smattering of snowflakes falling. I'm glad I had that super-charged coffee earlier and am ready for some more. "What do you say?" I ask Dean and glance at the house.

Scout prances up to him and drops his new ball. Dean chucks it back into the side yard near the rear gate and Scout bounds after it. "Two minutes?" Scout brings back the ball and Dean hurls it out again.

Eleanor's face is dark pink. I peek under the roof of Henry's car at his bright red nose and chin. I'm losing feeling in my fingers and toes myself. "Two minutes," I agree. "No more."

"Aww." Eleanor pouts and sticks out her bottom lip.

"We'll make hot cocoa!" I tempt.

Dean nods at the kids. "And I'll build a fire."

Henry leans out his car window, his coat sleeve on the door. "O-tay!"

The kids are wiped out after our busy Christmas morning. Dean and I feed them an early lunch and put them down for their naps ahead of schedule. They'll need their rest before the grandparents get here. With this being Christmas and us having guests, they'll likely stay up past their normal seven-thirty bedtime. Scout's worn out, too. He curls on the floor by Eleanor's bed and sleeps soundly.

This gives Dean and I a chance to pick up the house. New toys are scattered everywhere and wrapping paper litters the living room. "Gammy and Poppi really overdid it this year," I tell Dean. I pick up the handheld educational games they got the kids and flip over the boxes.

He chuckles and gathers a wooden train set in his arms, along with a hobby horse riding stick. "I could say the same of your mom."

The kids received loads of puzzles from Mom too, and gobs of storybooks and clothing from Miriam and Jack. Scout received his share of spoils too, including a stuffed Christmas tree doggie toy from Mom and a new leash, collar, and dog dish set from Dean's parents.

Dean got a sweater from his folks and a new spy thriller, and a winter scarf from Mom. Dean's sister, Jenny, gave him a neat bookmark and a fancy writing pen. Since she and I had already exchanged gifts, Mom showered all her attention—and excess—on the kids. Dean's parents gave me a nice glove, hat, and scarf set and a pretty pair of candy cane earrings.

I feel inundated by our family's generosity and worry over what we gave them. "Everyone was so thoughtful in their gift-giving," I tell Dean. "I hope they're okay with what we gave them?"

"Are you kidding?" He shares a big grin. "We got repeat orders for my homemade hot sauce and steak rub. Same as with the Christmas cookies you baked with the kids."

"Are you sure those things are enough?"

He chuckles warmly. "Sweetheart, you know that's all anyone ever asks for, and Eleanor and Henry have so much fun playing a part." I'm sad I missed that cookie baking session with them, but try to lighten my spirits with the knowledge that hopefully we'll be doing that again next year. For there's nothing I'd love more than spending another Christmas with Dean and our family. And then another Christmas after that, and then another.

"You look very nice," he says, noting my outfit. I put on the candy cane earrings from his parents to go with my ruby heart necklace and wear a snug-fitting, glittery red Christmas top, with black stretch pants and boots.

"Thanks, so do you."

We both dressed up a bit for the holiday, and Dean's in a dark red crewneck sweater and khakis. *Wait.* That's the outfit he wore to the faculty party. *No.* The faculty party that wasn't.

I recall what Mary Christmas said about it being impossible for me to be in two places at once and my heart stutters. Because I'm here, I can't be there. And maybe that other world doesn't even exist anymore? I'm starting to question if it ever did, or if the other reality was in fact the alternate one. I glance around the living room that's all tidied up and so holiday festive. I can't imagine forgetting any of this. Every moment that I've spent here has been so incredibly special. If I could have earlier memories from this life, I'd grab those in a flash. But, failing that fantasy developing, I'm content with what I have. *The present.* Dean enters the living room from the kitchen and smiles. *A future.* My heart beats happily. *A future with Dean.*

He nods over his shoulder. "What do you think? Want to get started on that lasagna?"

I check the clock on the bookshelf by the hearth and see it's nearly one o'clock. "Oh gosh, is it that time already?"

He steps back in the doorway and motions toward the kitchen. "I've already gotten everything out."

When I enter the kitchen, my jaw nearly hits the floor. The countertops are stacked with supplies and groceries, and two huge pots sit on the stove. One is larger than the other, and there's an enormous frying pan there, too. I note it's the skillet I used for the French toast.

Dean hands me an apron and I strap it on. "Might want to protect those nice clothes of yours from any flying tomato sauce."

"Ha. Yeah." I spot a mound of actual real tomatoes on the counter. The sort from the produce section. I pick two of them up. "We use fresh?"

He nods. "Always the most wholesome ingredients, you say!" There's a sweet onion too, garlic and parsley, whole oregano and basil.

"Wow!" I think of the frozen lasagna in my condo freezer. It was easy to microwave, but probably not as yummy as what Dean and I are about to make. Thank goodness he's going to help me.

"It's going to be delicious," he assures me with a grin.

I stare at the skillet. "You brown the meat," Dean says, "and I'll start chopping." I see a box of mushrooms by the cutting board, some yellow squash, a zucchini. He notes my apprehensive look and chuckles.

"Paige." He rolls his eyes. "You've made this loads of times before."

"Right." I swallow hard and switch on a burner. "I'm just grateful that *this time* you're doing it with me." I look around and find a packet of lean ground beef and another of hot Italian sausages. "Ground beef or sausages first?"

He shrugs. "You choose. It all goes in the big pot. Then once we get the sauce going, we'll boil the noodles."

"O-tay!" I say like Henry and blow out a breath.

"Don't worry." Dean winks and my pulse hums. "We'll pull it together in no time."

Two hours later, I'm dead on my feet and we're only half-way done. We gave Henry and Eleanor a snack and got them busy playing with their new toys in the living room. I dump the water from the noodle pot in the sink and the steam wilts my hair, buffets my face. Dean meanwhile places sheets of wax paper on the counter, then helps me take each long, flat piece of pasta and lay it out. "This is work," I say as he reaches over my arm with his.

Dean grins down at me. "Most good things are."

He bends down to kiss me on the lips, and suddenly I don't mind about the work, or my aching feet, or my sore back.

"Dean?" I say, looking up at him. "Do you think we were meant to be?"

His gaze sparkles warmly. "I don't just think it," he says. "I know."

Later, as we gather in the living room holding our plates, Miriam turns to me appreciatively and says, "Paige, I think this is your best Christmas lasagna ever. So tasty!"

Jack readily agrees. "Very good."

Mom says, "Hear, hear!" and Roger nods.

The kids sit at the coffee table near the fire. Eleanor perches on some pillows and Henry's in his booster seat. Both are gobbling up their dinners, and red sauce dribbles down Henry's chin.

"Thanks everyone, but I had some help." I blush, peeking at Dean. He and I brought in chairs from the kitchen and sit near the kids.

Mom and Roger are on the love seat, and Dean's folks are on the sofa. Dean's sister, Jenny, is with them. She favors Dean with her dark hair and eyes, and wears a ponytail, jeans, and a sweater. It's so good to see her and she's grown so much. Of course, in her mind, she saw me not that long ago, at Thanksgiving.

"Good for you, son," Miriam says and raises her wineglass toward him.

He toasts her in the air. "Thanks, Mom."

"I think it's good for guys to be involved in the kitchen," Jenny says. "After all, fair is fair."

Miriam confides to Mom in a teasing manner, "Jack's not much help in the kitchen." She shrugs. "But he's great with takeout."

"Takeout counts!" Jenny quips and grins. She's become a very attractive young woman, with a dimpled cheek and doe-like eyes. From the poised way she holds her wine, she seems more mature than twenty-one.

"How about Roger?" Miriam asks Mom.

Mom flushes with pride. "Roger's an excellent cook, aren't you, Roger?"

Roger's face reddens and he nods.

I shake my head at Dean, who purses his lips, hiding a chuckle.

"Thank you for the yummy salad," I say to Mom. "And the bread is so tasty."

She beams at Roger. "Roger made the baguettes himself."

Given my recent culinary escapades, I'm duly impressed. "Is that right?"

Roger nods and Dean chomps on his bread. "Wow," Dean says. "Delicious."

Jenny smiles. "I'm looking forward to Mom's pecan pie.

I spent a few Christmas seasons with Dean's family during college and recall it as being scrumptious. "Yum," I concur. "Me too."

Jack holds up his hand, not wanting to be left out. "I picked out the wine," he says, and the adults laugh.

"Excellent choices," Mom replies.

Eleanor looks up from her food. "Can we have Christmas cookies, too?"

"Of course!" I smile around the room. "We'll bring out a plate to share with the pie."

"I think we need a Christmas toast," Mom says brightly.

Jack volunteers. "Here's to family and to all of us being together!"

Dean casts a look at me and around the room. "Here's to love everlasting," he says dreamily with stars in his eyes.

That draws *oohs* and *ahhs* and sighs from the room, and I kiss him.

I tilt my wineglass in Roger's direction. "Here's to our new friend, who we're so glad could join us."

Eleanor holds up her milk and proclaims, "Here's to Scout!"

Chuckles fill the room and Henry grins. He stares at the grownups around him, absorbing the holiday vibe. "Merry Kissmas!" he says and folks laugh warmly.

Roger raises his wineglass high. "And God bless us, every one!"

"Dickens," I gasp happily.

Roger smiles, and nods.

After dessert, Dean challenges the others to a house-of-cards building contest. This is his specialty, apparently, and he enjoys showing off each year.

Jack shakes his head. "I'm out this time," he tells Dean. "You're the master there."

"Master Daddy!" Eleanor croons and the adults laugh.

"Merry Kissmas!" Henry adds, not wanting to be left out. I scoop him into my arms as everyone says *aww*. Hold him close, kiss his precious head. "Merry Kissmas, Henry." I hold him on my hip as Dean looks around. "What? No takers?" He glances at me, but I'm not about to partake. Riding a bike is the extent of my balancing abilities.

"I'll pass."

Roger waves his hand, signaling his participation, and I blink at Dean.

"A challenger!" Dean declares and people cheer.

I'm impressed Roger would join in. The man is growing on me, honestly. Mom could have done worse, and has done. Unfortunately. But things with Roger seem different. They look natural together. Comfortable. Don't get me wrong. I *hate* the idea of Mom moving to Wilmington. At the same time, I'm glad she's found her fit.

Before long, Roger and Dean have built midlevel towers out of their playing cards at either end of the coffee table. Each level has two cards leaning toward each other to form an upside-down V. Then those triangles line up with flat cards stacked on top to hold them steady as the next level's added.

Dean's up to level four now. Roger's astoundingly at level five.

Dean leans two cards together extra carefully, holds his breath, then lets go. They stay in position, and he begins the next set.

Roger's eyes travel to Dean's work, but he's still ahead. Now on level six while Dean finishes level five. The rest of us watch intently. What a fun game. Especially since I'm not playing. The very idea makes me antsy. Too much risk involved, and no guarantees.

"Nobody breathe," Miriam whispers.

We start to laugh but quiet ourselves when Roger glances over his shoulder, shielding our mouths with our hands. Roger begins level seven, standing up straighter from his hunched position. Dean races to catch up. He's taller than Roger so he's still bent forward. A card slips, knocking another and falling over.

A collective gasp.

We hear the clock ticking on the bookshelf to the left of the hearth. Dean's fire burns nicely, filling the room with its comfortable glow. I love the scent of the fire and the aroma from the piney candle on the mantel. The stockings are lying under the Christmas tree, the area now devoid of packages. Yet the lovely tree spreads holiday joy throughout the house and shines brightly out the streetside window for the enjoyment of neighbors and passersby.

Scout sleeps by the fire, all cozy, while Dean crouches with his arms outstretched. His tower remains steady, and he picks the errant card back up, lifting it with the tip of his finger, forming another triangle. Then the next.

"Son," Jack says in his gravelly voice. "Looks like you may have some serious competition."

The rest of us chuckle softly when Dean's neck turns red.

I've got Henry on my lap on the love seat and Mom's beside us behind Roger. Dean's folks are on the sofa with Jenny, who holds Eleanor near Dean's end of the coffee table. The child adores being around the older girl.

Dean lifts his palm for us to wait, and we watch as he expertly advances to level eight. Then nine. Roger's forehead beads with perspiration. Dean's caught up, but Roger sets his jaw, undaunted. Slow and steady in his work.

"Looks like it's neck and neck," Jenny giggles quietly.

Scout raises his head and looks around. Squints then blinks. Vigorously shakes his head in a doggie-like fashion, his shaggy hair drooping over his eyes.

"Paige," Dean says under his breath, as if having a premonition, "the dog."

Right. I pass Henry to Mom, who takes him and settles him on her lap. But before I can stand, Scout clumsily leaps to his four paws. Dean and Roger freeze, their hands suspended midair, their card houses stable. "*Woof! Woof!*" Scout wants to know what's going on. He trots over to Dean in big, swaggering steps and sniffs his pants leg, wagging his tail from side to side.

"Not now, boy," Dean whispers. He shoos the dog away, shoving gently with his hand and attempting to steer Scout toward the kitchen. But Scout isn't having any of that. He's a family dog and he wants to stay with his family.

Scout cocks his head then prances between the coffee table and sofa, cramming himself into the narrow space bracketing Dean's folks' and Jenny's legs. The dog advances on me and I lurch for his collar, but his big wagging tail zigzags back and forth, back and—*whacks into Dean's tower, nooo!*—bisecting it at level four.

The remaining three levels teeter ominously, then collapse like dominoes falling.

Our hearts stop and Roger smooths back his hair.

Wag-wag. Wag-wag.

Jack tries to grab Scout's tail, but it slips from his grasp.

Miriam catches it and grins. "Got it!"

But Scout yanks his tail away and it slices—in painfully slow motion—right through Roger's tall tower. "Scout," I gasp, but the poor creature has no idea what he's done, looking guileless with big round eyes. Cards tumble in a heap, fanning out across the coffee table and jettisoning onto the floor in a wild array. There's an equally large mess on Dean's end.

"Oh my," Mom says.

Scout shakes out his floppy ears and gazes innocently around, and we all groan good-humoredly, the tension broken. "It's okay, boy," Dean tells the pup, patting his head.

Henry claps his chubby hands together. "O-tay!" he chortles, and we all laugh.

"So." Dean sets his hands on his hips. "Who's ready for some eggnog?"

All hands shoot up.

That night we're so worn out from Christmas, we decide to turn in early. The kids fall asleep the moment their heads hit their pillows. Dean and I stand in the hallway, staring into Henry's room. "I'm so glad he got his merry Kissmas," I tell Dean.

"Yeah," he says tenderly. "Me too." Dean takes my hand, and we advance a few steps, peering into Eleanor's room. She's snuggled down in her bed and Scout sleeps at her feet.

I look at Dean, my heart swelling with love. "I'm so glad to be here. With you and our family."

He wraps his arms around me in the hall. "I wouldn't have it any other way." Angst roils through me. What if something happens? What if my new life gets uprooted? I can't be in two places at once, Mary Christmas said, so if I return to my former reality, this world will evaporate. My marriage with Dean, our darling kids, Mom's new relationship with Roger. *Poof, poof, poof!*

I stare up at Dean, my heart on the verge of breaking. "I couldn't bear for all this to be taken away from me." My chin trembles and my voice shakes. "Now that I've known this existence, I don't want to be anywhere else."

Dean steadies my chin in his hand. "Paige," he says warmly. "You're not going anywhere, okay?"

"But what if I do?"

He looks so deeply in my eyes it's like he's falling into my soul. "Then I'll find you." Heat burns in my eyes, but he holds me close. "I'll always find you, all right?" He brings his lips to mine in a tender kiss. "Hey," he asks gently. "What's this about? It's Christmas." He gives me a tender look. "We're supposed to be jolly."

"I've never been happier"—a sob escapes me, and I sniff—"than I am with you."

"Well then." He lays his forehead against mine and says smartly, "You'll just have to keep me, won't you?"

I share a happy grin. "Yes."

He kisses me again and warmth spreads down to my toes. "I'm counting on that." He bends and sweeps me into his arms, so suddenly I'm not prepared for it. "Dean!" I giggle quietly, darting a glance at the kids' rooms. "What are you doing?"

"It's Christmas." His voice grows rough as he carries me across the threshold to our bedroom. "I'd thought we'd play Santa and Mrs. Claus."

"What?"

Oh! Oooh.

My face heats, along with several other parts of me. Deliciously.

Ho, ho, ho.

He shuts the door.

CHAPTER
Twenty-Two

I wake to the sound of snow ticking against the window. The bed is empty. Cold. I stretch my arm behind me, feeling around under the covers. Is Dean up making coffee? Why so early? "Dean?" I call sleepily. It's the day after Christmas. Neither of us has work today and we were up late last night, playing Santa and Mrs. Claus. A rush of excitement tears through me.

Wait.

Where's the cozy smell of the cinnamon and clove holiday candle? The lingering scent of Dean's spicy bodywash beside me on his pillow? Henry noisily crashing into the room shouting "Merry Kissmas!" and Eleanor and Scout bouncing onto the bed?

The *tick, tick, tick*ing of the snow hits harder against the glass.

My pulse skitters.

Something's wrong.

I open my eyes and sit up. *No.*

I'm not dressed in Dean's large T-shirt. I'm wearing pj pants and a T-shirt of my own, and stark walls glare at me through the shadows. Panic crests inside me like a tidal wave, drowning me in fear. My eyes burn hot, but the rest of my body's icy cold. Gooseflesh rises on my legs, races up my arms and along the back of my neck. I huddle under the covers, blankets scrunched against my chest. Chilly, freezing.

This isn't our room. Our house.

Where's Dean? Where's my family?

Darkness closes in and my head reels.

No, no, no, no. No.

I don't want to believe it, I don't.

Shock shoots through me like a lightning bolt, bitterly hot and jagged, and I choke back a sob. "Dean?" Then another. "Eleanor?" I survey the room, and the open door to the hall, another to the bathroom. My eyes leak tears. "*Henry?*" My pitiful wail bounces off the ceiling. "*Scout?*"

But none of them are here.

Please, no.

Please, please, please. Noooo.

How? Why?

Mary Christmas said, "All right!"

I thought she'd given me her blessing to stay there forever with Dean and my new family. After I *begged* and *explained* how greatly I'd grown, all that I'd learned, and how I'd come to see what was truly important in my life. My heart breaks at another explanation. Maybe when Mary Christmas said "All right!" she was merely agreeing to let me stay through Christmas Day? And, if that's the case, maybe experiencing a once-in-a-lifetime Christmas *once* was better than never getting to experience one at all. But how gut-wrenching to lose it now.

But wait. Does that mean that Christmas is over? Has the magic ended? Is today December twenty-sixth? I lift the remote from my nightstand and press a button. The heavy curtains covering the plate-glass window drag apart, opening along their tracks. Snow-covered mountains form a jagged ridge in the distance, their spindly pine forests doused in white. The town of Boone's below, speckled with drifts like a Christmas village in a snow globe.

So what day is it now?

I push back the covers and stand. My legs wobble and I grab my nightstand. My dream journal lies open on top of it. I pick it up and read the last entry, dated December nineteenth. I'd written one thing: *Relationship with Dean.* Overwhelming sadness drenches me like pouring rain as I set my dream journal down. I didn't need to schedule my dreams in advance in that other world, because everything about it was picture perfect. Including my relationship with Dean. How could I have lost him? How could I have lost all of them? *How?* Was none of it real? Could it all have been a dream?

I steady myself on my feet and stroll zombie-like into my darkened kitchen. Flip on a light, turn on the coffee maker. The view through the living area window is even lovelier than the one from the bedroom, but a treadmill stands in the way. A robotic dog poses in a chair. A line of Christmas tree ornaments adorns the gas fireplace's mantel. I sigh weightily. No Christmas tree in sight.

My heart shatters in anguish and I press my hands to my ravaged chest to hold it in. Then turn slowly, slowly toward the advent calendar. The snowman's in the pocket for Day Twenty, the poinsettia's in the pocket for Day Twenty-One. A pair of ice skates are stuffed into Day Twenty-Two. A Christmas candle's in Day Twenty-Three. Santa's jolly round face waits in Day Twenty-Four. None have been removed from their pockets and placed on the advent calendar or attached to its felt Christmas tree.

Memories of the past six days flood me, filling me with so much longing and misty joy. What a truly wonderful world that was. What an amazing life we had. My soul cries out into the empty void that was my heart. Now everything's gone in one gigantic *poof!*

I glumly take the snowman from the Day Twenty pocket and paste him on the advent calendar's green felt Christmas tree, wishing this simple act could bring my other life back to me, instinctively knowing it won't. I run my fingers through my hair, tuck it back behind my ear. *Hang on. It's different.*

I hurry down the hall and into the bathroom and turn on the light. High-end fixtures gleam around me as I gape in the mirror at the woman with bluntly cut brown hair. I pull up my baggy T-shirt and slightly push down my pj pants behind me, stealing a look over my shoulder at my lower back. *No butterfly tattoo, either.*

My spirit flags. Which means no tight relationship with my girlfriends, more than likely. No real dog. No family. No homey bungalow brimming with love and joy. I frown at my reflection in the mirror, missing my pink highlights and flirty layers. Missing the person I was. Despite all I *didn't have*, I had so many valuable things worth cherishing. The love and support of a caring husband, the affection and adoration of two precious kids. The sweet attentiveness of our loyal dog. A mom that I was finally getting to know—and understand—better.

Mom.

I check my sports watch, seeing it's slightly after seven. I didn't have a high-tech watch to keep track of my steps or daily activities in the other realm. I chuckle sadly at the absurd notion that I didn't even have a working cell phone for most of the time I was there. Much less a computer, but still. I got by okay.

I find my cell phone charging on my dresser, and it's the newer model I remember purchasing. Today's date shines back at me: December twentieth of the current year. Right. I'm exactly back where I left off in this reality, which makes sense, according to what Mary Christmas told me. Since I can't be in two places at once, this reality didn't exist while I was in the other one—therefore, time here stood still.

I haven't missed a single day. Which means I'm back in time to launch Paws and Read! *Yes.* My heart thumps happily. The party in the gym's going to happen! So that's a *good thing* about being back. Though I've been torn away from the other world, there's joy present in this universe, and the potential to make *new* memories. I consider Mom and her medical tests. At least now I'll be here to take her for those on Wednesday, and together we can face whatever lies ahead. I issue a silent prayer that those will only be positive and happy things. But no matter what, I'm here for her.

Now that I'm back, will I get a second chance with Dean? And what about Mom meeting Roger? Maybe all is not lost. I learned so much in the other reality about the importance of love and family. Perhaps that's what I was meant to do all along. Similar to how Ebenezer Scrooge became enlightened in *A Christmas Carol.* My soul aches because I miss my kids, and Scout. But maybe they were specters of children, and a sweet pet, yet to come? I check my phone for recent text messages but find nothing from my old girlfriend group, only messages from Mom. The last one's a confirmation about our lunch at Beaumont's today.

I stare into the mirror over my dresser, still adjusting to my altered looks. My reflection shows my bland haircut and pale blue eyes. Incredibly sad and discouraged face. But, this time, something else catches my attention. A sparkly piece of jewelry hangs from around my neck, draping down the front of my T-shirt. My heart pounds. *No. Impossible.* I've never owned anything like this before. I lightly caress it with my fingers, hold the piece up in the light. It's a ruby heart pendant on a delicate gold chain. My Christmas gift from Dean.

Hope blooms in my heart. Could my keeping his necklace have something to do with our future? Is it possible it's not too late to find my happy ending? Maybe when I see Mom at Beaumont's, she'll be able to help me. She is, after all, my mom.

Mom gapes at me over her glass of Chablis. "I'm sorry, sweetheart. Can you repeat that?"

"Which part?" I take a forkful of my ham and cheddar quiche, enjoying its savory goodness. The burgers here *are* fantastic, but given that I had one only a few days ago, I opted for something different.

She takes a long sip of wine. "All of it?"

We opened our Christmas gifts to each other while waiting on our lunches. She loves her handcrafted blue and green earrings, and I adore my cute Christmas tree ornament that looks like a yellow labrador retriever wearing a Santa hat. She's so proud of me for starting my Paws and Read program, and I'm honestly proud of myself. Will the rest of my life work out, too?

"Okay." I lower my voice and lean forward so others don't overhear us in the bustling bistro. "When I went to bed last night I was here."

She points to the table between us. "*Here*, here? In Piney Mount, you mean?" She hasn't touched her chef's salad. Though she did devour her French onion soup before. I slurped up my tomato bisque too, along with a couple of yummy yeast rolls.

Who knew time traveling between different dimensions could be so hunger-inducing? I mull over the tasty treats I devoured in our cottage. The Christmas cookies, the butter-laden French toast. Oh my goodness.

"Yes," I whisper. "But here's the thing. I was in Piney Mount there, too."

"In this, um." She licks her lips. "Other reality?"

Yes. She's finally getting it.

"That's right," I continue. "But everything was different. I was married to Dean—"

She fans out her fingers over her heart. "I wanted to be sure I heard that part right."

I lower my voice and say excitedly, "We had two kids and a dog."

"What a lovely dream."

"It wasn't a dream, Mom," I whisper. "It was way too real."

Mom claps her hands. "Then a premonition!"

I sit back in my chair. I hadn't thought about that. But no. The necklace. "A premonition predicts the future."

"That's what we're talking about, isn't it?"

"No." *Wait.* Since today is the twentieth… I did get a small glimpse into the future, I suppose, but specifically in the alternate reality. That wasn't predicting my future in this world, though. Dean and I were the exact same ages we are now. It was our past that had led to a new and different place. I stare at Mom, who's desperately trying to understand. If I can't bring her on board, how will I ever convince Dean? I blow out a frustrated breath, and my hair spirals back from my face. I grab a lock of it with my hand, yanking it forward.

"Paige?" Mom asks, concerned. "What are you doing?"

"I think you were right about layers," I tell her, displaying my fistful of hair.

"Oh!"

"And highlights," I add, and she blinks. "I was thinking about pink."

"*Pink?*" she says like I've just told her I'm going to shave my head.

"Come on, Mom." I wave my hand. "Pink's not that drastic."

She twists up her lips. "Maybe not for the average person, but—"

"I'm also considering a tattoo."

I know I'm testing to get a reaction. She rewards me with one, her blue eyes wide. "Paige Pierce." She clicks her tongue. "What have you done with my daughter?"

I laugh and shake out my hair. "Maybe your daughter's loosened up."

She worriedly narrows her eyes. "You're not doing recreational drugs?" she asks quietly.

"Mom! No."

"Well." She shrugs. "You can't fault me for the question." She dumps the pot of blue cheese salad dressing all over her salad, swizzling it back and forth. When she finishes, she looks up. "What were you saying about the future?"

I try to remember where I was. *Oh yeah. Premonition.* "I was saying what happened to me couldn't have been a premonition, because premonitions are of events to come, and those things really happened."

She scarfs down her salad and recounts between bites, "The advent calendar, the lady dressed like Mrs. Claus at the market. Me and what's-his-name."

"Roger, Mom. His name is Roger and he's absolutely perfect for you."

"No one is perfect, sweetheart," she says wryly.

"I didn't say he was perfect for everyone. Merely for you."

"But I already told you, I'm seeing Stan."

"Not seriously, though."

"Not yet, but you never know." She pats down her red curls. "He's asked me to be exclusive."

I gasp. "What? Already?" My heart thumps. "Mom, no, you can't do that. Not yet. Don't rush into things."

"Why not?"

"Because you shouldn't compromise. Hold out for Mr. Right."

Her forehead lifts. "You have changed, haven't you?"

"I'm just asking you to slow down a bit with Stan," I say. "Maybe give things more time."

"Because?" Her eyebrows arch.

I huff. "Someone else might come along."

Mom chuckles and shakes her head. "What makes this Roger so ideal, anyway?"

"Well," I say, "for one, he's very agreeable."

"Agreeable's better than ornery." She slices into some larger chunks of iceberg lettuce, ham, cheese, and turkey, forming bite-size pieces.

"And," I say temptingly, "he's wild about you."

"Hmm." She acts like she's not intrigued, but I can tell the curiosity's killing her.

I eat some more of my ham and cheddar quiche and take a sip of wine.

After a beat, she leans toward me. "Are you sure about the drugs?"

"*Mo-om.*"

"Okay, okay." She shrugs and resumes eating. "But I do have to tell you, this all sounds like a fantasy."

Maybe it is too fantastic to believe. "I had trouble wrapping my head around it, too. But once I was in it?" I sigh. "It didn't seem fantastical at all. More like homey and natural, and right."

GINNY BAIRD

"Sounds to me like you're having regrets," Mom says sagely.

"My biggest regret is that I'm not there any longer." Tears prickle my eyes and I turn away. "I mean, I care about Paws and Read, and I'm *so happy* to be able to launch that program. But when I was in that other world, I couldn't help wondering if there was a way to start something similar there." I choke on my sobs. "A way for me to finally have everything."

"Oh my." Mom reaches for my hand on the table. "Paige. I had no idea you still carried such a torch for Dean."

I'm about to protest, but then I realize she's right. I do.

"I talked to you about this," I confess hoarsely. "When I was in the other reality, I tried to tell you what was going on in my life."

"I see." She puts on her best poker face. "And how did I take it?"

I tighten my grasp on her hand. "You urged me to hold on to what is good."

Her eyes glimmer softly. "That sounds like great advice."

"But Mom? How do I hold on to what's good when it's been taken away from me?"

"Don't rush to judgement, Paige."

"What do you mean?"

"From where I sit, your life isn't all bad in this reality, as you call it. You've got a great job that you love, a nice place to live, and you're establishing the charity you've talked about for ages."

My heart flutters happily. "Yes, that's all true."

"It's not over until it's over," she says in lilting tones. "Last I heard, Dean Burton was back in Piney Mount and working at Walton."

"Yes, but. What on earth can I say?" I've been puzzling over this since waking up this morning. It's been hard enough talking to Mom. My confession about the alternate reality will sound even more outlandish to him. "Certainly not the truth."

"Which truth is that?"

"About…you know." I dart a glance at the street. "The other place."

"What about the truth that's in your heart?"

I reach for my pendant necklace without thinking. Grip the dainty gemstone between my thumb and forefinger. *Everything in its place and all things in good time.* I felt like Mary Christmas was trying to tell me something when she said that. I'm just not sure what. Maybe that the timing hadn't been right yet in *this* reality for me to obtain what I had in the other?

"What a lovely ruby heart necklace," Mom says. "Where did you get it?"

I sigh, lost in the memories. "Dean gave it to me for Christmas."

"Wait." She sets down her wine. "The Christmas that hasn't happened yet?" She shakes her head. "Paige, did you buy that necklace for yourself? Because if you did, hon, that's perfectly great. It's healthy to indulge ourselves with—"

Her accusation puts me on the verge of tears again. "Mom, no."

She reads the sadness in my eyes. "I'm sorry, Paige. Of course you didn't. *Dean gave it to you*," she says, speaking slowly. "Four days from now."

"Yes." I heave a sigh, feeling discouraged. "You don't believe me, do you? You don't believe any of this."

She nods surely. "I believe that you believe."

Oh boy. I glance around the café and *stop*, my view landing on a familiar face with a reddish beard. *Roger.* He's at a different table, eating with a younger redheaded man, maybe his son. I can't believe my good fortune. "Mom," I say excitedly. "He's here."

CHAPTER
Twenty-Three

"**Who's here? Dean?**" Mom asks.

"No, no." I giggle and angle closer. "Roger."

"What?"

I hitch my chin in his direction and Mom steals a glance. "Who, him?"

"Yes, him. He's your one."

"Now, Paige—"

I stand up and grab her hand, tugging her to her feet. "*Paige Pierce*," Mom says quietly as I drag her toward Roger's table. "*What on earth are you doing?*"

"Roger? Hi," I say and he looks up. "I'm Paige Pierce. I believe we've met before?"

He cocks his head to study me but shows no hint of recognition.

His companion smiles cordially. "Dad's worked on a lot of cars. Maybe yours?"

"Yes, yes," I say. "That's it!" I pull Mom closer to my side, but she resists. I yank harder. Address Roger. "I know you're really great at, ah—what you do." Mom blinks at me in surprise. Too bad. She'll just need to tough it out. This is for her own good. "So, I wanted to introduce you to my mom, Rosemary. She's in search of—" Mom elbows me hard. *Ow.* Right in the ribs. I clear my throat and finish. "—a new mechanic."

"Oh, Dad's not in the business anymore," his son says. "He's recently closed his shop and retired. Haven't you, Dad?"

Roger nods.

Goodness knows why, but I find this endearing.

"That's a shame." I grin at Roger. "Maybe you could help Mom out? Recommend someone?"

Roger's gaze lingers on Mom, while she turns deeper and deeper hues of red. Finally, he says, "I'd be glad to help you, Rosemary." He takes out his wallet and hands her a business card. "The shop phone number's outdated, but my email's still good. Please, get in touch, and let me know about your car. I'll fix you up with the perfect person for you."

I try not to gawk. Those were more words than I've ever heard Roger string together in one sitting. I giggle inside. He must really like her.

I peer knowingly at Mom.

That perfect person will be *him* for *her.*

She grouses lightly as we return to our table. "I can't believe you did that."

"You'll thank me later." I polish off my wine and say sassily, "I won't even fuss if the two of you move in together."

"What?" She looks like I've floored her.

"On his houseboat."

Mom's mouth hangs open. "That is *not* happening." She sneaks a peek at Roger across the room and murmurs, "Although he is nice-looking, I'll give you that. Not in your typical manner. Still. He's got something."

"*See.*"

She beholds me proudly. "Who *is* this new you?"

"Maybe I had a secret side that was bursting to get out?"

Mom laughs at this. "Oh, Paige."

Our server walks over with the dessert menu.

"Want to split some apple cobbler?" I ask her. It looks tempting and is served warm.

She sits there looking mildly stunned. "Sure." She glances at the server. "And coffee for me."

Coffee sounds good. Although I recall sleeping soundly beside Dean, the alternate reality was a whirlwind, leaving me exhausted. But pleasantly exhausted, it's true. Happy memories flit through me of our many sweet family moments. *And our super private coupley ones.* "Make that two of those," I add.

The server promptly delivers our coffee and asks, "Cream and sugar?"

"Yes, please."

Mom blinks at me. "Since when?"

I square my shoulders and say, "A lot of things have changed about me."

She looks me up and down as I dump sugar in my coffee. "Apparently so."

Our dessert arrives as Roger and his son stand to leave. Roger waves to Mom. "Don't forget, now." *He winks.*

Oh. My. Goodness.

I experience butterflies on behalf of Mom.

I can tell she feels them too, but she tries to disguise it by taking a spoonful of hot apple cobbler loaded with ice cream. "So you're a matchmaker now, are you?"

"I just want you to be happy."

"Same." She considers me warmly. "Paige, what are you going to do about Dean?"

I'm racked with nerves. "I guess I'll need to talk to him. Try to explain things somehow." I sigh with frustration. "Unfortunately, I don't know where he lives."

"I do!"

My chin jerks up. "What?"

"His Aunt Jodi told me he moved into Mountain View Apartments. You know, the place with the nice amenities near the edge of town?"

"Do you know which unit?"

She shakes her head. "I'm not sure Jodi knows, either. I could ask her to ask his parents, if you'd like." Talk about awkward. Dean hearing from his parents I was trying to track him down through his aunt, who gets her hair done by Mom. Getting his Aunt Jodi involved will only expose the situation to town gossip.

Far better for me to handle this solo. I have a nice laptop here and can do some digging around myself. I can't show up at his place like a stalker, anyway. If only I had a way to get his number, I could text him about meeting somewhere, maybe catching up over coffee. That seems harmless enough. Unless I unload the truth on him and he bolts like a frightened rabbit.

Which is a very good possibility. I'd definitely look at him askance if he shared with me what I plan to tell him. But no. I can't let my apprehension stop me. I have to take this chance. Too many people depend on me. *Possibly.* If I believe in fate, and alternate realities influencing the future. I never used to, but now...?

"That's all right," I say to Mom. "Thanks, but I'll find a way to get in touch with Dean." And it will have to be soon. This can't wait until Monday. I'll absolutely lose my nerve, and maybe start thinking like Mom, doubting that any of this happened.

The necklace gleams against the front of my black crewneck sweater.

But it did happen, Paige, an inner voice says.

Funnily enough, the voice sounds *an awful lot* like Mary Christmas.

Mom smiles behind her coffee cup. "Well, the two of you do work at the same school," she says about me locating Dean.

Bingo! The teacher and staff directory. Although Dean's brand new at Walton, that information's on our school website and updated routinely. Since Dean's starting next semester, there's a good chance his data's already been entered. I jump from my chair to hug her shoulders. "Thanks, Mom! You're a genius!" I kiss her cheek, and she pats my hand.

"I'm glad you finally noticed."

Mom and I part with tight hugs, promising to keep each other updated. She's dying to know about how things go with Dean, and I'm excited to learn whether Mom follows through with Roger. Though I have a strong hunch she will. For now, the plan is I'm picking her up at seven in the morning on Wednesday for her medical appointment, and we both agreed to hold positive thoughts. Mom exits the restaurant in one direction, and I turn in the other—nearly running smack-dab into Heather! "Oh hi!"

Heather's long brown hair brushes her shoulders. It's dusted with snow. "Paige!" I blink, seeing Mia's with her. Her cropped black hair's cut at an angle, her dark eyes shining.

"Oh gosh," Mia says. "We were just talking about you."

I flush self-consciously. "You were?"

"Paige Pierce!" Kirstin says, scuttling up on the sidewalk behind them. She joins the group, her blond ringlets poking out beneath her red stocking cap. "Where've you been keeping yourself, girl?"

"Oh me? Um." I expect tense glances to pass between them, but all three women wear open and friendly expressions.

Heather rolls her eyes as snow pelts us. "I can't tell you how many times we've talked about texting you."

"Yeah." Kirstin nods. "Every time we go out, we're so sad you can't join us."

"Can't?" I don't understand.

Mia frowns. "You said Friday afternoons aren't good for you." She grimaces apologetically. "That's when you take advantage of the quiet at school to do your teacher planning. So, after a while"—she winces—"we kind of stopped asking."

Stupid. Stupid. Stupid, Paige.

"I'm so sorry," I say sincerely. "I want to do better." It's not like I don't have a planning block built into my day, for goodness' sake. Why hasn't that been enough? It's true I also have papers and quizzes to grade and district compliance paperwork to keep up with, but I've got evenings and weekends for that. Lunch breaks, too. Who does teacher planning on a Friday? *Sigh.* Evidently me. *No. Stop. The old me.*

"But you're always so busy," Heather says. I didn't know what busy was until I had a couple of kids. I don't know how all of them do it. They're my new heroes.

I sense an opportunity. A narrow opening, and I rush through it. "Then I'll *make* time," I tell them, meaning it absolutely.

"Are you still at Walton?" Kirstin asks, her green eyes sparkling.

"Yeah, teaching ninth grade English."

Heather gives a low whistle. "We've heard who's teaching physics there now."

Kirstin leans closer. "Dean Burton. Gregory told me," she says, mentioning her husband. "He heard it on extremely good authority from his dad, who's Dean's parents' dentist."

I laugh at their conniving. "No kidding?"

Kirstin reads my face and quips, "Something tells me she already knew this."

Heather huffs and plays along. "Of course she did," she teases lightly.

Mia sets a hand on her hip. "I heard he was in Colorado before. Has he started teaching at Walton yet?"

"No. He starts next semester."

"So you haven't seen him then?" Mia asks, big-eyed and with listening ears.

"No, erm. I have." I feel my face turning red. "I saw him at Walton's faculty holiday party."

Kirstin rubs her chin. "Interesting, hmm, ladies?"

They eagerly crowd in. "I hear he's not married," Mia says.

Heather spills more tea. "Or dating anyone, according to social media."

I gasp. "You spy on him?"

"No!" Kirstin giggles. "We've been keeping tabs on him for you."

Spoken in such solidarity, my eyes water. "I've missed y'all, I really have."

"Then come out with us next time," Heather says. "We go to El Bandito's happy hour."

Kirstin shares, "Their margaritas are excellent."

"Yeah, I've heard." I study their happy faces. "How are your husbands, kids?"

"All good," Mia says. "We definitely need to catch up." She winks at Heather. "Though somebody's drinking mocktails these days."

"Oh Heather!" I'm so happy for her. "Another baby?"

"Due in July."

I think of my pregnancy scare with Dean in our alternate

reality and feel a tug at my heartstrings. I didn't understand how much I wanted that kind of life until I experienced it. The sort my old friends have. "I think that's wonderful," I tell Heather. "Congratulations."

She playfully nudges me. "When is it going to be your turn for marriage and a family?"

My face burns hot. "Not sure."

Mia puts on a teasing tone. "Well, now that you and Dean are working together…"

The others grin and Mia holds up her hands. "We'll see what the future brings!"

The future. Right. Gusts blow snowflakes up from the sidewalk and into the street in billowy clouds, and I'm treated to a memory of me with Dean and our kids in our cozy cottage, all of us snuggled together on our double bed. Scout's there, too.

"Let's plan the more immediate future first," Kirstin says sunnily. "El Bandito on Friday at five o'clock?" she asks, as more snow cascades around us.

"That's the day after Christmas, isn't it?" I ask.

"Then we can share about our Christmases!" Heather says brightly.

My heart swells with happiness. "Oh gosh, I'd really love that."

Mia grins. "Can't wait!"

"Yay!" Kirstin joins in.

"Super yay!" Heather echoes as they rush me with happy hugs. Our arms fold over one another's in an enormous group embrace. "Oh, Paige," Heather says, holding on tighter. "We've missed you."

"Yeah," Kirstin agrees, and Mia adds, "We have."

"And I've missed all of you, so, so much."

We say our goodbyes, wishing one another a merry Christmas, and the women enter Beaumont's as I stride off in the snow. Chilly winds blow but my heart is light. *Everything in its place and all things in good time.* Maybe that's what Mary Christmas was getting at. First, I saw Roger at Beaumont's and introduced him and Mom. Next, I ran into my old girlfriend group and we're reconnecting. Paws and Read is back on track, which I'm ecstatic about. Is it possible I'll get a second chance with Dean, too? I pat down my coat over where the necklace rests close to my heart. I sure hope so.

CHAPTER
Twenty-Four

I hurry to my SUV and see some kids near the corner engaging in a snowball fight, ducking behind a park bench in one of the smaller town squares. "You're going to get it now!" one boy calls, lobbing a giant snowball at another kid. The other boy darts behind a lamppost, his arms spread wide. "Missed me! Again!"

They hurl snowballs back and forth amid happy laughter as I step aside to stay out of the way. I'm not quite quick enough, though, and a hard mound of snow whacks the bottom of my overcoat, leaving a big, white smudge. I turn around to see a younger girl with her mittens covering her mouth.

"Oh no! I'm sorry!"

"It's all right," I tell her gently. "No harm done."

The kids' parents wander over through the park. They're an attractive couple in their thirties wearing coats, hats, and gloves. "Everything okay?"

"Oh yeah." I laugh and dust off my coat. "Fine. Merry Christmas."

"Merry Christmas," the man and woman say before admonishing their kids to be more careful with their snowballs. My heart thumps at the pretty picture in my mind of me and Dean playing in the snow with our kids. That was such a special afternoon. All of them were wonderful, Dean and Eleanor and Henry. And Scout, can't forget him.

Then I see it. A cheery snowman standing tall in the park. He has a scarf wound around him and wears a floppy black hat, and—*nooo*. The carrot someone used for his nose was inserted with the skinny end first. Just like… My heart thumps and I inquire of the parents, "Did y'all build the snowman?"

The dad shrugs. "No. It was already here."

Just as he says it, the carrot sags on the snowman's head then drops to the ground.

Gasp.

The mom laughs. "Guess some kid put that in backward."

"Ha, yes." I trudge through the snow and pick up the carrot. Dust it off and insert it properly in the snowman's face. His eyes made of pebbles seem to gleam at me.

Ridiculous.

I stare up at the sky and snow dusts my hat and eyelashes. *And yet. How can this be?*

This snowman looks so much like the one I built with Dean and the kids, it has to mean something. Be some sort of sign. I press my lips together, knowing I never used to believe in those. Only in strong coincidences. Opening yourself up to *signs* is akin to believing in magic. But what could be more magical than the once-in-a-lifetime Christmas I shared with Dean?

My head whirls as I try to make sense of it while walking to my parking spot, but no part of my experience makes any rational sense at all. Most mystical happenings can't be explained logically. Isn't that what Charles Dickens hinted at in *A Christmas Carol*?

I climb into my SUV and fasten my seatbelt, my heart beating harder. I've got to find a way to *hold on to what is good*, like Mom said. Maybe I don't have my alternate reality anymore, but who knows what's possible in this life down the road?

I drive to the dry cleaners mulling this over, then stand at the counter while my laundry gets retrieved. The man working there hands me a collection of hangers cloaked in a dry cleaning bag and a heavy package of something else. Then I remember. It's my weekly laundry all done for me and folded. *Gone* is the heaping laundry basket and the bedroom chair piled high with scattered but clean children's clothing. Tears spring to my eyes, and I wipe them back.

I know I'm not crying over mounds of unfolded laundry. I'm not.

But when I reach my SUV, I fall apart and sob.

I wave to Lloyd at the guard house and pull into my condo's parking lot. It's so surreal that it's been less than a day since I saw him last night. The holly wreath greets me on the glass door fronting the elevator and I push the button for the sixth floor, hauling in my dry cleaning and package of neatly folded clothes. I've been treating myself to laundry service as a luxury here, but now I'd take unruly baskets of mismatched socks any day.

My place is eerily quiet as I carry my laundry to the bedroom, set the package on the dresser, and hang my clothes in the closet. When I return to the living room, afternoon falls across the valley outside my window and Elroy waits in his chair.

"Hi, boy." I pat his head. His automated *"Arf! Arf!"* used to cheer me. Now it just makes me sad. I miss Scout. I miss Eleanor. Henry. Everyone. Dean most of all. And it wasn't just about being with them; it was about how they made me feel. So special and loved, like an important part of their group. Our family. Goodness knows I fell hard for them. Like a ton of bricks.

I sink down in a swivel chair facing the view in my open overcoat. Bring my hand to my necklace and hold the ruby heart. I'm not sure how to approach Dean with what I want to say to him. It was hard enough trying to tell him I'd come from a different reality when I was in the alternate one. Attempting to share that I visited another dimension—and then returned from it—will be even harder. There's probably only a very slim chance he'll believe me.

Still. I need to try.

I spin the swivel chair using my boot heels to observe the kitchen. The advent calendar's arranged exactly like the one we had in our cute bungalow. Tomorrow's poinsettia day, December twenty-first, and the day after that, there's ice skating on December twenty-second. Which could be a fun thing to do after our last full day of school and before my big Paws and Read launch party. Then the Christmas candle ornament on December twenty-third. Will I still have a romantic dinner out with Dean that night? Mary Christmas's suggestion rings out in my mind. *Enjoy.* I did enjoy participating in those activities so much. But now—

Wait. I sit up straighter in my chair and stare at the advent calendar. If adding items to the calendar with Dean and the kids could predict outcomes, why not here? I did in fact see a snowman today in the park, one that looked strikingly like the one Dean and our family built in the alternate reality. When

I add the other elements to the calendar, will certain events continue coming true?

I gently drop the ruby heart pendant against my sweater and stand, walking over to the calendar, my mission becoming clear. I have to talk to Dean about what I've been through these past several days, even if it's difficult, even if he might not believe me. I at least have to try.

Hold on to what is good.

There must be hope for me and Dean.

I lay my hand on the ruby heart necklace.

Otherwise, why would I still have his gift?

Later that evening, I sit on the sofa with my laptop, locating the teacher and staff directory. It's on a password-protected portion of the website accessible by school employees only. Principal Peabody's information is at the top. I shake my head, recalling our "Boss Lady" conversation, and the lurid details she alluded to concerning her private escapades. If she honestly owns a mug like that, I'm never going to be able to look her in the eye without wondering about her secret life again.

I'm glad I don't have to work directly under her as her assistant anymore, and plan to pour myself into my teaching extra hard. Though the hours can be long and the paperwork endless, I'll remain thankful for my job every day. And when students act up, as they're bound to do on occasion, I'll remind myself of drowning in a sea of color-coded sticky notes and be grateful for my classroom management skills. It will be great to have therapy dogs in the school. I can't wait for my literacy program to begin in January, and the launch party on Tuesday will be so much fun.

Aha! I've found it! The section for Walton High School teachers.

I click the link open and scroll to the *B*'s for Burton, clicking that link next.

Dean's email is his professional account for the school, but his cell number's listed, too. All employees list both, since the school has a phone tree for emergencies. But finding Dean's contact information is only a start. I need to reach out next, and hope he responds.

What if he won't go for coffee?

What if he invents an excuse?

I feel faint.

What if he ignores me completely?

No. I recall his banter at the holiday party and that interested gleam in his eyes. I couldn't have imagined both things. Even if I possibly imagined Eleanor, and Henry...

Stop.

I pat my necklace, knowing I didn't invent those people. Just because they're not here now doesn't mean that they can't be around someday. That they very well could be a part of my future. My temples throb and I rub them.

How oh how am I going to explain everything to Dean?

Calmly and carefully so I don't leave anything out.

Mary Christmas's words come back to me. *Everything in its place and all things in good time.* Maybe the timing wasn't right for Dean to believe me about the dual realities when I was in the other realm. Is it possible I can convince him to believe me here? I lay my hand on my ruby heart necklace again. We did form a bond in that other universe, a very deep one, and this heart pendant is an expression of that love. So maybe?

I close my eyes and hope, make a silent wish.

Draw in a breath.

Okay, here goes.

I lift my cell phone off the sofa cushion beside me with trembling fingers and type in Dean's number, setting him up as a new contact. We've been out of touch for so long, he doesn't pop up as an already established one. Besides, his area code is not local to Piney Mount. Maybe it's for Boulder, Colorado? I open my text app and my thumbs hover over the keypad, doing a miniature tap dance in midair. I'm not sure how to start, so I decide to start simple.

> **PAIGE:** Hey Dean, it's me—Paige. Fun seeing you at the holiday party and about us working together. Want to grab a cup of coffee and catch up?

I have the immediate instinct to bail. But then I push myself to be brave—and hit send. I stare at the screen and the seconds tick by. Slowly. Painfully.

Maybe I've made a mistake.

Then, no!

A text alert sounds, and I read his message.

> **DEAN:** Sure. Where and when?

My heart turns cartwheels and I squeeze my hands into fists. *Yes!* I do a happy dance on the sofa. *Yes, yes, yes. Yes!* Take a deep breath. Two breaths. Tuck back my stick-straight hair. I'm definitely getting layers *and* pink highlights. Soon. *I can look fun and be a teacher! There's no rule against that!* Er. Unless maybe there is? *Okay.* I swallow hard. I'll check the employee handbook first.

> **PAIGE:** Cuppa Joe tomorrow at two o'clock?

Dots. Dots. And more dots.
My nerves skitter with each one.

> **DEAN:** See ya then.

CHAPTER
Twenty-Five

I'm *sweating bullets* waiting for Dean to arrive, severely overheated in my camel-colored cashmere sweater. I should have gone for a more casual look, like that flouncy dress I wore when I went to Beaumont's with Mom the first time. But nothing like that is in my current wardrobe. I'm also completely devoid of thongs. Which I should *not* be thinking about when Dean walks in. Or the way he cut one off me. *Snip-snap.* "*There goes Tuesday.*"

If my face burned any hotter it would catch fire.

He spots me and shares a lopsided grin.

My insides flip-flop, going all mushy.

How am I going to put this?

Dean, I have something to tell you.

No.

Do you believe in magic?

Too big a leap into the fantastic too soon.

You know that advent calendar you gave me?

Holds possibilities.

He strides over, removing his coat. "Well, hey there."

"Hey, you!" My mouth pinches when I try to look relaxed in my not-so-relaxed teacher-looking clothes. *Gah.* Why aren't I in jeans? He is, and he looks dynamite in an argyle sweater.

Dean surveys my coffee cup. I went ahead and ordered a double-shot latte, but the caffeine's not helping my nerves. The heel of my boot taps the floor and I press down on my knee. Then the same thing happens on the other side. He acts like he doesn't notice. Still. He sneakily peers under the table. "I'll just go and"—he points toward the coffee bar—"get mine."

"Great idea!" Why am I speaking! With! Exclamation! Marks!

Deep breaths.

Okay. I'll tone it down.

My left leg jiggles. Then the right. I grab my knees hard and squeeze. *Ahhh.* Better.

Dean returns with his order in no time. He got a self-serve regular coffee so it took him a nanosecond. His brow wrinkles. "Something wrong with your knees?" he asks, taking a seat.

"Er, nope!" I release them. *Bounce. Bounce. Bounce. Whyyy?*

He sets down his cup. "You're not nervous?"

"Who, me?" I rub my nose. "No."

He nods knowingly. "I remember that nose thing, Paige."

"Oh?" I straighten my spine. "Which nose thing is that?"

He sighs and settles back in his chair. "You really haven't changed." He says it good-naturedly, but he doesn't know how wrong he is. He reads my stricken expression. "I didn't mean that in a bad way. Most people would love to hear that at our age."

"Yes, ancient," I quip. "Twenty-eight and twenty-six."

A wry twist to his lips. "I *am* pushing thirty."

"Then you'd better break out the cane, grandpa."

He laughs and holds his coffee on the table, centering it in both hands. "It's really good to spend time with you again.

It's been what? Six years?" Depends on who you ask, and in which reality.

"Er. More or less?" I push my coffee cup aside, deciding I've had enough. That's what I get for sugaring things up, both at home and then here. "Dean?"

"Yes?" How could I have forgotten the way his dark eyes sparkle and that sexy dimple in his cheek? I was sleeping with the man just yesterday. *Jingle all the way!* I blink and shove aside the memory. This Dean knows nothing about any of that. Much less Tuesday or Saturday thongs. Or the two children who resulted from that sort of behavior.

He peers at me in his ultra-dreamy way, and I lose my nerve. "It's just! Really great! To see you!" I'm exclaiming again and growing breathless. The room spins and I clutch the table. Dean passes me my water. I'd forgotten I'd poured myself a cup from the complimentary station.

"Paige?" he asks seriously as I mostly drain the cup. "Are you okay?"

"Yes." I set down the water cup. Crush it accidentally. Water seeps over its sides, dribbling down my knuckles. "Why would you ask that?" I wipe my fingers with a napkin. "Exactly?"

"You're just"—he tries not to sound judgmental—"acting a little odd."

"I've just been juggling lots of balls lately." I stare at him deeply, hoping he'll get the message that this is super important. And, more critically, *not* all in my head.

"Juggling?"

"Yes. Here and there."

"Where?"

"*Here.*" I lick my lips. "And *there.*"

"In Piney Mount or at school?"

"Both places." I take a slug of coffee. "Honestly."

"Ahh. Got it. You've been working really hard on that new program of yours, Paws and Read." That *is* a bright spot on this horizon. It was hard to put that dream off in the other reality, with only the hope it was eventually coming. In this world, I know it is absolutely. When I see our first volunteers and dogs working with students next semester, my heart will burst with joy.

"Yes, but that's not the only thing." I lower my voice. "I've had experiences."

"Experiences?" He wrinkles up his face.

Okay, yeah, that sounded a little too Missy Peabody.

"Not *experiences*!" I sigh. "Adventures!"

Dean drags a hand down his face. "I…see?" he says like he absolutely doesn't.

"Dean," I say urgently. "You know that advent calendar you gave me?"

"On Friday, at the gift exchange? Sure."

"I think it's working." There, I've said it. I sit back in my chair and cross my arms.

"Working?" He takes a moment to digest this and then asks, "How is it working?"

"Exactly like you said it would."

He narrows his eyes. "In predicting the future?"

A floral delivery person pushes through the café's front door. She's got a cart on wheels and it's loaded down with festive red plants with pointy petals. She addresses the manager behind the coffee bar. "Where do you want these?"

"*Ahhh!*" I spring back in my chair so hard I nearly knock it over.

"Paige?" Dean's more startled than I am, which is significantly. "What's wrong?"

I extend a finger toward the flower lady as she starts

unloading poinsettias from the cart and plunking them down on tables. "Poin—poinsettias!"

"And?"

"Dean," I whisper hurriedly. "I took the poinsettia ornament from the Day Twenty-One pocket in the advent calendar this morning and added it to the tree."

"The advent calendar?" he asks, trying to grasp this.

"Yes, and now—" I gulp, unable to finish. Flower lady puts a pot down right in front of me. "Merry Christmas," she says, and I blink.

"Paige," Dean says calmly. "It's the holidays. Poinsettias are everywhere."

"Yes, but why here?"

He grimaces. "They're decorating the coffee shop?"

"A little late for that, don't you think?"

"I have no idea. Maybe they got a late-season discount."

Nooo. I'm making a mess of this. "I think it's something more," I confide in hushed tones. "I think it has to do with what you told me about the calendar predicting the future." He stares at me askance, but I won't give up now. Now that I've gotten started, I might as well carry on. Unless Dean jumps up and runs out of here. Which he might do. I hope he doesn't, though. "Yesterday was the snowman ornament," I tell him. "That was Day Twenty, and then I saw this snowman in the park."

"Well, Paige, it is December—in Piney Mount."

"That's not it," I insist hoarsely. "His nose was put in wrong."

"The snowman's nose?"

I nod. "The carrot was shoved in *backward*. Just like Henry—"

"Who's Henry?"

"Our *child*." I gasp and cover my mouth. I hadn't meant for that to come out so directly.

"We have a child?" Dean pales. "Paige." He's aghast and also slightly filled with wonder. "And you never told me?" *He is sooo getting the wrong impression.*

"*Nooo.*" I hold up my hands. "It's nothing like that. We don't have a child here—in this reality."

"In this reality, right," he says. "Where is the other one, then? In the future?"

I groan, growing discouraged. "I would say that, but we were still our same ages somehow. But not here, we were *there.*"

"With a kid named Henry?"

"And Eleanor! Henry's older sister."

"Odd coincidence." He rubs the side of his neck. "Henry and Eleanor were my grandparents' names on my dad's side."

"Oh! Well, old-timey names are coming back in fashion, I hear. For babies."

His eyebrows arch. "Our babies?"

"We also had a dog named Scout."

"*Scout,*" he says like that's vaguely familiar. "Wow, Paige. That's quite an elaborate dream."

"That's what I thought at first, until I realized it wasn't."

"How could you tell?"

"I was awake, Dean, and not sleeping." *Not with all the sugar-laden coffee I drank.* "I went to bed in my condo on Friday night, the night the comet passed overhead, after putting up my advent calendar." I pause and then ask, "Did you see it? Your Christmas Comet?"

"Yes, it was spectacular. You?"

"I know it passed over Piney Mount, but I was sleeping." I recall the flash of bright light in my bedroom. "I mean, mostly sleeping. I may have caught a glimpse of its aura through my bedroom window, but only vaguely, and then the very next day I woke up in this sweet little bungalow on Chestnut Street. But that didn't have to do with the comet. It was more about the Christmas star on the calendar, I believe."

Dean pushes back in his chair, looking stunned. "Did you say Chestnut Street? Whoa, that's weird."

"Why—why is that weird? I mean, any weirder than anything else I've said?"

"Do you remember the address?"

"Yes. One two five."

"*O-kay.*" Dean pulls his cell phone from his jeans pocket and taps something in. He holds its screen toward me. "This the house?"

"That's it!" My heart pounds at the darling view, although it looked cuter when we owned it. There's no holiday wreath on the door, and the front porch is missing those pretty icicle lights. I squint at the screen and see listing details. Square footage. Three bedrooms. Two baths. Lot size. A price. It's a real estate listing. My heart gallops. "Why do you have that listing on your phone?"

"Because I'm scheduled to see it," he says. "Later this afternoon."

Wait. I try to make some sense of this. Dean's buying a house, and he's looking at ours? The house that was ours in the alternate reality and could be ours again? I understand I'm jumping the gun. Dean and I would at least have to move in together or marry. In the other life, we didn't just share kids; we shared a mortgage.

Dean rakes his hands through his hair. "I didn't tell you, did I?" he asks like he's not sure. "Didn't mention I was looking for a house when we talked at the holiday party?"

"No. You said nothing about that."

"I've been saving for a while," he explains. "Figured buying a house might be a wise investment, but I didn't want to buy in Boulder. Something made me wait until I came home."

Home, yes. We made our cottage so cozy, with its wood-burning fireplace and cheery rooms. "It's a great house," I say emphatically, because I fell in love with the place. "It's even got a dog door in the kitchen for Scout." I purse my lips, realizing that might not be the case yet. "At least, that's a possibility. For a pet. Potentially. Meaning, a potential pet."

You're babbling now, Paige. Stop.

Dean chuckles at the absurdity of the situation. "What kind of dog is Scout?"

"A very big and fluffy white one. I think he was a rescue."

"I like that about Scout."

"He also gave himself a job," I can't help sharing. "He brings in our morning paper every day. Nothing stops him. Not even snowy weather."

Dean smiles proudly as if taking credit for this himself. "Good boy!"

My heart blooms with hope. "So. Wait. You believe me?"

Dean sinks back in his chair. "I believe you experienced something, but Paige? Is that the only reason you wanted to meet with me today? Because I have the feeling it was also about something else."

His expression's compassionate, kind, and I gather my courage and say, "It is. Dean, my wanting to talk with you today is not just about that magical advent calendar, or whatever other sort of life I believe I saw." My nose twitches and I rub it. "It's about what happened six years ago when you left for Puerto Rico. We never really talked afterward. In some ways, never resolved things."

He hangs his head and stares at the floor. "You don't know how many times I've thought about that over the years."

"Have you?" I thought I was over Dean, but something deep in my heart must have known that wasn't true.

He slowly looks up. "Yeah. That was a real turning point for the two of us."

"More like a breaking point," I admit sadly. "And I know I'm the one who broke things off. I'm sorry about that now. I wish I'd given you a chance. Given us one."

His eyes gleam with regret. "Have you ever wondered what might have happened…? I mean, if things had been different? If maybe I'd turned around and come back?"

"Did you consider it?"

"Honestly? Yes." Shame washes over his face, but he has nothing to be ashamed of. I'm the one who canceled us. "I was at the airport and there was this cute family boarding the plane ahead of me."

"A mom and a dad and their little girl?"

Dean's jaw unhinges. "How could you know that?"

"Because you told me." Heat builds in my eyes, but I need him to know the truth. "Dean. In the other reality, you did come back."

He sets his elbows on the table and rubs his forehead. "Are you saying you saw what might have been between us, if we'd stayed together all this time?"

"That's as close as I can come to explaining it."

"And?" He's genuinely interested and not faking it. I can tell this about Dean. This only encourages me to share more.

"It was wonderful," I say dreamily. "Our life was amazing. *We* were amazing together, as a mom, a dad, a family. I mean, it wasn't *perfect*, because nothing truly is, but close."

His expression grows foggy, like he's remembering, but he can't possibly be. "Will you tell me about it?"

Butterflies flit around in my chest because I'm so happy that he wants to know more, but I'm also frightened that sharing it all will be too much. "Only if you promise not to freak out."

He nods and drinks some coffee. "I want you to start from the beginning."

"Er. Okay." I weigh how much to tell him, deciding to deliver the recap in broad strokes while skipping the sexy details. Otherwise, he'll think I've been fantasizing about him. So I'm *one hundred percent* not mentioning naughty Santa and sexy Mrs. Claus—or thongs. A woman's got to have some mystery, and if Dean and I somehow wind up together, he'll have to find those things out for himself.

"Wait." He's staring at something on my sweater. Great. Have I spilled my coffee? I glance down, but no. It's not a coffee stain he's glued to. He's mesmerized by my ruby heart necklace. "Paige." He sounds like he's far, far away. "Where did you get that necklace?"

CHAPTER
Twenty-Six

Dean looks into my eyes, questioning. Like he's searching for answers.

"You, uh." I shift nervously in my chair, wondering if he'll buy this, even though it *is* the truth. "You gave it to me." My smile trembles. "For Christmas."

"This Christmas?" He reaches toward me and holds open his hand. "May I?"

I nod and remove my necklace, placing the jewelry in Dean's palm. He closes his fingers around it and shuts his eyes. "That's impossible," Dean says with his eyes still closed. "I distinctly remember helping you with this clasp...you holding up your hair. Wait." His eyes fly open as he grips the necklace. "You got pink highlights?"

Oh my gosh. A breakthrough.

My heart hammers.

Is it on account of the necklace?

He winces, pressing his hands to his temples. "Ow!"

"What's wrong?"

"It's like I had a brain freeze, but not a brain freeze. More like a jumbled info dump. Wild. Is your mom dating someone named Roger?"

"Dean!" I murmur excitedly. "You saw it, too?"

"I'm not sure what I saw. It was extremely compressed." He frowns, thinking. "Like a zip file ripping itself open. Scattered images were everywhere… Hang on." His eyes go wide. "Holy cow. Did you get a tattoo?"

I giggle and cover my mouth. "What else did you see?"

"A sweet little girl in pigtails. A boy saying 'Merry Kissmas.'"

Tears spring to my eyes. "That's Henry."

"Henry," Dean says distractedly. "Right." He shakes his head then chuckles. "He's a cutie, isn't he? So is Eleanor, and Scout?"

"It was a good life in so many ways."

"It couldn't have been perfect."

"No. But it was perfect being there with you."

"That's very sweet, Paige."

"You were sweet," I tell him. "The ideal husband and dad."

"I like the idea of being a husband and dad." Fear washes over his face, and something else: panic. "*Someday*." He opens his hand and stares down at the necklace. So do I. Was it this token of our love that enabled his sharing in my memories? An emblem of our unity that binds us across time?

I think so.

I look up at him and he stares at me, frozen in his chair. This has all been a lot for him to absorb. "I know. I get it," I hasten to add. "We're not talking about anytime soon. For you, or for me. Or, er, either of us." I laugh awkwardly.

"It is a big leap," he agrees. "We hadn't seen each other in years until Friday."

"My thinking exactly." *In this world.*

"So we don't want to rush into anything."

"Who's rushing? Haha! Not me."

"In fact," he says like he's trying to convince himself. "I think we should take things slowly."

"Good idea," I concur. "Super slowly. Like molasses dripping on a hot Sunday afternoon."

He surveys the poinsettias in the room, ending with the one on our table. "Coffee was a good start, though."

"Yeah, it's been fun!"

"And, extremely informative for me."

"Ha." That makes two of us. I had no idea about the powers of my necklace. I am so very grateful that Dean was able to see some of my memories, too.

"So," he asks. "What's on the advent calendar for tomorrow?"

"Ice skates."

"Hmm. And the day after?"

"A Christmas candle."

He shakes a finger at me and squints. "I took you out, didn't I? To a fancy restaurant."

I smile from ear to ear and whisper, "*You're remembering?*"

"Paige, I'm not sure why I'm sharing some of your memories now, but I seem to be catching glimpses of what you went through." His face reddens and his eyebrows shoot up. "'*There goes Tuesday*'?"

I sink down in my chair, my cheeks hot. "Oh gosh."

"We *did* get along, didn't we?" he asks huskily.

My pulse hums. "Uh-huh."

Dean chuckles. "Look. I don't know what any of this means, but it's hard to argue with the mysteries of the universe." He gingerly returns my necklace, and I put it on, watching it drape prettily against my sweater. "Especially when they're *this mysterious*." He rubs his chin. "I wonder if the lady who sold me the advent calendar could help explain what's going on. The one dressed like Mrs. Claus?"

"Mary Christmas?"

"Sorry?"

"That was her name. M-A-R-Y Christmas."

Dean laughs. "Fitting."

"Yeah," I reply. "We can try to find her and ask. I spoke to her in the other world, but then she disappeared."

"Oh yeah? Did she lend you any insight?"

"She mostly encouraged me to enjoy my life as it was happening, and to try not to second guess things. I really wanted to stay through Christmas Day and was so glad I did. It was a once-in-a-lifetime Christmas, or so I thought."

His gaze lingers on mine. "What do you think now?"

"That maybe my very special Christmases are just beginning."

"You know what I think?" Dean asks. "I think we should go to the holiday market and look for that advent calendar seller."

"Don't you have an appointment to tour the house?"

He nods. "We'll go before." I'm touched he's including me in his plans. "Then, after we speak with Mary Christmas, maybe you can come with me to Chestnut Street?" I grin when he adds, "I'd love your opinion on the house."

Dean and I walk to the town square, which isn't far from Cuppa Joe. The holiday market lights shine up ahead and snow falls around us. "Nice out this time of year," Dean says. "Nippy."

I stare up at his handsome face, reliving the memories we made in the other realm, wondering if there's a way to make them real. "It is nice," I answer. Wind blows back my hair beneath my pom-pom hat, pushing it over my shoulders. "Everything's so Christmassy."

He surveys the wintry scene. The cheerily decorated

streetlamps adorned with festive greenery, and holiday banners draped from their arms. Storefronts boast decorated windows filled with fake snow and covered in snowflake stickers. "Yeah." We pass by the smaller square on the way to the large one. Dean cocks his head in the direction of the snowman, who stands near the center of the square beside a frozen fountain. "That your guy?"

"Yep. He's the one."

Dean laughs and strides over to him. I follow him through the snow. "Wait. Where are you going?"

He stands with his hands on his hips, addressing the snowman. "Hey there, fella. The lady here seems to think we've met before. What's your opinion?" He leans toward the snowman like he's listening. "What's that? Wait!" He lets out the biggest, fakest gasp. "Did you see that, Paige? I think he winked at me!"

I playfully shove Dean's arm. "Did not."

"Well. It sure looked to me like he was thinking about it, anyway."

"Hmm. Maybe so."

Dean examines the snowman from top to bottom, paying particular attention to the carrot jammed into the center of his face. "His nose looks all right now."

"That's because I fixed it."

"Aha."

His eyebrows arch. "What else have you fixed?"

"Ask me in the morning," I say. "Unless all of this goes *poof*."

"*Poof*?"

"That's what Mary Christmas told me when I asked her about the time split and two different realities. She said there's no way for me to be two places at one time. So if I'm here, I can't be there."

"And if you're there…"

"Exactly."

"So the kids we had? The dog?"

"*Poof! Poof! Poof!*"

Dean frowns. "That seems very sad."

My heart sinks because I miss my family, even when Dean is here with me now. "It is sad, but since I've lost all that." I shrug. "I'm not sure how to reclaim it."

Dean's face shows real melancholy, like he senses a tremendous loss, too. Maybe he's absorbing my sadness, or simply being empathetic. He glances at the market. "Maybe we should go and ask Mary Christmas?"

We approach the main town square with its tall Christmas tree. I cast a look at the consignment store beside the bank, Second Chances, but it's a bakery now called Sugar Cakes. So, no telescope in the window—not that I'd need to buy one for Dean. He's been teaching for a while and on his own. Since he's considering buying a house, he's clearly stable financially. If he wants a telescope, he can likely get one for himself, if he doesn't own one already.

We duck under the main tent and out of the snow, where we see the popcorn vendor. The aroma of freshly popped popcorn fills the air, along with the scent of yummy hot chocolate. We both eye the booth. Maybe if we hadn't just finished drinking coffee, we'd be tempted to purchase a few cups.

"Will you look at this." Dean stops and picks up a mug from a ceramics table.

My heart stutters. It's got a painted starry night design set against the backdrop of the mountains. "It's great, isn't it?" he asks, holding it in front of me. Then he meets my eyes and I experience a jolt, almost like I've had déjà vu. But it's not me who's experienced a memory. It's Dean. "Paige," he whispers softly. "Did you—give me a mug like this?"

"Yes. For Christmas."

"And something else?" He darts a look across the square at the bakery.

"I did. A telescope. It was secondhand, but money was tight."

His eyes mist over. "You loved me," he says like he intuits this very deeply.

"Yes."

My ruby heart necklace lies beneath my coat, and he stares at the spot where he knows it hangs. "And I loved you."

My fingers find the delicate chain below my neck scarf, verifying the precious gift that rests close to my heart. While I'm glad he's catching glimmers of the life we had together, I so badly wish that he could see more.

"Paige," he asks. "What was wrong with the other place? You said it wasn't perfect."

My shoulders slouch as I answer honestly. "It was small stuff, when you look at the bigger picture. Money was tight for us, like I said. We had two kids on your teacher's salary and my income, which was lower than yours. I was Missy's administrative assistant."

"*Nooo.*"

"Yeah, and that had its—interesting moments. But I had other ambitions like I did here. I wanted to be a teacher, like the one who helped me when I was a teenager, and you encouraged me to go back to school."

"Back?"

"I dropped out early when—"

He nods. "The kids, right?"

"They weren't a mistake, Dean."

His lips pull into a smile that looks a little wistful. "No, I suspect not." His expression softens further when he meets my eyes. "I'm sure they were a blessing."

Hurt catches in my throat at my loss and longing. "They were."

We turn toward the far side of the tent and start snaking in that direction, and my spirit warms at our connection. It feels good being with Dean and on this mutual quest, but my heart wants more. My heart wants the love and laughter we shared in our cozy little cottage with Eleanor, Henry, and Scout. The life I never could have imagined, but now have a tough time living without.

I point ahead of us. "She was right over there, where the larger tent meets the smaller one on the side near the skating rink." Skaters glide by on the ice, the lights around the rink delivering a cheery glow. Happy laughter and shouts drift toward us on the wind, which carries the fresh scent of new-fallen snow.

"Right. I remember," Dean says about Mary Christmas, but I'm remembering other things. Thinking of our fun ice skating outing as a family and how we ran into Roger and Mom. Dean asking me out for our candlelit dinner. I knew then I was in so deep. Helplessly in love with my husband.

Dean leads me to the spot where Mary Christmas's booth had been, and we pause, peering around. There's no one here selling advent calendars. Only the actor dressed as Santa taking photos with kids. "But she was right—here," Dean says, confounded.

"She was the first time I saw her, too. But then she was gone. Just like—"

"*Poof*," Dean says sadly.

Then suddenly a voice sounds behind us. "Are you looking for someone?"

CHAPTER
Twenty-Seven

ean and I turn toward the apparition. "Mrs. Christmas!" I gasp. "You're here."

"This will be the last time I visit," she responds. "I'm needed elsewhere, and—just like you—I can't be in two places at once. Life is funny that way. It presents choices. Different forks in the road."

"What about my life in the other world?" I ask her. "What about our kids?" My heart breaks when I say their names. "Eleanor and Henry?"

She stares at me and Dean. "You both chose your paths, and those paths have led you to where you are today."

"But wait!" Dean holds up his hand. "What if we'd chosen differently?"

"You mean from the very start?" Mary Christmas asks.

Dean and I glance at each other, and we both say, "Yes."

"Then you would be *there* now, wouldn't you?" she says merrily. "With all the trimmings!"

"Trimmings?" I ask her.

Her eyes sparkle warmly. "All the things that make a life

complete, a past, a present, and a future." I gasp, getting her meaning. *Memories.*

Mary lowers her glasses and peers at me. "What you experienced was a bit of a preview, Paige, like a movie trailer." She slides her glasses back on her nose. "If you'd chosen differently from the beginning, you would have experienced the entire feature film. Naturally! And both of you would still be there now."

She turns to go but Dean stops her. "Mrs. Christmas."

"Yes, Dean?"

"I have a question. Will the magic of the calendar work next year?"

She frowns thoughtfully. "I'm afraid not. The window of opportunity doesn't last forever. After midnight on Christmas Day, its magic isn't valid anymore." She glances at the sky. "You were only given this gift due to a once-in-a-lifetime event this season."

Of course. The Christmas Comet.

Then as quickly as she'd come, she disappears.

Poof.

Dean sinks his hands in his coat pockets. Sets his chin and sighs. "I'm sorry she wasn't more helpful. It sounds like she was saying we are where we are."

I shrug disappointedly, not sure what else I'd hoped for. "Yeah." But something in the way Dean and I stare at each other says we're not sure.

"Well." Dean checks his watch. "As long as we're *here* now, how about we go and see that house?"

Dean and I stand on the front porch of one hundred twenty-five Chestnut Street. I rode here with him from the market, then he parked his jeep in the drive. We glance up and down the snowy street. "The realtor must be running behind," Dean says.

But I don't mind the wait. I'm absorbing the charming cottage that used to be ours, attentive to every detail. The railings on the front porch and its broad floorboards, the glossy black door that matches the house's shutters. I peek in the front window by the door, expecting to see the rocker stationed there, but the entire room is empty and freshly painted, as are the bare bookshelves on either side of the hearth. The heart pine floor gleams like it's been recently polished. "Thanks for bringing me with you," I say.

"Of course." He swallows hard. "It just seemed right."

Finally, a car pulls up to the curb. It's an old-model hatchback like the one I used to own before I bought my SUV. Dean lifts a glove and waves. "That must be her."

It's hard to tell from here, but it looks like the woman is older and wearing a red hat with a wide white brim. Almost like a Santa hat. No. That would be silly. Unless she's getting in the holiday spirit.

"Hey," Dean says. "She looks a little like…" He shakes his head. "No."

I laugh, guessing he was about to say Mary Christmas. "That's what I thought, too."

Dean's phone buzzes with a text and he pulls it from his coat pocket.

> **REALTOR:** On a call and will be in shortly. Feel free to look around.

We glance at her car, and she holds up a cell phone. Waves. Dean peeks over his shoulder at me and chuckles. "Okay." The lockbox on the door in front of us goes through a series of whirring mechanical sounds. Then a green light on the box shines. Dean tries the latch, and it opens. His cell buzzes again.

> **REALTOR:** Hope it's just right!

He laughs and shows me the text as we walk through the door. "No pressure."

We enter the living room, and I can't stop staring at the walls, envisioning the artists' prints Dean and I hung there from our museum visits. I imagine Scout barking and bounding toward us. Eleanor and Henry tugging at our legs. Looking up at us with sunny faces. Tears prickle my eyes and I sniffle.

"What's wrong?" Dean asks worriedly.

I pull a tissue from my coat pocket. "Memories."

"Yeah." He scans the room. "I wish I had more of those like you do."

"And I wish I had the ones you did in the other place."

He turns to me. "What do you mean?"

"When I was in the alternate reality, it was awesome. So much about it was wonderful. The only painful part was that I couldn't remember. Couldn't say how I'd gotten to the place we were from where we had started."

"The day I left for Puerto Rico?" His brow creases. "Or didn't go, in that case?"

I unwrap my neck scarf. "Yes."

"So you couldn't remember anything before December twentieth of the current year?"

"That's right." I tuck my scarf in my coat pocket along with my gloves.

"Could I remember the past?"

"You could. When I asked Mary Christmas how that was possible, she said in your mind that had always been your permanent world. That version of you had never seen any other reality but the one we were living in together with our kids. I, on the other hand, was completely aware of the dual realms. Because I had my memories from here, I couldn't have them from the other world."

He digests this information. "Did you try to ask me about them, those missing memories?"

"I did, but it was a little hard to explain where I'd come from. You thought I was unhappy in our relationship, and longing for a different sort of life without you."

"Oh, Paige. You were between a rock and a hard place." He sets his jaw. "Maybe I should have listened to you. If I were in that situation again, I would, you know."

"Yes, I do believe you," I say softly. "But you're in a different place now, headspace wise. We've spoken to Mary Christmas again *and watched her disappear.*"

"Boy oh boy." He rakes a hand through his hair. "If I'd only known when I bought that advent calendar all the trouble it would bring."

"So? Maybe it wasn't a bad thing?" I smile up at him and he grins, too.

"You know, Paige. I think you're right."

"What do you say," I ask him. "Want to tour the rest of the house?" It's warm in here with the central heat turned on compared to the frigid temperature outdoors. We both unzip our coats, preparing to look around.

Dean points to a room on our left. "Let's start in there." We enter the kitchen, and he appreciates the amount of natural light afforded by the windows, and the updated appliances and cabinetry. He surveys the side door, which has no pet door in it yet.

I shrug sadly. "I suppose there is no Scout in this reality."

I hear a *Woof! Woof! Woof!* in the hall and shake it off. Then Henry's sweet voice rings out in my head, *Merry Kissmas!* It's like the other realm is calling me across a divide, but I've no way to get back there. My heart wrenches painfully. I miss my life with my family.

But this is my current world, and where I am right now with Dean. Mom has met Roger, thanks to me, and hopefully their relationship holds promise. I cross my fingers and lay them against my heart, wishing for her tests to come out okay, because that would be such a blessing. The biggest Christmas gift I could receive. And there are still more joys pending, like reestablishing my friendship with my girlfriends. I steal a peek at Dean and my face warms. *Everything in its place and all things in good time.*

Dean and I tour the rest of the house, then we stop at the juncture of the hall to the living room. He nods up at the ceiling and I see a surprise. "When they cleaned out this house," he says, "looks like someone forgot the mistletoe."

"Looks like it." I chuckle and scan the street, wondering if the sneaky realtor put it there to make this house seem more romantic and appealing to prospective buyers, who in this neighborhood are likely to be younger couples.

Dean stares out the front window at the realtor, who's still in her car. "Long call," he comments with a smirk.

"Maybe she's giving us space to make up our minds?"

"I've already made my mind up." Dean brings his arms around me. "If you have yours."

My breath hitches when he holds me close. "Dean, what?"

"Paige, please, tell me we can go out tonight. Grab something to eat. I'd love to spend more time with you. And I'd love to hear more about that other world, if you'll tell me, because it sounds spectacular, to tell you the truth."

I grin up at him and say, "All right." I consider the time

we've missed. "And I'd like to hear about your past six years. I want to know all about Puerto Rico and Boulder and your decision to move back here."

He holds me tighter. "Deal. But only if you fill me in on your life completely. I want to know about you and your teaching. What made you think up Paws and Read. How your old friend group is getting along."

My heart skips a beat. "Um. About them—"

"Yes?"

"Heather, Mia, Kirstin, and I kind of drifted apart for a while, but we've recently been back in touch. So I have a feeling things will get better."

"That's great." His grin says he means it. "I really liked the three of them." He whispers, "I always thought Mia would wind up with David, and Heather with Peyton." He scans my eyes, anticipating an answer.

"They did." I confirmed the details about their significant others when we chatted yesterday outside Beaumont's.

"And Kirstin?"

"She's met someone new, Gregory."

He snaps his fingers. "I might have predicted as much. I wasn't so sure about her and Bryce."

I chuckle at his intuition.

He pulls me closer still and scans the living room, and the open bedroom doors in the hall. "So. What do you think about the house?"

My heart pounds. "Honestly, I love it."

"Good. Because honestly, I love it, too.

"Paige Pierce?" he asks warmly, darting a glance at the mistletoe. "Can I kiss you?"

"Dean Burton." I stare up at the mistletoe and then at him. "I think you'll have to."

His lips meet mine and my whole world fills with joy. I can't help but think of all we've shared together, both here in this reality over time and in that beautiful alternate world. It's amazing to know that kissing Dean is just as wonderful across all universes. Pretty outstanding, actually.

He nods toward the front door and the street. "I'm going to tell the realtor I'll take it."

My heart wells with happiness. "I'm glad."

We step onto the front porch and we're in for a surprise. The realtor and her car are gone, and snow drifts down from the sky. Dean stares at my sweater below my open coat. "Paige, oh no. Your necklace."

My hand flies to my chest and I feel around on my sweater, run my hand under my hair and across the back of my neck. Pull my hat and scarf from my coat pocket and shake both things out over the porch.

I stare fretfully at Dean. "It's gone."

CHAPTER
Twenty-Eight

*W*e *retrace our* steps indoors. I also remove my coat and check under my sweater, but the necklace is clearly not in the house—or on my person. "When's the last time you remember having it?" Dean asks as we stand in the bungalow's living room.

"At the market, when we were looking at the starry night mug."

"Then we should go back there and check. Park in the same spot or nearby, and watch our footfalls along the way."

"Okay."

Dean's cell phone buzzes in his pocket and he checks his text.

> **REALTOR:** Sorry! Emergency. Don't worry about the house. I'll remotely lock the door. Did you love it?

> **DEAN:** Yes.

I'm heartened by Dean buying this house. Is it a sign about the future? *Our future?* I've made mistakes in this world and don't want to repeat them. Although Dean will have to want a future with me as badly as I want one with him for things to work out.

I put on my coat and Dean helps me slide my arms into the sleeves. The motion brings his face extremely close to mine. His dimple deepens when he smiles. "Don't worry," he says about the necklace. "We'll find it."

But the sad fact is, we don't. We scour the inside of Dean's jeep, looking under the front seat where I rode and in crevices around the passenger door and console, but it's not there. Not anywhere along the sidewalk during our walk to the market either, although it could have gotten buried in snow.

"Maybe someone else picked it up?" Dean says when we stop at the Santa Claus photo station, scanning the crowd.

"I bet Mary Christmas might know." But of course she's not here. When we saw her before, she said that was her last visit. She disappeared, enigmatically suggesting that when two realities diverge you have to make a choice. Since no one can be in two places at once, does the same go for inanimate objects?

Dean searches the area and then says, "Maybe we should try to contact her?"

If only it were that easy. "Might not work."

"We can try," Dean says softly. He whispers into the air, "Mary Christmas?" He cups a hand beside his mouth and tries again. "Mary Christmas!"

I do the same, turning the other way and calling out in hushed tones. A man walking a dog stops in front of me and smiles. "Merry Christmas, young lady."

"Oh no, I—"

Dean casts me a glance and turns up his palms.

"And merry Christmas to you," an older lady utters to Dean as she parades by.

Dean's neck turns red and then his ears.

I cover my mouth and giggle. I step up beside him. "So much for getting the real Mary Christmas to reappear."

Dean's mouth twitches when he says, "Maybe she's at the North Pole baking cookies?"

"Cookies!" I exclaim. "I have to make some for the holiday party."

"Wait. Didn't we already attend one of those?"

"Not the one for Walton faculty," I tell him. "The one for my students. We're having a party on the last half day." Which gives me tomorrow evening to prepare. I'm going to be busy, organizing my items for the Paws and Read party, too. But that won't take long and will mostly involve loading boxes into my SUV.

"Ah, yeah. I generally allow my students to have a party. Although, I encourage them to do the baking, so I won't have to."

I meet his dark gaze. "Crafty."

"No. Crafty was Mary Christmas, both in making her calendars and now in vanishing into thin air." He surveys the tent with its bustling booths, then studies the ground near our boots. The earth is parched and bare where the layer of winter grass has been worn thin and dusty. "I'm really sorry we didn't find your necklace, Paige."

"Maybe we're not meant to find it?"

He turns to me. "What do you mean?"

"The time split limitations might not only apply to me and you," I say. "Mary Christmas intimated neither you nor I could exist in both realities. Maybe it's the same for the necklace?"

"Then how did it slip through this way?" Dean questions.

"I don't know." The problem vexes me. "Maybe I needed to see it?"

"Maybe I did, too. After all, touching that necklace was how I came to believe you, because I got that uncanny glimpse of that other reality we shared." Dean wrinkles his forehead. "So do you think the necklace has gone back there? Been returned to the other realm, where it's gone *poof*?" He chuckles at the absurdity of what he's saying and shakes his head, but I can tell he's buying into it. Completely.

"Hmm. Possibly?"

We start walking back toward his jeep, exiting the big tent and getting lightly pummeled by swirling snow. I consider his time in Boulder. "Did you teach the first semester in Colorado?"

"I did." He nods. "But it was a private school and it let out for the break a week earlier."

"What made you decide on public education?"

His grin charms me. "I had a good feeling about working at Walton."

"Dean. Were you aware I taught there?"

He shrugs and says mildly, "Might have heard something through the grapevine."

"What grapevine?"

"It's called social media."

I swat him with my scarf and tease, "You stalked me?"

He wears a playful frown. "'Stalking' is not a very nice word. Unless you're talking about Christmas stockings."

I twist up my lips. "Punny."

His laughter rumbles. "No, seriously. I applied to the entire district and Walton was where they had the opening in physics. I was going to move next summer, but I thought, why not now? There's something pretty magical about new beginnings at Christmas."

I stare up into his dreamy eyes. "Yes."

My cheeks warm when I add, "I have a confession to make. I might have peeked at your profile once or twice, too."

He lays a hand across his chest. "Only once or twice?"

I laugh. "Well, how many times did you check in on me?"

"Dozens." He pauses dramatically then adds, "Daily."

I roll my eyes, not believing him. "Bet that got to Wendy."

"Wendy? What?" His mouth drops open but then he laughs. "You're a little jealous, aren't you?"

I gasp. "Am *not*."

"What about you?" He eyes me curiously. "Any serious boyfriends, or such?"

"Not a one."

"Why not?"

I hug my arms around myself as we're walking. "Maybe I was waiting for you."

"Hmm." His eyes twinkle when he says, "I'm glad."

"So?" I nudge his shoulder with mine. "Still want to go out for a bite?"

"I'd love to." His smile warms me. "And I do want to hear about that other place, as much as you're willing to tell me."

Later that evening, Dean walks me to my SUV.

"I'm really glad we spent this time together."

I sigh dreamily. "Yeah. Me too."

"And Paige." He lays his hand on my cheek. "Thanks for telling me more about that other world. It sounds like a dream."

"It was, in some ways." I cover his glove with mine, holding his palm against my face. "A hugely chaotic but happy one."

He steps closer, lowering his mouth toward mine. "That Santa's sleigh ride move was kind of sexy, huh?"

I flush deeply. "Maybe I shouldn't have told you *everything*."

His dark eyes twinkle. "Maybe you didn't have to. Maybe some of it was in that zip file I received."

My cheeks burn hot. "What?"

"No worries. Your secrets are safe with me. All of them." He covers my mouth with his and his kiss is tantalizingly warm. "We haven't forgotten how to kiss," he murmurs softly. "That's pretty clear." He lays another sizzling kiss on me and I melt.

"*Dean*." I slide my arms around his shoulders and link my hands behind his back. Wintry winds blow but I'm sheltered in his embrace.

"Paige." His lips meet mine, so silky smooth. "I have to see you again."

"Aren't we going skating tomorrow?" We talked more about the calendar over dinner.

"Yes." A lopsided grin. "But I was thinking about after that. Maybe for dinner on Tuesday?"

"I'd like that."

"We have so much more to discuss." He pulls back to grin at me. "Like Missy Peabody, Boss Lady." He wears a smirk. "Who knew?"

"Oh stop!" I laugh and shove his chest. "And please, don't you dare tell *a soul* what I told you about her." I purse my lips and giggle. "That part might not even be true in this realm."

"The other aspects you told me about seem to jive." He shrugs. "More or less."

"Okay, fine." I give him a quick peck on the lips. "But things are also different. Look at the two of us, for instance."

"Hmm, yes." His eyes dance. "Just look."

As much as I hate to break things up, I know I need to go. "We should probably say goodnight. We've both got school in the morning." Though he's not teaching yet, he mentioned at dinner he has meetings in the morning with Principal Peabody and his department head. He also has to complete some paperwork and check out his laptop.

"All right. It's true." He kisses me one last sexy time and helps me into my SUV. "Drive safely," he says before shutting my door.

Fifteen minutes later I basically *float* into my condo.

"Hi, Elroy." I pat the robotic dog's head. "How are you?"

"*Arf! Arf!*"

My heart pings sadly when I think of Scout, and then of Eleanor and Henry. But no. I won't be sad. I should be overjoyed by these new possibilities. Dean and I are together again in a way I never imagined only a few days ago. Maybe Mom was right, and Dean and I are fated? She's such a great mom and I love her dearly. She has got to be okay. That's the only thing that makes sense.

Maybe I didn't understand her as fully as I should have beforehand in this realm. Sometimes I questioned what she might have done better with me parent-wise, but that was before I'd grasped the rigors of parenting myself. While we've always been close, I feel even more bonded with Mom after getting to know her in the alternate reality. Plus, she gave me such dynamite advice about holding on to the good things. I need to stop lamenting what I lost and be grateful for my present opportunities.

It's exciting to think I could have a happy romantic relationship with Dean along with the full life I've worked for. One marked by the accomplishments of education, my teacher career, and the important bonus of starting my charity. It's a real dream come true. Who knows how things will transpire over time? Maybe we'll eventually have a family, and a sweet pup like Scout? Even as I think that my heart thuds dully. Silly to miss what's never actually come to pass in this world, so I push those feelings aside.

I stroll into my galley kitchen and flip on the light, peeking in the fridge and freezer. I'm looking for homemade meals that have been put away. Enticing leftovers, or homemade Christmas cookies. But of course there are no yummy snacks here. I'll need to grocery shop tomorrow so I can make holiday treats for my class parties. Maybe those delicious peanut butter sandwich cookies that were dipped in white chocolate? I can probably find a recipe online.

A piece of paper catches my eye on the refrigerator door. My old daily schedule, dismayingly enough from December nineteenth. I close my eyes and *breathe, breathe.* I don't need my days planned out in such excruciating detail anymore, but I do need a formal lesson plan for my teaching these next two days, in case the principal requests to see it.

I pour myself a glass of wine and haul my laptop over to the sofa. I was so swept away by Dean, I neglected this important duty, and it's *not like me* to be unprepared. Except for when I'm thrust into an alternate universe without warning, which was totally not my fault, to be fair.

I open my laptop and hunt down my lesson plans file. I've taught this topic plenty of times, and there's no better time for this lesson than right before the start of winter break. It's an easy ask of the students, a short novella and a simple overnight read. I'd love to learn what my students think of our hero's predicament, which was eerily similar to mine.

I raise my wineglass to the ceiling and toast Charles Dickens for his genius. Fiction imitates life, they say, and truth is stranger than fiction, but I wonder if Dickens ever experienced a journey as transformational as the one he gave his character Ebenezer Scrooge.

I glance at the advent calendar hanging in my kitchen, understanding my view on logic has changed. I never would have believed such a fanciful experience to be possible previously. And maybe I'm still imagining my time with Dean, Eleanor, Henry, and Scout. But something in my heart says, *I don't think so.*

CHAPTER
Twenty-Nine

I *distribute the slim-volume* books, laying one on each student's desk. "Your assignment for tonight, should you choose to accept it…and you should." I grin around the room. "Is to read Charles Dickens's *A Christmas Carol* and report back tomorrow with your thoughts." There are twenty four students, their desks lined up in four rows of six.

Nate raises his hand in the back row. "But tomorrow's the start of winter break."

I scoff lightly. "Precisely why I'm not assigning this tomorrow."

This brings low chuckles, along with groans.

I see two students passing notes. I snatch away the paper that one hands over her shoulder to another. "Care to share with the class?"

I take a quick peek at the note and close it. *New physics teacher's hot.*

Kendra slinks down in her chair, her face red. "No, thanks."

A girl in the middle row texts on her cell phone. I stride

over and hold open my hand. "Ms. Pierce," Eliza whines. "It's a necessity."

I take the phone and place it on my desk. "Which is why you can have it again after class." When I turn my back there are quiet complaints and grouses.

I face the kids and say pleasantly, "Listen, I know you're all excited about winter break, but this is a really easy read. A novella. Less than a hundred pages."

Jeremiah's jaw goes slack. "All in one night?"

"No." I lean back against my teacher desk. "I'm giving you a head start during the rest of this ninety-minute class. You can use it, or not. Either way, we'll discuss the story tomorrow."

Emily's in the front row. She sheepishly holds up her hand. "The half day before break we usually have class parties."

"And we shall!" This captures their attention.

Every person in the room sits up straighter in their chair.

"I'll bring cookies," I vow, "and you all can contribute some treats."

The cell-phone-less Eliza frowns. "But we still have to talk about Dickens?"

"All I want to know from each of you is how you might have handled things differently if you were Ebenezer Scrooge." This exercise always provokes discussion, and discussion is good.

Emily's hand juts up. "What if we would have done things the same as old Scrooge?"

I cock my chin and say, "Then I'll want to know why."

Collective sighs as students glance at one another.

I have my eyes on the clock. "Feel free to get started at any time."

One by one, their books crack open.

Dean pops his head in my room at lunchtime. "Hey, tiger. How ya holding up?"

"Things are going great so far."

"So. We still on for ice skating this evening?"

"Most definitely." My heart twists when I think of Henry and Eleanor. Those kids were so real to me. That whole life was, too.

Dean's near the threshold, standing in the hall. The strap of a laptop bag hangs from his shoulder. "Hey, you all right?"

I force a smile and say, "Yeah, good. You?"

His face creases uncertainly. "Sure." After a minute, he asks, "Pick you up at five?"

"Can we say six? I've got to make a quick run to the grocery store after school."

"Six sounds great." His dark eyes shine and he leans into the room, grasping the doorframe. "And for the record?" he whispers devilishly. "There *is* a Boss Lady mug."

"What?" I cover my mouth with my hands and giggle. "*Ooh.*"

Later that evening, Dean and I sit on a park bench by the skating rink. It's not snowing for the moment, but everything is blanketed in white and the pretty town Christmas tree gleams along with the lights from the holiday market. He takes another bite of chili dog and says, "This had been lots of fun. Thanks for coming out with me."

"Yeah." I smile, likewise enjoying my food. "You too." We took several turns around the ice and laughed and chatted. The truth is, Dean was much more than my boyfriend in college; he was my best friend. It's been easy to step back into those roles. There's probably nothing I wouldn't tell him. I've already shared more than I ever thought I would.

"I'm really sorry about your mom, Paige," he says gently, and my heart aches in a very tender spot. "I wish I'd known what the two of you were going through back then."

"It's all right. We got through it."

He lays his hand on my coat sleeve. "And you'll get through it again." He scans my eyes. "You've got to stay hopeful. Believe the doctors are just being thorough, like she said."

"Yes, I hope you're right." I think over the things Mom told me at Beaumont's in the other reality. "Mom really appreciated you in that other world. She said it was the two of us who helped her through her cancer treatments, and you played a very big part. You were a really great son-in-law."

Dean purses his lips and then says, "I'm glad I was there to help."

We finish eating and pack up our trash, staring at the skating rink for a long time. Families skate by, moms and dads holding hands with their kids, and my heart aches because I'm missing Eleanor and Henry. I hate to think we've abandoned them. No, that can't be right. Not if the world they lived in is no longer there—but that seems just as bad.

Melancholy hovers over me like a gloomy storm cloud. Silly. I should be ecstatic. I'm here—on an actual date with Dean—and the rest of my life's back to normal. My teaching, my plans for Paws and Read. I've got concerns about Mom, but I'm trying to stay positive, like Dean's urging me to do. Dean reaches out to hold my hand.

"This might not make a lot of sense." His Adam's apple rises and falls. "But I get it. I do." He feels the absence of our family, too. The void of what might have been. Maybe I shouldn't have shared so much detail about the alternate reality. Its disappearance has been hard enough on me, and now I've burdened him.

I try to add a positive spin. "Maybe everything will look brighter at Christmas?"

He nods surely. "Yeah, of course it will. Speaking of... What are you and your mom doing on Christmas Eve? My folks and I generally go to the eleven o'clock church service, the candlelight one that ends at midnight. Jenny comes, too. Do you think you and your mom would like to join? I mean, I understand if she's not feeling up to it after her appointment."

"Aww. That sounds really nice. I'll ask her." Somehow, though, I suspect there will be a big hole in my heart if we're sitting there and not attending the family service while watching Henry play a shepherd and Eleanor an angel.

Dean scans my eyes. "I hope we're still on for dinner tomorrow, because there's nothing I'd love more than spending more time with you."

"I'd like that, Dean."

He wraps his arm around me and holds me close. It's chilly out, but next to Dean I'm warm and cozy. "You know what we need?" he says, half joking. "Another dose of holiday magic."

"Oh yeah?" I peer up at him. "And what would happen then?"

"Maybe that would give us a chance to experience that other life."

My heart hammers. "But what about this life? Your folks? Jenny?"

He hugs my shoulder. "Aren't all of them there, only better?"

Heat builds in my eyes. "That's what I thought, but, you know." I shrug. "I could have been wrong. I was viewing things through my lens and what I saw as important."

"That's so like you," he says appreciatively. "Trying to be fair-minded and kind."

I'm hopeful for a moment, but then logic slams down on me like a lead weight. "Dean, even if we wanted to go back, I wouldn't know the way. Would you?"

His deep voice rumbles. "Then maybe what we need to do is move forward?" Shadows from the lights rimming the skating rink cloak his handsome face and I snuggle up against him.

"I'd like moving forward with you."

His smile touches my heart. "Yeah. Me too."

We sit together, absorbing the warm holiday vibe as skaters glide by beneath a canopy of stars. I relax against him and sigh, enjoying this special moment. I love sitting beside him and feeling his body warmth seep into mine. He's the other half of my heart. My soul mate. I believe that now more than ever after having seen the kind of marriage we'd have.

"I'm glad we've gotten so much out of that advent calendar," he says.

I smile up at him. "Thanks for giving it to me. It's been a revolutionary gift!"

"It's not such a bad life, Paige," he says and holds me closer. "The one that we've got here." His mouth moves nearer, and I go a little breathy.

"No, it's fantastic," I say and melt into his kiss.

CHAPTER
Thirty

My students are alert as they arrive with their paper plates of Christmas goodies. "Ms. Pierce," one girl says. "I know what I'd do if I were Ebenezer Scrooge. I'd go back and ask Belle to stay my girl-friend. Maybe even marry me."

"But Scrooge loved money more than her," a boy intervenes as they all take their seats.

"Doesn't mean he couldn't rethink things," the first student retorts.

Rethink things, yes. The way I'd like to do with Dean.

If we could go back to that night at my apartment, the night before Dean left for Puerto Rico, and start all over again, like we hinted at last night, would we? Would that give us the life I saw? What about my work here with Paws and Read? Is that something I could lobby for and build in the other realm? Not immediately, but eventually?

It's been tons of work, but so worth it. Given the positive outcome, I wouldn't mind putting in the elbow grease again.

I'd have to go back to school first to earn my teaching degree. I didn't think that was possible at first, in light of our financial and family demands, until Dean found a way. Dean always finds a way to make things better and touch my heart.

I have a great time with my students and am pleased to see everyone engaged. Each student has their own theories and opinions, and it's fun to hear them arguing with one another, getting into the literary spirit, so to speak.

During my final class of the day, one boy comments, "You know, Ms. Pierce, for being as old as it was, the story wasn't half bad."

"It's a classic piece of literature," I assure him. "An original best seller."

The class laughs at this, but I hold up both hands. "No, seriously. Though Dickens wrote it quickly—in only six weeks—between the time it was released on December nineteenth, eighteen forty-three, and Christmas Eve, just five days later, the first printing completely sold out."

A kid in a middle row waves their book. "So it was a hot commodity."

"The hottest."

December nineteenth. Wait.

That was the day the once-in-a-lifetime comet passed overhead and the day I was affected by my advent calendar's magic. By December twenty-fourth—just five days later—I was head over heels in love with my new family. But one thing couldn't possibly have anything to do with the other. Could it?

I shake my head, thinking I've buried myself in too much Christmas lore.

"Ms. Pierce?" a shy girl in the front row asks, for apparently the second time. "Can we pass out the cookies?"

"The cookies!" I laugh and clap my hands. "Of course."

The student assembly's held next, with teachers putting on some humorous holiday skits for the students and Principal Peabody wishing everybody a good break. Before she ends her address, she motions me toward the podium. I'm pleased to have Beth and Adrian with me, and their dogs Cooper and Bailey are here, too. We've also got a cute goldendoodle with his handler, Rodrigo, and a King Charles spaniel with her handler, Mae. Our final therapy dog is Bella, a young German shepherd with a sweet face. Her handler's name is Louise.

All the dogs wear therapy dog vests and Cooper has his bells on. The volunteers wear Paws and Read T-shirts and ID badges on matching lanyards. Beyond them on one side of the gym we've set up tables with informational flyers and blue and white balloons. We have Paws and Read T-shirts for sale as well as buttons and are selling pawprint cookies for a dollar each, donated to our effort by a local bakery.

I lean toward the mic and speak. "Hello, everyone! I know you're excited about winter break." Kids whistle, clap, and cheer, stomping their heels against the bleachers. "I wanted to let you know about a new program in our school called Paws and Read." I've changed into my T-shirt and point to the logo on its front pocket. "We'll have five therapy dogs working at Walton during the new semester. Some of your teachers have requested time with them already, but any of you students can request a canine visit for your English class, as well.

"Pet partners are also available to attend reading groups in the library. There's a signup form on the school website under the special programs link." I can read their glowing faces. There's lots of excitement over this, and that does my heart good.

While the program working one-on-one or in small groups with struggling students is a priority, improving students' morale by providing the calming influence of therapy dogs in classrooms is a paramount objective, too.

"So, please come over to our tables and get more information on our program to share with your families. Our friendly dogs and volunteers can't wait to meet you!" Resounding applause echoes to the ceiling as Principal Peabody walks toward me. "Congratulations, Paige," she says, and my heart lifts. "It looks like you're off to a great start."

That evening at dinner Dean toasts me with his wine. "Here's to getting Paws and Read off the ground today!" He's dressed nicely in a suit and tie, and I'm in a red tailored dress, tasteful but a bit boring compared to the things I wore when I had highlights in my hair.

I clink my wineglass to his. "Thanks, Dean. I'm excited for next semester and seeing it implemented." I imagine Cooper bounding into a classroom with his vest bells jingling and the faces of all the students sitting at their desks lighting up.

He tilts his wineglass thoughtfully before taking a sip. "Walton couldn't have done it without you."

My cheeks warm at his admiring look. "Oh yes they could have, but I'm happy to have their support." My stomach tenses at the thought of our other realm. There was no literacy program there, and I had such a long road ahead of me before even getting a teaching degree. Still. That world was wonderful and warm, embracing my soul like a loving hug.

I drink from my wine and set it down, staring outdoors. We're at the same table as before, with the same Christmas candle, nestled in the front window with a view of the main town square. Occasional pedestrians pass by on the sidewalk, a few individuals, a family, a couple huddled together. Falling snow coats their hats and shoulders in glistening white flakes that catch the streetlamp's glow. Colorful lights from the holiday market glimmer in the distance and I ponder Mary Christmas's advice. *Everything in its place and all things in good time.*

"You can't stop thinking about it, can you?" Dean intuits correctly. "Your alternate life."

"I wish I could explain so you'd understand."

"Paige," he says sweetly. "You don't have to. It's like I have this thing in the back of my mind." He motions behind his head. "This far away memory that's just out of reach."

"Your zip file?"

"Yeah, yeah. I've got that." He frowns, thinking this over. "But the zip file is almost like a catalog, I guess. A compilation of things that happened, snapshots from that realm. But I'm missing what you've got." He pats his chest. "The heart."

He stares at me seriously. "I've been thinking about this a lot these past few days. You know that thing people say about wishing on a star?"

"Yes?" I unroll my napkin, laying out my silverware. We've ordered but our food has not yet come.

His temples go slightly red, his neck too. "The night the Christmas Comet passed overhead, I made a private wish myself," he says tenderly. "I wished for a second chance with you."

I reach out and hold his hand on the tabletop. "You're getting it," I say softly.

His lopsided grin warms me through and through. "I'd give anything to see that other reality, to know how our life might have been. It sounds pretty wonderful."

"It was." He tightens his grip on my hand and I squeeze his.

"You know what I wish now?" His voice goes a little husky. "I wish I'd never gotten on that plane to San Juan. That I'd turned right around and come back to you."

I look deeply into his eyes. "That would have meant a different life." I can't help but tease. "No Wendy."

Our dinners arrive and we unlink our hands, sitting back in our chairs.

Dean chuckles. "You *are* a little jealous, aren't you?" he asks in joking tones.

I playfully scoff, "*Wendy Schmendy*," but I'm not seriously jealous. Although I'll admit I liked it better when I knew Dean had spent his first post-college year with me, and not with her. I turn my gaze to my plate to hide my blush. "Ooh, this looks delicious."

He studies his dish. "Sure does."

I've ordered chicken carbonara and Dean's gotten the lasagna, reminding me of the Christmas dinner he and I put together in our cozy cottage. Such teamwork, but we can make a great team here, too. Of course we can. All signs keep pointing in the right direction. "So how are things going with the house?"

"Pretty excellent." He grins and picks up his fork. "The seller's accepted my offer."

"How awesome! I'm excited for you."

He tenderly meets my gaze. "I'm excited for us, and our future." *Our future.* Were there ever weightier words? I had a future with Dean in the other reality, too. Only there, I had no recollection of our past, which is not so unlike here. Since we've been out of touch these past six years, we hadn't formed any new memories together, until recently. Although each and every one of those has been stellar. I raise my wineglass again. "Here's to the future!"

He toasts with his glass. "May it be merry and bright!" he says with Christmassy cheer.

CHAPTER
Thirty-One

The next morning, I sit anxiously in the waiting room of the outpatient clinic. I feel like I've been waiting forever, but in reality, it's only been two hours. At last, Mom's surgeon emerges, dressed in his scrubs. His expression is stony at first and my heart races. I get to my feet as he approaches me in the small seating area at the side of the large room.

"Paige." I hold my breath, then he says, "I have good news." My eyes warm but I hold in my tears, give a sniff, as he goes on. "The shadows we saw on the scans that caused us concern were just scar tissue from your mom's earlier surgery. Everything else looks good."

Relief and joy flood me and I shake his hand. "Thank you, doctor." I try not to cry and fail. Hot tears leak from my eyes. "Thanks so much."

He gives a subtle grin. Compassion's in his eyes. "I hope you and your mom have a very merry Christmas."

Much later that night, Dean and I exit the old stone church with our families. He has his arm around my shoulders, and Mom's on my other side. His folks and Jenny are with him, and snow gently falls from the darkened sky.

Mom sighs. "Thanks so much for including us. That service was beautiful." Snowflakes dot her red curls and she dusts them off before tugging on her hat. After I brought her home from her appointment, she slept soundly for a few hours, then was up and eager for dinner and to come to church.

"It sure was," Dean's mom, Miriam, says, wrapping herself in her scarf.

"Very moving," Dean's dad, Jack, agrees. He glances at Mom. "Sounds like we have a lot to be grateful for this year."

Mom smiles softly in return. "Yes."

Dean's eyes twinkle at Mom. "We're glad you could join us."

I'm so happy about Mom. So happy about everything. Including being here with Dean. "Merry Christmas, Paige." He bends down to kiss me on the front steps of the church as others bustle past us, and my heart flutters. It's a little past midnight, so the holiday's officially here.

Jenny gives a happy smirk and Dean's parents smile.

Mom's eyebrows shoot up and she addresses Miriam and Jack, nodding my way. "Perhaps we should leave these lovebirds alone?" she says, and the rest of them laugh goodheartedly. My face burns hot but Dean doesn't seem to mind.

Before we depart, Miriam insists to me and Mom, "Please do come to dinner tomorrow at our place. We sit down at five, so come around four."

"I wouldn't miss it!" Mom quips.

"Thanks," I add, smiling. "I'll be there, too." There's only one thing I could imagine that would make me happier than Mom and me spending Christmas with Dean and his family.

Having Eleanor and Henry there too, and naturally Scout—
and Roger.

The group exchanges cheery holiday wishes and goodnights,
and Mom walks to her car, which is parked close to the church.
Dean's family goes farther down the block.

As Dean and I stroll down the snowy sidewalk and toward
his jeep, he asks, "Can I buy you a nightcap somewhere?"

I feel the same way he does, not ready for the evening to end.
But it's already after midnight on Christmas Eve. "I'm not sure
there's going to be much open." Maybe in some larger towns,
but not in sleepy Piney Mount.

He checks his watch. "We could go back to your place,
or mine?"

I blush deeply. "Paige," he says kindly. "It doesn't have to
be like *that.* We can just talk some more." I have no reason to
feel giddy and nervous. Dean and I had a serious love life in
the other realm, after all. But we haven't had one here, so this
feels different.

I smile at him and say, "I like talking with you."

Not long afterward, we appreciate the pretty view outside
my condo window. Dean comments on the darkened landscape
showcasing the mountains and the snowy sky. "Looks a little
like that mug you gave me." He shrugs. "In the other place."

"Yeah." I snuggle under his arm and we both drink our wine.
The gas hearth blazes before us, but I miss the coziness of a real
wood-burning fire and our cottage. Wouldn't mind having a
scotch *if* I bought hard liquor, which I typically don't. "Except
we have a snow-speckled sky outside our window instead of
one studded with stars."

He absorbs the gorgeous view. "I like the stars."

"I know you do."

"But now," he says, "I'm partial to comets"

I laugh and roll my eyes. "Who knew you could wish on a comet?"

He strokes his chin. "It's true they're made of rock and ice rather than gases, but that doesn't mean that *this* Christmas Comet wasn't extra special. If it hadn't appeared this year, maybe the magic in your calendar wouldn't have come to life?" We both turn toward the kitchen to admire the enchanted decoration. It's now complete. I put up the Santa face this morning and all of its pockets are empty, with the star at the top of the tree.

He considers the advent calendar and its spot in my kitchen. "It looks good there. Very festive." He chuckles and shakes his head. "I'm still grappling with everything you told me about your time split adventure."

I blow out a breath and say lightly, "You and me both."

"Funny how you returned on the twentieth, the exact next day. It's like you were gone no time at all."

"In this reality, yeah." I think of the Dickens novella. "Dean, do you know the Dickens tale *A Christmas Carol*, about Ebenezer Scrooge?"

"Of course I do, who doesn't? It's about the miserly old man who learns his lesson.

"Wait." He leans forward to peer at me. "You don't think your experience was something like that?"

I set my chin. "No. It was distinctly different. Though I did get a chance to reassess my life, the way old Ebenezer did."

Dean chuckles and holds me closer. "There are some major differences, though. You're certainly not the Scroogey type. Just look at Paws and Read. Setting up that charity was a completely selfless act."

"That's what I thought at first," I admit honestly. "But then I started to reflect on the sorts of things I've valued, like financial security and a steady job."

"Paige Pierce," he says seriously. "Nobody would fault you for wanting stability. That's an extremely common and reasonable goal. Plus, I understand how things were with Rosemary. You explained about your upbringing when we dated in college. You knew you were loved, without question, but your life was also chaotic. You two moved around a lot, and she was often out of work. You took odd jobs shoveling snow for your neighbors to help pay the bills."

"All that's true," I tell him. "But in some ways, I wonder if I threw the baby out with the bathwater when thinking about my past. There were so many good things about the life I had. *This life.* Mom was carefree, and fun. And, yes, she had—goodness knows—a gazillion boyfriends. But no matter what else was going on with her, she was always there for me."

His dark eyes twinkle. "Sounds like you've developed some good perspective."

I nod. "My experiences these past several days have helped. I also feel a new appreciation for Mom, like I better understand her."

He gently clasps my shoulder. "Sounds like a win-win."

"Yeah." I sigh and sip from my wine. After a minute I add, "You know what else is funny about that Scrooge novella? Its release date was the same day my whole life changed. December nineteenth."

"That's wild. Though, obviously, not in the same year."

I laugh. "No, in eighteen forty-three. The book sold out its first printing by Christmas Eve."

Dean whistles. "Talk about a runaway best seller."

"Sometimes things happen fast."

"And sometimes"—he looks deeply into my eyes—"they take six years longer than they should."

"Dean, I'm so sorry—"

He gently presses his finger to my lips. "No regrets now. I know we both have them and for different reasons, but Paige? Maybe it's time we let those go."

I nod and heave a deep breath. "Letting go sounds like the right answer."

He lifts the wine bottle off the coffee table, offering me some more, and I hold out my wineglass. He refills it and his. "Our situation does present some interesting metaphysical questions, though."

I giggle at his choice of words. "Metaphysical? Oh?"

He sips from his wine. "Say, for example, we had a choice. Both of us, about that alternate reality."

This piques my interest. "What kind of choice, exactly?"

"What if you knew you could return—"

"But I don't think—"

"Humor me."

"All right."

He takes another sip of wine while I sip mine. "My question was, what if you knew you could go back to that life, the alternate reality you experienced, would you do it?"

"Erm, that depends. Part of me would leap at the chance, but there were compromises, and I'm not talking about losing my fancy condo or SUV. It wasn't even fully about the job."

"So then?" he asks, waiting for more. "What?"

"Well, there's Paws and Read, for starters. I'm hugely proud of the charity that's going to help so many people and pets. It's hard to imagine jettisoning that when its contributions to the school and our community are so very important. On a more personal level, it was frustrating not having any historic memories, Dean. Not knowing what my life had been like up until that point. I loved seeing what it was in the moment, but there was a gaping big hole there called my past."

"Uh-huh I see." He tips his wineglass slightly. "So the trade-off is getting to a good place with home and family, but at the expense of recalling actual past experiences?"

"Yeah, that's what I'm getting at."

"Knowing what you know now, do you think you could build that kind of life here?"

"With you?" My face heats. "It's aspirational. I mean, maybe someday. Like you said."

"But it wouldn't be the same life, would it?"

"What do you mean?"

"The baby who would have been born five years ago—Eleanor—wouldn't be the same child as one born to us in the future, or would she?"

My heart twists because I don't know.

"Same with Henry."

"Maybe they were just representations," I say, "of 'children yet to come.'"

He sighs heavily. "Yeah, could be."

"I guess we'll never know."

"We might know," he says sweetly. "Someday."

That sounds amazingly wonderful, but risky, if Dean is right. I see Henry's smiling face, hear his cute voice saying "Merry Kissmas," and my soul aches. "I suppose I'd want it both ways. To have those specific kids, eventually in this realm."

"Yeah, eventually." He grows distant, staring at the snow. "But it's a gamble, I suppose."

My heart hurts at the thought of gambling with Henry and Eleanor. Two precious babies, mine and Dean's, the ones we might have had. "What would you do?"

"If it were up to me, and I'd bonded with those two the way you did, I'd find a way to save them." My pulse pounds, because there's only one thing that could mean: switching over to the alternate reality and staying there. "Theoretically speaking," Dean says, rubbing his chin.

"But I can't imagine leaving here now." I search his eyes. "Not after everything I've told you." I swallow hard. "And now that we stand a second chance."

Dean stares at the advent calendar in the kitchen. "I never said you'd have to go alone."

"Dean? What?"

"What if we were there together?"

"But we were there together."

"No," he says gently. "I mean what if we both made a conscious choice? Decided together that's the path we should have taken? No regrets." My pulse skitters nervously. "Paige," he proposes, "what if—when he was shown his past—Ebenezer Scrooge had been allowed to alter it, and wake up married to Belle?"

"But that's not how the story goes."

He takes my hand. "This is our story now."

"But I didn't choose to go there the first time. I've no idea how to get back."

"I've been thinking about something." Dean meets my eyes. "What if the magic that caused your transition is still working? It's Christmas Day now." My heart skips a beat, because I know what he's saying. We're not yet out of time. There's still a chance for that different life.

Dean stands and carries his wine into the kitchen, and I walk with him. He leaves his wineglass on the counter and removes the advent calendar's Christmas star ornament to examine it. "You told me that the night you put this up, you thought you saw it glowing."

He turns it over in his hand to peer at its Velcro back. "Maybe this star is the key to that other dimension. A way to open the door and return." He flips the star over in his hand again. "'A calendar that can predict the future,' Mary Christmas said." He's thinking out loud, postulating in his teaching-physics voice. If I were a student in his class, I'd crush majorly. I'm crushing majorly now. He looks at me and his eyes twinkle. "'Change lives,'" he says in a thoughtful tone. He steps toward me and asks, "But was it really the future Mary Christmas was talking about, or something else?"

"The calendar did predict the future in a way," I answer. "There were those appearing poinsettias—in both realities. Henry's snowman. The ice skates. The Christmas candle."

Dean considers the calendar. "I wonder what would have happened if you'd put this star slash quasi comet up on the calendar today."

"Another astronomical event?" I venture.

"Maybe astronomy's not big enough."

Says the man who teaches about black holes.

"What's bigger than the mysteries of the universe?"

His lopsided grin warms me, fills me with tingly joy. "The mysteries of the human heart."

I sense so many possibilities. A different kind of future with Dean. A brand new life. But not one I can plan for or program specifically. One fraught with unforeseeable surprises. In my current reality, Dean and I can carefully navigate our new relationship. Responsibly prepare for a deeper commitment in the future. Orchestrate an ideal family. Or. We can jump right into the deep end and let things get messy. "Dean, what are you thinking?"

He places my wineglass beside his on the counter and takes me in his arms. "I'm wondering, what would happen if we both made the same wish? Wanted the same things?"

"And?"

He nods at the calendar. "That just might change things."

Anticipation courses through me—anxiety, too.

"Paige." He holds me tighter. "Maybe to *hold on to what is good*, we need to let go of any guilt we're both feeling over the past, and the choices we made. Maybe it's not too late to choose differently and to have all those amazing things in one package. Our sweet bungalow, our cute kids and great family dog, a future for you in teaching where you can start Paws and Read all over again."

My eyes burn hot, because that sounds so totally perfect. "I won't mind the hard work of starting over again." I say honestly, and my eyes fill to brimming. "Not if you're there with me. Not if we have Eleanor and Henry, and our precious pup Scout."

His gaze locks on mine and he holds the star ornament out in his hand. "What if we put this up together? Took that leap of faith, united? Made the very same wish on the very same star, this Christmas star on your magical calendar? Today is Christmas Day. Maybe it's not too late for its magic to work."

Hope blooms inside me, but my voice shakes. "What if it doesn't work?"

He shrugs. "What if it *does*?"

I gasp and stare up at him. "Dean, maybe this is what Mary Christmas meant when she talked about going *all in*. She said when I made my choice, I'd have to make it with my whole heart and not partway, either. One hundred percent. I thought I'd made that decision in the other world but something must have been holding me back."

"Your worries over losing Paws and Reads? Concern about your Mom?" Dean asks me.

I shake my head. "What about my concern about choosing *for you*?"

"But I wasn't aware of the two realities then."

"That's just it," I say, understanding settling over me. "You and I are a team, Dean. We've always been a team. Maybe it didn't seem fair for me to make that decision for our family entirely on my own."

"You're not making it alone now, Paige." He smiles fondly. "I'm right here with you, *all in* all the way."

My pulse hums when he holds out the Christmas star, so I can grab part of it while he grasps the other end of the delicate cloth object. We press it to the tippy-top of the felt Christmas tree and wait. I expect the floor to open up and swallow us whole, for the white-tipped mountains to crumble into the snowy valleys outside my window, for the earth to tremble and shake.

Nothing happens.

I am so crestfallen.

Then suddenly the star on the calendar starts to quiver and glow, sending out thin ribbons of light. The beams grow wider and brighter, bouncing off the appliances in my kitchen and stretching across the room, hitting the large plate-glass window and making it shimmer like hundreds and hundreds of glittery snowflakes, now magically dancing around us.

Dean brings his arms around me securely. "I said if you left, I'd find you. Paige," he says soft and low, "kiss me." He dips his chin closer. "For luck."

His swoony lips meet mine, and bursts of light shine out around us. Glowing brighter and brighter, and bathing us in their warmth. Soon we're flying. Soaring—traveling at the speed of light—seemingly on the wings of angels.

We're in the center of a white-hot star.

Then everything goes black.

CHAPTER
Thirty-Two

I'm falling, falling through an endless dark stretch. Then I land with a springy bounce in a safe, sheltered nest. I stir under the blankets, basking in the cozy vibe. Someone snuggles against my back, his strong arm wrapped around me, holding me tightly. The scent of cinnamon and cloves cloaks the air—along with hints of vanilla. Nutmeg. My heart skips a beat and then it pounds harder. Am I there, or dreaming?

My eyes fly open and I'm staring at our room. The parted bathroom door, an unruly pile of laundry, snow falling through the windows beyond the partially raised blinds. He leans forward and kisses my shoulder. "Morning, tiger." *That voice.* Husky, caressing, familiar. Heat floods my eyes. *Dean.* I shift under the covers to face him. A smile spreads across his lips. My exceptionally handsome husband, with his smattering of morning stubble, my soul mate and my one true love. I reach up to touch his face, fearing he'll disappear. "We made it."

"I always knew we would," he says warmly. "That's why I asked you to marry me."

My hand darts to my chest and my fingers comb the front of Dean's large T-shirt, but my necklace is still gone. Maybe lost to eternity forever. "So you don't remember?"

Dean nestles me in his arms and kisses me. "Of course I do. Every precious moment." *Of this reality. Oh no.* He has no recollection of the other, but how could he? He's been right here the whole time. But now, so have I, right? Where are my memories?

"Mommy! Daddy! Yay!" Eleanor races into the room holding her Highland cow. She jumps up onto the bed and my heart bursts with joy. "Can I ride my bike again today?" *Eleanor.* I've missed her so much.

Dean and I sit up in bed, and I tug her into my arms. Kiss the top of her head, breathe in her little girl sweetness. Hug her so tightly that she squirms and giggles. "Of course you can." I dart a look at Dean. "So today is?"

"The day after Christmas," he says cheerfully. "December twenty-sixth."

Yes. I've returned to this world exactly when I left it—without missing a day. And I don't want to miss another day of being here with Dean and our precious family. My heart aches at the hole in my past. I remember nothing before December twentieth, when I came here the first time. But no, I won't be sad. I've got the beautiful present to hang on to forever and will treasure all the new memories we make.

Henry toddles into the room with a cheery gleam. "Merry Kissmas!" *Our baby boy.* My heart aches with affection. How I've missed him, too. He lumbers toward the bed, his Nessie hanging by the tail, and Dean scoops him up and into his lap. He hugs Henry close and kisses his head. "I think 'Kissmas' was yesterday, buddy."

"O-tay!" Henry croons.

My heart melts and I hug Eleanor tighter. Reach out and stroke Henry's chubby little boy cheek. *My babies. I'm here—and I'm never leaving you again.*

"*Woof! Woof!*"

Scout. My heart brims over. *Our sweet shaggy pup.*

Scout bounds into the room, but his bark sounds more like "*Moof! Moof!*" He's got something clenched in his teeth and it's not our morning paper. It's shiny and narrow, like an ultra-thin cord, dangling from his mouth and twirling. *Wait.*

Scout jumps up on the bed and sits down in front of me, squeezing in between me and Dean while pawing across the blankets. A delicate gold chain hangs from the dog's mouth and my ruby heart pendant glints in the morning light. I can scarcely believe it.

Dean stares at the jewelry. "What do you know? You must have lost it somewhere in the house yesterday during all the Christmas activity."

I hold out my hand and Scout cranes his head forward, opening his mouth and releasing the necklace. It drops into my palm, its gold chain coiling like a silky ribbon, the pretty ruby heart resting on top.

"Thanks, Scout." I pet him, and he hops off the bed, retreating from the room. A recollection tugs at me, and I gape at the open door to the hall.

When Dean and I toured this real estate offering in the other dimension, I thought I heard Scout elsewhere in the house while we were in the kitchen. Of course. Scout was in the other realm briefly, hunting for his family. He must have retrieved my necklace from that world, just as surely as he brings in the morning paper.

My eyes water when I grasp the truth. *Scout wanted us to come home.* He fought against nearly impossible odds, forcing his way through the fog of a realm that had gone *poof.* Because our pup wanted what we did, a Christmas miracle of the heart. I pass the necklace to Dean so he can help me put it on, and he closes his fingers around it.

"Huh." He blinks and stares at me. "That's weird."

"What is?"

He furrows his brow. "I just had a sudden blast of memories, but not from here. A snowman in a park? A bunch of poinsettia plants in a coffee shop? Walton's faculty holiday party? But you're there, and you're a teacher—what?" He reads my eyes, questioning. "Paige," he asks cautiously, "did something happen between us in a, um"—he swallows hard—"different place?"

"*Yes.*" I thank the heavens for this second chance and the opportunity to share everything I've learned on my travels with Dean. "I can't wait to tell you all about it."

"So wait." He blows out a breath. "When you woke up after the margaritas, and said you came from another world…" He blows out a breath. "Oh wow."

"Yes, Dean. Yes," I whisper, so relieved he can see it. Even if it's just a glimpse into my alternate reality, that lays a foundation for me telling him more. I grin and pivot away from him, holding up my hair. It feathers through my fingers in layers. *Yay!*

Dean closes the necklace clasp at the base of my neck and the pretty red ruby heart pendant rests on the front of my sleep shirt. *My necklace—of course.* This link between the two realms binds us, just like the love in our hearts.

"It wasn't a bad life, was it?" Dean asks dreamily, as if he's putting bits and pieces together. Getting little snatches here and there of what might have been, if he'd left for Puerto Rico. He peeks at the necklace then grins. "But this one's better."

"So much better," I sigh, my spirit soaring like a kite. Or maybe a shooting star. *No, a comet.* The most spectacular kind.

I lay my hand across my ruby heart pendant and memories flit through my mind, circling around and around one another.

> *Dean sweeps me into his arms. We're college age.*
> *Tears stream down his cheeks and mine.*
> *"I'll never leave you," he says and kisses me.*

Images flip, flip, flip.

> *I'm with Dean on our wedding day in his parents'*
> *backyard. He's so handsome in a suit and tie, and I*
> *wear a white dress. Mom holds my flowers, and my*
> *friends are all here.*

Flip, flip.

> *"Yeow-wee!!!" Holy cow. It wrenches, but Eleanor's born!*
> *"It's a girl!" the doctor says.*
> *I beam up at Dean and hold our baby in my arms.*
> *Eleanor.*

Another memory flip in a truly dizzying fashion.

> *Scout's a floppy-eared pup, dragging the paper through*
> *the door flap.*
> *It's nearly as big as he is.*

Flip, flip.

> *Dean proudly cradles our newborn son. "I like Henry,"*
> *he says. "It suits him."*

Flip, flip, flip.

I barely get the button done on my too-tight white jeans.
"Do these make me look fat?"
Dean winces and says, "Hon, you just had a baby."
I burst into tears and race into the bathroom, slamming
shut the door.
Dean pounds on it from the bedroom side. "Paige?
Sweetheart? I'm sorry!"

Flip, flip.

Ow! I glance over my shoulder at the tattoo artist.
"You said it wouldn't hurt."

"Dean." I gasp happily. "The trimmings."

He stares at my necklace and smirks. "We've got a lot to talk about, don't we?"

I laugh with giddy delight. "Yes."

Eleanor beams up at me in her cute pigtails, her dark eyes shining, and Henry wears his happy little grin beneath his mop of golden hair. Dean and I move closer in our cozy warm bed and form a giant family hug with our kids. My heart's so full it's bursting. I'm so glad I haven't forgotten about that other world and what might have been. I've learned so much from my experiences. An unforgettable lesson in what I value most, love and family.

Scout trots back into the room carrying the morning paper in his mouth, his wagging tail held high. He pounces up on the bed, sits back on his haunches, and drops the newspaper roll down in front of Dean. Dean's joyful laughter fills the room.

"Good boy!" he says and pats Scout's head.

Mary Christmas's words chime through my mind like tinkling holiday bells.

Everything in its place and all things in good time.

I can't wait to see what the future brings.

ABOUT THE
Author

New York Times and *USA Today* bestselling author Ginny Baird has published novels in print and online and received screenplay options from Hollywood for her family and romantic comedy scripts. Whether writing lighthearted rom-coms or spine-tingling romantic suspense, she delights in delivering heartwarming stories.

Ginny is the author of the Christmas Town series, the Holiday Brides series, the Summer Grooms series, a Romantic Ghost Stories series, and several standalone books, including wholesome romance novels from Hallmark Publishing and sweet romantic comedies from Entangled Publishing. Ginny invites you to visit her website to learn more about her and her books:

ginnybairdromance.com.

www.ingramcontent.com/pod-product-compliance
Lightning Source LLC
Chambersburg PA
CBHW030525190726
48283CB00006B/1779

* 9 7 8 1 9 4 2 0 5 8 4 9 6 *